THE GOVERNOR'S DAUGHTER

The GOVERNOR'S DAUGHTER

by

DENTON WHITSON

PEOPLES BOOK CLUB

CHICAGO

Library of Congress Catalog Card Number: 52-14023
PRINTED IN THE UNITED STATES OF AMERICA

This is a special edition published exclusively for the members of the Peoples Book Club, P. O. Box 6570A, Chicago 80, Illinois, and 25 Hollinger Road, Toronto 13, Ontario, Canada. It was originally published by The Bobbs-Merrill Company, Inc.

To My Mother

History is full of the errors of states and princes.

—BENJAMIN FRANKLIN

THE GOVERNOR'S DAUGHTER

CHAPTER *One*

THE girl lay listening. In a pocket of her mind lingered some sound that had awakened her; but out of the muffling gray darkness came only the tock-tock of the big clock belowstairs—faint, yet prodding to urgency.

Clytie, wide-eyed, sat up with a jerk. Had the clock clanged the hour—the *right* hour? She had told herself over and over again before she went to sleep last night that she would awaken when the clock struck *three.* She threw off the covers and reached with a foot for the steps beside the big four-poster bed. But she rejected the steps; they might creak. With her long, slim legs dangling now from the bed, she clung to the covers—and to the joy of her awakening. She must make no sound. Her cold toes touched the rag rug, and she stood erect, shivering.

Beyond the draperies of the bed a ghostly light washed through the west window of her room. Daylight? Oh, no! Cautiously she moved to the window. Through the budding trees outside she saw the orange blob of the moon lowering toward the western horizon—just what Mike had said would be happening when it was time for her to escape from the house.

Then the clock *had* struck three. Oh, Mike, are you waiting?

She tiptoed back to the bed and doubled down beside it to reach for a bundle concealed beneath, cautious not to bump her head or let one of her heavy clogs drop from the bundle of garments and hit the floor. The Hubers, belowstairs, were heavy sleepers, but she must not count too much on their not waking.

In the wan light she stood up, unbuttoned her nightgown and let it slip to the floor.

As she stood in her tall, lissome, young strength, naked except for a money belt about her middle, the cold nipped at her slim shoulders and firm little ankles. She adjusted the belt and patted with satisfaction the small padded pockets. Not heavy. She had slept in it last night without discomfort, although it was stuffed with gold crowns. A little key, dangling about her neck by a silken cord, was now between her shoulder blades. She brought it around to hang in front.

She snatched up her woolen drawers and drew them on. Ugh! They scratched. Now the shift. That on, she eased down to the floor to pull on her cotton stockings and took out the garters that Lottie had stuffed in the toes. Good, faithful Lottie! But hurry! hurry! Mike had told her not to put on the clogs until she was out of the house. She sprang up, put on her cotton petticoat and tied the strings just above her money belt. . . . Poor Mike! Her heart gave its sympathy for the dangers she was leading him into; yet well-remembered words of her father's comforted: "Mike and the sunrise–I have come to trust one as well as the other."

She slipped the skirt of her brown linsey-woolsey dress on, then drew on the bodice, her fingers icy as she fumbled with the buttons, and the thought of their long wilderness journey squeezed at her heart. . . . But no! no! *Beauteous* wilderness! Though a wilderness of darkness and terrors, it held mystery, too, and beauty and sun shadows–spring wilderness.

She buttoned her bodice up all the way to her neck, smoothed down the little round collar, stuck out her chin marked by its dimpled cleft, while the mind of her heart repeated: I won't fail your colonies, Grandfather. I won't fail. It was more of a prayer than a promise, but after she reached the washbasin and dashed her face with cold water, she was hopeful of its truth.

Her hair brushed, she tied a brown ribbon about it the color of her dress–not that she could define color or line in the little mirror. In the uncertain moonlight her face was a ghostly blur, her blue eyes dark and uncanny. She bared her even white teeth at her reflection, and shuddered. Would she look like that when the savages in the wilderness had scalped . . . Her hands clung to her hair. But her courage stiffened, and she flipped at the ends of her ringlets that now touched her shoulders.

A pretty time to be indulging in scare-thoughts!

She and Lottie had cut her hair shorter last night; it would be easier to handle on the wilderness journey. But she must not dawdle.

Clytie took another bundle from beneath the big wardrobe, and this she handled with tender care; it was her cloak and head scarf, but within these wrappings was something *precious*. And on an impulse, not to be denied, she sat down on her heels at the west window to make sure the treasure was intact.

Moonlight on the trees outside inked a pattern of feathered fingers about the box she uncovered—not a big box. It was eight by four by three. Mike had measured it. The painted flowers and cupids on its tin surface were almost worn off—an old box. But it was watertight. Mike had tested that, too.

Her fingers trembled a little as she took the little key from about her neck and unlocked the box. Suppose . . . suppose she had only dreamed that . . .

She tore off a layer of cotton wool to disclose a glittering array of jewelry—rubies, diamonds, a string of pearls—but such sparkle in the moonglow did not interest her. It was the thing beneath the jewels, *if* it were beneath.

Never in all her eighteen years had truth so mingled with the fanciful as she ran long slender fingers down beneath the jewels. Her possession of the letter must be a dream, a dream that she had been able to steal it last night from the locked cabinet belowstairs.

When her fingers touched the parchment, smooth, brittle, her shoulders slumped with relief. It was there! The official letter, with the great seal of His Majesty King George the Second's forces in America on it, *was there.* The April moon sliding down the western sky looked real again, and Clytie's spirits lifted.

She assured herself that the contents of the box did not rattle before she tied her head scarf about it, put the key again about her neck, and fastened her cloak about her shoulders. She took up her clogs and headed for the door. But when she closed it softly behind her and started to feel her way toward the stairs her heart pounded wildly. One false step would bring down on her the sound of Prissy Huber's shrill voice: "Thief! Thief!"

How Clytie ever got down the steps, which threatened to creak at every touch of her stockinged feet, she never knew. And never had the tock-tock of the clock sounded so ghostly as she tried to listen for any sound that might cut off her progress toward the back door. Lottie had left it unlocked, but her heart was in her throat as she moved toward it, fearful of stumbling against something in the dark.

Then the sound that cut off her breathing. It filled the old house with an ogreish rumble and stopped with a snort. Never had a snort so reassured her. She breathed easily again. The sound was Uncle Aaron Huber's snore.

When the door latched softly behind her, the sting of the chill night air gave Clytie courage, and she ran. Not until she had cleared the corner of the house and was headed across the lawn toward the gate of the driveway was her progress slowed. The soggy ground sucked at her stockinged feet and dark tree shadows confused her direction. Yet her heart sucked at freedom; in another moment she would reach the gate and find Mike. . . .

A fearsome howl ripped into the silence. It froze the darkness. "The fiercest watch-hound in all Philadelphia country," Uncle Aaron Huber had said. Clytie quickened her racing strides, terrified, and dropped one of her clogs. She turned back. Her need for the shoe rivaled her fear of the watchdog's fangs, and she had just stooped to retrieve it when from a black shadow something leaped . . .

"He be chained up, missy."

"Oh, Mike! Mike!" She wanted to laugh and cry all at once, but only followed his hurried lead toward the gate, where sight of their three horses materializing out of the shadows steadied her.

She gave Mike the precious box to put in her saddlebags and sat down to put on her shoes—difficult over her wetted stockings, but urgency was vital with continued howl of the watchdog.

Mike was just giving her a hand-up onto her horse when through the trees she saw the light in the Hubers' window. "Oh, Mike, look!"

The Hubers were capable of any pursuit, any cruelty to thwart her escape. Clytie straightened herself in the saddle and took up the reins. Mike too was mounted now, leading their pack horse. Never had his voice been more reassuring.

"They'll no' be lookin' into your room, missy, nor knowin' ye be gone till arter sunrise." His big, kindly face, lighted by a streak of moonlight, gave her courage. "Ride straight ahead, missy."

Clytie put her horse into a fast canter along the moon-shadowed wilderness road.

"Easy, missy! Take it easy till it's lighter. No trouble reachin' Chester by noonday." Mike was just behind her, and they had struck a strip of corduroy road.

Clytie brought her horse to a walk. They had covered several miles over the loamy tract that was the King's Path, easy to follow amid the towering trunks of the great trees with the moon not yet down. But they had dipped now into a hollow where a mist swam through the feathered April undergrowth and dimmed the lightening sky. They could scarcely see the road a few feet ahead. Eager to put as much distance as possible between her and the Hubers, she had had little time to think of any dangers the dark forest might hold for them; yet, as they had passed through one wooded glade, she had had the eerie sensation that eyes followed her. Knowing, sinister eyes. But she had brushed it aside, for both she and Mike had been told in Philadelphia that the road to Chester was patrolled, and her mind had accepted the fact that this first stage of their journey would be safe.

Now Mike's reference to noonday caused her to question, "Might not noonday be too late, Mike?" Her voice had an unreal quality amid the sleepy dawn pipings of woods creatures, and unconsciously she lowered it as if the wildwood had curious ears of its own. "This Captain Appleton you hope to meet up with in Chester . . . Suppose he has ridden away to Baltimore?" she finished anxiously.

"Steady, Malt! Steady, boy!" Mike's soothing of their pack horse prevented his answer. The road wound upward now out of the glade, and a low-hanging limb had scraped the high pack on Malt's back.

Clytie rode on ahead and gave consideration to this Captain Appleton of Maryland Colony of whom Mike had told her. He had learned that the captain had ridden into Philadelphia on business for his colonial colonel, and that on his way back to Frederick he was to enlist recruits to fight the French and their savages. "He rides to *Frederick,* Mike?" she had questioned unbelievingly, since Frederick in Maryland Colony was their own destination. But Mike had been repeating only what he had heard, and had told her, "So if we could meet up wi' him and his troopers, missy, by ridin' in his wake, t'would bring us safe to Frederick."

She had been mightily cheered at the thought of having such protection for the important letter she carried. But before Mike was able to locate this captain who served the king and colonies, he had left Philadelphia for Chester. So now their only hope of meeting up with him was that he might still be recruiting around Chester.

Appleton, Appleton, Clytie found her mind repeating, hovering over the name almost as if it held mystical significance instead of hope for the safe delivery of the letter. More like salvation. Or the fulfillment of some promise made to her in the long ago. The crunching sound of Mike's horses behind her repeated: Appleton! Captain Appleton!

Mike rode up closer now to answer her question. "Could be we'll miss him, if he ain't dallied long to pick up his troopers." Mike's voice was heavy. Then more hopefully: "Could be too he might dally a day to pick up more recruits at Queen o' France Mill. Hear tell that's some ways t'other side o' Chester on the King's Path. And where a body can find a roof to put over his head."

Clytie did not reply. His vague hope of meeting the captain had given over to his worry that she should be forced to sleep unsheltered in the wilderness. Foolish worry. She was prepared for any hardships they might encounter.

They were mounting the hillside now, and ahead was an archway of light that signified a clearing. Woods creatures stirred amid the thick undergrowth. Frogs croaked with ringing sound, and when the arc of light had broadened into a wide clearing a dog barked in the distance. Daylight had come. Mist and fog still hung low over the cultivated fields that bordered each side of the road, but the fields were green—so green that in the nacreous gray-white dawn they had a liquid, unreal quality. Wood smoke scented the air, and in the misty distance sounded the clip-clop of a woodsman's ax.

"Clippity-clop, clippity-clop! Appleton, Appleton, clippity-clop!" Clytie's spirits were mounting. And refusing to abandon hope of meeting up with the captain, she made up a cheery song. Song of the morning—a glory morning.

"What say, missy?" Mike called against the ring of their horses' hoofs on the well-packed earth of the trail.

"I said it was going to be a fine day."

He did not answer. But then Mike was not eighteen and entering upon the first adventure of his life as she was, she must remember. Nor had he been told stories in his childhood of the beauty, majesty and illimitable vastness of the great wilderness by an adored grandfather. And as the green fields slipped away and the road plunged again into the forest of trees that nudged into the brightening sky, Clytie looked back at his solemn and homely face, furrowed by fifty years. Good, loyal Mike! He was inspecting the musket that swung from his shoulder along with his powder horn. He had tied the lead rope of their pack horse to his saddle, and rode close behind her now. The trail was light enough to see their way clearly, but his eyes searched the undergrowth and he balanced his musket close to his shoulder.

Clytie, too, became watchful. It might be true that the King's Path to Chester was safe for other riders, but she must not allow her joy of the wilderness to dull her senses to the fact that it might not be safe for those who bore a letter with the great seal of His Majesty's forces in America on it.

CHAPTER *Two*

THE Queen of France Mill lay some eight miles southwest of the town of Chester. It racketed on the edge of a millpond made from a small stream, and was on an elevation of ground that incorporated a sizable clearing within which stood two log huts. One was occupied by the miller, his wife and six small children; the other was reserved for any wearied travelers who might find themselves on the King's Path at nightfall with no other roof to shelter them.

It was a poor roof, patched and leaky. The hard bunks were flea-ridden. But the guest cabin had proved most profitable for the miller. He was a long-nosed, dour and mingy little man, Ezra Jones by name, who had in the past proved capable of exacting the last penny from any hapless traveler who wished to enjoy the luxuries of the cabin.

But today Ezra's business acumen had failed. Four stalwart young men had ridden in on four stout horses, declared themselves as recruits who had "jined up to fit the French," and rejected the price of his hospitality. But—devil take them!—they had not rejected such lawless action as bedding down on his clearing. *His* ground on which to lay their ruffian heads. And making use of his mill stream to water their horses. With greater insult still, they were making a fire over which to cook their supper. And without a half-penny profit to himself!

Ezra raged. But he did not despair. With envious eyes on the strongest of their horses, he began to wheedle: he offered all the snug comforts of his cabin with only the generous proviso that but one of their "spavined nags" be left in his keeping until such day as the owner could return to redeem it.

Yet the young hell-rakers guffawed at his generosity.

You can't argue with lusty bandits, so Ezra took refuge in fistshaking and screeches. "Aimin' to fit the French be ye?" he threw at them, and demanded, "*What* French?" But when their good-humored laughter increased, he shouted: "Ye be lyin' scalawags! There be no French in these parts. Nor Injuns nuther. Hit be excuse to thieve your way by poachin' on me land."

One of the lads made a threatening gesture, and Ezra scurried to a safer distance, which but called for a louder outlay of voice. "But I'll git me pay fer your poachin'," he screeched. "I hyeared ye say your capt'in be ridin' in come mornin', so 'tis him I'll make pay fer your thievin'. Or ha' the law o' the king's colony on ye."

As still louder laughter bore him down, Ezra retreated into his mill. Yet, had he known it, he was to be fully requited for the use of his cabin that night.

Two wayworn travelers were even then watering their horses in his stream. They had made their approach under cover of the troopers' raucous laughter and had heard the miller's maledictions while they kept sheltered from sight by the wooded embankment of the stream.

"They are here, Mike," Clytie whispered. "And did you hear what was said? *The captain is expected in the morning.*" The news so revived her drooping spirits, Mike had to gesture to her for quiet. Yet she was conscious of the relief that brightened his troubled face.

They had arrived in Chester only to find that Captain Appleton and the small quota of his recruits who possessed horses had ridden away several hours earlier. Yet the alewife at the little inn where they had eaten a hearty dinner vouchsafed them a ray of hope; perhaps, Clytie thought, because she felt sorry for her, after being convinced she was Mike's daughter.

"Thought she be your doxy," she told Mike with shrill laughter. Then regarding Clytie as if she were some plumed tropical bird that had strayed northward, she said, "Ne'er in all me versal life saw sich a purty gal!" Nor had suspicion quite left her voice when she said, "Ye ain't arter talkin' like your pa. An' got manners like ye be better 'n common folk like him."

Whereupon Mike denounced the alewife with such vigor that Clytie was hard put to suppress her laughter. "Why, ye old nanny goat!" he stormed. "More of sich bleatin' an' I'll lay boot to your behind. Me darter be in service to a fine lady—finer than ye are like to see. Cert, she'll no' talk like her pa." And with an authority that set everything right: "She be talkin' an' actin' like she be taught, come these six years. More ale, ye ignorant woman!" He banged his mug on the table.

The alewife had been docile enough after that, and she and her husband had told them that their own son, Jed Hawkins, had "jined up" as one of the captain's recruits and had ridden away with him on their only plow horse.

"Kin't do nothin' wi' a lad as makes up his mind to fit them French an'

Injuns. Might as well let him go, handsomelike, ahorse. 'Stead o' hoofin' it to Frederick." But Jed's father went on to say that it was like as not Jed and the captain had "rid over to Si Weaver's farm to pick up Si's son, John." In which case Captain Appleton and his troopers would be likely to tarry the night at Queen o' France Mill.

Nor had Jed's mother neglected to confide that there "ne'er be a finer lad born i' the land. Stringy he be, red-haired," and should they meet up with him, would they "give him his ma's love."

Tears were in the alewife's voice as Clytie promised and said good-by.

And now their shadow of hope and the added hardship of an eight-mile ride had been rewarded. It was the first time Clytie had spent a whole day in the saddle, and although she was prepared to spend others as well, her muscles ached. She was so tired when they reached the clearing and Mike had bargained for use of a cabin and feed for their horses that she welcomed the hard bunk on which she lay down.

And slept. Her need for sleep had drugged her healthy young body. She remembered nothing more until she opened her eyes on the morning light that streamed through the chinks of the windowless cabin. For a moment she knew a sense of bewilderment that was near panic. Where were the silken curtains of her bed at home? The soft light that streamed through the rosy draperies of her windows? There was not even the harsh severity of the Huber guest chamber to reassure her.

Then she heard a raucous voice outside the cabin door, and the world righted itself.

"What kin' o' darter ye got, man, as makes her pa sleep outside wi' his horses?" It was the same screechy voice she had heard when she and Mike rode into the clearing.

A rumbling growl followed the screechy voice—Mike's growl.

Clytie suppressed a giggle, got up from the bunk and scratched herself. She had not taken off her clothes, only her clogs, and the stale, moldy scent of the blanket with which she had covered herself made her put fingers to her nose. She slipped into her clogs, straightened her hair a mite, and listened again to the miller's voice.

"Had a darter like that I'd lar'up her, what I'd do." His snort contested with Mike's growl before he went on: "Ain't no good gonner come o' a darter walkin' high-headed like she be better 'n other folks."

Clytie did not giggle this time. That was the second reference made to the fact that she did not deport herself as though she were Mike's daughter. That was not good. She must try hard to remember always how Lottie, his true daughter, would act. Yet that was not easy. Lottie was always respectful and obedient to her, but with others Clytie had reason to suspect she was pert, saucy. Maybe if she herself tried that . . . She broke off her speculation with a startled "Oh!" Her saddlebags were on the bunk; she had slept with them under her head. Mike must have put them there.

She hurried to the cabin door and flung it wide. "Good mornin', Pa! Good mornin', miller!" she called cheerily.

The miller snorted and turned toward the mill. Mike was just disengaging himself from his bedroll, which lay practically under the horses' feet, and she was reminded of the curious stares people in Chester had given their three horses. And when Mike had told the landlord of the inn the purpose of their journey—a tale she and Mike had agreed upon—he had said to Mike, "Then ye'd best keep close guard on them fine horses, man. Or before ye reach your master an' mistress in Virginia Colony, ye are apt to be shy one or more o' them thoroughbreds."

So Mike was taking no chances. He told her he had slept like a rock and that he would soon have breakfast ready. Then he followed the miller toward the mill to buy feed for the horses.

But now that morning was here, would not the captain soon be riding in? Appleton, Appleton, clippity-clop! She wanted to sing his name aloud, it offered such reassurance for their safe journey to Frederick—safety for the precious letter in her saddlebag. For should she and Mike be able to ride all the way in the wake of his troopers . . .

She heard lusty laughter from the direction of the water trough, and through the morning mist she saw stalwart, rustical figures moving about a fire. The troopers she had seen when she and Mike rode in. Were they cooking their breakfast?

The appetizing smell of salt pork was in the air when Clytie went toward the water trough to wash her face. It needed it. She had slept with almost thirty miles of dust and dirt upon it. She was glad now that she had put an extra supply of jellied olive-oil soap in her saddlebags. Towels too. She ignored the four troopers while she bent over the trough and soaped and scrubbed her face and hands, rinsed them in the cold spring water, then buried her face in her towel; but when she heard a gay, youthful voice call, "Mornin', sister!" she uncovered her face and flicked the towel at them. That was what Lottie would doubtless have done. She wanted no more of this saying she was "better 'n other folks." She even called in a gay voice, "Top o' mornin', sirs!" to be answered by good-natured laughter.

She might need their friendship, she thought as she went back to the cabin to collect her saddlebags.

Atop a little knoll in the clearing near the highroad, Mike had made a fire and was cooking their breakfast. The horses were tethered near by. "Sit down on that log, missy, and drink your tea," he told her, and gave her a steaming cup.

Nothing had ever tasted so delicious, except possibly the eggs, fried ham and rice cakes with molasses that came later.

"Sun's breakin' through," he mumbled, munching his own food. Then anxiously: "That capt'in ought to be gittin' in soon."

Clytie felt anxious, too. Could there be a mistake as to what they had heard about Captain Appleton rendezvousing here with his men?

After they had eaten they saddled their horses, and Mike strapped on Malt's back a supply of feed he had bought from the miller.

"How, Capt'in, sir!"

"Hi, Jed! How, John!"

Clytie swung about at the sound of the troopers' greetings. A rider, followed by two other men ahorse, had appeared on the trail leading up from the brook.

Captain Appleton had arrived.

From this distance he appeared all of a color with his brownish horse, a tall, parasitic growth on the animal, rooted there.

"No dawdling now, men," he called sharply as they gathered about him. "Got feed for your horses?" His voice carried so clearly it was like a padded hammer on a brass gong. "Miller! Miller Jones!" He rode toward the mill.

They could not hear what he said to the miller, but the latter screeched out, "Ye'll git no feed till I be paid fer them fellers poachin' on me——"

"Silence!" snapped the captain. "You'll be paid for the sacks of corn meal and bran you can furnish, and nothing more."

The miller started whining. The captain ignored him and wheeled back toward his men. "Seen any Indians around here?" he asked.

Clytie and Mike hung on his words. The troopers shook their heads. Then, loud enough for the miller to hear, he said, "Down the King's Path, no more than a mile from here, a postrider has been found *scalped*."

The words were a whiplash in Clytie's face. "Mike! Oh, Mike!" she moaned, and cowered behind the bushes through which she had been peeping. And as Mike's face grew hard and grim, she whispered, "It must have been the same postrider, the very same, to whom we thought of entrusting the letter——"

"Sh, missy!" he cautioned, and looked about as if the bushes had ears. Then more gently, "Since we didn't do sich, it ben't our fault—" Mike crossed himself—"that the poor man be butchered." He crossed himself again and muttered words of his faith.

Clytie was too sickened to contradict Mike; yet she knew that he too was thinking that the savage spies had assaulted the postrider, believing he carried the letter that was in her saddlebag.

"I know no more about it than you do," sounded the captain's voice. "Yes, yes," he answered the growls around him, "you can bet it was the French savages who have penetrated this neck of the woods. Likely looking for any documents being carried to Braddock's camp in the south." He swung from his horse and headed toward the mill. A long, lean, purposeful figure followed by several of the troopers.

Those words about Braddock's camp in the south prickled at Clytie's spine like ice.

Mike's face was drawn when he came closer to whisper, "Don't look like ye heard a thing, missy. Be your bright self. 'Twill likely be nought in our favor should the captain suspect . . ."

"Yes, Mike, yes." She could understand that a colonial captain would not wish to add to the hazards of getting untrained troopers through the wilderness by being called on to protect a document valuable to the king's forces; but their intention had been merely to advise the captain that they were traveling in his wake, without imposing on him undue burden. No need for it. Their safety from savage attack would lie in the fact that they traveled within call of the troopers' assistance.

But when the captain came out of the mill, Clytie saw that this plan had gone awry. The miller was directing attention toward her and Mike. In another moment the captain, mounted, was headed toward them.

"Don't slip up on our story, Mike," she whispered as he stamped out the embers of their fire.

But her whole mind and being were riveted on this man whom she depended on as their possible protector, now more a menace as he approached—a centaur, at one with his mount. The horse, with strong play of muscles, was beautiful—Arabian stock, she thought, thick-necked with slender limbs. And the rider—she thought of a Roman legionnaire riding forth to join Caesar. Or was he more the ruthless Spanish conquistador boding ill to all about him? Yet this straight-shouldered, grim-faced captain, who might have belonged to any era of time, was not timeless in his dress: He wore the fringed buckskins of a colonial trapper. A coon's tail dangled from his cap. A musket swung from his shoulder.

When he drew rein Clytie's heart was a riot of misgivings, but she stepped out from the shelter of the shrubbery to meet with a smile the hard gray eyes in his bony face—a face carved of rusty iron, cleanly carved: the nose straight, brow high, protruding chin and full lips covered with a blondish-brown stubble of beard. And of no age at all, neither in the eyes nor face. Ageless.

"Good day to ye, Captain Appleton, sir," she said brightly.

Mike echoed her greeting. But the captain's eyes were on their horses—thoroughbreds, although one carried a pack. Her two sizable boxes, not heavy, were affixed pannierwise, and above them were stores—pots and pans, and hay for the horses.

"Where do you hail from?" he threw at Mike.

"From New York town, sir." Mike's voice did not waver. "We be on our way to Winchester in Virginia Colony to join our mistress, lately married and removed there, sir."

"This your daughter?" The captain jerked his head in Clytie's direction, but with no look at her.

"That be right, sir. Mike O'Day I be, an' me darter, Lottie O'Day, be maid to me mistress——"

"So you figure that by riding in our wake as far as Frederick you'll be safe, hey?"

But how could he have known? Clytie thought quickly. Except that to reach Winchester, which destination was but part of their tale, you had to pass through Frederick.

"We'll no' be of trouble to ye, sir," Mike said.

"You won't, for a fact, my man," the metallic voice assured. "My recruits and I are riding hard and fast under military orders, and if you figure to hold me up because of any trouble you get yourself into, you were never so mistaken. I'm stopping to lend assistance to no man fool enough to set out over this road at *this* time," he emphasized. "And with a woman." His eyes pin-pointed Clytie.

She met them unflinchingly, although she longed to consign this impertinent bumpkin and hope of his friendliness to limbo. "Likely, sir, we will not be needing your assistance," she said mildly. But when he made a scoffing sound in his throat her anger flared, and she continued in a caustic tone, "However, we thank you for your courtesy and kindness, sir." She turned her back on him, picked up her cloak, and started toward her horse. Her linsey-woolsey dress felt, all at once, hot and scratchy.

"I offer neither courtesy nor kindness" was thrown after her. "I but serve the colonies . . . and the king, when it is for the good of the colonies that I do so. So 'tis my duty to warn you of the perils of this road."

Clytie swung quickly about, but not for the reason he doubtless thought. That pause in his voice when he spoke of the king had warned her that this colonial was not to be trusted too far. Mike started to speak, but the captain gave him no time.

"Or didn't you know that the French and their savages are warring on the colonies?" He eyed them both. "Haven't heard, hey, that the King's Path is watched by spies, savage spies, for communications carried from the northern forts to Braddock's forces in Maryland?"

"But, sir," Mike began, "we be nought but peaceful servants——"

"Bah! If a postrider can be suspected of carrying military documents, why not such as you?" His eyes again took in their horses, then narrowed on Clytie.

"If you would imply, sir," she fought down her anger to say quietly, "that documents of value to the king's general would be entrusted to us, you do us too-great honor." She even found courage to give him a mocking smile, which to her amazement dimmed the baleful quality of his scrutiny. Not that she could identify the meaning behind his eyes, yet whatever it was made her blood race.

"I wonder now, Mistress O'Day," he drawled with but the ghost of a smile hidden in his stubble beard.

"You need not, Captain Appleton," she said quickly in an effort to disguise her quiver of fear at such suspicion. "We would be pleased to serve His Majesty, or His Majesty's forces."

"Which Majesty? *Which* forces, ma'am?"

Clytie froze inwardly at this monstrous impertinence, yet met it with gay laughter directed toward Mike. "We are French spies, Pa. Did ye know that?" Mike looked bewildered, so she strode toward her accuser and winked into his frown. "In confidence, Captain, I be the mistress of old Louis of France, and me pa his minister." She whirled on Mike. "Straighten your peruke, ye sweet gentleman, and off with this colonial's head!" Her laughter mounted.

But Captain Appleton was not amused.

"Lawful pert for a *lady's maid,* ma'am," he accused her. Then, turning to Mike, he said, "My warning to you is to turn back to Chester. But if you are bent on Frederick, understand that you can hope for no help from me. The safety of my men is my one concern."

Clytie caught his quick look that added to her disquiet, challenged her. But her reply was cut off as he wheeled his horse and bellowed toward his troopers, "Forward, men!"

He headed at a swift pace toward the highroad. The clatter of his mounted troopers sounded across the clearing. In a cloud of dust they followed their captain.

"What day of the month is it, Mike?"

Clytie was forced to raise her voice to call back at him because of the speed they were making in order to keep on the heels of the troopers. Riding hard and fast, were they? No harder than she and Mike could ride. And despite the outrageous insolence of that Captain Appleton, the King's Path was free. And, ride as he might, her own plans were unchanged: she would follow the troopers and not be shaken off. It might be that the dour-faced captain would proffer her no help should her life be endangered, but not even a red-savage French spy would doubt that such colonials as the troopers would protect their compatriots.

"What say, missy?" Mike had ridden up closer behind her now. They had sighted the troopers only once as they passed across a clearing, so they were far enough ahead not to hear her voice.

"I asked what day of April it was. . . . The twelfth?"

Mike had to think a minute before he agreed with her that it must be the twelfth.

Yes, that was right. And important, because she was trying to figure out what day her father must have traveled this same road on his way south. The seventh, likely, since she had left New York with him on the third. Then if she was not to miss him she must arrive in Frederick not later than the sixteenth. . . .

Time . . . Clytie's mind lingered on the word. Could there be time in this vast illimitable wilderness that for her would roll on and on in mystery? And in danger—that was why she must remember the second of April, that it might stiffen her courage and her resolution not to fail her beloved father in carrying out this mission. For it was on that day that he had summoned her into the library of their home on Pearl Street. . . . It had been raining, Clytie remembered. . . .

CHAPTER *Three*

On April 2 Clytie DeLancey had been delighted at her father's summons; she had not expected him home from the fort so early and had rushed down to the library, only to stand agape at sight of the grim look on his face. James DeLancey, acting Royal Governor of New York Colony, was standing with his back to the glowing fire. It was a characteristic stance, hands on the small of his back beneath his velvet coat. But there was nothing characteristic about the deeply troubled look that caused him neither to see nor to hear his daughter's entrance. . . . Nor about the way his shoulders drooped.

He was a soldier, Clytie told herself. His tall, straight figure *never* drooped. Oh, he could snake down into a chair as if he had not a bone in his body, but that was only when he was in a playful or philosophical mood. He was in neither of these moods now.

She backed up against the heavy curtains of the doorway, fear in her heart. What had happened? Great washes of rain beat against the windows, but he appeared not to notice that either. Could it be that the doctor had told him about his weak heart? Her reason resisted that, for Doctor White had said it was best that he not know, that no one know but old Manners, their housekeeper, and herself, unless worse symptoms developed. Not even her mother knew, Clytie was glad to remember.

He moved toward his desk with heavy tired steps, and the whole room seemed to dissolve into a threnody of tired, doleful colors. The cheerful mood created by the sparkle of the fire on the richly patterned carpet, tapestried chairs and gold velvet draperies at the windows was blotted out by her fears. She did not make her presence known, because she had learned never to disturb his thoughts. He was so cruelly overworked.

James DeLancey was not only acting royal governor, he was still serving as lieutenant governor as well. Governor Osborne had hanged himself, and the king and parliament had sent no one over to replace him. Clytie often thought they delayed in sending a new governor because they knew no one could work so well with the colonial assembly as her father, since he was a colonial himself. And he was trusted and honored after his long service as chief justice of the highest court, and, later, as lieutenant governor.

As he took up a paper from his desk and put it down again with an impatient gesture, his expression in the brighter light of the candles looked more troubled still. Clytie moved toward him.

"Papa," she said softly.

"Oh–ah–yes, yes, my child." He swung about, but with such effort to concentrate on her that she threw her arms about his slender waist and buried her head against him.

"You . . . are all right, Papa?"

"Yes, yes." He patted her shoulder. "Sit down, my dear." He seated himself at his desk, took up several papers his secretary had left there, and signed them hurriedly.

When a sigh of relief escaped him, Clytie relaxed in her chair. So that was it! He had arrived at a decision after long and careful thought, as was his wont. Now he would be his precious self again. And she would learn why he had sent for her: to tell her of some lovely social event, likely, to which he would take her, and for which she must have a beautiful new dress. She had never gone out anywhere or had any lovely dresses until these last wonderful months when she and her father had been alone together, after her mother, her elder sister, Olivia, and the boys had sailed for England.

But when her father, still in somber thought, went back to the hearth-rug, her anxieties returned.

He was a tall man with a spare but well-knit frame. And because at no time had he ever neglected his military training, he had whipcord muscles. His face was lean below his high, wide brow, his hair powdered and tied back neatly with a ribbon. He wore a peruke only on ceremonial occasions. Wondrous handsome, Clytie thought him. His chin was indented, just as hers was, below full lips. Only, his cheeks did not settle into foolish dimples like hers. And whenever he fixed someone with his penetrating gray-green eyes, his lips curling into a cryptic smile, she always recalled what that overstuffed woman at the DePuyster ball had said of him: "Deliciously saturnine." Maybe that was because the woman knew he saw through her, as he did through most people. But for the most part, his smile was so benign it threw this picture of him out of balance. That is, it did if she did not recall the impressive occasion when, as a child, she had been permitted to see him bewigged, robed and august—and a little terrifying—seated on the supreme-court bench. There his eyes rapier-pointed evildoers.

But it was nicer to remember him as lieutenant governor, when all cares seemed to fall from him in his happiness with his militia. Then came Governor Osborne's awful death. . . . Clytie had watched him anxiously since then, while her mother fluttered and preened her lovely feathers as the wife of the royal governor. True, her mother had not known what she and Manners knew about the effect of these dreadful responsibilities on him. The doctor had thought it best for her father that her mother not know.

"You have known, of course, my child, that I intend soon for Alexandria for a conference with General Braddock." Her father spoke so suddenly that Clytie was shaken out of her reverie.

"Y-yes, Papa."

"I am leaving tomorrow at sunrise. And because of the uncertain conditions here, I see no other way—none for my peace of mind—" he pulled at his embroidered waistcoat—"but to take you with me."

"M-m-me, Papa?" Then, as full realization of this rushed over her, she bounded to her feet. "To Alexandria? That is so close to Frederick, where Aunt Monica Chester lives! Oh, Papa—!"

"Quiet, please, my child." He strode across to a window, then turned back again. "Assuredly, I am not taking you all the way to Alexandria. Nor to Frederick. What sort of a father would I be to take you into that troubled part of the country, exposed—but for the general's army, lately come to our aid—to enemy raiders?"

"Aunt Monica—you mean, Aunt Monica is . . ."

"I shall know more of the dangers besetting your aunt and her family when I arrive there for the conference with other royal governors." He was still walking about, with shoulders bent. "Presence of the general's headquarters in Frederick will solve the Chesters' problem of safety for a while; but he intends, at the earliest possible moment, for the northwestern fort of Duquesne." He stopped and looked at her with anxious eyes. "Meanwhile, it is *your* safety I must consider."

Clytie could only stare wide-eyed and appeal unsteadily, "New York—you mean, New York—?"

But he did not seem to be listening. He went to a window and looked into the gray mist and fog. A cart rumbled over the cobblestones of Pearl Street. A sudden downpour again pelted the windows. Memories pelted Clytie as she looked up at her grandfather's portrait over the mantelpiece—memories of what he had said long ago when the French and their savages threatened the northern borders of New York Colony:

"They must be driven back. Not one inch of our blessed free soil must we abandon to French tyranny. This vast new country of ours can prosper only under the Magna Charta—under British laws, British love of justice and freedom." Yet her grandfather had been born *French,* of a French Huguenot family who had fled the wrath of "old Louis, the Sun-God," and had taken refuge in England before coming to America—"the greatest land on earth, child. . . ."

"I do, indeed, mean that New York is endangered," said her father, turning back toward her. "All the colonies are endangered. What with the French fleet patrolling our shores and with only our thin line of forts, poorly manned, to guard our northern boundaries, it will be but by God's mercy that we are not swept into the sea."

He was talking to himself, as much as to her, as his restlessness carried him from point to point about the room. When he relaxed and his voice became milder, Clytie relaxed with him.

"The point is, I must make this journey. There is no way out. And since Philadelphia is about the safest part of the country, as I see it at the moment, I must take you there and leave you with your Aunt Priscilla Huber, until I can pick you up on my way back."

The pleading protest Clytie would have made died on her lips as she saw behind his eyes an appeal for her co-operation. But Aunt Prissy!

Aunt Prissy Huber, her mother's sister, gaunt and raw-boned, had filled Clytie with fright and awe ever since she had been a child. Aunt Prissy had married a Quaker "to outquake all Quakerdom." Her mother had laughed—her beautiful mother, whom Aunt Prissy had called "a vain, silly, frivolous creature," to which remark her mother had answered: "Better than being a religious fanatic."

Clytie's father spoke also of his own peace of mind, so she only answered softly, "Yes, Papa."

"It won't be for long, my dear—" he laid his hand on her bent head and stroked her hair—"not more than a fortnight at best."

Clytie reached up for his hand and rubbed her cheek against it. He could take her to the devil and leave her there, if it would help his peace of mind.

"Now, best run along and pack." He moved toward his desk. "Nothing frivolous, you know," he cautioned her, with a smile. "Quakers, and all that. . . . But, yes, yes—one pretty dress—for the night that I remain in Philadelphia. I shall take you to dine with Governor Morris."

Clytie was able to return his smile. But from the curtains at the doorway she again regarded her grandfather's portrait. It was that of a white-haired, elderly man with wide-set blue eyes. Strength and nobility were in the features. He was half smiling, as though about to wrinkle his big nose, put his finger to it and tell a wondrous tale of the vast wilderness through which he had once journeyed.

But to Clytie the portrait was more than a likeness. It had sometimes come alive since he died, four years ago, to counsel and comfort her. And her superstition, that nothing ever turned out well unless she invoked advice of the portrait, had grown, and at this moment she needed advice badly if she were to find the fortitude to remain with the Hubers for two weeks. Help me for my father's sake, Grandfather, her heart appealed. Old Etienne DeLancey's eyes, that held hers, appeared to glow, and at the sound of her father's scratching pen, Clytie added: Watch over him on this journey, Grandfather. Keep him safe!

She closed the door softly behind her.

It was the next morning when, coated and bonneted for her journey, she made a more memorable appeal to the portrait. That was because she had had a strange dream during the night.

She and her maid, Lottie, just before she went to bed, had finished packing her boxes with the drabbest dresses her wardrobe afforded, except for one—a lovely blue satin she was to wear for dinner with Governor Morris—and Lottie had asked what jewels she would wear with it. Clytie had pondered that. The bracelet, necklace and earrings set with diamonds, left her by Grandfather DeLancey, or those set with rubies, lately given her by her father?

Unable to decide, she had given Lottie her big jewel box to pack.

"'Tis awful heavy, missy," Lottie said.

And it was. She must make her boxes as light as possible since they must be strapped atop the carriage.

Searching about for another box, she had come upon one of her childhood treasures. It was a box of black tin, painted with flowers and cupids, that her grandfather had given her on her eighth birthday, and because she had not found a better use for it, she sailed her dolls in it on the fish pond at his farm on the Hudson. So she had dumped the contents of her jewel box into this one, after Lottie had lined it with cotton wool.

Her dream that night had been about the box. She herself was sailing in it, over murky troubled water, and out of the darkness around her sounded wild savage yells such as her grandfather had told her were made by Indians in the wilderness.

Still disturbed by the dream, she had stopped in the library to say good-by to her grandfather's portrait.

In the darkish room she lighted a candle and placed it on the mantelshelf, and because of her dread of the Hubers, she had been glad to remember one of her grandfather's sayings: "Never give others the power to make you unhappy, chickadee. Hold your happiness tight within you, so that no one can get at it to destroy it." (That was because Olivia so often conspired with her mother to make her wretched.)

Yes, Grandfather. But, oh, how I long to visit Aunt Monica in Frederick! her thoughts had just said, when a rush of cold air came into the library from the outer door.

The candle flickered, cast strange shadows on her grandfather's face, and to Clytie's amazement and awe he was looking down on her in stern admonishment. Unbelieving, she stepped back from the portrait. But there it was! The same look he had given her once when he had told her not to go near the fish pond, swollen by the spring rains, and she had gone and fallen in, and had almost drowned.

Unmistakably, the portrait wore a *frown.*

"But why, Grandfather? Why? . . ."

Maybe she had breathed it aloud, for at that moment old Manners bustled in and said, "Sayin' your prayers, the Lord love ye? No time for that. Git along wi' ye, dearie," she urged, "else ye keep the governor waitin' at the ferry. The carriage be waitin', Mike and Lottie on the box."

She followed Clytie to the outer door. Then Clytie, still haunted by her grandfather's frown, turned and hugged Manners before racing down the steps and toward the carriage.

It was befitting that the daughter of the royal governor should travel by carriage, but Clytie envied her father, his aides and small squad of militia, who were ahorse.

Since leaving the ferry at Perth Amboy she had kept her eyes close to one of the little draped windows to see the green sprouts that sprang up from the earth like solemn gnomes, or little green gods in council, while the brooks and streams babbled wisely in their own tongue. And at every wayside stop her father's spirits improved; he joked and laughed with her and Captain Saxon as if they were on a holiday. This only pointed up the truth of what dear old Manners had said: "Don't ye go worryin' about the gov'ner long as he be ahorse."

Manners, who had been with the DeLanceys since "the gov'ner" was a little boy, had tut-tutted as well Clytie's fears that he would lead his militia into battle. "Kin't be spared to mix in the fight, dearie," she had said. "He'll but appoint fightin' men. 'Tis like enough he'll be ridin' to Albany soon. Maybe to the forts. Well and good," she had emphasized. "Git him away from all the taxin' worries in New York."

This had proved true as he rode through the sun and soft winds. But when they reached Bordentown, on the Delaware, where they were to take the scow ferry the next morning for Philadelphia, her father seemed depressed. At supper in the little inn, with her and Captain Saxon, he brooded, as if something weighed heavily beneath the surface of his mind and made him drink more of the fine port wine he had brought along than was his wont.

Clytie succeeded in enlivening him for a time by the jokes she made with Captain Saxon, a big blond giant of a man. More brawn than brains, she thought—for when she told him she would have preferred being ahorse to sitting in the carriage he blushed from shock.

At which her father laughed heartily. "Why, she can outride and outshoot a trooper, Saxon," he bragged. "And swim like a duck."

The poor captain reddened all the more. He had a little birdlike wife as bright-feathered and nesty as Olivia DeLancey, who had never baited a worm on a hook in her life. All Olivia wanted was to chirp and flutter in drawing rooms like their mother.

"All my father's work," James DeLancey went on proudly. "He had Clytie and her brothers taught many useful things, the same things. Woodcraft. How to make a meal if they had to. My father always maintained that in this vast new country young people should be prepared to pioneer if necessary, for one never knows . . . never knows."

He seemed prepared to settle into gloom again, until Clytie said gaily, "You see, my grandfather was preparing me to marry a colonial." She wrinkled her nose at her father.

"Should the right Mister Colonial come along, my pet." He answered her smile and attacked his spring lamb, hominy and applesauce with more appetite.

Clytie was reminded of how they had laughed together at so many of her suitors who had come along since he had been taking her to official functions, after her mother, sister and the boys had sailed. "Too much snuff on his ruffles," he would sum up. Or, "What that lad wants is to be wed to his grog, not a wife." Then one evening he had said quite seriously, "Would God I could find for you the right husband! A man, not a puppet of damask and lace." And she had known too well why the matter so deeply concerned him, for, once her mother was home again and Olivia's marriage arranged to suit her mother's pleasure, her own turn would come. And protests would avail her little should the suitor be able to advance her mother's ambitions.

"Time rides a man hard," her father was saying with that troubled look again on his face. He slumped deeper in his chair. "Had I been able to make this trip a week ago, I might have encountered General Shirley, who has no doubt by now welcomed General Braddock and sailed north again."

There had come a moment's weighted silence. James DeLancey sipped his port. Clytie opened her ears and heart. It was as though some key to her father's late worries had been found.

"But is it not likely, sir, that General Shirley would have been able to supply General Braddock with the information your delayed dispatch would have contained?" Captain Saxon spoke hopefully.

But James DeLancey fixed unseeing eyes upon him before he said sharply, "Impossible. Shirley has been patrolling the seas from Nova Scotia to Boston. And what with this long trip south, he could have had no late report from Oswego, and likely not from Niagara." He fell into brooding silence.

So that was it! thought Clytie. That was the cause of his deep depression in the library at home when he had told her of this journey. He was awaiting a dispatch from the fort of Oswego that had not come.

"What we dare not forget," he aroused himself to continue, "is the cunning of our enemy, of their murderous savage spies, doubtless dispatched to watch our trails from the northern forts all the way to Braddock's encampment in the south."

A clammy hand squeezed at Clytie's heart as she watched her father's deeply troubled face and brought out some foreboding that transferred his anxiety to her. It rested heavily on her shoulders, and because of this she asked, irresistibly, since it was not her nature to question her father, "When your document from the forts arrives in New York, Papa, won't they dispatch it to you in Alexandria or Frederick?"

"Hey?" He looked startled. But after he had gulped his port, he said, "Yes, yes, no doubt, my child, if . . . it arrives there."

His very hesitation had seemed to brand her mind with some awareness of danger. Whether for herself or for him her conscious mind made no accounting. But after she had gone to bed that night the thought of her father's messenger riding hard and alone through fearsome stretches of dark forest haunted her.

It was still haunting her when they reached Philadelphia. It lingered in her consciousness after her father continued on his way southward. . . . So that deep in her heart she knew she had been mystically forewarned when the bloodstained, wounded messenger bearing her father's dispatch arrived at the Hubers' and lost consciousness at the doorway.

CHAPTER Four

CLYTIE and Mike had ridden hard on the heels of the troopers all day with scarcely a stop. It had been easy enough to keep them within sight and hearing during the first seven miles to Wilmington village; but after they had left the little settlement, to trail through bogs and woods and barren stretches, the pace they set had left Clytie saddle-worn.

Not that she minded being tired and hungry; her chief unease was about Bob, her horse. Mike had bought him for her the day before they had left Philadelphia. Bob had stood up well during their first day's travel, but the grilling pace of keeping up with the troopers had left her unsure of his stamina. She feared his heart was not too strong, yet she could not bring herself to mention it to Mike. He was so worried about the other two horses.

Salt and Malt were her father's carriage cobs that had brought her to Philadelphia. They were strong and well-muscled, but poor Malt was not accustomed to serving as a pack horse, and during the last few hours Mike had been talking to him as though he were a child on whom had been imposed an undue burden. When they had crossed the Christiana bridge, and one of the troopers—not the captain—had turned to wave at them, Mike had muttered, "Mind ye, Malt, nought but a plow horse he's got. Ye be not lettin' the like o' him outdo ye, hey?"

They had just climbed to the top of a low ridge amid cultivated fields, and Clytie was not surprised to hear Mike call, "Draw up, missy!" He dismounted and loosened Malt's girth. "Troopers or no troopers," he growled, "I got no mind to git these horses stove in. Tryin' to throw us off o' his track, that captain be," he went on in a tindery voice. "But less 'n they stop to rest their nags, they'll be afoot 'stead of ahorse time they git to Frederick." But he added, "Ain't many horses in as fine fettle as that captain's mare be."

Clytie was glad to slip to the ground and exercise her legs. A sidesaddle always made her feel cramped. Several times to rest herself she had thrown her leg over the saddle and ridden astride as she had on her grandfather's farm. Long ago in England and France, she considered, women had ridden astride on long journeys. Maybe she should have dressed herself as a boy on this trip; yet since she was so poor an actress that she could not even imitate Mike's accent, the gimlet-eyed captain might have suspected her of worse things than being a French spy.

She gave each of the horses a lump of the sugar with which she had stuffed her pocket this morning at breakfast. She gave Mike a couple, too, and ate some herself since there was not time to unstrap the stores and take out some bread. But as the horses rested she stretched her legs. The fresh wind flapped her cloak, and high in the larkspur-blue sky white clouds tumbled over the far vistas of the wilderness. Down a rutted little lane was a settler's small log hut, and she thought of all the tales her grandfather had told of the dangers of such brave settlers. Had dear Aunt Monica, after she married her Maryland planter, ridden this same road? But no, they had taken a boat to Baltimore, Clytie remembered being told. She had seen Aunt Monica only once in all her life; that was when she and Uncle Peter Chester and their two sons, Jamie and Pete, had come to New York for a visit seven years ago. But, oh, how she had loved them all!

"Aunt Mony, Aunt Mony, I'm on my way to you!" She covered the distance back to Mike and the horses in unmaidenly leaps and bounds, her sunny-brown ringlets flying in the wind.

"How far to Elk River, Mike?" she said when she had mounted her horse. He had told her he thought the troopers would make camp there.

"Depends on where we cross it, I reckon." He adjusted the gun strap over his shoulder and squinted at the sun. "About three hours to sunset, and less 'n that captain be more fool 'n he looks he ain't gonner swim no horses, hot from travel, over that river."

They were riding briskly over a good stretch of road when Clytie asked, "Swim a river, Mike?" There had been a ferry at the Brandywine.

"Body dunno what he be apt to meet up with," he said, close behind her now.

The forest trail grew darker and darker. A copse of evergreens, sprinkled among the great sky-nudging trees, with their feathered branches, and the thick undergrowth made a gloom that was eerie. Not even a bird note sounded.

Clytie was picking her way along the soft loamy path when Bob stopped, snorted, pranced and caracoled. "Steady, Bob! Good boy!"

"Whoa, Salt! Whoa, Malt!"

Mike was struggling with his horses when Clytie saw the big, dark, shadowy creature lope across the road not twenty feet ahead. With a crackling of underbrush it disappeared. But scent of the bear had so frightened the horses that they had to give them their heads and gallop along the trail with the fear of Malt's pack coming to grief at any moment against the low, overhanging branches.

Anxious now that the troopers had got too far ahead for them to catch up before the sun went down, they kept up a good pace after leaving the dark woods. The birds sang again. Their orchestration became a din, until Clytie could not distinguish the trill of a wren from the squawk of a jay.

"There, Mike! There they are!" From the brow of a hill she sighted the troopers winding along a sparsely wooded valley road, strung out like a thin, dark thread. Never had the sight of fellow beings so comforted her. Since coming on the bear, her joy of the wilderness had been tempered by thought of the lurking sinister things beneath its beauty.

Clytie had lost sense of time and distance when she and Mike reached the valley floor, where the trail led through tall swamp grass; but after they climbed a hill and sighted the river winding broad and yellow amid a green tapestry, she knew they were not far behind the troopers. She was too tired now to take account of anything but that the sun squatted low over the green and copper glow.

As they were winding through the river valley she had the unreal sensation of swimming through a blue mist that mounted into the wide branches of giant sycamores. The sandy soil took on a nacreous, golden light. . . . Everything swam, nixie-wise, leaves, pebbles. . . . The tree trunks were purple giants waving saffron clubs trimmed with green feathers. Clytie clung to her saddle.

"Hold these, missy." Mike gave her the reins of the other horses. But when she heard his voice again she had to struggle out of a fog. "They be makin' camp, thank the Lord," he said fervently. "Hear 'em?"

Yes, she heard the purple giants laughing—gold and blue sound. Clytie untangled herself from it and slid to the ground.

"Best wake up an' eat your supper, missy." Mike was standing over her. Clytie sat up, startled.

She was wrapped in one of her blankets and had slept with her saddlebags under her head; she could not remember when she had lain down. She yawned prodigiously, saw the fire he had made, and smelled the good scent of cooking. Their horses within the light of the fire seemed to be munching on the surrounding blue twilight.

Through the windows of the great tree columns she could see another fire in a clearing beside the river, sending up bright sparks—the troopers' fire! They were calling to one another with jests and laughter. What did their uncivil, rustic captain think, now that she and Mike were so close behind him?

Mike's supper of ham, boiled potatoes, corn-meal cakes and applesauce was wonderful. She drank three cupfuls of good hot tea. But after Mike had eaten and was puffing at his corn pipe, he shook his head at her dolefully.

"It ain't right that ye sleep unhoused."

"But, Mike, I love it!" She kept her voice low for fear the befuddling captain might be eavesdropping. Yet there was no use trying to make Mike understand how truly she loved these vast, silent places. It was as though something were released in her spirit, which she did not quite understand herself. More as though some missing part of herself—lost after her grandfather died and his beloved farm was sold—had been found and fitted into place.

A big, gibbous moon was rising and glimmering down on the river shadowed on the far side with a violet wall of forest. Yet this lovely world was not so silent after all. Near at hand a brook dashed out a tune on its rocky way to the river, and there was the ringing sound of tree frogs to which bull frogs along the riverbank added a bass note.

"There be a ferry," Mike said. "Seen it down aways a piece."

When he had gone off to wash their supper vessels in the brook, Clytie sat lulled and contented, watching the fire sink to red embers. The troopers' fire was dying low, too, and she reminded herself that she must not judge the incivility of the captain too harshly. Her father often said you must know all the circumstances connected with a person's action before you had a right to judge. Aunt Prissy Huber was likely judging her unjustly at this very moment for the theft of her father's letter from the cabinet where Aunt Prissy had locked it.

Thoughts of the dour, forbidding woman and of the unhappy days she had spent at her house flooded Clytie's mind.

The Hubers had received her with courtesy—in her *father's* presence—not unmixed with resignation toward the Lord's will that permitted invasion of their house by such godless kin. Nor had the Hubers objected when she dressed herself in her lovely blue satin and Mike drove her away to the governor's mansion for dinner, where her father was stopping for the night.

"I think that they were relieved, Papa, at the saving of food I might have consumed this evening." She found time to giggle before they joined the other guests.

He had laughed with her. "Whatever could Prissy have done with all the Heathcote money? She received as much as your mother."

"Hid it in the walls, likely, with the corpses."

"Corpses, my child?"

"Doesn't the whole house smell like a moldy tomb?"

They laughed together until he sobered. "Your aunt is a God-fearing woman, my dear. Eccentric, but kindly."

Clytie was to find, later, that this was one of his rare misjudgments. Her aunt's *kindliness* proved but that of a wily cat left in charge of one of the fine-feathered DeLancey birds. Clytie was even convinced that her aunt's mouth had watered long for such a chance, for the morning after her father had ridden south with Governor Morris and Benjamin Franklin, Aunt Prissy cast baleful eyes on the dark-blue dress Clytie wore.

"Your mother being the lightheaded, ungodly woman she is, I might have expected you to offend me with such garments," she remarked.

Clytie had made no answer, having promised her father to keep her temper. She had gone to her room and changed to the black silk dress she wore at funerals, which met with almost as much disapproval.

It was the sinister silence in the clammy house that oppressed her most. Only one small fire was kept going in the dining room. None in the parlor, not ever. Nor in her room. Mike and Lottie slept in the barn loft where there were dreadful rats.

Speech had been tabooed in the Huber household because of some religious implication. Sandwiched in between a silent supper and an early bed hour was the observance Clytie dreaded most: a séance in the cold parlor, that she was given to understand she must attend. This was the hour in which the Hubers communed with God.

Communed but poorly, she suspected, since she had heard no kind word spoken in the house forever closed to sun and air.

For these séances Uncle Aaron Huber would sit with his little button eyes closed, his scrawny beard lowered on his chest, his waspish little black-clad figure shriveled to even smaller proportions. Sleeping, Clytie supposed. Aunt Prissy, raw-boned, upright, lips set grimly, appeared to be a totem-pole effigy. And that they were not true Quakers, Clytie soon learned. They were merely religious fanatics such as may dishonor any creed. This was evidenced on the morning the messenger arrived, bearing the letter for her father from the northern forts.

Clytie was in her room when she heard Lottie's scream from the hallway below. She raced down the stairs and saw a disheveled soldier leaning against the front door.

"DeLancey . . . message . . . Gov . . . DeLan . . ." The thick words struggled out, his eyes appealing to her, as he slumped to the floor.

"Get Mike! Quick!" Clytie knelt beside him, and, her mind alert to the importance of the document he carried, managed to roll him over, unbutton his jacket and feel for it, feverishly. Her hand first touched warm blood, but she searched on, her father's troubled face before her.

She had just drawn out the letter, with its big official seal, and was ramming it into the pocket of her dress when Prissy Huber's voice shrilled behind her.

"What's this? Who's this? Blood on my carpet! Blood——"

"He is my father's messenger from the forts," Clytie tried to say in a quiet voice, at which the other's fanatical cry mounted in rage.

"War messenger! War blood! War! Get him out of my house! Out!"

It was the inhuman screech that had caught Clytie off guard. The big letter still protruded from her pocket, and as she looked up into the distorted face a bony talon snatched at the letter and tore it from her.

"Hiding something from me, hey? Hiding——"

"It is my father's letter." Clytie was on her feet, face flaming. "Give it to me at once, Aunt Prissy. It is important."

But Prissy Huber only shook the letter she held high and headed for the parlor. "War! War! James DeLancey, barbarian, making war!"

Beating back her fears, Clytie followed. "You must give me the letter, that I may dispatch it to my——" An angry shove sent her reeling backward. She lost her balance and sprawled on the floor.

"Must, hey?" her aunt's voice taunted her. "You, to say *must* in my house!" And before Clytie could get to her feet, Prissy Huber thrust the letter into a cabinet and locked it. She shook the key at Clytie. "The letter was delivered to my house, my fine lady, and here it stays!" She turned back into the hallway, where Mike and Lottie bent over the wounded man, and cawked like a buzzard. "Out! Get him out! War blood in my house!" She hurried from the sight of the wounded man.

Clytie shuddered at the recollection of those next two days in the Huber house, convinced as she had been that her aunt was half demented. But in making their plans to get possession of the letter and dispatch it to her father, she and Mike had been forced to go slow.

She sat up straight now to see Mike moving about in the moonlight; the moon was climbing in the sky, silvering the water and filtering through the tall sycamores. What was he doing? Oh, dear, kind Mike! He was cutting boughs to make her a bed, piling them under a tree.

It had not been easy to convince Mike that they must carry her father's letter themselves through the wilderness. They had taken the wounded messenger to a doctor in Philadelphia and had seen that he was well looked after. But Doctor Benton, a kindly man, had assured them that the messenger, with such a bullet wound in his side, would not be able to ride again for weeks.

Their search had begun then for another trustworthy messenger. And after fruitless days of looking, Doctor Benton had summed up their difficulties accurately.

"You see, Mistress DeLancey, the forts are now poorly enough manned, with none but a raw recruit to be spared. It would be a poor gamble for ye to take, since t'would be better that your father and General Braddock not receive news of the northern forts than have such fall into enemy hands. Besides, whate'er ye pay a man of whose honor ye cannot be sure, 'tis likely a French spy would pay more." He shook his wise old head and counseled further: "With Governor Morris and his staff departed with your father, there be none to concern themselves about a letter for the governor of New York, each colony but holding, as it does, jealousy of other colonies."

But yes, Clytie had heard her father lament that fact.

And so she and Mike had spoken of entrusting the letter to the post-rider, with herself protesting.

"It would not be right, Mike. Mr. Franklin's riders serve peace, not war. It would be disloyal trickery."

Yet she had been sorely tempted to obliterate His Majesty's seal and dispatch it as a peaceful document. Memory of the kind-faced Mr. Franklin, her father's friend who was postal commissioner for the colonies, had precluded that. (She had sat next to him at Governor Morris' dinner and had later confided to him—oh, many things. . . .)

The inevitable had caught up with her then, and the burden she had felt with such strange prescience fall upon her shoulders in Bordentown became more weighted. "Mike, I shall carry the letter myself," she had said, as though her intention were to go alone. Mike was bound to her father; she had no right to dispatch him alone on a mission of peril.

"Y-you, missy?" Mike's hair had all but stood on end with fear. And when she had revealed her plan to take him with her, it had been no better. "I be servin' the DeLanceys nigh on to thirty years—" he had groaned—"an' for the gov'ner I'd lay down me life, but I'll no' be risking the life of his daughter in the fearsome wilderness."

Yet, when he sensed that nothing could divert her from her plan—that she meant to go with or without him—he had set about preparations with a craft and wisdom that amazed her. He had told her how to effect secrecy in their escape from the Hubers, and had purchased and gathered together all their equipment. She still felt that in all these long years the DeLanceys had underrated Mike.

They had postponed theft of the letter from the Huber cabinet until the evening before their escape, fearing the letter would be missed. After the Hubers were in bed and Uncle Aaron snoring, Clytie had crept down the darkened stairs in a long, blinding fear as shapeless and menacing as the darkness. She had opened a shuttered window, and Mike had entered and pried open the cabinet. She could still feel that awful sensation of groping blindly for the letter, fearing that it had been removed. The old clock in the hall had ticked an eternity, until her hand came in contact with the great seal. . . .

"Best be beddin' down, missy," Mike said.

"Oh, yes, Mike." Clytie sprang up and dashed away her memories. "Oh, thank you for the wonderful bed, Mike." She wrapped one blanket about her and lay down to cover herself with the other. "Do you think I might take off my clogs?" It would be nice to wriggle her toes.

"There be nought to trouble ye. One of the troopers be on guard." He covered the fire and bedded down close to the horses.

Yes, one of the troopers was on guard. She sat up, and through a pathway made by the moon she could see a long-bodied man doubled up on a log near the embers of the troopers' fire. Such a lonely figure in the vast moon-washed night. As she watched him, he stood up and stretched himself. Then, with his hands at the small of his back, he looked out onto the silvered water. . . . The captain. It was Captain Appleton, and with a shape, stance and outline just like her father's. Odd that she had taken no account of that when she first saw his lean bony face, his long-stemmed body. No man could be truly bad who was so like her father. . . . "Riding hard and fast on military duty," he had said. Or was he riding fast to his wife and children? Even a hard-eyed man could have a loving wife and children . . . an unpredictable man who, with that queer, sardonic smile he had leveled on her, had made her blood race. It was as if for a moment she had seen a different man behind the mask. She would like to see him really smile.

A woods creature scampered in the branches over her head. A twig dropped. The frogs along the river croaked in chorus. The captain still gazed over the river as Clytie tucked her saddlebags, with their precious box, under her head and slept.

CHAPTER *Five*

NOTHING moved. Nothing rubbed against anything else or made a sound. There was only a sea of mist, with the world not yet in the process of creation; then a groan. The birth pangs of something being born? A bird twittered sleepily. More twitters . . .

Clytie lifted her head and saw the fog-bound shapes of their horses nosing at their feed. A crunching sound . . . Mike, a phantom shape, was treading the gray sea, but, happily, carrying a very real kettle of water.

Clytie got up and shook herself out. "But the troopers, Mike?" She saw only the troopers' horses tethered to the limbs of trees.

"They be downriver a mite, lookin' at the ferry."

She noted an odd tone in his voice, but went off gaily to wash herself in the little brook. When she came back her breakfast was ready.

After Mike had gulped his own food and had gone off to find the troopers, she, eager to bestir herself, saddled Bob, tied up her own blanket roll, and fastened it securely as Mike had taught her. She led Bob into the clearing beside the river, and when she recognized the captain's beautiful horse tied up some distance away from the others, she tethered Bob near him. This might afford her a chance to say a cheery good morning since she had not handled their other interview very tactfully—she had not done justice to her father's diplomacy, although Mr. Franklin that night of Governor Morris' dinner had called her "a very diplomatic little lady."

How wonderful Mr. Franklin had been! Her thoughts leaped toward him as she felt a hungry desire to be on her way. He had traveled this same route with her father toward Frederick, toward Aunt Monica. He was an old friend of the Chesters and had told her all about Pete and Jamie—Pete was a born soldier, and Jamie meant to be a doctor. . . . No wonder she had confided to Mr. Franklin that her father's heart was not too strong. "And, oh, sir, won't you please tell Aunt Monica that she must guard against my father's receiving any sort of shock," she had pleaded, "for the doctor says that would be mortal bad for him."

Mr. Franklin had been all sympathy and kindness, to shame her for her first impression of him. When she first saw him, a man in drab homespun dress among a bevy of damasked and peruked gentlemen and handsomely gowned ladies, she thought his dress queer. Her opinion changed after she had met him and had been warmed by his smile. Mr. Franklin's eyes were as wide-set as her grandfather's, but deep-set, too, beneath a wide brow; his brown hair lay limp and unpowdered about his collar. In spite of his homespun appearance, everyone at the governor's table had hung on his words when he had spoken in his mellow-voiced, impressive way. Of course, she had heard of the postal commissioner before; her father was always quoting something he had said. She had read the *Gazette* Mr. Franklin published, too, but never had she met anyone whose charm and friendliness so lingered in her mind.

She heard shouts from the direction where Mike had gone, and now that the mist was lifting she could see the ferry drawn up half out of the water and men gathered around it. She gave Bob a lump of sugar and started toward them along the pebbly river shore.

"Ain't got no nails," someone shouted. "Sent me son to Baltimore town to git some."

That must be the ferryman. Clytie walked nearer. The captain and some of the troopers were examining the flat-bottomed boat.

"Mebbe we kin peg her up, Capt'in," one of them said.

"Kin't do no more 'n I could of done," yelled the ferryman, "an' I had the timber to mend 'er." Whereupon Captain Appleton told him angrily that it was his business to keep the ferry in good condition. He only screeched louder: "Got plenty time to cut timber, seein' me son won't be back fer couple o' days."

The troopers were now arguing so angrily with him, Clytie thought it best not to move closer.

" 'Tain't my fault she got stove in takin' all them horses, so'jers and big officer fellers across nigh a week ago."

Oh, that would have been her father's party. . . .

"I wonder they got across, you lazy old gaffer," the captain shouted. "She's rotten clean through." And to his men he said, "Take a day to fix her up, if we had the time—which we haven't. Make ready to swim across, men. Jed, Zeb, take a look along the bank—see where we can ford without getting in too much mud. I'll have a look down this way." He disappeared among the bushes that lined the downstream bank.

Clytie's insides grew cold. The yellow, sluggish river was wide from the spring rains, and the far bank seemed a long way off. At midstream—or was it nearer the far shore?—a current appeared to swirl. At the crunch of a step, Clytie turned to see Mike.

"We—we can camp here wi' the ferryman, missy, till the boat be mended," he tried to say cheerfully. He rubbed a hand along his thigh and looked away from her. " 'Tain't no other way."

"In which case we lose protection of the troopers, Mike." She had already made up her mind about what she intended to do, but tried to break it to him gently. "And remember, time is as precious to us as to them." She noted the spasm of fear in his eyes, but steeled herself. "If they can swim that river, Mike, *we* can."

"No, missy, no!"

His fright was so painful that she put a hand on his arm. "Listen to me, Mike. You told me what I might have to face, so the responsibility is mine."

"No, missy, no!"

"Their horses are no better than ours. Take my boxes off Malt and throw them away. That will lighten——"

"B-boxes ain't—ain't heavy." He was sullen now with despair.

"But not important. Do as you think best." Then she said with finality, "We are following the troopers, Mike."

Clytie went toward her horse. She was sorry for Mike, very sorry, as he went toward his horses, dragging his feet.

The troopers were now gathered about their horses, making loud, rustic jokes with one another, some distance away from where Bob and the captain's horse were tethered. They were loosening the girths of the saddles and piling their equipment high upon them, while Clytie noted how strong and hardy their horses were.

But Bob . . . She rubbed her hands over his forelock and nose, haunted by her misgivings of yesterday. "Good Bob! Fine boy!" He was a good horse with a lovely, sleek, red-brown coat. "Oh, Bob, please carry the box and letter to safety and——" A sudden, striking thought cut off her plea, and a force outside herself yanked her around to regard the well-muscled strength of the captain's horse. He would be sure to breast the evil-looking current in that river. The weight of a breath-taking decision was now upon her.

Clytie scanned the direction in which the captain had gone and glimpsed him in the distance headed her way. She stood between her horse and his, and through no volition of her own, seeming to act only on instinct, she removed the black painted box containing her jewels and the letter from her saddlebag. Without giving herself time to think she crossed to his horse, opened the flap of his saddlebag, and crammed the box down under a welter of garments her hands found there.

She had rebuckled the strap on his bags and had headed back toward Bob before she started to tremble. She put her arms about his sleek neck to steady herself. But, yes, she had done right; the box would reach the other side of the river safely. With luck she might reach it herself. After that the outcome was unpredictable. No use to think or plan now. No use . . .

Conscious of footsteps, she looked up and saw the captain approaching. He stopped to regard her as if she had been created for no other purpose than to annoy him.

"So here you are!"

"Begging your pardon, sir." Clytie forced a smile and dropped him a mocking curtsy.

He did not return her smile. He reached his horse with long strides and untethered him. Would he look in his saddlebags? Her heart hammered in her throat. He was but stroking his horse's neck.

"Such a beauteous horse, sir," she ventured as he led the horse past her. To her surprise the flicker of a smile crossed his face. His eyes met hers with curious scrutiny. She was glad she had brushed her hair and tied the ribbon about it so neatly.

"Ferry'll be patched up in a couple of days," he said mildly.

"I shan't be here to see that, sir."

His eyes stared then with the old hard look. Clytie only gave him a wider smile. "O'Day!" he bawled in Mike's direction. "You fool enough to let this girl swim that river?"

There was only an indistinct answer from Mike, who was still hidden by the trees.

"I was minded my horse might do the swimming for me, Captain Appleton." She was enjoying his anger.

"*Can* you swim?" He seemed to forget his anger, for he came toward Bob, eyed him critically, ran a hand over his chest, and then put his ear to it.

Clytie hoped her fear would not overrun her eyes. "W-well, Captain?"

"Fair," he said, and gave Bob a pat.

"I—I can swim," she now volunteered.

"Not in those clothes, my girl." He eyed her—too keenly this time—then led his horse away, washing his hands of her.

For some reason Clytie's face burned. Not from anger. Yet no man had ever eyed her with such indifference before. He was pulling off his coat, his waistcoat, shirt, and piling them atop his saddle. He was naked from the waist up, his long, white, body gleaming, when Mike came from the trees and gaped at him.

"This mission of yours must be damned important, O'Day, that you can't wait for the ferry."

"Oh, it is important, sir. Mortal important," Clytie answered quickly for Mike. And because of the suspicion in the captain's voice she hurried on: "Our mistress will be anxious about us, about her fine horses should she learn that——" She broke off, horrified.

The captain was taking off his breeches.

He stood in tan underdrawers, strapping his boots and other garments atop his saddle. If he had heard what she said, he gave no sign. Another moment, and then he vaulted onto the rump of his horse.

"Keep those guns dry, men!" he shouted. "This is the best ford right here." He lifted his musket high and headed toward the water. "See that white birch leaning over the other side of the river? Head for that to avoid the bad current below."

With never a look back, and with his long bare legs adangle, he plunged into the water. His horse was up to its belly in the water now, swimming.

The box is watertight, Clytie thought; she offered a little prayer for it, for the horse and the rider.

The other men were stripped of all but their underdrawers; one, naked except for his breeches tied about his neck, leaped onto the rump of his horse. "Ice! Woogh!" he yelled as his dangling legs struck water. "Hell and yellow devils!" from another. One boy was kneeling beside his horse in prayer. "Come on, sweetheart," was yelled from the water. "Hit ain't your soul ye want to save, but your hide."

The boy got up, mounted and followed. He was lean, almost frail in a whipcord way, and so young. They were all young—no more than her own age, Clytie thought. And perhaps the boy could not swim. Not that they might have to swim, but they should be prepared for . . .

"Missy, not—not your bodice!"

She had taken off her linsey-woolsey skirt and her petticoat and had thrown them over the saddle.

"Why not?" she answered. "I couldn't swim with it on."

"But ye won't ha' to——"

"Would you rather have me dead in clothes or alive without them?" She stood only in underdrawers and shift now, with no feeling of shame. The troopers were acting through love of the colonies; so was she. Mike strapped her clothes atop her saddle, and she mounted astride them. Then, because he looked his despair, she said, "We *must* follow now, Mike. I put the box with the letter *in the captain's saddlebag.*" She headed toward the water.

"Wind the reins about your wrists, missy. . . . Don't let go!" followed his frantic appeal. No word about the letter.

The shock of the cold water on her legs shut off her breath for a second; then across the wide yellow flood she saw a horseman climbing the bank. The captain!

"The dispatch is safe, Mike, safe!" she called back.

As the cold water slushed about her knees she thought frantically, Never mind the cold. Reins about wrists. She leaned over Bob's neck. Good boy! Take it, Bob! . . . He was swimming now. No bottom, no end to the yellow flood. . . . Liquid copper filled all time and space. . . . Above the white sapling . . . above the swirling . . . She tugged at the right rein. They were breasting a stronger current now. From across the water came an agonized scream, then curses, shouts.

Strong Bob! Brave Bob! The water sucked at them, climbed her thighs, boiling. They were making no headway. Bob's strength, his heart . . . Relieve his burden. Slide off, clutch the saddle, swim beside him. . . . Irrationally, Clytie was prepared to slip from her saddle when she heard a bellow from the shore ahead: "You are all right! He'll reach shore!"

Warmth in the voice, life in the voice. Life, life, Bob! Her frozen hands steadied on the reins, her frozen heart resisted the swirl of water around them. Her mind leaped toward the waving figure on the shore, clung there, clung to the tall captain's shouting.

"Head for the bank *here!*" he called.

A green world was looming out of the yellow. Bob's forefeet struck earth, his shoulders lifted. . . . Clytie realized much later why someone's arms had yanked her off Bob's back: he had headed for the low branches of a tree.

"Brandy, Jed!" Strong, muscular arms were about her, and she clung, numbed, trembling, gulping the fiery liquor held to her lips. Then came a yell as she was put aside: "Cut the load off, man! Cut the girth!"

Clytie's senses righted. Salt was emerging from the water, riderless. "Mike!" she screamed.

A piercing animal cry came from the water. Only Malt's head was visible. And Mike? Where, where?

"Mike! Mike!" she screamed again. There were other shouts from shore, then she saw Malt's back rise above the water, a gleaming copper pot, and Mike clinging to the horse's tail, a knife in his teeth.

Her boxes, cut free from Malt's pack, bobbed a moment on the current and drifted out of sight.

They rode through a tunnel beneath a green sea. The emerald billows peaked so high overhead that the sunshine was like golden rain awash on shimmering waves. It was midday, and for the most part the wilderness rolled gently along; yet since leaving the river they had forded rocky brooks and dipped into boggy depressions.

But now the "pack road"—as the troopers called it—had leveled off and they could travel at a brisk canter. "Best keep us in sight," Captain Appleton had said after they had dried themselves at a common fire. He had given Mike some dry powder with which to fill his horn. Mike had cleaned and oiled his fowling piece and also Clytie's, which had remained, so far, strapped to her saddle. Jed Hawkins, whom she had recognized from his red hair, and to whom she had given the love message sent by his mother from the inn in Chester, had helped her clean her pistol, which had become wet in her saddlebag.

"Beautiful weapon, fine, ma'am," he had said, admiring it. "Kin ye use it?" He had a lovely grin on his broad, healthy face.

Clytie had grinned back and had fitted the pistol into the big pocket of her cloak. They had all been most kindly.

"Gal with guts," said the boy who had screamed when he got entangled in some driftwood.

But Clytie feared that the captain's civility only cloaked suspicions of her that had deepened when he heard her call her *father* "Mike."

Yet she was ready to forgive him any sort of suspicion, because his voice had thwarted her mistrust of Bob and had saved her from the peril of trying to swim to shore. Her face was still red from remembering the way she had clung to him before he dosed her with brandy. With such a hold on her half-naked figure, had he felt the money belt about the waist of a "servant girl"?

"Mike," she said as they walked their horses up an incline, "there was no chance to retrieve the box from the captain's saddlebag." She felt chagrined now not to have trusted Bob to carry it to safety.

"Leave it be, missy," came Mike's laconic answer—no censure, which surprised her.

"But if he should find it—?"

" 'Tain't likely. More 'n likely he won't open them saddlebags." He spoke as if he had been thinking it out. "Seen troopers afore, pressin' along a trail, ne'er mindin' saddlebags but to lay their head on 'em o' nights and sling 'em on horses ag'in come mornin'."

"You mean leave the box where it is until we get to Frederick?" She was uncertain about the wisdom of this.

"Ain't a safer place for it," he said grimly. "That captain—he'll git to Frederick, if nobody else does, what wi' the strength o' his horse an' his own quick thinkin'."

Clytie thought this over; she was in no mind to challenge any hazards that might occur along the route—not after that river. "Then in case . . . I mean—" she did not seem to be sure what she meant—"would he deliver the box to my father?"

Mike did not answer immediately. Then he said thoughtfully, "The lad's a patriot, for all his crusty talk."

"*Lad?*" She looked at Mike accusingly: the captain must be nearer her father's age.

"Reckon he's got a few years to go afore he turns thirty. . . . Mind the rocks down this grade, missy."

Clytie minded the rocks, not her thoughts which declared that Mike was nimtopsical. That man, who both repelled and attracted her, could *not* be young.

"Take it slow, Sid." They heard his voice, mingled with the sound of rushing water, from below the hillside.

To their left was a wide marsh, and Clytie had been watching two blue herons rising against the deeper blue of the sky; she had not noticed that the trail ended halfway down the hill. The scene they came on was so frightening that she caught her breath. A ledge of rock jutted out over a declivity like a yawning mouth with giant teeth that did not meet. Into this thundered a waterfall with a veil of sunlit spray, which filled the chasm with rushing water. It was spanned by a narrow footbridge, across which a trooper was leading his horse. Three troopers were already on the other side.

Clytie fought down a sick feeling in her stomach long enough to meet Captain Appleton's eyes, which merely noted that she was there.

"Keep going, Zeb, and don't lean on the rail," he said to the heavy-set, large-boned trooper, whose long arms swung in front of him as if he missed the plow he had so long operated.

Clytie, dizzied, watched him as he led his horse over the bridge. The handrail was only one strip of timber on either side of the bridge. When he was across she slid off her horse and turned her back to the bridge. She had never been able to conquer her terror of high places from the time she had climbed to the top of an apple tree and had not been able to get down. Her grandfather had sent a farm hand to rescue her.

She was giving Bob a lump of sugar and patting his neck when Jed Hawkins said, "Horses don't mind sich a crossin' much as ye'd think, ma'am—leastwise, when they know who's leadin' 'em."

Yes, Bob would need confidence in her now. It made her regret that her confidence in him had wavered so at the river.

"Best take your horses across yourself, O'Day," the captain said to Mike.

Nothing could have stirred and sealed Clytie's courage more. She watched Jed cross without even feeling sick in her stomach.

The bridge was supported by an island in the gorge and did not shake as much as she had first thought it would. Maybe it was the roar of the waterfall, which she could imagine knocking down the rocks that held the bridge and swamping it, that made her nervous.

Captain Appleton started toward the bridge but turned back to say, "Don't depend on the handrail if you get dizzy. Sit down and wait for your father to help you across." His half-smile was so wise, so knowing, penetrating her fears, that Clytie was certain she had never hated anyone so much.

But that was it: she hated him. Hated his suspicions, his twisted smile, his impertinence. But she watched him cross the bridge—there was an easy, confident strength in the firm way he planted his big feet, the way he put his hand through the bridle so that his horse's nose was close to his shoulder. No one had to tell her that he loved his horse.

The troopers left their horses and disappeared into the woods for some reason, a private one, maybe, as Mike took Salt across and then came back for Malt.

"I'll come back an' git Bob, then you, missy. Just you wait," he said.

She made no answer. She was thinking of what her grandfather had often said: "Don't cross bridges until you get to them." As if you *could!* Yet, of course, if you ever wanted to get anywhere you could not afford to be afraid of crossing bridges. You simply could not be *afraid,* not of dizziness, not of anything.

While Mike was tying up Malt on the far side, and the troopers were coming back for their horses, Clytie led Bob to the opening of the bridge.

"No, missy, no!" Mike shouted.

Clytie did not stop; she only looked up for a minute to see if the troopers were watching her. Her pride did the rest.

You dare not falter or get dizzy with eyes on you—not even when the bridge begins to rise and the earth to sway. . . . No, no, the earth was not swinging her into space. . . . Planks . . . the earth was made of planks with slits of eternity glistening between. The sound of Bob's hoofs behind her on the planks . . . Bob's nose near her shoulder. He was depending on her. . . . There was no roaring void beneath . . . For one agonizing second the sound, light and planks merged into a line too thin to follow. . . . Thud, thud. Bob's breath on her shoulder . . . Her feet found the thin line, the planks broadened, the world opened its arms. She was across the bridge.

The troopers were mounted and riding away. Their forms blurred. Sounds blurred. Clytie staggered to the support of a tree.

CHAPTER *Six*

THEY had reached a lovely valley when Captain Appleton rode back to join Clytie and Mike.

"The valley of the Susquehanna," he said as he wheeled his horse to ride beside her. "The river, ferry and boat landing are less than a mile away." His manner was unexpectedly friendly but scrutinizing. "You folks aim to take the boat here for Baltimore, I reckon?" His voice drawled as he looked back at Mike.

"Oh, no, sir!" Clytie denied quickly. Take a boat and be separated from her precious box? Not likely.

"We ben't allowed no money for takin' horses on a boat, sir," Mike said wisely.

That is, Clytie thought it wise until the memory of her money belt, that Captain Appleton had doubtless felt about her waist, came to mind. And in spite of her flushed face she hurried to say, "It would pleasure me to ride on and on through the wilderness, sir, till we come to the end, the very end, where we would see the other ocean." Then, to keep his attention diverted, she said, "Would it take long, sir—I mean, many weeks?"

"Many months, more likely." For the first time now his smile fastened on her. A real smile—it transformed him. It was wide, white-toothed, young, almost boyish. "Better part of a year you'd travel, so the Indians say," he told her. "Over great rivers, mountains, plains—no telling what."

Clytie had to close her wide-open mouth and swallow before she could say, "Just the same, I'd admire to travel it."

He smiled again as they cantered ahead, and Clytie's spirits lifted high into the fragrant breeze. Long afternoon shadows spread across marshy fields, and against the open sky was silhouetted his profile—high brow, outthrust chin, straight, thin nose—handsome, arresting. Yet, she thought, it was not strong in the way her father's bony face was strong and wise and astute, for the captain's strength was not mature.

Mike was right: he was young. And maybe because he was unsure of his real strength, he hammered home his authority as a fledgling would. Often her father had said of some colonial protégé: "He is crude now, but with the right self-discipline he will learn."

"Used to riding you are, hey?" he said, with only a half-smile to cover his suspicions.

Clytie's face reddened; she lifted her hand to adjust a lock of hair loosened from the ribbon that bound it. Her head scarf and cloak were tied to her saddle because the day had grown warm. She was not prepared for his question, but she made her answer gay.

"Otherwise, would my mistress have left her favorite saddle horse for me to ride to Winchester, sir?"

"Lives in Winchester, hey? What's the name?"

"Crockett." She was prepared for that. "My mistress but lately married Captain——"

"*John* Crockett?"

His surprise brought her most friendly smile. She could afford it. Her cousin Ariana DePuyster had truly married this Virginian and had gone to live in Winchester. "You know Captain Crockett?" she said.

"Sure do. He is in my colonel's regiment."

"And he will be beholden to you, sir, for your kindness to my father and me."

His eyes narrowed on the trail ahead. In the next moment a stiff breeze, catching at Clytie's skirt, blew it high over the pommel of her saddle, and as if it were a flag of warning, the captain spurred his horse ahead and rejoined the troopers.

The ferryman hoisted his sails and made ready to push off with the long poles. They had been detained because the troopers and Mike had had to purchase feed for their horses and get it aboard. Mike had had to move fast to get enough feed for three horses, but Clytie had helped, glad enough to stretch her legs and muscles.

She moved about the broad flatboat now and watched the sun sink below the wildwood on the far bank. How hungry she was! But at least she did not have to swim this wide, muddy river. Her mother would have fainted with horror had she seen her this morning. And her father—he must never know. Never. She would have to think out ways of guarding him from the shock of knowing the things that had befallen her on this journey.

"Purty, ain't it, ma'am?" Jed Hawkins was beside her, his freckled face smiling. His orange hair curled about the collar of his homespun shirt. Clytie was certain his mother had dyed his stockings to match.

Clytie remarked that the blue-and-pink sunset clouds reflected in the bronze gleam of the water were lovely, as well as the white blossoms in the far green woods. Then she asked him if he wasn't hungry.

"Could eat a whole ox, ma'am. . . . I reckon Capt'in Adam will make camp on t'other side afore dark."

Adam. His name was Adam—Adam Appleton. It had the sound of *first* things—the beginning of all things.

"Plumb prettiest boat ye ever seed," they heard the ferryman telling Adam Appleton. "It was waitin' here for them big officer fellers when they rid up. Took 'em to Baltimore—so'jers, horses an' all."

"*Two* royal governors, blast your eyes!" one of the troopers sang out. And another said mockingly, "Shake your lace ruffles! Dip your snuff, ye royal scum!" The other troopers laughed raucously. "And git nipped for taxes, ye dastard colonials!" The last speaker kicked at his fellows and a scramble ensued.

Clytie moved quickly to the other end of the boat. How unfair! How cruelly unfair! She wanted to turn on these rustics and say, "There is no colonial on this earth today who works harder for the good of the colonies than Royal Governor James DeLancey." She held tightly to herself; she must not judge these ignorant boys too harshly. Yet, recalling the riots that had occurred in New York against the authority of Royal Governor Osborne, before her father succeeded him, she was reminded of how much royal governors were hated by many colonials. Perhaps by Adam Appleton. She hungered to get her father's letter into her possession again. Perhaps tonight while the captain slept . . .

The ferryboat scraped the shore.

The red glow that came from the hole in the earth was like the devil's caldron. It lighted the boughs of a tree at the edge of the clearing and threw the rest of the forest into deeper gloom.

"Fire's made Indian-fashion," Mike said. "Troopers dug a hole and found a burnt-out tree stump. Charcoal don't make no smoke." They did not want smoke, he said, because a farmer had told the captain that Indian runners, thought to be Wyandots, had been seen "hereabouts."

Their ride after they left the ferry had been so grueling—riding on and on, single file through boggy places and over hillocks, with muskets ready—that Clytie had dropped into an exhausted sleep when they stopped to eat supper. After the troopers had finished their meal Mike awakened her to eat her own hot food.

Revived, she sat on a mossy place, her back against a great tree near the edge of the clearing, watching for the moon to rise. The wide clearing was bordered on two sides by the forest, and the other two sides dropped away toward swampland. Beyond this and the far fringe of woods the sky was lighted by the rising moon. It was too beautiful a night to sleep.

Mike had found plenty of cedar boughs to make her bed, off to her right, deeper in the woods where the horses were, and she had told him to bed down himself and not wait for her. Nothing must rob her of the magic of this forest night. I am here, Grandfather, her heart was saying, in this wilderness of which you have told me so often. It seemed protection enough in a night too beautiful to hold perils.

The heavy-set, long-armed trooper they called Zeb was on watch in the clearing. The others had gone off to bed down with their horses. The captain, too. She had watched him swing away from the glow of the fire, the coon's tail adangle on his cap. The very rhythm of his movements were those of a mountain cat at home in the illimitable wildwood.

Adam Appleton, Adam Appleton, she had said over and over to herself, tugging at the roots of her mind to bring up some memory that seemed to have been planted there in the long ago and that made her feel a loneliness as vast as the beauty of the night.

Clytie sat down and then wrapped her blanket more closely about her. The great orange orb of the moon was peeping over the far trees. . . . Had he opened his saddlebags, or merely put them under his head when he bedded down as Mike said he would?

"Not sleepy, hmm?"

The voice behind her was unreal. She had not heard anyone approach. The silence had seemed to stretch to the moon; yet Adam Appleton stood beside her, his hand on the tree against which she leaned.

"Oh!" was all she said. And again "Oh!" But her welcoming smile broke through. "It's too beautiful here to sleep."

He swung the musket from his shoulder, balanced it against the root of a tree, and sat down beside her. "Good trooper you are—" he grinned, his face full in the moonlight—"seeing you've got someone to wait on you hand and foot." A knowing quality crept into his voice.

Clytie was startled but not trapped. "He *is* a kind father, isn't he?"

she said with easy emphasis. But when Adam, with low, mellow laughter, merely leaned back against the tree, she added defensively, "If you had a daughter, not so strong as you, wouldn't you wait on her when she was all tired out?"

"Haven't got a daughter." He lazily stretched out his long legs. "If I had, she wouldn't call me by my *first* name."

Clytie laughed. It was her best defense. "Perhaps you have never been in service, Captain Appleton. Never heard your father called but by his first name. Would it be fitting that I say to my mistress, 'Pa is waiting with the carriage'?" She giggled. Then, breaking into his silence, she said, "Why do you think it is important?"

"Wouldn't be if other things added up." His drawl was so good-natured that she looked around at him quickly. "You really think you convince a body that you are a servingmaid, don't you?"

He seemed so amused now that she was frightened. Had he found the box, seen the jewels, and . . .

"You with that voice, speech," he went on, "and those soft, white hands!"

"Oh, thank you, Captain!" She relaxed. Then he had not found the box. Now the game amused her—her wits against his. "Now if I were *not* my lady's personal maid and had not been taught to speak as my mistress, but were married to a settler, my hands would be coarse and red, wouldn't they?" She held her hands, with their long, lovely fingers, up before her and turned them about for inspection. "Does your wife have roughened hands, sir?" She felt his eyes nibbling at her hands, felt the tingle, and was not prepared for the imitation snore he gave.

"Smart gal. Make up another story to keep me awake." He pulled his cap down slantwise over his eyes.

"Oh, then she does have roughened hands." Clytie sighed.

"Got no wife."

Her low laughter was genuine this time, but for a reason somehow confused with the stir of her pulse. The washes of moonlight, her sentient awareness of the primeval world around them, the vast silence, only deepened by the April wind in the treetops, was like a song of the night. And this man beside her was compounded of iron muscles, the driving force of mule teams, and a personality that could play on your senses according to his unpredictable moods.

"Ha! A wife!" he said, stretched out now, hands behind his head, addressing the moonlit branches that extended over the clearing. "What would a man do with a wife, with French and Indians to fight?"

"Perhaps *she* will wait for you until the fighting is over." Her instinct caused her to probe softly.

"Did I say there was a *she?*" His eyes were now on her face, stark in the moonlight.

Clytie kept her own on the silvered clearing, feeling the moonglow seep all the way through to her spirit. Then came a thought to make her smile softly: What if her grandfather could see her now? Would the ecstasy with which she was abandoning herself to the arms of the wilderness night delight him?

"Did you ever have a grandfather—one you remember, I mean?" she said irrelevantly.

Adam sat up, followed her gaze across the clearing, and without appearing to think her question odd, said, "Never saw either of them. Ma and pa came over in 'thirty, to Virginia. I was born the next year."

Had the night wrapped up his spirit with hers, combed out his suspicions and resistance, and bestirred him to confidence in her? She computed quickly, too, that if he were born in 1731 he could now be only twenty-four. Adam Appleton only twenty-four years old! She found herself adjusting gladly to that.

"They came from England?"

"Dundee." He was watching Zeb, silhouetted against the deep-blue night sky out on the clearing.

"My grandfather of whom I was thinking," Clytie said, "came from Cornwall. But he was born in France, and used to tell me tales—"

"French, hey?" He turned on her with such quick suspicion that she gasped. "I thought it would come out," he drawled.

She fought for a moment with her anger, but it won out. This provincial bumpkin to dare . . . She threw off her blanket. "Since you choose to be so unmannerly . . ." She was getting up when a strong hand shot out and caught her arm.

"Not so fast, my pretty!"

Clytie slapped quickly at his face. Ducking, he grinned and caught both her arms. The blow had not landed.

"There now, be the high-bred little princess you are, my servant girl!"

He settled her against the tree as if she were a fractious *poupée.* No point in making an unseemly struggle, she told herself.

"The complete gentleman. I might have known," she said coldly.

"Smarter than I thought." He even had the impertinence to gather up the ends of her blanket and tuck them around her. "There now!"

He sat back on his heels in front of her with an infuriating grin on his face. "Of course, a man can't know the truth behind those big cornflower eyes, though it's easy enough to know you are the prettiest lass a man ever set eyes on. But there's more to it than that, what?" He settled himself beside her.

"I find your compliments as offensive as your infantile suspicions, Captain Appleton. And if there is anything you would like to know about me, I would suggest that you query Captain Crockett and my mistress."

He doubled up with soft laughter. Hang him! Oh, hang him! He was getting the upper hand. She must do better than this.

"One thing I know—you are a bad actress. You just speak your piece. But a man's got to believe you, or he's a skunk."

"How right you are, Captain."

His laughter was so infectious that she might have laughed with him if it had not been for a strange cry that rose from beyond the clearing and chilled her blood.

The captain sat taut. The cry lifted in savage laughter, ending in a sepulchral moan.

"It's a loon, all right," he said with relief. "They can't imitate that sound."

"The—the Indians?"

"Always go wrong on the last note."

"What—what is a loon?"

"Web-footed bird. There's a swamp beyond the clearing. Scare you?" He leaned back against the tree, his shoulder touching hers.

"It was eerie."

"Now then, let's talk about you."

"But the enemy Indians," she said quickly. "When the great General Braddock drives back the French and their savages, the country . . . the country will be safer, won't it?"

"Changing the subject, hey? Yes, *if* he drives them back."

"*If!* . . . Oh!" And before he could interrupt, she said, "You and your men are marching to the forts with him, aren't you?" From his silence she sensed she had struck on a subject to divert him.

"Depends on how my colonel gets treated. How the dunderheaded royal governors shape things up with Braddock." He dug the heel of his boot into the moss.

"Dunderheaded?" She suppressed her resentment. "Are all royal governors dunderheaded?"

"Looks like it."

"They represent the king."

"Body wouldn't say old George was overloaded with brains."

Clearly, it was not a safe subject to argue about if she hoped to keep enough peace with him to be able to follow him and her box to Frederick. Yet she was forced to say, "Our own royal governor, James DeLancey, is beloved in New York Colony." She was fearful that there was too much pride in her voice.

"Don't listen right, not for one of those tax diggers." He broke a small stick into fragments and threw them away. "Couldn't we talk of skunks instead?"

"Oh!" she exploded. "Because your own Governor Dinwiddie is—is a—a poltroon!" She relaxed when he grinned. "Oh, well, let's talk of your colonel."

"Look, lady, when you speak of my colonel, speak softly—" he eyed her grimly—"for you talk of a man who *is* a man."

But before she could reply he was on his feet, rigid as a statue. The high, shrill note of a night bird was sounding. It grew into a full-throated whistle. Adam Appleton grabbed his gun and moved away from her, in the direction of the cry, with the silence of a shadow. Not a twig cracked beneath his feet. He vanished from her sight as though he had never been there.

Clytie moved to the darkened side of the tree trunk. There was little undergrowth in the woods; the towering pines were like columns of a great temple, its lacy vaulting pierced with slits of unearthly light. The cry of the night bird had died. Had it been a mystic cry from the temple altar, where heathen sacrifice was made to the ancient gods of the wilderness? And the man who had moved from her side like a woods creature stalking its prey, was he but a part of a magical forest that had reclaimed him?

She drew her cloak tighter, chilled more by a sense of loneliness than by the mist creeping amid the columns of the temple riding on the moonglow. She should go to the bed Mike had made for her, but she could not. Not until the disquieting, uncivil Adam Appleton should reappear, *if* he reappeared. Every nerve in her body seemed alive with expectation as she searched the shadows for this object of her hatred, her fear. Yet there was more to it than that, truth told her, for some primitive urge from the core of her had tangled in his moonlit smile. . . .

She flattened her back against the tree trunk as the low, mellow sound of the night bird came from the other side of the tree; she saw a moving shadow, and in her instinctive flight she stumbled over a root of the tree.

It had happened so quickly that she did not recover her wits until she was limp in Adam Appleton's arms, which held her as though the forest night had put out tentacles of iron to bind them together.

"Didn't mean to scare you." His voice was hoarse, his breath warm on her cheek. His stubble beard was buried against her neck, the contact of his lips pulsating . . .

"P-p-please . . ." Her struggle was feeble, her heart feeble, against the hand that moved over her head, tilted it backward, forced her eyes to meet the glow in his. She could not think, could not act; her every fiber was at his mercy. For a second of eternity his arms strengthened but he only pressed her head downward beyond reach of his lips, and released her so quickly that she staggered.

He walked off a few steps, beat his fists together, and kicked viciously at the root of the tree. "Hang my fool soul!" he said in low-voiced anger. "I–I'm sorry, ma'am."

Clytie's wits returned. Nothing could so have retrieved her senses and poise as the humility in his words. Besides, she was in no position to effect a DeLancey pride, which she did not feel. She felt something quite different and unrecognizable. How would Lottie O'Day have dealt with this unpredictable man's embrace? she thought quickly. She'd have shrugged or slapped him, likely.

But there were no shrugs or slaps in Clytie DeLancey's reaction.

"It's all right. It–it was stupid of me to stumble," she said as steadily as she could, yet knowing in her heart that it was one drowning person's comfort to another–both had fallen under the liquid mystery of the night. He wheeled around and smiled at her. It was the most welcome smile she had ever encountered. Full in the moonlight, it held gratitude and admiration.

Her blanket still lay where they had been sitting before he dashed away into the forest. She picked it up and wrapped it about her. She was throbbingly conscious of his surprise as she settled herself against the tree, but instinct told her they had struck the wrong note on which to separate for the night. She had no intention of letting him think she was silly and too maidenly to be afraid of him. Besides, she needed his friendship, all of it she could get, while that box was in his saddlebag. Or was she just deceiving herself, yearning only for further beauty of the night, further joy in the unfathomable things he had stirred. "Never deceive yourself," her father often said. "Deceive others if it makes for the general welfare, but face the truth within yourself."

Well, she was facing it. "Not afraid of the lady up there in the moon, Captain?" she invited him.

His smile broadened. "When do you figure to travel back up there, moonwoman?" He sat down beside her. "Shouldn't go haunting men in forests, you know."

"What if I've lost my broomstick and can't get back?"

"Serve you right."

"Besides, it's lonely up there. . . . Know what would be nice? To have you tell me a story."

He gave her a quizzical look, but stretched out his long legs contentedly. "Could tell you a heap, I guess."

"First, about your colonel."

"My colonel?" The faintest note of suspicion was in his voice.

"Only because you said he was 'a prince'—no—'a man who *is* a man.' "

"Somebody tell you he started this war with the French?" His suspicions were on the rise.

"But I don't even know his name. . . . Did he?"

"The French say he did. Washington's his name—George Washington."

"Never heard of him. But go on."

"You will. But what they said about his starting this war is a fool lie. The British added to the French tales, wanting to make out some colonial had run amuck. Why, blast the fools, they have been fighting the French for years, centuries, off and on!" He kicked at a tree root. "What'd they expect a man to do—stand there and get shot at? And that frog, Jumonville, waiting to ambush us. I ought to know. I was there." His voice tensed with resentment.

"Please, I can't quite follow you. Begin at the beginning. Sounds like it would make a wondrous story, since you were there." She turned her head toward him and smiled. In the drenching moonlight his smile was warm and responsive.

"Too long a story." He relaxed. "What with those eyes of your addling a man till he's apt to try to take a bite out of the moon."

"Ugh! It's made of green cheese."

"That what you are made of?"

"I want to know why you and your colonel went looking for this Jumonville. Where'd you find him?"

"At the forks of the Ohio. That fool, Dinwiddie, sent us there to build up the forts."

"The *Ohio?*" Clytie sat up amazed. "That must be almost to the other ocean. And you—you have been there?"

"It's not that far. Though far enough, once you tackle the Alleghenies, dragging cannon, bridging streams. Last April it was. But nothing daunts my colonel." He sat up, hugged his knees, and gazed across the bright clearing. "But I'm telling you no other man alive but George Washington could have got one hundred and fifty men through that savage country alive. Well, as I say, it's a long story." He leaned back. "Nothing pretty about the men, cold, hungry, in rags, by the time we got to the Mingo chief—a friendly tribe—only to learn that the French were surrounding us."

"What—what then?" Clytie's anxiety was real.

"Ambush." Adam Appleton shrugged. "What else? But, thank God, we were traveling single file, Washington in the lead. Then 'Fire!' he snapped. And did we fire? Oh, man!" Adam slapped his thigh. "The colonel's got eyes like a lynx. He sighted Jumonville with his gun cocked, and beat him to it. That's all there was to it. Down that froggie went. Ten more of his dastards dead, and the rest took to their heels. And so, Washington started the war because he didn't stand there and get shot. Hell an' hocum! And that's not all," Adam growled. "What I say is, that if those men now in conference in Frederick want this war won, they'd better let George Washington tell 'em how to do it. That's paz!" He leaned back against the tree.

Clytie felt his shoulder rub hers, but she felt his closeness this time with a drowsy sense of comfort. "It—it *was* a wondrous . . . s-s-story. . . ." Her heavy eyes closed, her tired muscles no longer responded, her head dropped, wobbled and came to rest on Adam Appleton's shoulder.

THEY arrived in Baltimore in a blinding rainstorm the next day around noontime. The troopers led the way through the sprawling little settlement they called Jonestown to the blacksmith's shop. Several of their horses needed to be reshod. Bob and Salt, too.

When Clytie and Mike rode under the smithy's shed, they saw the other horses, tied up, unsaddled, and Jed Hawkins sitting atop the heaped-up saddlebags, dolefully watching the red-hot anvil.

"Inn's a piece up along the water front, ma'am," he told Clytie, "where ye kin dry out. Maybe git some food, if ye got the price." He was watching the water drip from Clytie's cloak into a little pool at her feet. "Troopers ain't got no more 'n I got, I reckon," he went on with an effort at a grin, "but they kin git 'em some ale."

Clytie, shivering, managed an answering grin.

After Mike unsaddled the horses they left their things in Jed's care and went out again into the cold wind and rain to find the inn. Mike had to see about replenishing their stores.

Clytie, blown through the door of the little tavern, was struggling to close it behind her when she heard the inhospitable welcome.

"A drowned rat ye be. Lawful heart! What ye want here?" A hard-faced woman stood in the narrow, smoke-grimed hall.

"F-food, please. My father and I—"

"Where be your pa?" The woman flayed her with suspicion.

Clytie, blinking, wiped the raindrops from her face. "We have the money to pay, madam," she said, and summoned up her courage. "I should like a room, please, a private room, where I can dry myself out before a fire."

The woman sniffed, scowled, but ended her inspection and questioning with "Come this way."

Clytie was led into a little sitting room. But not until she had paid for the room and her dinner—she had taken money for this purpose from her belt before setting out that morning—would the alewife consent to strike tinder to the readied fire. For extra pay she agreed that Clytie's dinner should be brought into her "hotter 'n the devil's tongue."

Nothing had ever offered more refuge and comfort than the snug room and blazing logs of the fire. Clytie hung her cloak and skirt on a chair beside it and watched them steam as she took off her clogs and wriggled grateful toes at the flames. It was good, too, to be wholly alone for a bit, so that she could think out with more sense what had happened last night after she went to sleep on Adam Appleton's shoulder. Or *had* it happened? Surely, no—it must have been some form of hallucination. . . .

"There ye be, dearie!" The alewife re-entered with Clytie's big tray of food, her attitude servile because of the coins the "drowned rat" had produced. She placed the tray on a table near the fire. There were baked wild fowl, sweet potatoes, hominy, steaming coffee and brown Betty.

But until Clytie could think up a ruse for getting all the troopers fed, she could not enjoy such a dinner. She extracted a gold crown from her money belt, and when Mike entered during her meal, she gave him the coin.

"It is to buy dinner for you and all the troopers," she told him.

"Oh, no, missy. It ain't right fer the likes o' us——"

"Let me finish. Give it to the landlord and explain that you want it to appear that he himself is generously offering food to the troopers—the best there is, mind you—because they are on their way to fight for their country."

Mike looked doubtful for a moment, then his homely face beamed as he counted on his fingers. " 'Twill leave enough to fee the old skinflint fer so doin'."

"See that Jed gets his dinner, too, and—and the captain. . . . Oh, be careful, Mike, that he does not suspect . . ."

Mike would be careful, and she hoped he thought her flaming face was caused by the hot fire. When she had finished her dinner she was able to think more rationally about last night.

Of course, she could never be sure how long she had lain there on the mossy ground with Adam Appleton's arms tight around her, but the moon was high in the sky when she awoke. Never, never could she ever forget that awakening—not a slow awakening, but a quick consciousness of his easy breathing just above her head, which rested on his arm. Her blanket was tucked tight and snug around her, and his body was stretched close to hers. She had held her muscles still and had made no sound until reality seeped through to her senses. She was grateful for those few moments that had given her time to think what she must do. Yet, with a delicious sensation of life tingling in every fiber of her body, it had been difficult to make any decision at all. A night breeze had stirred in the branches of the tall trees, and there had seemed to be no world beyond the wilderness, which must roll on and on to seas beyond the moon and sun. And there would be warm possessive arms around her all the way.

She had been wrapped in timelessness with this man who so bestirred her.

Then out of the silvered silence a twig had broken. A woods creature scampered through the boughs above them—a nameless thing that had crept out to enjoy its little hour. That moment had been her own hour in which to become aware of the magic of life as never before dreamed of, with Adam's quiet breathing beside her.

Not until he had stirred and she had felt his chin leave the top of her head had she been able to move without awakening him. His right arm lay heavy across her body, but the left arm, on which she had rested, was limp on the ground. Slowly, cautiously, she had moved, trying not to yield to panic, yet knowing that, should he awaken, anything might happen—to her or to him. *That* she must avoid. . . .

Clytie's hypnotizing thoughts were interrupted by joyous shouts and the clank of ale mugs from the taproom. Oh, Adam, Adam! Are you feasting too? . . .

Never had she believed anyone could sleep so soundly as he had slept while she moved from beside him and got to her feet. No doubt he was as tired as she from their long, weary ride. Never had she been so filled with compassion as she carefully spread her blanket over his inert body—the strong, wire-strung man, a child in his sleep. She had even waited to watch him roll over with a little groan, so that she might tuck the blanket tighter about him. She had made her way silently in the shadows to where Mike had made her bed and covered herself with the horse blankets. . . .

But reality did not return until she saw the troopers ride away in the morning mist.

The rain washed in great gusts against the windowpanes, but Clytie slipped into her skirt and pulled on her dry clogs. The captain would not tarry long here; she must be ready to ride when Mike came for her.

From Baltimore they traveled due west. If Adam Appleton had been ruthless in the pace he had set the two previous days, he was devil-ridden now as he led the little company over ridges, through hollows and rock-bedded creeks. They had crossed Swan Creek and Bush Creek, but at Gunpowder River there had been a ferryboat ride, which rested riders and horses briefly. Over a corduroy stretch of road a trooper permitted his horse to stumble.

"Stupid dullard!" the captain called back, and added as a warning to all, "You'll take the brunt of your own carelessness. We are halting for no accident."

"He's hyeared somethin' in Baltimore to upset him," Mike said. "Don't know what. But makes him reckon he's gonner put some stretch o' road behind him afore dark comes."

Clytie was in no mood for comment. Adam Appleton had taken no notice of her presence and Mike's, except to call back once when they had lagged behind a bit in the mist: "For pity's sake, O'Day, keep closer behind." But her faith in his wisdom was not wavering, in spite of his determination to bend man and beast and the forces of nature to his will. His was a purposeful will, even though she did not know its purpose. She knew only that her letter was still in his saddlebag. That was enough to reckon with for the present.

The rain had slackened soon after they left Baltimore, then it had stopped; yet the somber gray clouds had not lifted. Climbing a rocky hill in an ocean of mist and fog, they were forced to a detour because of a great tree which had fallen across the road. Clytie had felt sorry for Adam then, sensing his need to reach the destination he had set; she had felt admiration, too, for the grim stoicism with which he led the way back down the long hill, through a hollow of brush and trees, to mount the precipitous hill again and come to the roadway on the other side. Meanwhile, on the detour she had been forced to straddle Bob in order to lean with more safety over his neck, so as not to be left swinging, like Absolom, by her hair. This Adam Appleton was a good woodsman.

Nightfall was not far away when they reached an open space of wide cultivated fields. They met two men in a bullock cart who hailed them as they trotted past. But they did not stop. On the far, western horizon the red arc of the sun had escaped the dark clouds and was pouring out a glorious light, which seemed to transform fields and the world into glimmering vistas. In spite of danger and fatigue, the wilderness again became for Clytie a place of enchantment. It did not last. The murky clouds closed down before they entered a somber wood. The trail led downward, winding tortuously down. . . .

At her first glimpse of the swamp below, over which a gray twilight had settled, a premonition of danger caught at the pit of her stomach. She tried to shake it off, ashamed of fears that mounted at the lonely cry of swamp birds and the din of croaking frogs.

The place was sinister, and she knew the minute she and Mike rode up to join the others on the valley floor that this was the place Adam had hoped to put behind him before nightfall. He was off his horse, giving low instructions to his men.

"Can't be helped now. . . . Do the best we can," she heard. And to the murmured question of a trooper, she heard: "Sure, sure, could have cleaned them out. Too late now. That's their hideout—an old Indian lookout. . . ."

Clytie followed his glance to a perpendicular shaft of rock that rose from the swampy water at their right. It had the shape of some savage monument, scraping the desolate, low, overhanging sky.

"I don't think they have any reason to attack us," Adam went on. "Nothing to gain but trouble. . . ."

Nothing to gain! Clytie's conscience reproached her. What if he knew the savage spies had much to gain? What if he knew of the box in his saddlebag?

"Been trouble here of late, and I was warned," he went on, ". . . right. Trust to luck that they'll get no bead on us in this light. . . . Clean 'em out in the morning. . . ." His voice was now inaudible.

So, his stop here was for the darkness to gather.

Clytie took in the terrain. A corduroy road led over the narrowest part of the swamp to the foot of a wooded hill. The towering lookout would be the best vantage for an attack with arrows on the road.

They were preparing to gallop across the causeway.

"Time your start, men—not too close. Keep some distance between you—" Adam was mounting—"lean low to the left and keep going. Fast!"

The cawking cry of waterfowl re-echoed against the great rock as the low-flying birds winged across the causeway and lost themselves in the purple distance to the left.

"Miss O'Day—" Adam rode up close beside her—"straddle your horse, lean low in your saddle, and when you start going move fast."

No time to answer. He wheeled his horse and was off across the causeway—a gray phantom streak. The hollow thud of hoofs were the only sounds, except for the raucous frogs.

What Mike had said comforted Clytie: "He will make it if no one else does."

Another trooper started off. Another and another. Louder, hollower ring of hoofs mounted toward the menace of the monument.

When the last trooper had leaped into the gray-blue mist, Clytie was astride Bob and ready.

"Lean low! Hold tight, missy!" warned Mike.

Bob's hoofs were pounding the causeway . . . halfway across now. . . . "Whoa! Whoa, Bob!" She tried to pull him up short at sight of the sprawled figure on the causeway, then a whip fell on his buttocks, from Mike behind her. Bob leaped ahead. . . . Dark streaks shot across her vision, above Bob's neck, below. Something struck a rock with a splintering sound. . . .

"Whoa, Bob!" She had galloped up the wooded trail.

He was still trembling from the sound of musket shots when she slid from his back. She patted his neck. "Steady, Bob!"

"Keep your head down! Get behind him!" cried Mike as he galloped past and stopped just ahead. The shots multiplied, sounding farther away.

"Mike! Malt–Malt is wounded!" she cried. Something dripped from the horse onto the dry leaves. At the same moment she spied atop his back a feathered arrow sunk into a beer keg that Mike had bought in Baltimore. But an arrow! Then the dark streaks she saw before her as she crossed the causeway had been . . .

Clytie swallowed the lump in her throat.

Mike yanked the keg off Malt's back and grabbed his musket. "I got to help, missy. Ready your musket." He hurried away in the direction of the shots, toward the monumental rock.

Not until Clytie was alone in the dim forest, the darkness thickening around her, did she realize that if all the troopers had run such a gauntlet of arrows, more than just the one trooper must have been felled. But no; she must have been the principal target, and because of the growing darkness . . .

But that figure she had seen on the causeway? Not the captain. . . . No.

She tethered Bob, then ran swiftly along the trail to where the troopers' horses were tied. *Seven,* she counted. They were all there. Then how? . . . But, of course, the wounded trooper's horse had followed the others. Before she reached Bob again she had made a quick decision. The trooper out there on the causeway might be dying and . . .

She did not know much about tending the wounded, but she tore into strips a linen shift from her saddlebag, put her brandy flask into her pocket, and led Bob toward the causeway. Then a thought struck her, and she stopped. She had never been so irresolute: the captain's saddlebags were now *unguarded.* She could slip back, transfer the box with the letter to her own. . . . "He will reach Frederick if no one else does." . . . A man lies wounded out there, her conscience said. Wounded by an enemy seeking scalps. *Scalps!* Her own scalp!

As Clytie reached the causeway the fog and darkness battered at her courage. . . . She must not let Bob slip into the bog. "Oh, careful, Bob, careful!" She edged outward, farther outward. There was no trooper. Had she been dreaming? "Careful, Bob!" . . . She almost stumbled over the trooper before she saw him.

He lay on his face, an arrow buried deep, protruding from his right shoulder. But his heart was beating.

"Zeb!" She spoke softly. It was the big, long-armed man. She lifted his head and put her brandy flask to his lips. "Oh, Zeb, can't you drink?" She knew no way of forcing it through his closed lips.

Her bringing Bob along with her had been an instinctive action. Into her mind had flashed a picture of childhood days: a laborer on her grandfather's farm being dragged by another across the fields by means of his horse's bridle, after an accident. Now if she could get Bob's reins under Zeb's shoulders . . . Never had the world seemed so silent, so menacing. But she could not leave him here. . . . Scalps . . .

Clytie never quite knew how she effected it, but now Bob was dragging the great bulk while she clutched at Zeb's clothes, holding him so that the protruding arrow would not scrape the ground.

"Slowly, Bob! Easy, boy!" Bob was the hero.

They were climbing the wooded slope when she heard a groan. She released the reins and propped Zeb up, using all her strength.

Holding the flask to his lips, she said, "Drink, Zeb. Oh, drink!"

He stirred, groaned. She got the flask between his lips; and then he grabbed it. She was so startled she almost let him fall back against the arrow. He gulped and gulped.

At last he spoke, but with a rumble in his throat. "Got me, hunc . . . got me." He drank again, dropped the flask, and tried to lie back.

"No, Zeb, no—the arrow! Mike!" she screamed. "Mike!" She was suddenly terrified by the silence. Had Mike been killed? The captain? Her knees were planted firmly in Zeb's back.

"Arrow—devil—swine." He raised his long arms, felt for the arrow, gripped it, his body twisting as he tugged.

"Oh, no, Zeb, no! Mike!" she yelled again. . . .

The arrow was out, and he fell back on her with a gush of warm, oozing blood, which her hands and the clothes she pressed to his shoulder could not stop.

"Where are you—where?" It was Adam's voice. "Lottie!"

"Here—here!" she cried. "Adam—Adam!" She sobbed with relief and fright when he knelt beside her.

"You dragged him here? You, alone?" His hands covered hers amid the blood. Zeb groaned. "Jed! Hank!" Adam bellowed. "My lantern! Build a fire! . . . You'll be all right, Zeb." He rolled him over on his face and pressed the fresh linen Clytie gave him to the wound. "You wonderful girl—Lottie, Lottie——"

"Lottie! Darter!" came Mike's cry.

When he too knelt beside the wounded man, Clytie got up and staggered away. She sat down beside Bob and wept.

CHAPTER *Eight*

A BRIGHT fire burned in an open place along the trail. Zeb lay wrapped in a blanket. On the other side of the fire, farther away, a prisoner the troopers had brought in sat bound to a tree. His head was bent over his breast, a bloodied leg stretched out before him. He wore the fringed buckskins of a trapper. "A Frenchman—a murdering skunk!" Mike had said. The troopers had killed the three Indians who were with him. "Ain't no more. Can't fool the capt'in—a wild Injun himself—by havin' his troopers ambushed."

Had it been because of the letter she carried? Clytie had asked herself, not daring to voice it even to Mike. She had not eaten very hungrily of the cold roast lamb Mike had brought along from the tavern in Baltimore, for when she had caught the prisoner's eyes looking at her she had become a little weak and sick. He had tried to kill her with his arrows. *Why?* What did he know? How?

"He'll be tended to proper when we git to Frederick tomorrow," Mike said, following her eyes to the Frenchman.

Frederick tomorrow! Her father's letter safe. And her father, Aunt Monica, Uncle Peter, the boys, and Chestermere, their plantation she so longed to see, only one night away! She should be cheered, but she was not. Adam Appleton sat across the fire from her, his elbows on his knees, lost in some reverie. What? His voice had so comforted her when he had knelt beside her and Zeb, she had wanted to throw herself into his arms and . . .

He got up now with one of his quick, decisive movements, took his canteen from his pocket and a corn pone from a skillet, and went over to the prisoner. He nudged the man with his boot.

"Eat," he said, and held out the corn pone.

The man raised his head, took the bread, and eyed the canteen. "Water, *m'sieu?*" he said.

"Liquor. Drink."

The prisoner drank, gulped, made a wry face, and returned the flask. "Worse than water," he said in good English.

Adam ignored him and walked across the lighted space toward the tethered horses, not toward the troopers' saddlebags, all piled now within range of the fire. Clytie watched his swinging, purposeful stride, her thoughts disorganized. He was a part of the dark woods into which he disappeared, yet he possessed a nameless poise that, she felt, contained a steely arrogance and self-discipline. That was just it—she sensed and *felt* him, irrationally.

Mike was repacking the stores, Jed refueling the fire, and one of the troopers patrolling the woods, when Clytie found the eyes of the prisoner again centered on her. Evil, dark eyes, bloodshot under shaggy brows and strings of matted hair. She shrank back with an instinctive terror but steadied herself.

Adam came from the woods, his cowhide whip in hand. He went directly to the prisoner.

"Now's the time for you to talk, Frenchy."

The man's shoulders were bound by ropes but he managed a shrug.

"Where'd you come from?" Adam raised his whip. "I'll give you one second to answer."

"Onondaga."

"You lie. Those savages with you were Wyandots from the northwest country. You came from Duquesne, hey? The forts your bloody friends stole before Trent and Washington could reach it."

"Onondaga," the prisoner said again.

"Could be, Capt'in." Jed's voice sounded from the shadows. "Travelers from the north, stoppin' at Pa's inn, tell how Wyandots are mixin' with Ottawas to harass General Shirley in the north. Could be this frog and his savages were sent down——"

"So that's it!" Adam caught up the words, and accused the prisoner. "You were sent down to spy on the King's Highway for messages to Braddock. So! It was *you* who scalped the postrider. You and your devils, hey?" The whip hung, threatening. "Answer me!"

Clytie regarded with revulsion the leer on the prisoner's face. It could be he who had wounded her father's messenger, trailing him . . . The thought bred another more terrifying: Trailing *her*? Had he spied on her and her father? Did he *know* her?

The weird cry of a nightjar had drawn Adam's attention from the prisoner. Jed raced off in the direction of the sound. "You too, Hank," Adam said to another trooper who grabbed at his musket. "It's a goat-sucker, all right. We cleaned the vipers out, but we'll take no chances. Sid," Adam yelled, "you there?"

Sid was guarding the horses. "All's well, Capt'in!" came in answer.

The prisoner's head was limp on his breast. Adam pushed it up, forced liquor down his throat. "Faking. You got but a flesh wound in the hide of that leg. I'm not through with you yet." He followed the troopers into the woods.

Clytie was alone by the fire when the prisoner's stare, that of a poisonous snake ready to strike, again centered on her. But Adam's voice arrested her movement back into the shadows.

"Plain as day. His Indian runners attacked the postrider, then loped on through the woods to join this frog and his Indian guide with news of us." He and Jed came into the firelight. "Thing I want to know of you, Froggy, is what in all fire you expected to gain by attacking a bunch of raw recruits? Just what you got, hunc, to be taken to Frederick, and hanged?"

The Frenchman tried to move his wounded leg, and his face, distorted with pain, slipped into a venomous sneer. "Not quite, *m'sieu.*"

"What, then?"

"A letter, most valuable to French."

Clytie's blood seemed to cease flowing until Adam gave a snort of laughter.

"Smart scout!" he said lazily. "Now, maybe this letter would be from some bewigged royal governor, hey, to the big-boss general who's come to our shores to teach us poor colonials how to fight you rattlers. That right?" He was doubled onto a log by a scornful guffaw. "So a colonial captain whose sole business is to hustle recruits into training takes on such a darn fool mission as that. Blast me! You French snakes are so smart it pleasures a man to collect your hides." He unwound the leather thongs of his whip.

Jed threw another log onto the fire. It flared up and lighted the evil glint in the prisoner's eyes, which were turned toward Adam.

"You carry the letter, Captain," the Frenchman said decisively.

"What's that? You——" Adam leaped up, his whip poised. Then he lowered it slowly, to follow the Frenchman's glance toward Clytie.

Numbed, she could not look away from his leering face.

"Keep your cursed eyes off me darter!" Mike bellowed at the Frenchman.

"Silence!" Adam lashed out at him.

"So, Captain," said the prisoner, "the beauteous lady has deceived you, ha?"

Adam's face became a mask of rage directed at her and Mike. "Put down that gun," he commanded Mike, who had seized it, his Irish temper out of control.

Clytie whispered to him under her breath, and he quieted.

The silence was oppressive.

"You know this girl—these people?" Adam Appleton's voice knifed at the prisoner, whose eyes were still on Clytie. "Answer me, or, by heaven——"

"Oui, m'sieu . . . and no." His bloodshot eyes made him appear even more evil. "Bonnets—bonnets conceal a woman's face. . . . There was a woman on the box with that man—" his eyes focused on Mike—"and one inside the carriage. So which she is——"

"What carriage? Whose carriage?" Adam's words came quick as musket shots.

Clytie's fears were realized; ice seemed to clog her veins.

"The carriage of Governor James DeLancey on its way to——"

"Lying hound!" Mike yelled, and grabbed again at his gun.

For a wildly hopeful moment Clytie thought the scuffle and words between Mike and Adam would divert attention from the Frenchman's tale, but then Mike accused Adam of heeding the lies of a spy.

"We'll see who's lying," Adam bawled. "So this man is a coachman for Governor DeLancey, hey? And the girl—?" He leaped toward the prisoner, whose head had dropped low. Adam shoved it up and forced brandy down his throat. The glazed eyes opened. "Go on, hang you! Talk."

"Girl—" his words came weakly—"not know . . . Know only girl ride—ride from house where messenger leave . . . letter for . . ."

The voice died, the man's head rolled to one side and hung limp. Adam forced it up, but the eyes did not open. The man had fainted.

"Jed! Sid! Hank!" Adam shouted. "Search the belongings of these two." He strode toward Mike. "Take off that coat." Rage had transformed him into a dangerous foe.

Mike did as he was told and submitted to being searched.

And while the troopers searched for what Clytie hoped they would not find, she assembled her thoughts. It was not likely that Adam would have his own bags searched; yet if he should have the bags of all the troopers searched, fearing one of them was in league with her and Mike . . . He was capable of having everything turned inside out, and once he had found the letter he was capable, as well, of destroying it. He hated royal governors, and one of his recruits had been wounded because of the letter. She must find some way to divert his rage. . . . *Some way*

. . . Her instinct found it; she said a solemn prayer that it might work.

Adam was probing the sole of Mike's shoe with a knife when Clytie aroused herself from muteness and said with all the scorn she could muster, "So my father and I stand accused on the word of a French spy. And of what, Captain Appleton?"

"Of not being what you represent yourselves to be."

"My father *is* a coachman."

"For Governor DeLancey, hey?" He threw down Mike's shoe and wheeled on her. "Carrying him a message that brought on my men a deadly ambush, and——"

"High and mighty patriotism from you, sir," she said, taunting him. "What sort of patriotism is this—even supposing we *did* carry a message, which we do *not*—that causes you to denounce us, when that message is of such importance it calls forth the activities of a murderous spy?"

"And the near death of one of my men by your lies and trickeries."

"And your great skill at pursuit and capture, Captain," she said in a conciliatory tone. Anger would get her nothing—it would not serve her plan.

"Nothin' in their belongin's, Capt'in." Jed came into the circle of light made by the fire. "Made a thorough search, sir."

"Not of *all* our belongings. You have not searched me, Captain," Clytie said, mockingly, delighted when he gaped.

"Get the men back on watch," he told Jed. Then he faced her with such a threatening scowl that for a brief moment she cowered.

She unbuttoned her linsey-woolsey skirt, stepped out of it, and tossed it toward him with an easy banter she did not feel. "It has deep pockets, my Captain." He threw it aside with such rage that she taunted him further. "Don't look so tindery. You have seen me with less on. Besides, surely you would not neglect to look in the *bosom* of my bodice. Isn't that where a lady would conceal so important a letter?"

"T-take it—take it off," he commanded her.

Clytie's heart cringed. Her fingers fumbled at the neck of her bodice. But a tremor in his voice had told her the truth: he had not believed in her from the beginning, but had permitted the glowing episode in the forest night to weaken his judgment. And for this he hated himself more than he hated her. It gave her courage to do what she must do.

"Come and take it off me yourself, my Captain," she said. "You are the accuser."

He glowered, then leaped toward her. His iron-hot hands were on her—a deer in the paws of a leopard. He yanked at the opening of her bodice. Buttons flew. Her shoulders stood bared. Clytie was dizzy with shame and outrage, until a moan was rung from him and his big body leaned over her, his hot hands gripped her arms, his lips were on hers—hungry lips. The earth swayed and she dangled, clung. . . .

"Swine! Dastardly cur!" The butt of Mike's musket was raised.

Clytie staggered, suddenly released. Adam caught the gun before it come down on his head, twisted it from Mike's hands, and flung it aside. He wheeled on Clytie, caught her arm, and flung her at Mike.

"Take your crafty wench, old man!" Adam cried.

He walked with long strides to the edge of the woods. Clytie came to her senses.

"No!" She grabbed at Mike as he started after Adam. "Get out of sight. Obey me!" she cried fiercely. "Get out of sight!" She snatched up her skirt and followed Mike out of range of the firelight.

When she looked back Adam had disappeared. He would not go searching further for her father's letter—not tonight, he would not. That was all she must think of, all she dared think of, that her desperate *plan had triumphed.* Yet she sobbed even in her fitful sleep.

CHAPTER *Nine*

By early afternoon of the next day they reached Parr's Ridge.

"Valley of the Monocacy's not far away," one of the troopers called. "See Frederick soon."

The French prisoner, for whom Malt had been commandeered, and Mike and Clytie rode sandwiched between the troopers. All three were prisoners now, except that she and Mike were not strapped to their horses as the Frenchman was. They had left the wounded Zeb at a settler's house which they had reached just after dawn. But Clytie had been so unhappy about him that when no one was looking she slipped the settler's wife a crown for his keep.

"Lawful mercy!" The woman had regarded Clytie's torn skirt muddied with Zeb's blood, her ripped stockings that had been caught by briers and underbrush, her bodice held together only by thorns Mike had cut. "Ne'er in me versal life saw a purty gal so ragged," she said.

Clytie had laughed. When Adam came from the house and looked at her angrily, she had laughed even more. True, she had been kept awake last night by outraged pride and anger, and also by an impious joy, which had seemed to last the longest.

"Ride!" he had yelled to the others, and when she could not find an upping block from which to mount Bob, Adam had caught her up as if she were a bag of meal and set her on her horse.

Since then he had let his horse kick mud in her face as she followed him and Jed. She did not mind; she had welcomed it, welcomed her tatters. It all fitted in with another plan she had been forced to devise, to counteract the shock her father might suffer on learning too suddenly of her ride through the wilderness. She had no way of knowing he had yet reached Frederick or if he had been detained in Alexandria; but if the former were true, the more muddied and ragged her appearance, the better chance she had of not being recognized by him or anyone else. She would keep her head scarf well down over her face.

But what then? What about Aunt Monica? She had not seen Aunt

Monica nor any of the Chesters since she was a little girl. Was Aunt Monica watching her father's diet and guarding him from shocks, as Mr. Franklin had promised to tell her to do? . . . Mr. Franklin! *He* could help her. He could give her father the letter. No, she must not plan too far ahead. *Could* not until she knew where this Captain Beelzebub was taking her. While she was his prisoner anything could happen. At the moment he was setting a pace fast enough to kill the horses on such a warm muggy day.

"There she be—Frederick," Jed called back from the brow of a hill. "Looks good to me."

The troopers behind Clytie yowled delight.

It looked so good to her that she could scarcely believe it. From the hill she glimpsed the winding, shining river; and near it two white church steeples rose out of the surrounding green, like unopened lilies. Frederick—and her father's letter safe. But was it safe? Not until it was in her possession. Nothing was safe or sacred to the iron-muscled leopard that was Adam Appleton.

"Top o' day, Adam!" "It's Captain Appleton!" "Adam! Adam's back!" came the cries from all along the village street.

Men, women and children were pouring out of doorways, crowding the highway to greet the bedraggled little cavalcade riding through. "Prisoners? Ye got prisoners?" "Oh, look! One's a woman!"

Clytie, her head scarf low over her face, looked neither to right nor left. People were following them, Adam was calling greetings. Oh, why did he not ride faster and get wherever he was going? "Who be the gal?" she heard. This must be the way one felt when put in the stocks for all to gaze on and deride.

They were passing a greensward when she saw the red-coated soldiers, General Braddock's soldiers, come to save the colonies, as her father had said. "Blimy, a hero!" one shouted amid the other calls and cries. "The colonial's bagged him some skunks. One a female!" The other redcoats with him laughed raucously.

"Laugh, you red-coated monkeys!" a trooper called.

"Hello, purty!" A heavy voice was beside Clytie. "Uncover your head, wench." A red-coated arm reached for Clytie's ankle, adangle from her saddle horn.

The sequence of what followed, after she screamed and kicked at the man's strong hold on her leg, she did not remember. She heard Adam's bellow, saw his whip lash at the man's head. The noise became a tangled medley of shouts, curses, cries of the townspeople, as the troopers beat at the heads of the redcoats with musket butts.

She did not know how she managed to pull out of the melee . . . She was galloping down the street.

At a turn in the road near the river she waited for the angry colonials to overtake her.

"Shut up! And fall in line," Adam shouted.

Order was restored, and they followed his lead.

Clytie saw now where they were heading: for a stockade surrounded by a high piling. Just before they reached the gate a rider trotted out and hailed them.

"How, Adam, my boy! What you got there?" He drew rein. "Glad you are back." He was a stout, florid-faced man with a voice like . . .

Clytie suddenly remembered who . . .

"Top o' day, Colonel Chester, sir!" was Adam's greeting.

Uncle Peter! Oh, Uncle Peter! But only Clytie's heart and tired, wearied spirit voiced it. She dare not speak. She was not yet in possession of her precious box, nor was there any hope of his recognizing the bedraggled creature she was. And this was well, for if he did, he would take her to her father and bring on the shock, the awful shock, she *must* avoid.

He and Adam had drawn away from the others and were speaking in serious voices that she could not catch. Then Colonel Chester said, eying the Frenchman, who sat his horse like a wooden man, "Good work, lad! Washington will get the truth out of him, hey? May get a clew as to what's happened to that dispatch from the forts the governors over at my house are on their ears about. Send us word, my boy." He rode swiftly away.

Clytie had felt his eyes on her; yet as the wearied cavalcade followed Adam into the stockade, she reasoned that Adam likely had not told him of the prisoner's accusation of her and Mike.

The stockade was a large place with log huts surrounded by pools of rain water. A squad of soldiers was drilling; others were loading or unloading carts. The wail of a trumpet, the bark of a dog, the ringing of an anvil and the braying of a mule were all discordant sounds that mixed with her anxious thoughts. What would happen now?

"Nort, take these recruits to quarters and feed 'em!" Adam said as he drew rein before a small hut. To the other men who had followed the riders, he said, "Sam, here's a frog for you. Get Doc." He dismounted, ripping out orders to others. "Feed the horses. Hey, that sorrel the prisoner rode—bring it back here when you unhorse the frog." When he reached the cabin door he turned back and said, "Not *my* horse, Tom. Leave him here." He disappeared into the cabin.

Clytie breathed again. When she had seen his horse being led away, her box inside the saddlebag, she had known a moment of panic. Now it was over. The horse stood docile near her and Mike, the only ones of the cavalcade left. She slipped to the ground and darted toward him. Fevered, that Adam might reappear at the door, she unstrapped one side of the bags and ran her hand inside. Her heart seemed to stop beating. No box! The other side; he might have reversed the bags. The horse's tail brushed her shoulder as she went around to the other side; she plunged her arm into the bag and, limp with relief, she drew out the box with the same heart-throbbing sensation as when she had placed it there.

Voices sounded from the cabin.

"In here, O'Day," Adam called from the doorway. "Where—where's the girl?" He saw her beside his horse, saw her with the box clasped tight to her breast, and leaped toward her. "What—what's that you took from my bags?"

Clytie's movements were those of a rabbit. She darted around the horse and rushed into the cabin before he could catch her. She had no idea what she might find there, but she had heard a voice that might protect her.

"It's my property, sir. Mine!" she cried, and rushed to the protection of a tall man, who stood behind a table. "Mine, sir!"

"What'd you take from my—?" Adam broke off as the man, behind whom Clytie stood, raised a hand.

"Just a minute, Appleton. What's this?"

"Don't know, sir. But she's got something there I saw her take from my saddlebag." Adam glared at her.

The big man looked down at Clytie and said in a quiet voice of authority, "So this is the girl you brought along? Who is the man?"

Mike was entering the doorway.

"Calls himself O'Day, sir," Adam said. "And says the girl's his daughter. Said they were headed for Winchester. But the French prisoner identified him as a coachman for Governor James DeLancey."

The big man took his eyes from Mike, who looked uncertain of what he should say or do, met Clytie's appealing glance, and directed her to a chair opposite him at the table. "Sit down, young woman."

Clytie edged toward the chair. She could not see the tall man's face too well because he stood with his back against the light of the only small window in the cabin, but his resonant voice gave her confidence. Was he Adam's colonel?

"Are you Governor DeLancey's coachman?" he asked Mike.

"Yes, sir, he is," Clytie answered quickly.

"Lying to me all the time," ripped out Adam. "You see, Colonel——"

"Oh, are you Colonel Washingstone?" Her eyes brightened.

"Washing*ton*," Adam snapped.

"At ease, Captain." The big man sat down.

Clytie was certain she had seen a half-smile on his face. "I'm sorry, sir," she said. "But he told me how wonderful you were, and . . . I mean, I was just sure if I could get to you, you would . . . Oh, I don't mean that Adam—Captain Appleton—" she rushed on—"was not brave and wonderful, too. He saved our lives. And without him we never could have got here with the letter safe, and—"

"Letter?" But Adam's fierce outburst did not stop her.

"—and I did not mean to be distrustful of him, only it did not seem right to tell anyone about the box, not even when he became so angry over what the prisoner said, and searched our things, and——"

"Where *was* this box—letter?" Adam's question was hurled at her so hard that Clytie flinched, but she kept her eyes on the colonel's kindly gray ones.

"In—in your own saddlebag," she said, fearing to look at Adam. But she heard his gasp. "You see, Colonel Washington, I hid it there when we had to swim a swollen river, because I was sure about the strength of *his* horse but not about my own. I feared his heart——" She broke off before the colonel's curious and perplexed stare. He seemed to be taking in her muddied face, tattered garments and—and something else she could not fathom.

"This letter you speak of, to whom have you brought it?" He leaned forward; eagerly, she thought.

"To my . . . to Governor DeLancey, sir." She caught the relief in his eyes, before they could again bore through her. Then he leaned across the table, his hand outstretched for the box.

For only a moment she hugged it closer, then slowly surrendered it. She had to trust someone, and since this man with the somber face and honest eyes had so successfully fought the French in the wilderness . . .

"Oh, the key!" He was attempting to open the box. She reached for the key which hung around her neck.

"Where did you come by this letter?" The colonel said quite gently.

"From the messenger from the northern forts, who arrived in Philadelphia, badly wounded. And since we could find no other . . ." She stopped, an appeal in her eyes that indicated her concern at Adam's presence. To her relief the colonel responded at once.

"Appleton," he said, "you'd best have a look at your prisoner. See that he is in condition to be questioned."

"Er—yes, sir." Adam moved unwillingly toward the door.

Clytie felt greatly relieved. The sight of the jewels might force her to confess her identity, which just now she felt she could not endure—not with the memory of his embrace of last night so hauntingly in mind. As Lottie O'Day she could endure it, but not as Clytie DeLancey. Yet her heart followed his soldierly figure . . .

"And, Captain," the colonel added, eying the key in his hand, "report back here. I shall wish you to complete your mission of bringing this young woman safely through the wilderness by delivering her and her letter to Chestermere."

Adam's only response was to wheel about and give a quick salute. "Yes, sir." He did not look at her, but swung out through the door and away.

While the colonel's perplexed eyes were on the jewels he had uncovered in the box, Clytie studied him, amazed that she had not realized how young he was. No older than Adam, she thought now; but there was a force and strength about him she could not define. She could only feel it—a quiet, unassertive strength that came from some inner wisdom and knowing. As she stared at his broad face and large head, his powdered hair with a queue tied neatly at the neck, glistening in the light behind him, she had the oddest sensation of being reduced to the dimensions of a child before a towering personality and authority.

Clytie brushed her hand over her eyes. She was tired and her thoughts were vaporous. "Oh—oh, sir," she said, "beneath the jewelry is the letter."

His eyes searched her, with a faint smile, a wise smile. He emptied the box onto the table and came upon the letter. Solemn now, he noted the great seal and turned the letter over in his big capable hands.

"Blood stains?" he said questioningly.

"The wounded messenger's, sir." Then quickly she said, "Oh, sir, is—is Governor DeLancey in—in Frederick?" She knew her voice trembled with anxiety, but she had not expected the wide smile that centered so approvingly on her.

"Yes, Mistress DeLancey, your father is here."

"Oh—you—how did you—?" She fell back in her chair.

His smile broadened as he replaced the jewels in the box, to disclose an irregular line of white teeth. "It was a very dangerous mission you undertook. But I am certain your father will be relieved to have the dispatch from the forts. Gladder to have you safe." His long fingers lifted her string of pearls. "Your Grandmother DeLancey's, hey? I have heard my own mother say there were none more beautifully matched in the colonies." He wrapped them in a piece of cotton wool, placed them in the box, and fitted the letter atop the jewels. He locked the box, rose to his tall height, and gave her both the box and the key.

Her eyes were moons. But there was something in his kindly admiration of her that brushed away all her mud and tatters.

"Oh, sir, my father will be so grateful to you," she managed to say, hugging the box again.

"Then we will see that you get to him and to your aunt's home without delay. Appleton!" he called from the doorway. . . .

She had to shake Mike to arouse him from his slumber on a box against the wall.

CHAPTER *Ten*

Adam had not spoken to her all the way along the river road. He was well in front of her; Mike, Salt and Malt were some distance behind.

Yet since he had not learned her identity she felt comforted. And for all his rudeness she could not find one protest against him to rub against another. Last night he had revenged his distrust of her by accepting her challenge to search her bodice. But instinct told Clytie that it was not all revenge—not his embrace, his kiss. Afterward he had hated her more for his weakness. Then, before his colonel, he had suffered a defeat over the box, and her lies had been made plain. What if he knew she were Clytie DeLancey? Oh, she dare not think!

He drew up now at a little lane that led to the left of the river road and wheeled about. When she drew closer he said, "Reckon the Chesters will be willing to bed you down tonight in their Cabin of Refuge, being as you are Governor DeLancey's servants." His eyes were hard.

"Cabin of Refuge?" she echoed, pleased that there had been no suspicion in the word "servants." Yet even as she repeated his words, it seemed that a long-buried memory welled into mind. Had she heard of that cabin before? "Cabin of Refuge," she murmured again. It had a solacing sound. But as they turned into the lane, walking their horses, she knew that the words were not concerned with memory, but impinged on her future.

It was so strange a prescience that she looked at Adam's upright figure in his saddle, at the clean profile of his bronzed face, with the bewildering sensation that they were imprisoned together in some continuity of time, flowing out of the past, flowing on and on.

"Tired?" he asked.

Yes, that was it—she was bone-tired; but she tried to smile.

"That's what the cabin's for, such tattered travelers as you." He looked her over now, grinned and then whooped with laughter. "Ought to see yourself! Body can't tell if you are white or black with all that mud on your face. *Could* wipe it off, you know."

Wipe it off? Never. But she did not say it. She only grinned, thinking she might need a stronger disguise if she were to encounter her father.

"You'll sure be scaring the Chesters with your rags and tatters." He laughed again.

"Tattered in a good cause, Captain. Nor do I regret a tatter—" it was wonderful to be laughing with him—"if that relieves your conscience."

"*My* conscience?" He gaped, flushed, then grinned. "Look, next time I'll take you by the scruff of the neck——"

"Will there *be* another time, Captain?" she said, taunting him.

He kept his face averted. They were riding amid great oaks and chestnut trees in the domain of Chestermere. She looked back to see Mike following, taking his time about it.

"You'll see there's not another time, I reckon," Adam said with such unexpected reproach that her heart joyed.

But she could not force the joy into her voice; she was too concerned, too anxious about what would happen when they reached the house, which she sighted now amid the trees.

"No—no, I hope . . . I mean, I don't know—not about tomorrow, not about any tomorrow that I can reckon with. . . ." Her voice trailed. Her mind and heart were trying to reckon with today, with her father's heart and how best to . . .

Clytie drew rein with a little gasp. They had mounted a rise of ground where the woodland fell away, and Chestermere, set amid wide lawns, was before them. So she was here. Truly here at last.

This was Aunt Monica's home, about which she had heard all her life, listening enraptured to tales of Aunt Monica's marriage to the Maryland planter. The house, with its rose brick and small white-columned portico, gleamed in the lowering sunlight. It was a stalwart, hospitable house. One arm stretched to the south, another northward from the main structure—just what her grandfather had told her of this wilderness home.

Grandfather! She suddenly remembered how his portrait had frowned when she said good-by.

"What's the matter? Seen a ghost?" Adam was regarding her with so strange a look that it increased her forebodings concerning the portrait's frown.

She had just told the portrait that she so longed to visit Aunt Monica, when the frown appeared. Had he been trying to warn her of danger here? "Oh, no, Grandfather. Not danger—not here." She turned to meet Adam's eyes, yet her forebodings increased, encompassing him also.

"Y-yes, a ghost," she said faintly.

His laughter was mellow as he rode forward. He dismounted on the graveled space before the portico and hurried up the wide steps.

Voices were sounding from open windows at the right of the portico, and Clytie slid quickly from her horse, fearful that she heard her father's voice and that she might be seen before she was prepared for it. She took the letter out of the box and slipped it into the pocket of her cloak; she relocked the jewel box and hid it under her cloak, wrapping the cloak around her. When Mike rode up she hurried toward him.

"Take the horses behind the tall boxwoods there, Mike." Plans were coming to her more clearly now. Her father must not catch sight of the horses. "And wait there, Mike, until I call."

She found some muddy earth under the boxwoods and smeared it over her face. She tied on her head scarf and pulled it well over her forehead. Much of her anxiety now died as she mounted the steps and crossed the portico toward the open door.

"Colonel said to deliver her and her letter to Governor DeLancey," Clytie heard Adam say as she entered the cool, wide hallway.

"Letter? Message from the forts—this girl?" Uncle Peter Chester's voice was excited, but to avoid his stare and the hand that stretched out for the letter, Clytie slithered down onto the sofa. Not to anyone but her father would she surrender the letter.

"You have a dispatch, girl?" When she made no movement, he asked, "Who is she? Where'd she come from?" Without waiting for Adam to speak, he hurried to a door, opened it on the sound of men's voices, and said, "Excuse me, gentlemen, but Captain Adam Appleton is here with a dispatch for Governor DeLancey."

The mingled sound of voices frightened her for a moment. Then her father appeared in the doorway.

"From the forts? From Johnson?"

The moment Clytie had feared had come. Yet her heart bounded at the sight of the silk-clad legs, the velvet knees within her vision. Head down, she held out the letter unsteadily.

"Dispatch—from—a girl?" He took the letter from her dirty hand. "Thank God! But how? Where? Who is this girl?" His voice was eager, yet not *too* excited. But her joy that the letter was in his hand did not overcome her fear; letting her head fall back on the sofa, she pretended to faint.

"This is Captain Appleton, Governor DeLancey," Uncle Peter said.

No one was noticing her. "He met the girl in the wilderness and brought her and her father to Washington, who sent her here."

"My deepest gratitude to you, Captain Appleton. Noble of you, sir. Splendid service to the colonies and to the king." Clytie peeked around just in time to see her father grip Adam's hand.

"Not my service, Your Excellency, the girl's," Adam stammered.

"The dispatch, Governor? Good, good!" boomed another voice, Governor Morris'. "This should soothe General Braddock, what? Come inside. Let's have the news." Then he turned to Adam and said, "Good day—good day, sir."

Governor Morris and her father had started out of the room when her father turned back and said, "Look after the girl, Peter. Keep her here. Give her anything she wants. I'll question her later. My thanks again, Captain. Heartiest gratitude."

The door closed after him. And nothing had been said about Mike. Clytie's swoon threatened to become real, so great was her relief.

"She's fainted. The gal's fainted. Eph!" Uncle Peter called.

"She'll be all right, sir. Tired, hungry—that's all. You all right, Lottie?" Adam's hand was on Clytie's shoulder.

She lifted her head, gulped, and nodded.

"Well, she's yours, Colonel. Feed her. I'm off," said Adam.

"What's your hurry? Where you off to, Adam?" Uncle Peter followed him across the portico.

"Colonel Washington is waiting, sir. Things to get done before I ride with him to Virginia tomorrow."

He seemed in a mighty hurry, but now that he was mounted Clytie saw him looking around. For Mike? Oh, no! If he told Uncle Peter that Mike was her father's coachman . . .

Clytie let out a beseeching groan and doubled up again on the sofa.

"What's the matter, girl? Sick?" Uncle Peter was beside her.

She heard the hoofs of Adam's horse thud, and her heart cried after him, Come back soon! Oh, come back soon! She stood up, revived.

"It be me father I be worried about, sir," she said, again attempting that awful accent of Mike's.

"Father?"

"It be me father brought the letter safe through the wilderness, and he be a tired old man——"

"Brought it from where, girl?"

"It be no time to bandy words, sir," she reproved him with impudence. "He waits out there wi' our horses needin' to be fed." She went out to the portico and called, "Father!" When Mike appeared with the horses she said, "He be pinin' to rest hisself on a good bed and be given food."

"Yes, yes." Uncle Peter went down the steps, shouting, "Jake! Solomon! Blast your hides!"

Clytie waited for no more. She slipped back into the house. One glance at her bedraggled self in the long hallway mirror told her it was no time to make herself known to Uncle Peter or anyone. They would only call her father, and the shock she had so far guarded him against would surely come. But if she could find Monica . . . Mr. Franklin had warned her aunt; yet not even her aunt would believe . . . Oh, Mr. Franklin, if only you were here! If she could only hide until . . .

She started up the broad stairs, stopped at a sound from above, turned back, and darted into a narrow hallway. The first door she came to she opened softly. There was no one inside. She closed it quietly behind her and stood dazed. A bedroom. A big canopied bed swung round and round in a blue haze, and her tired, numbed body yearned toward it as toward a phantom of half-forgotten things. . . .

Clytie's cloak dropped to the floor; her jewel box followed. Relieved of these she swayed, groped toward this invitation to paradise. Her hands fastened instinctively on her clogs. She tugged; they would not come off. Then her hands touched a downy softness, her body fell onto the bed; she stretched out her wearied limbs . . . and floated beyond sight and sound.

"Lawzy me! Ooooo! Lordy, Lordy!"

The screech ripped into Clytie's deep sleep. Her heavy eyelids tried to open, but she saw only through a slit the little black girl who stood at the foot of the bed, her hands raised in horror, her eyes popped wide.

"Git off'n dat bed! Dat Miz' Mony's bed!" The cries mounted. "Git off'n, you po' white trash!"

Clytie's muscles made no response. She closed her eyes to shut out the apparition, and heard from afar the sound receding: "Sis' Phyly! Sis' Phyly!"

Clytie moved away on tumbling clouds. . . .

Then out of the darkness issued a belly-deep chuckle. "Sotweed an' cider! The little wench!"

A woman's soft gasp was added. And, conscious now, Clytie lifted her long eyelashes cautiously, ever so little.

"Squire Chester, who is this girl?" said the woman.

"I cum in hyar an' seed her, Miz Mony—dar she was——"

"Quiet, Sapphira. Squire—?"

"I just told you, Mony," he answered. "George Washington sent her here when he found out she had a dispatch for James."

"The one he has been so worried about?"

Their voices droned around Clytie as her veiled eyes fixed on Monica's face, a face so long held in loving memory—the same blue eyes, the strong classic features—yet she was not so tall as she had remembered her. Away off in time sounded her mother's voice: "I did not say that Monica was not handsome—but pretty, no. Too rigid. Not flexible. Dress her in breeches and she'd make a handsome man." Clytie remembered her mother's low, light laughter. "Dress my sister Prissy up with four feet and a snout and she'd make a handsome pig."

Clytie heard half-whispered words and Uncle Peter's continued chuckles. The little black girl dashed out a door that opened into the garden, calling loudly to someone. Clytie saw gray streaks in Aunt Monica's sandy-blond hair when she came closer to the bed—her eyes grew wide on seeing the bundle of rags and grime that lay so inert.

A heavy hand shook Clytie's arm. "Come, you little wench. This is no place for you—in a lady's bed." She only expelled a groaning sigh at Uncle Peter's touch. She had to think first.

"Let her be, Squire, until Phyly comes. Her clothes are bloodstained. Was she wounded?"

"Fainted when James took the letter from her."

"He does not know who she is? What's this?" Monica stooped to look at the cloak and jewel box Clytie had dropped on the floor and drew back from touching them. "It was brave of her to have brought James's dispatch. But to throw herself onto my bed! Such filth!"

"Where's Phyly?"

"In the weaving house."

Monica's revulsion was rousing Clytie's pride and anger. Clytie DeLancey might have become a pitiable spectacle, but not one to cause revulsion and derision. She'd do some deriding herself. She would be hanged!" as Adam would say, if she had not been buffeted about enough. A spirit of mischief crossed her anger.

"Phyly, Phyly, look at this!" Aunt Monica uttered in despair.

A tall, straight grenadierlike black woman came in. Her big eyes gleamed white for a moment in startled alarm. "Lawzy, lawzy!"

Clytie wanted to giggle.

"Take her down to the Cabin of Refuge, Phyly, and——"

"I won't go to the Cabin of Refuge," Clytie said as she sat up with a suddenness that startled them all. The very mention of the cabin to which Adam had condemned her, and that had so inspired her awe, stirred her to brisk resistance. "I'll ha' nought but the best in your house—" she lifted her clogs from the bed and with an agile leap stood to her tall, straight height—"the best, I sa'iy." She defied the gaping mouths.

"Sotweed and——"

"Merciful heavens!"

"I be a guest, ben't I?" She hurled her words among their exclamations. "Was it no' the tall, handsome gen'man hisself—he wi' the shapely laigs an' velvet riggin'—I gi' the letter to, told ye to gimme what I want? Hey?" she tossed at Uncle Peter. Her attempted dialect was not much good, but her wide-legged stance, fists on hips, was determined. "So, then! Hit be a fine room I be wantin', an' a soft bed, an' a beauteous, *beaut-i-ous* warm bath." She stretched her arms with joy at the thought. "An' food—hunks and heaps o' food."

"Saints preserve us! Look here, my fine baggage . . ." Uncle Peter said.

But when Clytie grinned at him through the mud that streaked her face, the squire's protest ended in a wheezy guffaw.

"Squire Chester!" Monica reproved.

"And ben't the handsome gen'man's dispatch worth that?" Clytie grimaced. "What I want be but me roights." She snapped her fingers under Uncle Peter's nose, enjoying herself now. It was like one of the charades she and Pete and Jamie and her brothers had staged in the nursery at home when Aunt Monica and Uncle Peter had brought her cousins on a visit to Pearl Street.

"By the Lord High Jinks!" Uncle Peter slapped his thigh. "You shall have what you ask, ye sassy wench."

"Squire, call James. James will know what to do."

Clytie hoped that her eyes had not popped too wide with horror at this. But Uncle Peter's laughter reassured her.

"How can I call James, Mony, when the general has just arrived? No, by thunder! We'll dress her up and turn her loose on James. Handsome, hey, my pretty? Good. We'll give him a lark."

"Oh, sir," Clytie pleaded, "could he but see the likes o' me handsome dressed——"

"Have done, please." Monica directed her words at both Clytie and Uncle Peter. "Phyly, get a clean cotton dress——"

"I'll ha' no cotton dress," Clytie defied her, scratching herself. "Silk or satin, or no dress at all I be havin'."

"Lady for a day, hey?" said the squire. "Come, Mony, where's your sense of humor? Give James a laugh. He'll need one after that conference he's in." When Monica dropped into a chair with a despairing sigh, he continued, "Get one of your mistress' fine dresses, Phyly——"

"An' satin shoes, an' silk stockin's, an' a bonny ribbon fer me hair." Clytie strutted and scratched her head.

"Squire, you don't know what you are doing!" It came sternly from Monica. "I won't have James set upon."

"Why, the gal's a heroine. Don't you know a heroine when you see one?" It was clear nothing would stop Uncle Peter's zest in his joke. "Out you go, minx! Up the stairs!"

As Clytie made for the door he spanked her bottom. She squealed, clapped a hand over her laughter, headed through the corridor and for the stairs.

"First door on the left," he called after her.

She raced upward toward it.

As Clytie opened the bedroom door softly she heard Phyly's footsteps on the back stairs. Those stairs must lead toward the kitchen. Phyly had told her the dining room was just beyond the parlor where the royal governors were in conference with General Braddock.

"And Mr. Franklin?" Clytie had asked eagerly.

Phyly had said yes, she thought he was there, and looked at her so curiously that she had had to break off her questions. But Mr. Franklin's being there was all-important to the only sensible plan she had been able to make.

She listened for other sounds in the house before venturing into the hallway and toward the stairs; hearing someone speak below, she closed the door again softly. She must not be seen by any of the Chesters, must *not* be seen until she had reached Mr. Franklin and implored his help.

For nothing had changed, not really, although she had on a lovely blue dress of silk brocade. After the unmannerly way she had behaved, Aunt Monica and Uncle Peter would never believe she was their niece until they had called her father. And then the silk dress would not prevent his shock at her being here.

No. There was only one way. Mr. Franklin was wise and kind; he would know how to cushion the shock if only she could reach him. The conference in the parlor could not last forever, and if she could get to the dining room and wait there . . .

Clytie in muddled indecision sat down on the bed. She had told Phyly that she was so fagged from her long ride she must rest a bit before presenting herself to the Chesters. Phyly's agreement had served her well. But she felt nervous over the way the nice black woman had looked at her all the time she was taking her bath and getting dressed.

She had stripped, and the little black girl Sapphira had taken all her rags out to be burned. Then Phyly and Sapphira had brought in a big tub of hot water, with salt in it to kill the chiggers.

As Clytie stepped into the water she tossed her money belt to Phyly, and Phyly smiled so wisely that Clytie asked, "Why do you look at me like that?"

"Jes' thinkin', honey, how like you is . . ." Phyly, her arms folded across her spare stomach, had shaken her turbaned head slowly. She had a big, strong-boned frame, but she was lean and angular, with a truly lovely face. It had strength and character and goodness.

"Like—like what—whom?" Clytie had doused her head in the water and lathered her hair with the glutinous soap.

Phyly had not answered until she brought a pitcher of clear water to pour over Clytie's head. Then slowly, softly, she said, "Like Miz Mony's little girl might o' been, had she lived." She occupied herself then with taking out undergarments for Clytie to put on.

Clytie lay back in the tub, thinking of Aunt Monica's little girl who had died, she had been told, when she was two years old.

It had not been easy to keep up her pretenses with Phyly, especially when the blue dress was being fitted to her. The skirt was all right as to length, for she was as tall as Monica, but the waistband had to be taken in. After Phyly had fitted and sewed the seams of the bodice, so that it looked as if it were made for her, she had had to express herself in her own way.

"You are a sempstress without compare, Phyly."

But from the shining smile Clytie received, she might well have thought that she herself was beyond compare. The dress *was* becoming—the same blue as her eyes. Her hair was all fluffy ringlets—it was so fine-textured it dried easily—and Phyly had given her a blue ribbon to tie about it. She had felt very much like Clytie DeLancey again.

Now she felt frightened. She went to the door again and opened it softly. She heard nothing but the sounds of low voices from the conference room. Monica was lying down, with a headache, Phyly had said. Poor Aunt Monica!—because of her, of course, Uncle Peter had gone out to his office. Pete was still at college in Virginia, and Jamie had not returned from his tutoring in Frederick. All this she knew. So if none of the family saw her as she headed for the dining room . . .

Clytie pulled off her blue satin slippers. They were loose on her feet and she might drop one. She tucked them under her arm, ventured out to the stairs, and raced downward. There was no one in the hallway. She headed toward the back door, which opened into the sloping garden, turned right along a brick walk that run beside the house, ducked low when she passed the parlor windows, and came to a door that was opened into the garden. The dining room? A voice from across the garden startled her. She rushed into the half-darkened room and hid behind a screen.

CHAPTER *Eleven*

"Now then, sirs! Two thousand miles ha' I come wi' my troops through storms and perils of sea to protect your colonies," pronounced the speaker. "Other countless miles must I make my way through your ungodly wilderness to this—this Fort Thing-a-me——"

"Duquesne, General." Governor Morris supplied the name, and for a moment the angry voice with its burred Scotch accent stopped. But the general went on more angrily than before.

"And wi' what am I met when my demands on ye and your colonies are stated? Wi' *promises*." The voice cannonaded. "I am met wi' glib promises of provisions and supplies. Aye, even of transport for my ammunition and supplies. Yet where be these supplies, Your Excellencies? Where be my transport—two hundred wagons and twenty-five hundred horses—to haul my supplies?" Indeterminate sounds came from the others in the room before the general's voice fired its parting shot: "It is *that* I demand to hear. Forthwith and now!"

At that very moment the speaker strode into Clytie's view. From her position behind the dining-room screen, she had been impressed by the authority in his voice. Now she gaped and held her breath. He was magnificent, august. Against the background of his red coat his decorations glistened, his epaulets gleamed. A ray of the setting sun slanted through a window of the parlor and lighted his great hand that gripped his sword hilt. With his other hand he twisted the walrus mustache that swaggered down his florid cheeks. The oh's and ah's and clearing of throats from the others in the room seemed to re-echo, like hapless groans, around the tall, strong frame of the grim warrior. This could be none other than General Edward Braddock, the king's general, come to save the colonies.

There were wheezings from another man who was well within Clytie's vision. He was Governor Dinwiddie of Virginia. He had dined with her father one evening at her home on Pearl Street, and she recognized his grotesque figure. He was so fat he oozed out from beneath the arms of his chair. His feet could not reach the floor, and he had no neck—just a jowly face, topped by a powdered peruke, that sat on his shoulders; his eyes were little pin points. That was one of the reasons she had giggled when Adam called him a fool.

There was another man whom she could see, dressed in black. Governor Sharpe of Maryland, maybe. He had been a fine military man, her father had said, but now his health was not good.

But where was her father? Where was Mr. Franklin?

She moved cautiously and peered through another slit opening, where the panels of the screen joined. She could see a little better now—their group was composed as though they were on a stage, a stage of history. Two steps led down to the dining room, and the broad door stood wide open to the fresh breeze. She was eavesdropping, which was sinful. Yet didn't she have a right to know something about these important matters since she had brought a dispatch from the northern forts? Apparently it had not put the general in the good humor Governor Morris had hoped it would.

Words and phrases were now so mingled in the room that she could not catch what was said. Then came the general's snort.

"It does not signify. Promises—bah!" He walked to a chair, lifted it, then set it down again hard on its feet. "Promises will not save the king's lands, nor ye colonists from butcheries. Now, sirs, I shall act." He emphasized it. "Act with dispatch. Unless my demand for wagons and horses be met *forthwith*, be it well understood that I shall entrain my troops and set sail for home." On finishing this ultimatum, he spread the tails of his coat and clanked into a chair.

"Brandy, General?"

Clytie caught her breath. That was her father's quiet, mellow voice. Contrasted with the blare of the other's, it was music. He came within her sight now, poised, gracious, a decanter in one hand, a big snifter glass in the other. At the general's nod of approval her father poured. The glass was almost full before the general's hand stretched forth for it.

The general sniffed. He gave a satisfied "Ah!" and poured the liquor down his throat. He smacked his lips loudly. Her father took the empty glass. She knew he wanted to grin, but he did not.

"Are you aware, General," she heard Governor Morris say, "that our postal commissioner for the colonies, Mr. Benjamin Franklin, has been sent down here by my assembly to give heed to your need of transportation of supplies? And he has promised——"

"One moment, Morris," James DeLancey put in. "General Braddock has expressed himself as to the value of promises. And even in his short acquaintance with Ben Franklin, I am certain he would adjudge him to be a man who makes no promises he cannot fulfill. Now, in this matter of horses and wagons—an astounding quota—I am convinced Franklin could never have promised such."

"Wh-what—what be that, mon?" The general's voice mounted to a roar.

"A simple fact, sir," answered DeLancey. "The colonists do not possess such a quota of either horses or wagons as you demand."

The general gasped.

But Governor Sharpe said irascibly, "Nor do they show a disposition to co-operate with officers of the Crown."

This brought the general's anger down on him. "And whose flibberty-jibberty policy be that, hey?" roared Braddock. Then he leveled at Dinwiddie. "So, ye be forced to shift your Crown duties to the back of a colonial, hey. To this—this Franklin!"

The widening of Governor Dinwiddie's beady eyes and the flap of his jellied hands on the arms of his chair made Clytie want to giggle, even amid her desolation that Mr. Franklin was not attending the conference.

Then, what should she do now? No need to stay here any longer and listen. Voices from another quarter caught her ears—from behind the door that led toward the kitchen. If she were found eavesdropping by one of the servants . . . She would have to run, only she did not know *where* to run. She might never get upstairs again without being seen. She calculated quickly: near the high screen that stood close to the parlor doorway was a lowboy that stood out from the wall, and if a servant entered she could crouch . . .

"Franklin!" boomed Governor Morris.

And the others cried, "Mr. Franklin! Thank God you have come, man!"

Clytie forgot all peril as she heard the voice she would have recognized anywhere by its calm authority.

"Your Excellencies! General Braddock!" answered Franklin.

She glued her eyes to the screen to see his brown-coated figure. He was shaking hands with the general. Then, calamity! The pantry door opened, and Clytie slipped down, crouching, beside the lowboy. An old white-haired Negro entered the room. He placed two candlesticks holding fresh candles on the mantelpiece, went out again, and re-entered —she scarcely breathed—with two more double-stemmed holders, which he placed on the table. Half-blind he must be, that he could not see her, though the light in the room was dimmer now.

When he went away she again peeked through the screen opening, her ears alert, regretting all she had missed.

Mr. Franklin, seated beside the general, was saying: "We understand your needs, General. Our difficulty is to supply them. Few planters or farmers in this part of the country have wagons. As for horses, this is the planting and sowing season, and should that be neglected because the colonists' horses were relinquished for your expedition to Duquesne, untold hardship would accrue for their families."

"Relinquished, sir? Relinquished?" volleyed the general. "If these colonists be so disloyal to the king as not to offer freely their property, *take* the horses. Take them, mon." His hand pounded his thigh. "*Confiscate* the horses."

In the silence that followed, Clytie could hear a thrush singing in the gathering twilight outside in the garden. Breathlessly she waited for the general to continue. She knew what his emphasis of that wicked word meant. Her grandfather had so often talked against the too high-handed use of royal authority. . . .

"The assistance I was delegated to render to you, General," Mr. Franklin said with calm authority, "did not include confiscation of the properties of colonials."

"And why not, sir," the general barked, "when, for preservation of the king's colonies, these horses must be procured?"

Mr. Franklin met the angry eyes, but his voice lost none of its uncompromising intent. "What liberty of conscience and action we have, General," he said, "must be preserved. Should an enemy rob us of our freedom it would be dire. Should we rob *ourselves* it would be direr still."

The general's face became purple. His mouth opened, but he only yanked at his mustache. A red afterglow from the sky flashed through the windows. Benediction on what Mr. Franklin has said, Clytie thought as she awaited the general's outburst.

It did not come. He swept the room with a glance, and delivered his opinion with bitter scorn.

"So that's it!" he said. "I ha' come two thousand miles to defend colonists who be disloyal to their king."

Protests were voiced but he did not heed them.

"Or could it be, Mr. Franklin, sir—" he spoke with an oily voice—"that whispers I ha' heard be not unfounded: that the colonists be inclined to *accept* invasion from the French?"

"A lie. Who whispered that whispered a lie." It was James DeLancey's voice, modulated, but scalding.

No one but the Royal Governor of New York, as all the listeners knew—Clytie as well—could afford so to challenge the king's general. He was not concerned with this unprecedented demand for horses and wagons; he was merely an interested observer. All appropriations from his own colony were committed for the defense of the northern forts.

No one is so fearless as Father, Clytie thought joyfully.

"Permit me to advise you, right here and now, General Braddock," DeLancey went on amid the hush, "that our colonists *are* loyal to the Crown. Malcontents exist everywhere—in Ireland, hey?—in Wales, in Scotland. Some exist here—"

A snort from the general did not stop him.

"—and make themselves but poorly heard. Our settlements that stretch five hundred miles back from the sea are British to the core. We have, as well, a small per cent of Europeans—Scandinavians, some French. But tell your whisperers, General, that ninety-nine per cent of our colonists are loyal, sir. And you might inform the king and parliament," he said emphatically, "that when disloyalty threatens, those to be held responsible must be those who impose burden after burden of taxes on us, without permitting us to derive any benefit therefrom. Tell them that, General."

Then, out of the silence came the general's soapy-smooth accusation "Born a *colonial,* hey, DeLancey?"

"And proud of it, sir," was the quick reply.

With a rattle and snap the general got to his feet, and with a more menacing rattle shook himself out.

Clytie trembled. But to her surprise the general said mildly, "Damme, DeLancey! Ha' it your own way, for I ha' not come two thousand miles to talk politics. I ha' come to fight—to fight the king's enemies, sir. Gi'e us a drink, mon."

The parlor was now brightly lighted by candles. Clytie had been discovered by the elderly servingman, who said his name was Ephraim, after he had taken the lighted candles into the conference room.

She had told him that she was waiting for Governor DeLancey, and at once dispatched him for a goblet of cold water. He went without comment. Now Clytie's eyes were again on Mr. Franklin and the general.

"Since ye opine these horses and wagons may be obtained in Penn Colony, Mr. Franklin," the general said, "I will dispatch Colonel Dunbar to collect . . . Hey?"

Mr. Franklin handed him a paper. "I have set down in the paper the terms on which these may be obtained, sir. They are terms that require *rent* of the wagons, *hire* of the horses, and *pay* for the drivers."

"R-rent? Hire? Pay?" the general countered explosively.

"The exact stipulations of which we may agree on at your convenience, sir," Mr. Franklin stated firmly.

The general made a fearsome noise in his throat. It died away.

"Of a number to accommodate me, sir?" He was being more co-operative now.

"I devoutly hope . . . even believe so," came Mr. Franklin's measured and impressive words.

Ephraim came in with Clytie's glass of water and the conversation from the parlor became confused, but she heard Mr. Franklin say something about twenty days in which to assemble the wagons and horses, Lancaster farmers and a printing press.

"A printing press to drive about the country, Franklin?" Governor Morris asked.

"I shall need to drive words about the country, Governor. And awe, superstition, even fear and terror, into the hearts of our beloved countrymen, so that their wagons and horses may be driven out of their fields and into the general's camp."

Even Ephraim seemed to be listening when Mr. Franklin finished by saying solemnly: "I shall need, too, gentlemen, the help of God."

She put down her goblet of water, almost spilling the remainder on the sideboard, when she realized the conference was breaking up. Mercifully, Ephraim went out toward the kitchen. The parlor doors into the hallway opened, and Clytie feared that Mr. Franklin might be leaving. She risked detection by moving closer to the door just as her father and governors Morris and Dinwiddie passed into the hallway.

Mr. Franklin was talking to the black-clad man when, in her desperation, Clytie whispered, "Mr. Franklin, sir." It came out like a hiss.

Mr. Franklin turned around, his face blank, but as the black-clad man, Governor Sharpe, continued to talk, he went with him to the door. Governor Sharpe left the room, and Mr. Franklin turned back again.

But Clytie ignored his startled look of surprise; when she saw her father follow Governor Sharpe onto the portico, she flew past Mr. Franklin, closed the parlor door, and snapped the bolt.

"Oh, sir, I am in fearsome trouble——"

"Mistress DeLancey!"

She had no sooner wheeled on him, her back to one door, than she realized there was a second door leading into the hall. Toward this she leaped, not heeding his wide-eyed astonishment, and bolted that door, too.

"Oh, sir——"

"Your father did not tell me——"

"He doesn't *know*." She had no time to be mannerly. "That is just it—he doesn't know I am *here*. Nobody does." She grabbed his arm, and when the dignified postal commissioner started to speak, she put a finger to her lips and propelled him toward a sofa at the far end of the room, away from the candlelight.

"Bless my soul!" He chuckled as she flopped down on the sofa and drew him down beside her. "Am I seeing a vision?"

"Yes, sir—no, sir." Never had she been so apprehensive of discovery. "I mean——" She stopped and giggled as he stared; then some vestige of poise returned. "Oh, I am in dire need of your magic wand, sir." She joined in his soft laughter.

"So, you have lost the Aladdin's lamp that brought you here, and the jinni has vanished?"

It was so urgent that she tell him her tale and plead for his help that she could not remember afterward just what she *had* told him—only that he had listened, disturbed and amazed, to the tale of her trip through the wilderness. And maybe she used Adam's name too often, explaining what a hero he had been, although she caught herself several times and called him Captain Appleton instead, for she saw Mr. Franklin smile, a very subtle and knowing smile. So she cut the tale short.

"And what must I do now, sir," she pleaded, "so that my father will not find out too suddenly that I am here? The shock—his heart——"

"What's the matter with this door? Open the door!"

Clytie started up in terror. Someone in the hall was rattling the door. Uncle Peter!

"Don't be alarmed. It will be all right." Mr. Franklin was standing beside her. When Uncle Peter tried the other door, Franklin started toward it, saying, "No time like the present, my dear, to get everything all smoothed out."

"But . . ." Suppose her father was there and followed Uncle Peter in?

Taking no chances, Clytie slipped behind one of the long heavy curtains at the window.

"Yes, sir. Vanished—poof! Like that! The little wench has vanished," Uncle Peter told Mr. Franklin.

Franklin had turned about and saw that she had hidden, but he did not interrupt Squire Chester's tale, which went forward, interspersed with chuckles.

"Strangest thing you ever heard of! That ragged little wretch demanding a satin dress and the best room in the house. Yes, by sassifras! Got it, too. Phyly fixed her up—said she was the prettiest little baggage you ever set eyes on. Now she's flown the coop. Gone. But where? Left a money belt filled with gold behind—that's a fact. And an old box and a cloak. Searched the place for her, but no gal. What do you make of it, hey?" But before Mr. Franklin could answer he said, "Ephraim, seen any strange woman about the place?"

Peeking out from behind the curtain, Clytie saw that the old Negro had come in with a shovel of red-hot coals with which to light the fire on the hearth. But she was not excited now, only tickled at Uncle Peter, for whatever Ephraim said, Mr. Franklin would make it right.

When Ephraim said he had seen a woman in the dining room, who was waiting for Governor DeLancey, Uncle Peter's hearty laughter broke out anew.

"Making a play for James. All set to make him pay for that letter she brought."

"Just a minute, Squire——" But Mr. Franklin did not get far.

"Where'd she go, Eph? Not—not to James's bedroom . . ." He heaved himself to his feet. "He's asleep, and Mony won't have him disturbed."

"Asleep? Oh, is he *asleep*?" Clytie was so relieved at this respite that she could not contain her joy. She stepped from behind the curtains as she spoke. But when she met the squire's staring eyes, she feared for the shock she was administering to *him.*

"Sotweed and cider! This—you?" He was taking in her transformed appearance and her wide smile as she linked her arm in Mr. Franklin's. "Why, you——"

"Squire Chester, allow me to present to you your niece, Mistress Clytie DeLancey," said Mr. Franklin.

Uncle Peter gasped, but steadied himself as she threw her arms about him and kissed both his ruddy cheeks.

CHAPTER *Twelve*

MONICA'S voice, making a jumbled sound, came from behind the closed door, and Clytie strained her ears, hoping to catch her father's replies. They were more jumbled still. Monica had stationed her here while she went into her father's room to tell him Clytie had brought the dispatch. Clytie had hoped for Mr. Franklin's wise intervention, but Monica had taken the situation over with authority and caution.

"I shall first make him understand how long I have dreamed of having you with me here at Chestermere," her aunt had said, "then ease into the fact that my dream has come true."

That had been after Aunt Monica had stared coldly at the interloper who claimed to be her niece. But her coldness had not lasted. "Clytie! My little Clytie!" Monica had gathered her into welcoming arms. But because of Monica's fears caused by her niece's wilderness journey, Clytie had recounted none of its dangers. She had spoken only of the loss of her boxes and Aunt Prissy's theft of her father's dispatch.

Now, as indistinct murmurs came from her father's room, she thought she heard the Huber name; she moved closer to the door. Anxiety turned her hands and heart to ice. There was a louder sound of voices. . . .

"Old scarecrow! Traitor as well, hey? Never would have left my girl there if . . ." Her father's voice died away.

Clytie held her breath. Oh, Aunt Mony, be careful! She heard only murmurs. Then again: "Mike . . . Lottie . . . Girl brought my dispatch was . . ."

Monica's words were muffled, and it seemed to Clytie a lifetime before she heard again: "Don't know my girl, hey?" He snorted. "No De-Lancey alive is more of a credit to . . ."

Monica's voice, so close to the door that Clytie jumped back, overlapped his: "Now that you agree, my brother, that no girl is braver . . ." The door opened. "Come in, my child." Monica beckoned.

Clytie's knees almost buckled. From the doorway she saw her father, seated in his dressing gown. His dear face seemed to be swimming in a blur. But she pulled herself together, advanced, and drew up before him in a smart salute.

"Corporal DeLancey reporting, Your Excellency," she said.

"You—you wanton! You little heathen!" He lifted his arms; she dropped on her knees before him. He hugged her close.

And now with that crisis over, another loomed; it was already, in fact, sitting like a tombstone on Clytie's chest. While her father had been dressing he had sent for Mike.

She had waylaid Mike, who was on his way out of the house, and had asked him, "Mike—what?"

His homely face, transformed with smiles, had assured her that he had been dealt with generously, but her heart seemed to have heard only ". . . so we be settin' out for home come daylight tomorrow."

Tomorrow! Home! Clytie now sat, bowed in thought, on the parlor sofa. Her thoughts dangled and clacked against each other as if they were being blown about by a chill wind. To leave Chestermere so soon meant that she would never see Adam again. Not ever. She tried to shake such cruel thoughts from her mind, but her body was too tired to co-operate. Besides, how *could* she ever see him again, see his eyes crinkle in that wondrous smile, hear his voice drawl, when she did not know where he lived and could not write to him? And he did not even know her true name. Her heart was stricken. It was like being tied up alone in the dark, unable to make a sound—not to Monica, not to her father. . . .

"Oh, there you are, darling!" Monica stopped on her way toward the dining room. "Tired? Of course you are." Monica sat down beside her. "Now as to your leaving in the morning with your father, it is sheer nonsense. I won't allow it."

Clytie's eyes brightened, but her pleasure contended with loyalty to her father, and she said, "He needs me, Aunt Mony. I could not——"

"He won't need you where he is going, my dear. Immediately he arrives in New York he sets off for Albany and the northern forts." Clytie looked up in alarm, but Monica hurried on. "So you see it would be much wiser to leave you here than alone in that great house with no one but old Manners to look after you. That is what I must make him see, since with the general's forces here we are in no danger."

"O-oh, Aunt Mony!" Clytie wavered between joy and fear. "But—but Albany—the northern forts . . ."

"Only for the purpose of making disposition of his militia, and for keeping in touch with General Shirley. Don't worry, he will be better off away from New York."

"Yes, yes, that's what Manners said." She was truly brightening now. Yet when Monica said he might remain there for months on end, she was not so sure.

"The important thing is, I must make James see that he must leave you with us." Monica again started toward the dining room.

Clytie quickly put out a hand to stop her, then withdrew it. What she wanted to say, she dare not. Instead she said, "No, please don't force him to a decision—not about *me*." She felt overwhelmingly that this was a crossroad in her life: to go, or to stay and see Adam again. Then she realized the decision was not Monica's, nor her own, but her father's. She trusted him in all things concerning herself, and the *right* way must be determined by him.

"As for the loss of your boxes, my child—" Monica turned back from the door—"Phyly and her sewing girls can fit you out with an entire new wardrobe. Shoes and slippers, too. Our shoemaker tans hides and works with satin." She lifted her gray satin skirt to display a satin slipper. "We shall plan lovely things for you." Her smile drenched Clytie with fond delight.

But after Monica had gone Clytie sensed that there had been a wistful sadness about her smile. Had she been thinking of her little girl, of whom Phyly had spoken, who would have been only a little older than herself? A drowsy warmth stole over Clytie. She admired her aunt; there was authority about her, but serenity, too, and wisdom and understanding. Would she understand her, Clytie DeLancey, who had never had understanding from her own mother, but only from her father?

She heard his voice in the hallway and got up eagerly to greet him. He was followed by Mr. Franklin and Uncle Peter. He put his arm about her, but without breaking off what he was saying.

"Quite an enterprise," he said, "cutting a road all the way to Fort Duquesne, Franklin, for those supply wagons. Yet if Morris and Sharpe think they can effect it over those mountains——"

"Jamie!" Clytie interrupted her father in a most unmannerly way.

But he laughed with everyone else as a loud voice, raised in song, came to them from the driveway.

"Young rascal gets home later and later from his tutoring," Uncle Peter said.

Clytie, enlivened by the song, hurried into the hallway. It was one Jamie had taught her when the Chesters came to New York on a visit.

When she reached the portico she saw in the blue dusk a lanky figure on a shaggy pony coming up the drive. One leg was drawn up on the saddle, the other dragged the ground, as he sang lustily,

> "I wish I had a load of bricks,
> To build my chimney higher,
> For every time the rain comes down,
> It puts out all my fire.
> It puts out—"

"—all my fire!" echoed Clytie in a high clear voice. She had scurried down the steps and concealed herself behind one of the boxwoods.

"Whoa, Rozinante!" Jamie drew up at the upping block and looked around for the mysterious singer.

His long face, with its irregular features lighted by the lantern, startled Clytie. He was not the Jamie of their childhood. His red hair was unbound and dripped in snakelike curls down his neck.

"Who in the name of Beelzebub?" His startled eyes were as big and as blue as his mother's.

Clytie peered from behind the boxwood, then rushed toward him, crying, "Jamie! Jamie!"

"The furies are upon us, Rozinante!" he yipped, vaulting his pony. Then he chanted from the other side, "*Aeternum servans sub pectore vulnus.*" He pretended to shiver.

"Silly gander! Don't you know me?"

"Bet your broomstick I know you. I know harpies, witches an' sich when I sees 'em."

"Then I shall turn both you and Rozinante into brown bears." Clytie waved the imaginary wand that had served them in childhood.

"Great horned toads and buttercups, it's true!" He shouted her name and ran toward her. Then he grabbed her up as if she were a bag of meal and bounded up the steps with her. "Ma! Pa!" he bellowed. "Look what I found in the bushes!" He did not put her down until they were among the company in the parlor.

Now, with supper over, Mr. Franklin, accompanied by Jamie and two of the slaves, was setting off for a conference with General Braddock.

Clytie waved good-by from the portico and was about to follow her father, Aunt Monica and Uncle Peter back into the parlor when, in the blue April night, she thought of Adam and felt again the weight of the impending decision: to go with her father, or to stay *and* . . . That little word seemed pregnant with so many speculations. It seemed to tie her to Adam riding to that faraway Fort Duquesne, to involve her with all of Mr. Franklin's horses and wagons. At supper there had been little talk of anything else, except when Jamie had quipped at Poor Richard.

Poor Richard was the name under which Mr. Franklin wrote for his *Almanack.* When Monica had reproved Jamie for getting home so late from Frederick, he had said it was all Poor Richard's fault.

"Ever hear of that mental Robin Hood, Uncle James," he asked, "who flays about him at those who would rob the hours of thriftiness? 'Leisure is the time for doing something useful,'" he quoted, from Poor Richard's sayings, with a grin at Mr. Franklin. "So after the professor gives us tea, I use my leisure to work at my Latin."

There had been more talk of Poor Richard, whom her father said Mr. Franklin had made immortal. But when not even Poor Richard could divert attention from the miracle needed to help Mr. Franklin secure the horses and wagons, Clytie had offered him a suggestion.

"When a man can bring down lightning from the skies to serve him as you can, sir," she said, "I'll warrant he could make some arrangement with Pegasus for those horses. It is said his constellation is full of them, each hitched to a star."

Mr. Franklin had chuckled, and answered, "Might I borrow your chariot then, Mistress Aurora, to cart the horses to the general's camp, or is it too loaded already with your bright cargo of dreams?"

It had been almost as if he read in her eyes her dreams of Adam.

She heard Uncle Peter's voice from the parlor now and hurried in.

"Safe as a church here, James," he was saying, puffing at his churchwarden pipe. "Let the girl stay with us. Could be June before the general sets out for the forts, and by that time . . . Here's our dispatch rider," he greeted her.

Monica was putting in her plea, so Clytie drew up a footstool and sat down beside her father, her eyes and ears for him only.

He brushed back the ringlets from her forehead and said, "You would like to stay on for a while, my pet?"

Clytie's mouth opened but the words would not come. He was passing on to her the decision she dare not make.

"Of course she does, with you away at the forts, James." Monica's easy voice saved Clytie from a reply.

"Yes, yes, there is *that,* too." Her father considered Aunt Monica's statement, but not as if it were the main issue. "The chief difficulty would be to get her home after the army moves."

"No difficulty about that—solve that easily," Uncle Peter said. "My ship the *Queen* will put in from London about that time, so we will hoist her aboard and sail her home in record time."

Monica agreed. Her father smiled. And Clytie gulped, whether from joy over his easy agreement that she should remain, or vague remorse over separation from him, she was not sure; she only knew that fate had decided. Then came a memory, sharp, irrational, of the frown on the face of her grandfather's portrait, as it had loomed between her and her first sight of Chestermere. "Seen a ghost?" Adam had said.

"Meanwhile, we'll rastle a husband for her from among our Maryland planters." Uncle Peter's chuckles had the quality of a robust fawn conniving with Eros.

"I am ahead of you there, Peter," her father said. "I have a candidate of my own." Clytie could believe neither her ears nor the thoughtful smile that her father turned on her. "What would you say, my pet," he went on, "if I told you I had found a princely fellow down here whom I should be happy to know might find favor in your blue eyes?"

Clytie's widened eyes focused on him; her heart and mind refused the question, except as a jest. Yet on one occasion he had spoken of a suitor for her, and he had not been jesting. He had said: "Would God I could find for you the right husband! A man, not a puppet of damask and lace." The memory of those words flashed across her mind as Monica asked eagerly about this "princely fellow" and diverted her father from Clytie's bewilderment.

"Remember my telling you of my encounter in Alexandria with Major Sir Jason Mayne of Braddock's staff?" he asked. "He is the son of an old school friend of mine at Oxford and one of the most outstanding young men I have met in a long time." His eyes twinkled now at Clytie. "I am not suggesting, my sweet, that you ensnare this young man without giving him a chance to escape, but I am willing to wager you will like him as much as I do—if more, all the better."

Clytie forced an answering smile, but knotted cords seemed to squeeze her heart. So this was the price of her deception in not telling her father about Adam? Adam's arms about her in the wilderness night, his hungry lips on hers. Her efforts to keep all knowledge of the perils of her journey from her father, which had prevented her, also, from telling of its joys, had boomeranged. It was her own voice, yet not her own, that answered him now.

"Your unworthy daughter does not accept your wager. She would be too certain to lose." Her half-jest savored of all the harmony and trust between them.

But as Monica took over the conversation with questionings, Clytie wondered if she understood correctly that her father's real reason for leaving her here was because of this favored suitor. *And all because of her mother.* As their talk went on she lowered her head to her father's knee. It had long been a source of unease to him that when her mother had made a match for Olivia, her own time would come to be parceled off to someone, however unworthy, if her mother's ambitious requirements were to be met. Nor would her father be able to save her, without disrupting his home or threatening his career; nothing daunted her mother when set onto a course.

". . . no thought of inheriting the title until his eldest brother . . . one of the oldest titles in England . . ." The words she heard now held little meaning; Clytie was hearing other words of her father's from the long ago, as he comforted, shielded her from her mother's slights; yet he had been unable to save her from such denunciations as: "A DeLancey you are, through and through—prideful, disdainful . . ." Then, when Clytie had protested: "Oh, no, Mother, no!" her mother had snapped: "Silence. You are fusty, bookish, proud as Lucifer, as all the DeLanceys are, of being colonial. *Colonial!* Heaven!" She had a way of tossing out that word as if it were waste matter. Clytie's true liberation had come only after she had been left alone with her father. Then the wilderness had opened her mind and heart—moon shadows now danced a rigadoon amid the tall forest, in the scent of wildwood—"Adam, Adam," sounded the night birds. . . .

"The child is asleep—worn out from that cruel journey."

"Come, sweet! Time for bed," her father said.

Arms were about her, she was clinging to a tall, spare figure, battling against her dreams—these were her father's arms, not Adam's. She clutched him tighter in shadowy remorse, obscure disappointment; then a light shone in a crevice of her heart: Adam and her father were rooted there in one ideal, one grace of body and spirit, with a grave modeling of features and an unwavering devotion to duty.

Expressions of sympathy for her exhausted state were mingled with the name of Sir Jason Mayne as she climbed the stairs with her father.

But Sir Jason Mayne was not available for the matchmaking, which Monica had taken over with such approval. When Squire Chester called at Braddock's headquarters the day after Governor DeLancey, his staff and Mr. Franklin had ridden away, he learned that Major Mayne had gone to Will's Creek, the general's supply depot, to where the main body of the army had been dispatched. It was not known precisely when Sir Jason would return.

Dutifully, Clytie had concealed her satisfaction over this, as she had been forced to conceal her haunting desire to learn more of Adam Appleton. But after she had been at Chestermere almost two weeks and no word had been spoken of him, she determined to down her self-consciousness and question Jamie. His teasing on the first evening of her arrival—"Big, strong hero rescued beauteous maiden, what?"—had made her wary; but she *must* know what her chances were of seeing Adam again. She knew he had ridden away with Colonel Washington. But for how long? Did he live in Frederick? And if that were true, *what* would his reaction be when he learned she was Clytie DeLancey? He hated lies and deceptions, and this one, piled atop all the others . . . The more she thought about it, the more uncertain she became; for Adam was not like other men. He would not be impressed by the fact that the daughter of the Royal Governor of New York had slept in his arms, that he had mauled her and embraced her. . . . In the middle of the night her face would grow red and hot as she remembered—Adam the ruthless, the tender, who had hated her the most when he held her closest, and who had adored her when he denounced her—Adam the unpredictable.

Meanwhile, her joy in the life and varied activities of Chestermere was unabated. Jamie had shown her everything—the dairy, chickens, pigs, new calves and colts, the pond where the wild ducks nested and were fed. She had ridden with Uncle Peter over his tobacco fields, where the new plants, like a vast army of green-hatted gnomes, marched toward the blue hills in the distance, and where the slaves sang as they hoed. At the tobacco barn and drying shed, which stood on high ground above the river, not far from the house, she had watched the flatboats being loaded with the primed tobacco—Uncle Peter called it "sotweed"—that would be floated the long distance down the Monocacy to his wharf on the Potomac. There the *Mary Monica* was being loaded. She was the sister ship of the *Queen* that would take her home. It was these ships that brought all the lovely materials from which Phyly was making her dresses.

The one she was wearing this morning was made of pink dimity, for the weather was getting warm. After breakfast she went out into the rear garden, on her way to the stables to give Bob his lumps of sugar. She had tied on her bonnet, made of the same material as the dress—Monica was fearful that she might display a freckled nose to Sir Jason—and had started down the garden walk, lifting her skirts to avoid contact with the dew. Her shoes of soft calfskin, with silver buckles on the insteps, had felt so springy that she would have enjoyed racing to the barn, but to Monica this was "unmannerly deportment."

"Clytie! How!" It was Jamie calling from the compound that bordered the garden. But before Clytie could close the wicket gate of the garden he had disappeared into the little cabin he called his "laboratory."

She stopped then to look back at the house, which seemed to brood in such quiet peace amid the blossoming vines and shrubs. But a memory impinged quickly upon her: Her grandfather's tale of an Indian raid on Chestermere. It had happened when Jamie was an infant, and the story of Uncle Peter's brave defense of his home and family had always stirred her with admiration and terror. That was why she had been so frighened when her father, in the library at home, had spoken of possible danger to the Chesters.

"Hi—wanna see something?" Jamie called again.

Clytie waved and started across the compound. But what she wanted most to see was the blossoming pear orchard. It bordered the compound to the left, and she stopped to breathe in its wondrous fragrance. To the right of the wide compound, which contained but one towering tulip tree, was the path that led to Uncle Peter's office, the storehouses and laundry. Jamie's little cabin was nearer the fence that gave onto the broad meadow, and from both its door and window there now issued volleys of wood smoke.

"Jamie, whatever are you doing?" She peered inside. In the center of the room a fire burned on a frame of ashes, and over it, in a big caldron, was a brown bubbling liquid. Jake, Jamie's own servant, was stirring it with a pole, grinning.

"Boiling dried seaweed," Jamie told her. "I distill it. Pretty, what? Cures cuts and wounds."

All about the room stood mysterious vessels and jars, filled with concoctions. His ambition was to become a doctor, and his father said he had real genius: "Cures everything—slaves, cattle, his family and jay birds."

"Call me when it's ready, Jake," he said as he followed Clytie out of the cabin. "Know what I've found good for bruises? Cow dung. All right, laugh!" He grinned with her. "But I found it in old Penn's book on physics, and it's got some quality I can't get at. But it works. Fall down and sprain your ankle and I'll prove it."

He opened the gate of the compound that led into the meadow, and Clytie laughed again. Not at his cure, but at him. He wore soiled, ragged breeches, his shirt was stained and torn, his red hair loose in the wind, and he had withal a look of complete content. He was a wonderful companion.

They took the left path, toward the barn and stables. Questions about Adam hovered on her lips, but the far vistas of the valley intrigued her. The river glinted between its wooded banks, and the sloping meadow was tapestried with wild flowers.

"Jamie, Jamie, it's all so beautiful—a little world in itself!" That was all she could say. Then she put to him another of the many questions she had asked since she came: "Why are the slave cabins enclosed by the stockade?"

The cabins were on high ground to the right of the meadow, and beyond that was the little chapel where they worshiped.

"Pa's granddad built it when he first acquired a few slaves. Made 'em feel safe, I reckon, because of the Shawnee."

That Indian terror again! But the morning was too lovely to speak of it. Besides, she must concentrate on how to ask about Adam, without letting Jamie suspect how much it meant to her.

But to her surprise and confusion he spoke of Adam before she had an opportunity. It was after she had given Bob his sugar, when they were coming out of the stables onto the lane that led to the highway. They were going to circle back to the compound through the pear orchard.

She had taken off her bonnet, and was just pulling a blossoming bough down to her nose, when he said, "With a rosy nymph like you loose on the farm, what we need around here is a lively young Satyr." He pranced around her, piping an imaginary flute.

"Silly! A pear orchard is no place for Pan. He lives in the forest."

"Ho, ho! So that's where you found him, hey?" he taunted. "Only you called him old *Adam*. When you offered him that apple, did he bite?"

Clytie felt her face grow scarlet. "You—you anthropophagus!" She walked ahead of him, yet this was the time to ask her question.

"Know what, my Sibyl," he said, pursuing her, "your divination was likely all wrong—thinking you had hoodwinked old Adam."

"Wh-what do you mean?"

"Bet you a green persimmon he knew you were not the miller's daughter—I mean, Papa Mike's. Wise old fox, Adam."

Her heart beat violently. Could this be true? Was that why he had made no effort to see *Lottie* again? She turned on him with determination. "All right, Mr. Oracle, since you know so much, maybe you'd better tell me what else Adam is." Anything she could learn would be helpful.

"That's easy, milady. He is Nimrod, Oberon, *Curx criticorum*. He is what the pretty lasses cry for, and don't get. Unless, of course—" he eyed her slantwise—"they set a bear trap for him on a ride through the wilderness." He broke into lusty laughter. "Ho, ho! Bet old sober-boy would squirm even in your trap. He's the fightingest rascal in ten colonies."

Clytie had just framed an important question when Jamie's dog, Monk, came racing toward him, drowning out her voice with his barks.

Then came Jake's voice: "Look like it's b'iled enough, Mas' Jamie."

Jamie loped toward his precious caldron.

It was from Phyly that Clytie found out a little more about Adam. It came about because of a plan Clytie had thought up to lessen the shock for Adam, when he learned her real name, if he did not already know it—which she thought unlikely. It was not much of a plan, but it was the best she could think of as she lay awake at night, wondering.

She and Monica and Phyly had gone into one of the storehouses to select material for the dress she would wear when Sir Jason came to supper, after his return to Frederick. Most of her dresses had been made of cotton or linen for the warm spring climate—all her petticoats, underthings and nightgowns, of the finest linen—but this dress was to be very special. Clytie's eyes widened at the lustrous lengths of silks and brocades that had been unpacked.

"This, I think, would be wondrously becoming." Monica took up a piece of blue satin and wound it around Clytie's shoulders. She had just stood off to admire it when a protest came from the doorway.

"No, Ma! No!" Jamie came in, and without listening to any arguments he tossed aside the blue satin and draped a rosy-pink satin about Clytie. "There you are!" he said with satisfaction.

"Oh, Jamie, don't confuse me. A girl should dress to her eyes," Monica protested.

"Wrong, Ma. Sure, she's got Persian-kitten eyes. Damme," he marveled in scrutiny, "if both pupil and iris aren't blue. Just the same, the pink has more allure—gold-brown hair, rosy cheeks, bloom of spring—what?"

Clytie made a face at him, but she was glad to see Monica weaken. She preferred the rosy color herself, yet since she was not asked . . . The truth was, she more than suspected that she had become Monica's *poupée*. But her aunt's generosity so overwhelmed her that she could not summon up resistance. Then, too, it was the first time in her life anyone had been interested in what she wore. At home the only pretty dresses allowed in the DeLancey household were those for Olivia—that is, until after her mother had sailed and her father had told her to order what she liked.

So now, after another look at the blue, the pink was decided on and Monica was saying, "White, I think. Her dress should be white for the general's ball." She took up a length of lovely white brocade.

"What general—what ball?" Jamie asked.

"Jamie, don't be foolish. The ball we will be giving General Braddock, of course, before he leaves for the fort." Monica spoke as if it were incumbent on Chestermere.

Jamie whistled. "You mean *if* he leaves. Better not count those horses and wagons until Mr. Franklin has hatched them."

"I wish you would not say such disrespectful things, Jamie," said Monica as she wound the lustrous white fabric about Clytie. It was sprinkled with little silvery stars of Bethlehem. "Besides," she admonished him, "has Mr. Franklin ever failed in an enterprise?"

"No, Ma. But maybe horses just ain't hatchable. In which case you've got to give a man time to sow horse-an'-wagon seed, then plow 'em an' reap 'em."

"Jamie, go away," his mother commanded.

Phyly cackled as he swung out of the door, then swung back.

"Course," he said, "you could give the ball for Colonel Georgie and his colonials before they leave to clean up a mess too hot for the regulars." He grinned and went out.

But Monica called to him to wait; she wanted him to go with her to visit one of the sick slaves. So the beauteous white material had been decided on, and Clytie and Phyly were left alone in the storehouse.

"Phyly, I can sew," Clytie began, eager now to consummate her plan. "Mike's wife, Jessie, taught me. And I'd like to practice sewing"—she hurried on as Phyly repacked the big hampers—"because my grandfather said a girl should learn everything, by making myself a homespun dress."

There! it was out—as much of her plan as she could explain without giving herself away. But she thought it safe to add: "You know, Phyly, a dress like the German girls wear in Frederick."

This plan had come to her when she remembered the village girls waving at Adam on that first dreadful day they had ridden through the village. His calls to them had made her think he felt at home with them; so, if she should wear such a dress, maybe he would feel at home with Clytie DeLancey. But Phyly had turned to her with such a perplexed smile that Clytie was forced to use other arguments.

"You see," Clytie continued, "a homespun skirt will not tear on the briers, when I race about with Jamie and Monk, nor on the rose bushes in the garden, where I tore my blue-flowered lawn the other day. Now, don't you think——"

"I cert do, missy—yessum." Phyly nodded deep approval. "Heap o' homespun pieces in de weavin' house, an' it would be a fine way to practice what yo' gran'pa say. You come along now—we go see."

Clytie had never been in the weaving house before, and she marveled at the great skeletal looms being worked by the slave girls, making a clacking sound. One of the girls was weaving a big blanket of yellow, red and brown.

"Knot dem threads careful, Lindy," Phyly cautioned her. "Mas' Pete wants dat blanket wove close and warm. Hit's for his friend Capt'in Appleton, time dey be off for de forts." She moved toward another loom.

For *Adam*. Clytie gasped. He was a friend of Pete's, and Pete would be home next week from college. Her heart was dizzy with high hope. She watched the girl throw the shuttle back and forth as the threads were beaten into the lathe, and recalled the night she had wrapped her own blanket around Adam and how his own blanket roll had been thin and worn.

"Dis piece would dye pretty, missy—any color you like." Phyly had opened a big hamper and had held up a piece for Clytie's inspection. It was a stout material, not too heavy.

"Y-yes—oh, yes! A maroon—would it dye a lovely maroon?"

"Yessum."

"That for the skirt. And for the bodice, this." Clytie seized a thinner, whitish piece. "This I can gather—fullish—about the neck and make little puff sleeves." . . .

So it had all been settled. That is, everything had been settled except what Monica would have to say about it; and what she said was not encouraging when she found Clytie, absorbed in activity, two days later.

"Child, I don't mind your learning to sew, but why a peasant's dress?" It was delivered with the fond disapproval of which her aunt was mistress.

Clytie was standing before the mirror in the sewing room, wearing her handiwork. The white bodice was almost finished, and it fitted perfectly. She had got the dyed material for the skirt only this morning, but had already sewed up the seams and gathered it into a broad belt; now Sapphira, who had become her worshipful shadow, was on the floor beside her, turning up the hem.

"But for wet mornings in the garden, Aunt Mony . . ." Clytie began, with a slight flush of guilt, "and—and it will never wear out." She rallied and smiled broadly at Monica's scrutiny. "This shall be my souvenir of Chestermere. I shall say to my grandchildren, 'The material was woven on your great-aunt's looms.' Won't they be proud? Is the ankle length all right?" She twirled about for approval.

Monica conceded that it was. She settled herself by the window with her knitting—the sewing girls were not at work this morning—and when Sapphira was dismissed Clytie settled herself to baste the hem. She was pleased to have this moment's companionship with her aunt, who was always so busy with her multiple duties. For if Uncle Peter might be termed Commander of the Plantation, Monica was Captain General. Her genius for co-ordination of so many enterprises amazed Clytie.

They talked of how her dress should be made—for the supper party for Sir Jason—and agreed on it. As to Sir Jason himself, Clytie had so far registered no resistance to her father's approval of him as her suitor; but Monica's assumption that the whole matter had been transferred to her own authority was disturbing. Clytie feared, as well, her aunt's dominant personality, which sought to govern her. And she was not governable. Nor was she the type to be gobbled up piecemeal by Monica's possessiveness. Yet she must give no hint that she understood this.

". . . George Washington, if he is here." Monica had been talking of the supper guests as Clytie's mind wandered. "Yet it is always so difficult to find a supper companion for him."

"Why, Aunt Mony? Doesn't he like women?"

"I think it more likely that women don't like him." She sighed.

"O-oh!" Clytie was startled. Then, remembering that somber face with its grave smile, she said, "I can understand that. They would not like him because they could not understand him." Monica's surprise forced her to add, "I mean, he has such quiet authority, reserve, as though weighty responsibilities set him apart—apart from youth."

Monica gave her an odd look and twisted her knitting about. "I never heard that George had responsibilities—his mother, perhaps, or this muddle about the colonial troops."

But the look had thrown Clytie into near panic. Could Monica suspect her of being infatuated with . . . "It may have been all the brave things Captain Appleton told me about him that made me think—" Clytie broke off. In her effort to refute her aunt's suspicion of Colonel Washington she had brought up Adam's name. Her voice was small as she ended—"think of Colonel Washington that way." She bent to her sewing.

The silence trembled. When she had recounted Adam's prowess in the wilderness, Monica had said with distaste, "I trust the man's behavior was seemly." Now she spoke in an even voice; the discussion about Colonel Washington was forgotten.

"I must remind your uncle," Monica said, "that Adam Appleton is to be given a substantial reward for lending you assistance through the wilderness."

"Re-reward?" Clytie stammered.

"Certainly, my dear. We are obligated."

There was such underlying distaste in the tone that Clytie's mind went blank. Could she have so revealed to Monica her feeling about Adam?

"He—he did not even know I was your niece," she said, trying as hard as she dared to defend him from this humiliating reward.

"No matter. For the son of a poor farmer, a fitting reward would not be amiss. That his father tilled the soil for the Washingtons no doubt accounts for George's interest in him." Monica twirled her knitting with a jerk of disapproval.

Clytie scarcely breathed—she was eager for more information; yet the source of her aunt's deep distaste for Adam was so baffling. . . .

Monica's next words were revealing: "He came here to farm for his uncle, Gabe MacLoughlan, after his parents died. But I understand he lives now in camp with the militia. And because of his military knowledge, my son . . ." Her aunt's voice hardened, paused, and then was lightened with half-humorous annoyance. "I am afraid your cousin Pete shows small discrimination in his friendships."

Clytie breathed again. So it was Pete, not she, who had caused this dislike of Adam. Relief brightened her spirit, while her heart blessed Pete for his superior discrimination as to friendships.

CHAPTER *Thirteen*

CLYTIE was wearing her homespun dress on the morning that Adam came to Chestermere. But she never quite knew whether it was coincidence or knowing design that had caused Jamie to tease her into adding a cap to her costume on that particular morning. She had worn the dress before—even Monica approved of it when dew was on the grass—but with a ribbon about her hair which Phyly had dyed the same maroon as the skirt. Then Jamie had suggested the cap.

He was setting off to Frederick for his classes, while she fussed with her hair before the long mirror in the hallway.

"We've got ourselves a sassy little *Fräulein,* Eph," he said to the old Negro. "But as a first-class servingmaid there's something missing. I've got it!" He yanked a big kerchief from his pocket, tied knots in the corners, and stuck it on Clytie's head.

"You are mussing my hair," Clytie objected.

"Now, Eph, you can make her scrub the floors," Jamie teased.

Clytie grinned with him, but tossed back his kerchief. "If it's a cap you want, I can do better." She took out her own lace kerchief, put it on her head, pulled one corner under the ribbon above her forehead, and pinned the opposite corner to the ribbon near her neck. "That suit you?" she demanded.

"It'll help to remind you to mind your manners, my gal." He raced out the door, whooped at Jake, swung himself onto Rozinante, and was off for Frederick.

Clytie forgot about the cap, she was so absorbed in gathering jonquils and syringa sprays for the house. Monica had approved her arrangements of flowers and had told her that she had a talent for it. Ephraim had filled with water the bowls and vases that she wanted to use for the long parlor; she set one of them down on the hearthstone beside her basket of blossoms and plumped down, cross-legged.

She was using her shears, making quite a litter, when she heard a voice in the hallway that she would have recognized on the mountains of the moon: "Morning, Ephraim! Squire Chester home? . . . Right. Just got back this morning."

Clytie's heart turned topsy-turvy. When a tall figure strode past one of the open parlor doors, she was just able to emit huskily, "Adam!"

It served. The figure that appeared at the doorway filled all space. He saw her on the floor engaged in her task.

"Ghosts and goblins!" he cried.

He swung in on his pine-tree legs, spread them wide, his arms akimbo, and stared down into her smile, speechless.

She was speechless herself. It was Adam, and yet not Adam. No buckskin dress, no stubble beard. His dark smallclothes were neat and correct, if plain. His white neckcloth added youth to his face, and a cleft was visible in his square chin. Never had she seen his eyes so bright as now, regarding her in her cap and peasant's dress.

"So! they kept you here, hey? Well, I'll be bound!"

There was such delight in his voice that Clytie gaped for a moment. Then those long-meditated fears over this first meeting skidded into secret places behind her widened eyes. She clapped a hand over her giggle. There was no denunciation here, no anger at her deceptions: *he still thought she was Lottie O'Day*. She got quickly to her feet and made a proper little bob, scattering remnants of flower stalks on the carpet.

"Oh, yes, sir, Captain." Her joy in this deception expanded. "The master and mistress have been mortal kind." To hide her confusion she bobbed down again, onto her knees, groping for the litter she had made on the carpet.

"I'm hanged! Didn't ride back with your father and Governor DeLancey, huh?"

"Oh, sir, I was that pleasured to stay." She was on her feet again, grinning with more assurance now.

"Were, hunc? Little liar, giving me all that gammon about Winchester." He moved toward her with a glow in his eyes that made her dizzy. She backed behind a chair.

"Me, gammon *you,* Captain, sir!" She mocked him with her smile.

Adam ran a hand over his sleek, queued hair, then regarded her, shaking his head. "Can't believe it. Sure it's you, Lottie? No muddy face, no tatters——"

"No prickly beard, no anger." She taunted him with a giggle.

"Why, you sassy little baggage! I'll teach you to gammon . . ." He took hold of the chair that separated them.

"Oh, do, sir!" She retreated behind a table.

"Capt'in Appleton, sir," Ephraim said as he came in. Adam wheeled about. "The squire—he's on one of them flatboats just pushed out in the river. You hurry, sir, an' you kin call to him from the bank."

"All right, Eph. Right away." But Adam did not hurry.

Ephraim went out. Adam gave her a look with delicious threats behind it, then moved to the door. And while she was still thinking desperately how to detain him—it must not end just this way, so soon—he turned back.

"Have any time free, Lottie?" he asked.

"Oh, yes, sir. Tomorrow." She spoke from her heart alone, suppressing the vision of Monica's ire. "Tomorrow afternoon."

"Good. I've got to ride to the Lenape camp. Can you ride a piece with me?"

The Lenape were a near-by Indian tribe Jamie had told her about.

"I'll ride *all* the way." Discretion had blown out the window on the spring breeze, carrying with it the last thought of Monica. "Know the trail by the river?" She pointed to the west. "I'll meet you where it joins the King's Highway."

His smile bundled her up. "That's paz?" When she nodded he started to the door again, but turned back. "By Hector, if this is another gammon—!"

"Never. Two-thirty," she promised.

He swung out the door and down the hallway.

Clytie plumped down on the sofa, her insides queasy, her heart racing after him. Adam! Adam, you precious, blessed fool! That's paz—that's truth.

The siesta hour in the Chester household was sacrosanct. Clytie had counted on this when she told Adam two-thirty. By that time Uncle Peter could be counted on to be snoring in the library or in his office, and Monica would be resting in her room.

But no such thing happened today, of all days.

When two o'clock came Monica was still sitting in the cool parlor, talking with Clytie about the way her pink satin dress should be made, and after they had resolved that, about Pete.

"He is so eager to get home from college and start training his company . . . A born military man. . . . And now that he has his commission . . . Your uncle has already recruited most of his company, but this war . . . frightening war . . ."

"Frightening, Aunt Mony?" Clytie tried to appear to be listening. And she was, but with only half her mind. Adam! A ride with Adam. And should she fail to appear on time . . . Oh, she dare not think what might happen then. He might come to the house and . . .

"Frightening in that . . . If it must be delayed because of the horses and wagons, it will give the French time to fortify the forts. It is *that* your uncle fears, and——"

"But, Aunt Mony, Mr. Franklin said but three weeks, and that's almost up." However nervous about Adam, she really *must* give heed to this.

"Yes, child, but Mr. Franklin's last letter was none too reassuring. . . . Is that Jamie?"

Someone was calling from the compound.

"I–I think it's Jake. I'll see." Clytie rushed to the rear door of the hall, terrified that it might be Adam. It was Jake calling to Moses.

"Is Master Jamie back, Jake?" she called.

Yes, he was back, he answered her, but had gone fishing. He had spent last night with Abe Wilson, a friend. Clytie looked at the big clock in the hallway: two-fifteen. Her nerves were in a tizzy. But when Monica came into the hallway on the way to her room, Clytie tried to relax.

"Jamie has gone fishing, Aunt Mony, so I will exercise Bob along the river road. I may meet him." She hoped she would *not*.

"Clytie, dear, I don't like you to ride without Jamie or your uncle."

Another obstacle. But Clytie hurdled it, though her laugh sounded strange and forced. "Darling Aunt Mony, all I'm afraid of on your lovely plantation are rattlesnakes. But Bob is not afraid. And the day is so lovely."

"Have you a bonnet to wear with that dress?" The question was caustic with disapproval of the homespun Clytie was wearing, but at least it implied that she might go for a ride.

"The blue one. I'll get it and tie it on tight," Clytie said as she dashed up the stairs.

When she came down Monica's door was closed.

She raced down the garden walk, through the orchard to the barn. She had feared to tell anyone to saddle Bob. Well, she would do it herself. She spied Moses in the harness room. He was a house servant and was not supposed to do such chores, but when he saw her with Bob's bridle he took it from her.

"Look like hit might rain, missy," he commented.

"Oh, no, Moses. It's a lovely day."

"Yessum, but hit's spring, and dem clouds over dar . . ." He fastened Bob's girth, then rubbed his own shoulder.

She knew what that meant. "Your rheumatism tells you it's going to rain? But I thought Jamie had cured you."

"Hit's bedder. But you ain't goin' far, is you, missy?"

She mounted at the upping block, and grinned as she answered, "Not too far."

Then she was off, heading down the trail that skirted the woods on the far side of the meadow. She was not so very late, thank goodness! When she crossed the brook near the Cabin of Refuge she was reminded of that day when Adam had spoken of the cabin. One day Jamie had taken her to see it, but the door had been locked. It looked quiet and peaceful now under the shade trees, with its white-washed log walls, and for some reason that tugged at her inner mind it still held a niche of its own in her consciousness. Was it a dream she had had about it as a child and could not quite recall?

The sun was hot as Clytie followed the trail through the cornfields, and she was glad she had not brought her coat, even if Monica objected to sun-browned arms and a freckled nose. Maryland ladies, she was told, kept themselves well covered when riding; they wore veils over their faces. Veils! She smiled. Here was another reason for Adam to think she was no lady. Last night when she was writing to her father she had wanted to tell him that she was going to ride with Adam to the Indian village. *Remember the tall soldier you thanked for bringing you the dispatch, when you did not recognize your bedraggled daughter?* Her father had a sense of humor, and if she told him that to Adam she was still Mike's daughter, he would have laughed, even if he had wanted to spank her. Her thoughts wandered. . . .

Monica was *worried,* deep down, about something. The expedition to the forts? But then Uncle Peter was worried, too, and fell into long moody silences. Was it about the refugees who, Jamie said, had reached Frederick with tales of Indian butcheries to the northwest?

She reached the shaded part of the trail along the river. Was Adam impatient as he waited near the highroad? She cantered more swiftly, atingle with expectancy; her heart seemed to be galloping ahead of her.

"In a hurry?" called Adam.

She heard his mellow voice beside her before she saw him or heard his horse. He had appeared out of nowhere. She reined to a walk, and beamed with delight on him and the buckskins he wore; he was the same old Adam of the wilderness, the one she had first encountered at the Queen of France Mill. He did not respond immediately to her smile.

"Are you the magician Merlin, sir?" She altered her smile to pretend fright. "But, please, don't change me into a beetle. I'd rather be a bird."

"Figure you are one without help from me." His grin gave her wings. "Not an early one at that."

"I'm sorry, Captain, but the mistress——"

"Thought those horses you and your father had belonged to Governor DeLancey." His eyes were on Bob.

So that was the reason he had looked grim! But Clytie was ready for that remark, even though she shrank a bit inside with fright. "The carriage horses, yes, but not Bob."

But he was not to be put off. " 'My mistress' favorite riding horse' was the way you put it when we rode along the valley of the Susquehanna."

"Oh, wasn't that a lovely ride!" But her effort to divert him did not work out. She sobered under his hard eyes but managed to ask with gay inconsequence, "What would be your solution, sir, for my return to my mistress—as of course I must—without her horse to ride?"

They walked their horses along the leafy path. He did not answer; he kept his shoulders erect, his eyes straight ahead. His suspicions of her, whatever they were, were subdued, she hoped, but he did not turn his sun-browned face to her again until she pushed back her bonnet and let it dangle on her neck.

"Set on returning, hey?" He eyed her, a flush beneath his tan, and broke into a smile that made her heart chirrup with the birds. But because personal things at the moment held a slight menace, she gaily changed the subject.

"I am that pleasured to be riding to an Indian village—a friendly village. I have never been to one." And she added, to divert him further, "Why do you ride there, Captain?"

"Heap o' reasons. See what's going on. Make sure no French Indians are filtering down."

"Savage Indians, you mean. I used to think all Indians were savages because of the stories I was told as a little girl about the cruel raid on Chestermere. You see," she hurried on, under his searching eyes, "I was born in the DeLancey household, and—and my father told me how Mistress Monica's home was raided, the cattle butchered, the tobacco fields burned, and how the squire fought from the shuttered house to save his family and slaves. Oh, it was a stirring tale! Did you know about it?"

"Heard about it. Everybody has. Those were Shawnee. No such Indians about here now. Colonel Chester's regiment drove them out."

"Then, if the Indian tribes in Maryland are friendly, could—could French Indians stir them up against the settlers?" She thought suddenly of Monica. Could *that* be the reason for her aunt's disquiet?

"Who gave you that idea?" he said so sharply that she sensed, with a touch of dread, there was truth behind it.

"N-no one, but . . . but isn't it true," she went on earnestly, "that if the general delays his expedition too long, the French may sneak their savages down, so that when the troops do depart, the country here will be defenseless against the marauding raiders?" The idea was terrifying in its suddenness, yet it had always been one of her father's fears.

"Trying to find some reason to be sorry you stayed on at Chestermere?" The granitic quality of Adam's face had changed so quickly into a smile that she was forced to smile, too.

"Never," she denied, with emphasis.

"Why *did* you stay, Lottie?"

It came so unexpectedly that Clytie reddened, but her smile deepened at the delicious implication behind his question.

"Because I love to hear roosters crow in the morning," she said teasingly. "I love wide fields and a big sky for a change, and all the scents and sounds . . ." Her voice faded out under his warmly approving eyes.

He yanked off his cap and dashed it, with boyish humor, against his palm. "I still can't believe it! And me thinking I'd never see you again. But here we are! Hunc?" He rode close, rose in his saddle, quickly put an arm about her shoulders, and . . .

His breath was on her face when she touched Bob with her whip, moving out of range. That look in his eyes was too tempting. She could not accept it—not yet. Her gay laughter taunted him as he righted himself on his horse.

"Little cheater." But his smile broadened. "So you don't figure you owe me a couple of kisses?"

"Oh, sir, are such to be bartered?" She pretended to be distressed.

He clapped his cap onto his head. "Well, now, seems to me I recollect a little unfinished payment. Course, I can give you an hour or two to think it over, time for you to remember what all I aim to collect."

Clytie's laughter soared with the call of a wood lark high overhead. "Dare I remember?"

"I figure dares are plum pudding to you, saucy face."

The sun filtering down golden moments onto them, the air vibrating with unspoken things, entangling them in the pure joy of being alive and together, and the river with its slivery glints reminded Clytie of the mystic promise made to her when she first heard the name of Adam Appleton.

"Hi! Hello! Blow me down!" It was Jamie's shout.

Clytie's first impulse was to flee. If her name were spoken now, all was ended. There would be no more precious moments. But Adam had reined in and answered Jamie's call. He came up from the river with his dog and fishing pole.

"What goes on here?" Jamie's grin was wide.

Clytie's heart was doing somersaults, but she made her frantic appeal before Adam could speak.

"Oh, Mr. Jamie, sir, don't tell the mistress I am out! She would be that angry——"

"Hunc? W-what d' ye say?" His big mouth gaped, but he saw the signal she gave behind Adam.

"She would scold tinderly. Please, Mr. Jamie. . . ."

"Why you—you dinged little devil!"

"Hey, young fellow, mind your words." Adam looked around at her, but she dropped her head. Jamie guffawed, and she knew she was safe.

"My apologies, soldier boy." Jamie exploded into more laughter and slapped his sides. "But watch out! She's the sassyest little wench this side of Glory."

"Don't mind Mr. Jamie, Captain, please," Clytie appealed to Adam's frown. "He is that handy with his jokes. But please, Mr. Jamie, don't let the mistress get angry!"

"You bet she'll be angry—you out riding with a handsome officer. Who d' ye think you are, my gal? Cottoned to me before you came around, Capt'in. So, look out. The gal's a Delilah."

"Is, hey?" Adam whirled his horse about and moved on. "Come on!"

Clytie stuck out her tongue at Jamie and followed.

"Where you going?" he called after them.

"To the Lenape village," Adam said, turning in his saddle.

"Good," answered Jamie. "Tell old Big Corn to send me those anise plants he promised me."

Adam waved. Clytie gulped down her giggles as they cantered away.

Adam did not speak to her again until they turned into the highway and set a faster pace along the rutted road.

"Delilah, hmm?" His eyes accused her.

Clytie's skirt was billowing, her bonnet bobbing on her shoulders, and her curls streaming backward, but she chirruped gaily, "Not to you, Captain. Your strength is not in your hair."

"Smart, ain't you?" His grumble was not reassuring.

"A body must do her poor best to keep up with you, sir."

He slowed their pace and turned from the main road onto a broad trail that led westward through green, sunlighted woods. A breeze had sprung up and was singing through the giant treetops. Clytie's heart sang with it in spite of Adam's sullen humor.

"Is Jamie the reason you stayed at Chestermere?"

"Partly." She wanted to tantalize him. "He is such an amusing bratling."

"Bet he is as old as you are."

"Three months older." She grimaced at him playfully, but he did not respond. There was only the thud of their horses' hoofs along the grassy trail.

"Why didn't you tell Mistress Chester you were coming out?" His eyes looked straight ahead, his shoulders were stiff, his whole bearing spoke disapproval.

Clytie said mischievously, "I feared it would demean you, Captain, to be riding out with a servingmaid."

"Gammon!"

Silence. The wind bent the tall trees and a dark shadow swept over the woods, casting an eerie light on the path ahead.

"Moses said it was going to rain," Clytie volunteered.

"Maybe I'd better take you home." He slowed his horse.

"You will *not*. I want to see the Indian village. How far is it?"

"Couple of miles."

"Lead on, my Captain!" As a smile slowly lighted his face, she said, "Talk to me."

"About what, Delilah?"

"About all that you did when you rode away with Colonel Washington."

He sobered again, his mouth set hard. "He is no longer a colonel."

"How? *Why?*" Colonel Washington was for her an important person. "Isn't he going to the forts? Does Squire Chester know?" Her questions poured out. "I mean—the squire looked so gloomy last night."

"Sure, I told him yesterday. Told him what that old fool Dinwiddie and Braddock had cooked up—no *colonial* to hold a rank higher than a captain."

"O-oh! That's outrageous! Just wait until I write my father!" She gasped. "I mean, he—he gets so hot over any slight to a colonial officer." She was making it worse. Had she given herself away? She hardly dared look at him. But he was smiling.

"Go on! Get mad. That blue blaze in your eyes comes near to setting the woods on fire." He became serious. "One thing sure, all the blazes this side of hell won't smoke George Washington out and away from his farm until they restore his title. That's paz."

"Then—he won't go to the forts?"

Adam laughed bitterly. "They haven't had a Virginia enlistment since they took away his rank. So if they want a thousand colonial troops to march with Braddock, they'd better restore it quick."

They cantered on against the rising wind, unmindful of the darkening woods. Maybe it would rain, but she could not think about it as she listened to his talk of riding to Will's Creek for Colonel Washington.

"They have got a colonel of supplies up there, a fellow named Dunbar," said Adam. "Biggest jackass this side of the water. Looks like they pick that sort to send over here." They laughed together and let their horses walk. "Beats me how a man can talk to you, Lottie, about all that comes into his mind, like you were——" He broke off, fearful of saying too much.

"Like what, Adam?" she asked softly as they rode slowly side by side.

"Look, Lottie, I . . . Damme! Sorry——"

"For . . . what?" Her voice was taut with the knowledge of their closeness in the vast green woods, suddenly so silent—silent but for the pounding of her heart.

Slowly they rode ahead. His buckskin-covered leg touched hers in the stirrup, and from the very earth a current rushed up as if to engulf them. His eyes were branding her, burning into her flesh, as he raised up in his stirrups and reached out for her. The ease with which he lifted her to his own horse and cradled her before him was a part of the swift magic that welded them. . . . The world swung into limbo with the first touch of his lips. . . . There was no past or future, until a flash of light stabbed through the woods and the bowl of the sky split with a crash.

"Want to start riding for home?" Adam asked.

She was again mounted on Bob when the rain started. It drummed down on the great trees like an assaulting enemy.

"Because of a spring shower?" She had to shout because of the drummings and rumblings. "How far is the Indian village?"

"Mile or more."

"Ride, soldier! Ride!" Clytie was already off at a gallop, a gallop in time with her heart that not even a cosmic upheaval could down, not with him beside her.

Galloping still, they reached a wide clearing, gray-veiled by sheets of rain.

He slowed down and asked, "Can you make it? The village is just beyond."

Clytie did not answer; the rain lashed at her face. She headed Bob out to the open trail that dropped toward a brook. When they reached it she was too blinded by the gusts of rain to do more than follow the dark shanks of Adam's horse. The heavens had opened, as though to wash them to kingdom come. At last they reached the far slope mired with sliding mud and pebbles.

"Don't let your horse slip," he shouted, reaching out and grabbing her bridle. He held it until they reached the woods.

A stockade loomed up and they saw an open gate. They raced through it. There was a dark ring of low brown huts, and Adam was calling, "Hello!" Shouts answered from here and there; brown figures appeared.

A big man beckoned from the door of one long hut and called out as Clytie slid from her horse.

"Go with the chief," Adam told her.

She raced toward the doorway as Adam led her horse away.

CHAPTER *Fourteen*

IT WAS no spring shower. The rain beat down on the rounded top of Chief Big Corn's bark roof, now and then washing over it viciously in a gust of wind. There had been little slackening of the rain since they arrived; Clytie was not certain how long ago that had been.

She was seated now, cross-legged on a woven mat, in a wide semicircle with Adam, the chief and a young Indian whom Adam called Joe Toads. They were not too close to the fire, for it was under a hole in the roof, through which smoke escaped from the long room, and when the rain blew in it splashed ashes around.

Adam was talking earnestly to the chief in the chief's own language, and they all seemed to have forgotten she was there. Listening to the droning voices made her drowsy, but she aroused herself to make mental notes of what was happening, to write her father.

She had been dripping wet when she entered the hut, which was gloomy except for the coals of fire. She had been a little frightened at all the eyes fastened on her by the shadowy, dark people she could not see plainly. As she moved closer to the fire, shivering, a hand had touched her arm, and an old Indian woman with a rusty-brown face and bright little eyes had made signs to her which she had not understood.

Then the young Indian, Joe Toads, from the other side of the fire had said, "You bad wet. Woman make dry. Go, take off wet."

"Oh—oh, thank you, but I—I will soon dry out."

Then she had looked down at herself; her clothes were so plastered to her that her breasts and stomach and legs might as well have been bare. When a pretty Indian girl with a reassuring smile came up to her with some garments in her arms, Clytie had gladly permitted herself to be led away.

The two ends of the long rectangular room were divided into little cubicles by low partitions that opened onto a narrow runway. The girl and the old woman had taken her into one of these cubicles that contained nothing but a roll of skins, and had soon made her understand that she must take off her wet clothes and put on the dry garments.

"Wet. Be sick," the pretty girl, whose name, Clytie discovered, was Omeme, said.

Clytie had been glad enough to get off her sopping bodice and skirt, but when those were off she found that her petticoat and chemise were just as wet, even her drawers. But she had left the drawers on. It had been wonderful to have the two women rub her dry with some kind of soft cloth.

She had thought they would give her a blanket to wrap herself in until her clothes were dry, but instead they put over her head a soft shirt of white doeskin, a skirt of the same, that Omeme fastened about her waist, and leggings—odd things that fastened above her knees—all fringed and beaded like the shirt and skirt. And so warm. They had taken her stockings and shoes out to dry with her other things, and had given her soft moccasins.

When she came out to the fire again and saw Adam's grin, she said with delight, "Mr. Long Knife, I am White Sea Gull."

When Adam had told the chief that that was her name, she had giggled with Omeme and Joe Toads. The chief's eyes had sparkled at her, but what he said she had not understood. Omeme had disappeared with a little ululative sound behind a partition at the other end of the room, and Clytie had sat down near Adam. She became conscious then of the figures of three men who, in the half-light, lounged against the upright posts that supported the roof.

They were not looking at her—it would have been a violation of hospitality, she supposed—but their faces were frighteningly grim. Their frames were wiry and muscular—warriors, perhaps, since their heads were shaved except for the scalp lock. One of them was naked except for a breechcloth, and there were colorful markings on his body. A sort of blanket hung from his shoulders, but he had not wrapped it around him as the other two had. The chief had thrown some guttural sound at them and they had turned toward the door, which was made of reeds that flapped like a curtain. Two of them had gone out into the rain, but before the naked one followed, he had turned back and looked directly at her. She had tried not to look too frightened, glad that Adam had not seen, for the Indian's long face—with high cheekbones, not round-shaped like the others—wore an ugly, twisted sneer.

Adam was watching the head-waggings of the old chief, and when he handed Adam his pipe Adam took it and puffed politely. She could not tell what sort of clothes the chief wore because his blanket covered him. His black hair was parted in the middle and hung down his shoulders in two plaits; his head band, with the big feather in it, was of silver, she thought, and his face seemed to be made of old, brown, crinkled bark—a kindly, solemn face.

Now as their voices droned on and Adam seemed to be appealing to the chief for something, she felt so proud of him. Her father had sent many of his militia to be trained in the Seneca or Iroquois language—necessary, he had said, in order to deal with the powerful Six Nations of New York Colony.

The chief was making a long oration to Adam, and sounding very dramatic. The smoke of the fire and the pipe, and the flying ashes, and all the queer smells she could not identify, tickled Clytie's nose until she had to sneeze. She had no handkerchief, so Adam gave her his. He looked anxiously at her, but could not speak through the chief's words.

These ended with a big grunt, then Adam said, "He has been telling me about the white men who sell his tribe rum, which sets fire to their heads. And I have told him we are trying to stop the mean, harmful traffic."

"One of the Indians who just went out must have been a little drunk, I think—the one who did not have his blanket around him," she said in a low voice.

"What makes you think——" Adam said quickly, but Joe Toads, coming from the shadows, interrupted.

"Wawa," he said grimly. "He bad Indian. All time drunk."

"Wawa means Wild Goose," Adam told her. "But he is harmless, I think—a half-breed of sorts."

He and Joe began to converse in the chief's language, while Clytie tried to erase from her mind the thought of the cruel, beady eyes that had fastened for a moment on her and her doeskin dress. Tired of sitting on her crossed legs, she got up and resettled herself on her heels.

Then suddenly the gloomy room became light. The sun was shining; it shone through the hole in the roof, through chinks in the log walls and cracks in the door, though the rain had not quite stopped.

"Clearing," Adam said as he got up. "We can set off for home now, White Sea Gull."

"But—but my clothes——"

"Wear those, honey. I'll fetch them back next time I come."

Joe Toads had opened the door while the old chief seemed to be protesting something, and they were just ready to say good-by when in came two Indian squaws bearing earthen dishes filled with steaming food.

The chief grunted and Adam looked perplexed, but he whispered to Clytie, "This is their hospitality. We can't refuse."

Clytie was not sure she wanted to; it was the first good smell she had encountered, and she was very hungry. She had been too excited about riding with Adam to eat any dinner at Chestermere. After they resettled themselves on their mats, the bowls of food were placed before them. There were roast duck, beans and little fried corncakes, and a two-pronged wooden fork to eat with. Adam ate with as much appetite as she did, but before they finished the room had become dark again. Joe Toads, who, Adam had told her, was the chief's nephew and a good friend of his and Jamie's, got up and lighted a torch that was fastened to a post.

"Can we go now, Adam?" she whispered.

"Nervous?" He looked anxious himself.

"At least I won't get drenched to the skin any more than you in your buckskins," she tried to say cheerfully.

But she did not cheer him, for the chief was saying something that made him frown. He shot back questions in the chief's language.

Then Adam said to her, "He says that the brook we crossed about a mile from here will have overflowed the hollow in this downpour—make a quagmire for the horses." He walked restlessly about. "Damn my gumption! Why didn't I bring a lantern."

"It can't be *that* late, Adam." Surely they could get home before night. She was thinking of Monica's worrying. Oh, if Monica could see her now! But at least Jamie could tell them she was out with Adam, and Uncle Peter would know that he would not let harm come to her. So if they did not get back until late . . .

Adam seemed to have made a sudden decision, for he opened the door and dashed out into the rain, Joe Toads after him. Clytie resettled herself on the mat, sorry that she could not talk to the chief, who puffed away at his pipe. A woman came in and took away the empty bowls, and Omeme walked over to Clytie, holding out a gourd of clear water. Clytie drank gratefully.

Omeme sat down beside her and said, "Rain not stop, you not worry. You . . . your man sleep *there.*" She pointed toward the cubicle where Clytie had changed her clothes.

Her man. She gasped, then held her breath. *Spend the night with Adam!* If it should truly become necessary to spend the night here, she would not let Adam get an inch away from her. The thought caught her so unaware she went hot from head to toes. As they had sat around the fire while the rain pounded, such an eventuality had not entered her mind. Rain and wind and darkness did not deter Adam from traveling—not all the way from Queen of France Mill to Frederick they had not. And now that his business with the chief was finished, and she had sensible garments to wear in the rain . . .

"You and your man sleep there" still echoed after Omeme had left her; it gave her a breathless feeling. Would she sleep again with Adam's arms about her, as on that wilderness night? But no, Adam would find a way to take her home; he was not the kind to permit wind or rain or quagmire roads . . .

He re-entered the hut like a thunder gust, rain dripping from his buckskins.

"Your Bob has lost a shoe," he said, all but accusing her. "The rain has put out the fire in their smithy, and who knows when they'll get it going again."

"You could lie down if you put your head at my feet, couldn't you?" Clytie whispered softly in the darkness.

There was no answer. She had never felt so lonely. This was not at all what she had expected when the black darkness had come, before the smithy fire had been set going. Big Corn had not permitted Adam to attempt to cross the quagmire and brook, and it had been too dark to make out the other trail back to the highway. Adam had told her she must sleep here in this little cubicle alone, while he slept by the fire with the other men; but when she would not leave him, he had come in with her and spread the big bear rugs for her to sleep on. He had not taken her in his arms, nor had he kissed her; he had not even spoken until he took her blanket from her, spread one end of it on the rugs, and told her to lie down on it and roll over.

When she was all rolled up in the blanket, he had knelt beside her and said softly, "I'll sit here near you, sweetest." His voice had quavered ever so slightly. "You do understand, don't you, and—and will go to sleep?"

He had wound her arms into the blanket so tightly that she could not get even one of them out to touch him, and she could not quite remember what she had said in pleading that he lie beside her—only that the more she had said, the more impatient he had become.

"Listen, Lottie—" he had kissed her forehead—"do you want to make this situation harder for me than it is?"

"It's no harder than in the wilderness, is it?"

"A sight harder, and you know it."

But she had not known it, and it had not made sense. He had wrapped himself in his blanket, sat down, and leaned against the post. Then the torch had been put out, and now everything was so black she could see only his vague outline. Maybe he was truly asleep.

There were many other people in the hut. She had heard a baby cry above the slapping of the rain on the roof. It sounded now as if the wind were throwing hard pebbles against it—hail maybe, for it was cold. The wind was blowing through the chinks, and she shivered. But she would not speak to him again; she bit her lips as his name almost escaped them. If he wanted to sit there, as remote as the big brown beast who had given these skins for her to lie on, let him. She had to work hard to get one of her arms from beneath the blanket, for something wet was running down her cheek and it was not rain. She angrily brushed it away.

Suddenly a terrifying shout sounded above the rain. Clytie sat up with a startled cry. It was not from this hut, but from another. It became a series of horrible whoops. . . . Those cruel-looking warriors, who—?

"Lottie," Adam said softly, "don't be afraid, sweetest. It's only a drunken Indian . . . rum sold him by the criminal whites." The sounds of shouting died away. "Scared?"

"Y-yes."

"Can't you sleep?"

"N-no." She rolled over and turned her face from him. "It's t-too c-cold to s-sleep." She was shivering, but she had not meant to let a sob creep into her voice; yet it was out, coming from deep down—because she felt so shoved away, maybe, and for a reason that was no reason.

He did not speak, but she heard him move; then suddenly the darkness vibrated. He was close beside her, grappling for her. He lay beside her, his arms tight about her. He had pulled her close, her back to him, her head on his arm.

"Blast you, papoose! Blast you!" His voice was a caress.

"Adam!" Clytie fitted herself into his curved length and sighed deliciously.

"Now will you sleep?" He tucked her blanket close about her.

"Are you wrapped in your blanket?"

"Yes. Stop wriggling."

"I—I'm not wriggling—just warm and happy."

"Why?" he said softly.

"Because I'm close to you."

Their soft whispers created a warm island in the darkness and the rain. Yet in the center of that charmed island Clytie sensed a tautness, something gathered up and held hard and tight, a restraint from the fibers of her being and his. She felt its ache and tingle, the vibration of an unknown ecstasy. It was to be cherished.

"I'm glad Bob lost a shoe," she murmured.

"Why?" His arms tightened about her. "Because you want to get sent back to New York? Get me in a peck of trouble with the squire? Or because it pleasures you to drive a man crazy?" He rubbed his cheek against her hair. His arms twitched ever so slightly.

"No, no. Why—why would you be in trouble with the squire?" She tried to turn toward him a little, but his arms pinioned her.

"Lie still."

Clytie lay still, except for the fingers of her free hand that caressed the back of his hand which was tucked about her.

"Because your hair is so sweet and soft." He breathed softly, his lips entangled in it.

Clytie, only half conscious of her action, ran her fingers up above his wrist to where the little soft hairs . . .

His body quivered.

The hard, tight core within the silken softness around them vibrated as she made an effort to turn her face to his. He aided her movement and bound her closer—his lips ranging her face found hers.

Rainbows glinted in the darkness. New dimensions asserted themselves. She felt a hunger of spirit and flesh.

"Dear heaven . . ." His lips withdrew, lingered on her face. "Give me strength . . ."

It was a tortured breath of prayer, mingling with Clytie's soft cry of his name. Then he held her ruthlessly, turned her about as if she were a log, until her back was again to him, and pressed her down.

"Now lie there quietly—you understand?" His voice was thick, shaky. "If not, I'll sit up the rest of the night."

Clytie lay still, trembling—he had thrust her so suddenly out of their closeness, into darkness. But awareness of his struggle kept her mute until she could say in a fairly steady voice, "Y-yes, Adam." She felt, rather than saw, that he was up now, wrapping his blanket around him, and she feared that he would again sit against the post. But he lay down beside her, not touching her.

A silence followed that magnified the clawing of the rain on the bark roof and the chill wind that penetrated the cracks in the wall.

Then she heard Adam's long-drawn-out sigh and his whisper, "Will you go to sleep now, honey?"

"Yes . . . better if—if you would let me put my head on your arm, I'd lie very still."

No answer. He sighed again, then said, "All right."

He worked his blanketed length over the bearskins, slipped an arm beneath her shoulders, and drew her close again until her head lay on his arm. His other arm slackened across her shoulders with his heavily expelled breath.

His arm was weighty now, but she loved its weight. When his breathing became easier Clytie's whole body relaxed, her tautness slipped away. Never had he been so dear. He had fought his battle with himself for her sake. And however ill-defined in her mind the results had that battle been lost, she felt its menace now that it was won—the menace of dark and forbidden things.

As his quiet rhythmic breathing clocked her happiness, another specter arose to make her heart shiver: her deception of him became an ogre lying in wait to tear them apart. Oh, Adam, dearest, Clytie DeLancey is only a *name!* She was forced to fight her own battle, else she would cry it out and tell him, and this one little moment of blessedness snatched out of time be lost. Besides, now that he loved her—oh, he did love her, he must!—everything would be all right. No anger, no pride, no resentment. He would laugh and tell her that even though her name were Circe, or Delilah, nothing was changed.

Clytie dreamed on, her disquiet drifted into peaceful rhythm, became one with the disciplined stillness of Adam's body. He breathed softly, and patter of the rain on the roof . . .

"You all right?" Adam called back to Clytie.

He was riding ahead of her along a narrow path, following an Indian runner who was showing them the trail to the highroad. The little brook they had crossed on the way to the Lenape village was now a muddy lake across the swamp, closing off the wider trail.

Clytie called a happy answer. The sun was coming up and reaching orange fingers through the fresh green of the forest. Diamonds glistened on the trees and sprinkled down on her with the cool breeze. But she did not mind; she was wearing the doeskin dress.

When she had awakened this morning Adam was gone, and Omeme stood beside her with a steaming bowl of corn mush and honey. And while she ate greedily, Omeme had fetched Clytie's homespun dress, all dry and smoothed out, her admiring eyes on it. The little Indian had been all sparkles when Clytie made her a present of it—petticoat, bonnet and all, even the stockings and the maroon hair ribbon. All Clytie had kept were her shoes, which she was wearing now. But she had made Omeme understand that Adam would return the doeskin dress and the beaded band she was wearing about her head.

The little Indian village had looked very different in the morning light, with its crude brown huts and brown naked children running about. Many of the small tribe had turned out to see them off—squaws with darling little babies on their backs—and all agape, all but the tall, strong warriors who had only grunted at Adam's friendly good-bys and had watched their departure with grim faces. Only Joe Toads and the chief had been friendly and smiling, and Adam had invited them both to come to see him at his military camp. It had been a wonderful visit.

Adam stopped his horse to listen to the Indian runner's directions as to how to follow the trail. Clytie drew up behind him. Suddenly, from the quiet woods around them issued a blood-chilling volume of yowls and yells. Clytie was too horrified to cry out. Were they being ambushed by those fearsome warriors? Multiple terrors assailed her mind as the awesome yells re-echoed. Was this a trap for Adam? Had they purposely unshod Bob and put out the smithy fires?

But Adam was smiling, waving at her amid the horrifying din.

Then, out of nowhere, the half-naked bodies of small boys appeared, leaping and running through the underbrush. The sounds died out, and the boys were gone, as though by magic. The runner and Adam were laughing.

Adam rode back to her and said, "Frighten you, sweet?"

"It scarified."

"Youngsters—little devils!" His face sobered. "Gives you an idea of what a full-blooded Indian ambush can be like." He spoke to the runner again, then they rode on without him. Clytie shivered until Adam called back, in high spirits, "What did you think of the Lenape?"

The trail was too narrow to ride abreast, but she was close enough behind him to ask, "Are they all Lenape? I mean, some of them don't seem so friendly as Big Corn and his nephew."

"Smart girl. The chief's tribe is made up now of fragments of several tribes—Patuxents, Piscatawas. The Lenape were once a highly civilized tribe—owned most of the land in the east. A proud people. Friendly to the settlers. Mostly a vanished race now." The path widened and he waited for her to ride up beside him. "Big Corn told me last night that he was an aged hemlock; that long the wind had whistled through his branches and that he was now dead at the top." He laughed, rode close to her, leaned over and kissed her lips. "Good morning, my beautiful papoose! You know, I feel like a big chief sachem myself this morning." He kissed her again, precariously, as their horses moved forward.

"Not in a mind to put your prisoner in a pot and eat her?" she teased.

"Might get around to that, too, some day." He grinned broadly. "Figure I'd better deliver her intact this time, and think out the sort of sauce with which she had best be eaten."

Clytie laughed. But her heart moaned, Oh, Adam, Adam! don't hate me when you find out the truth. Again her impulse was to stop and tell him. Again some hope goaded that there was a better way, that some way would present itself. . . . *A letter:* that would give him more time to readjust to her, to realize that nothing was truly changed.

The path had narrowed again and she hid her unease by riding behind him and directing their talk to impersonal things.

"What else did Big Corn tell you, Adam?" she asked.

"That if any French Indian came among his tribe, he would die a flea's death. Said his ears were closed to Shawnee or any other enemy of his white brothers. He means it all right, but the chief is getting old and some of his Piscatawas are getting hard to handle. No use borrowing trouble, but if old Braddock should get himself in a fix up around the forts, friendliness of the few Indian tribes round here could be mighty important. Look out, papoose!" He held back a low-hanging limb; when they passed under it the trail widened. He stopped their horses and kissed her hungrily again. But after she had abandoned herself to him, feeling again that swing into space, the haunting feeling of her duplicity returned and tears stung her eyes.

"What's the matter, sweet?" He looked anxious.

"Happiness, I guess. Let's ride."

They galloped along the grassy trail, but when at last they stopped to let their horses walk his mind was still on the foolish tears that had welled up.

"Look, blessed, if you are worrying about what the mistress will say,

I'll fix that up with Colonel Chester. He's the finest there is. Used to be a great Indian fighter, you know. It was the colonel who drove the Shawnee out of this country."

She answered with only a smile. They had reached the main road, and she was planning what to say to him when they came to the trail that turned into the Chester plantation. She must make him leave her, so that she could ride home alone. It was true that Uncle Peter would be the one to smooth her way with Monica. Maybe his intercession would cause Adam to forgive her. The hope cheered her.

Clytie needed all the cheer she could summon as she raced through the orchard in her doeskin dress. She had left Bob at the barn in Solomon's care. And, mercifully, she had been able to leave Adam near the crossroad. He had protested angrily at first—she had talked nonsense about his not going to the house with her—but after she had cajoled and entreated, saying how much more embarrassed she would be by his presence when she faced the mistress, he had laughingly consented.

"But mind you, my sweet," he said, "I'll be over soon to give my own version to the squire."

He had kissed her, and never had her own lips been more eager, never had she longed more for a moment to continue into eternity. Would it be their last kiss?

The thought had stung her eyes as she forced a smile, moving Bob ahead and calling back, "*A bientôt,* not good-by, my Captain!"

But his face had looked so solemn, his whole sculptured outline, slashed by the morning sun, so like a bronzed sentinel guarding over her fate, that her panic grew until she rounded the bend in the trail and was out of his sight.

And now it was ended. She was racing back into unreality—Clytie the shadow, the make-believe—while that other self had been the true . . .

"Clytie! Ho! Sotweed and cider! What's this?"

Precious, laughing Uncle Peter was coming down the garden walk. She headed toward him and straight into his arms, laughing with him.

"Where's Adam? With him, weren't you?" He held her off.

Somehow she managed to tell how she had not let Adam come home with her, and about the storm, Bob's shoe, the Indian village. She was forced to hurry, for Monica stood in the doorway, her unbelieving eyes focused on the fringed doeskin dress.

"Clytie *DeLancey!*" cried Monica.

It was the emphasis given the name that compelled Clytie's uncontrolled laughter. Suppose Adam was standing beside her! The thought of his astonishment made her laugh even more.

"I am White Sea Gull of Lenape tribe, madam," answered Clytie.

"You are disgraceful. Never—never would I have believed——"

"Come, Mony!" Uncle Peter interrupted. "Could the child help it if a deluge came, such as we have not had in years?"

Dear, helpful Uncle Peter!

"But that man—how could you ride out with *that man?*" Monica's dignity had almost vanished, and Clytie stopped laughing.

"Blamed lucky she was with Adam," the squire said. "What if she'd been alone?"

"And what if Sir Jason should hear of this escapade?" Monica's tone was one of which she alone was mistress.

Since that was the question, and the only question that seemed important, Clytie winked at Uncle Peter, laughed again, strutted, wriggling a little for his benefit, and followed Monica into the house.

Now Monica's hopes ran high, for news had come from the general's camp that Major Sir Jason Mayne was expected back tomorrow or the next day. Meanwhile, Clytie all but ran a fever—not over Sir Jason—over the report Adam had threatened to make to the squire concerning their delay at the Indian camp.

For two days after their return she had been afraid to cross the compound, to be seen in the garden, even outside the house, for fear Adam would appear and she would be lost.

"Guilty conscience, what?" Jamie accused her, grinning.

Unsteadied from anticipating that meeting between Uncle Peter and Adam, Clytie kept her eyes glued to a rear window in the parlor, watching for those long strides to the office that would be her undoing.

"Well, even the most gladsome charade must end," Jamie added, and draped himself over a chair.

"But not so—so soon. Not *this* way." She had told him all that had happened—well, *almost* all. "I just can't endure that he should learn the truth from Uncle Peter, yet I don't know how to——"

"Why not put on your best DeLancey air, and brush the poor fly away with a proud heroine's gay laughter?"

"Stop it, Jamie! I'm frightened."

"By Hector, I believe you are! Anything wrong, you figure, about being a DeLancey?"

"Yes. For Adam, yes."

"Could be right. Proud critter, Adam. What I can't make out is how you've kept his head in wool for so long."

"He—he just wanted to believe I was Lottie, that's all. Can't you see it?" *Maybe* that was it; oh, she did not know.

"Blamed if I can, seeing how La DeLancey is not so remote herself."

"You are not talking sense."

"All right, you talk it, and make it good." He stretched himself out, his long legs in front of him, and regarded the toes of his boots.

And he was right. It was about time she made her whole deception good to herself, unless she wanted to accept herself as a coward. Clytie sat down in a darkened corner of the shaded parlor.

"Look, Jamie, I know it doesn't seem funny any longer about my being Lottie, but—"

"Can run a joke ragged, you know."

"Of course I know. Look at me, I'm all frayed at the edges." Jamie chuckled, but she hurried on. "Yet it has been the most wonderful thing that ever happened to me."

"What?"

"Just being *myself* . . . with Adam."

"Yourself?"

"My *real* self. I didn't even know what sort of person Clytie DeLancey was until on the journey down here—"

"The hero appeared. Go on. It's been written of before by novelists. But speak on."

"W-what's been written?"

"Oh, about how in the springtime the sap runs high, and the birds and beasts and little maidens discover love and gender."

"J-Jamie Chester!"

"What's wrong with that?"

"It wasn't love. And it wasn't gender." Or was it? She was glad she was in the shadow; her face was flaming.

"All right, then, my pretty; it was innocence of such worthy urges that ruined a lot of pretty lasses—innocence. But never mind. You were saying?"

What was she saying? Jamie had a way of tangling her up.

"About how with Adam in the woods you felt the sap rising," he prompted, with a wicked grin.

"All right, if you won't be serious I won't talk at all."

"*Know thyself,* little one. Might as well get it out."

"Yes, if you would only let me. That's just it, I *was* myself with Adam, as—as I never was in New York." That's what she had wanted to say. It was all-important.

"You mean when suitors showed up? Came sparking?"

"Yes, because to them I was only the daughter of the royal governor. And worse: Clytie was known to have been left a fortune by her grandfather. Now do you understand how I was not *me—myself?*"

"By Hector! That's right! Granddad did sort of set you up. I'd forgotten. Never mind, he was pretty good to Pete and me, too. So, what you are trying to say is that as a gal without name or fortune . . . Listen!" He jumped up from his chair at the sound of a voice from the compound. Adam's voice.

"O-oh, Jamie. . . . " But Jamie was already out of the room, and from the window she saw him going toward the compound, and she heard him say: "Pa's gone to the Potomac wharf, soldier boy."

Was that true? She hoped so. She saw Adam wave—she could not hear what he said—and turn back through the pear orchard toward the barn where he had likely left his horse. She felt hysterical with relief that his exoneration of Lottie had not come about. Yet had she been wholly frank with Jamie concerning her dread of Adam's discovery of her identity? No, because she had not stated that it was his pride of class that frightened her. His Scotch pride. In her heart she knew that she could throw her fortune into the discard box, throw her long deception of him after it, and he would still fend off Clytie DeLancey. He would maintain his pride like a banner, his self-conscious pride: "The Appletons tilled the land for the Washingtons." She could hear Monica's voice sounding the truth that to Adam would be insurmountable. Yet her grandfather had said that such pride of class was a baleful thing. She could remember her mother's defiant protests when, up on his farm, her grandfather had let her play with his overseer's daughter, remember her grandfather's booming voice: "Ragtag today, Lucy, but tomorrow a respected landowner, thanks to this blessed country." In her mind's eye Clytie could see Adam Appleton turn stony-faced toward Clytie DeLancey, who was not of his world; the banner of his pride was not to be hauled down, not by life, not by love.

But, as Jamie had said, her joke was now ragged; it had to end. How? When? She must think it through, not to make it easier for herself, but for him. Oh, Adam, Adam, don't hate me!

In the next few days there seemed little time to think anything through, so many events came crowding together. First of all, Pete came home. And when Pete was home it appeared that all Chestermere revolved around him, around his stalwart, six-foot-two, blond strength. He was the light by which Monica measured all her blessings, while it was clear that the sum of his father's hopes sat with confidence on his eldest son's broad shoulders.

Jamie's attitude toward Pete held a sort of wistful adoration that was expressed mostly with sardonic barbs especially aimed at the army, which was Pete's life. His mind was so completely on his troopers, most of whom his father had already gathered from the highways and byways to fill his company, that after no more than an hour in the house he and Uncle Peter were off to the stockade. And when they came home for dinner that day, Clytie sensed another threat to Adam's belief in Lottie O'Day—a threat that might be realized before she could properly compose the letter she had resolved to send him. If only she had not torn up six versions of it already! The danger was upon her with Pete's first words as he flung himself from his horse.

"Sure, Pa, with Adam to help me get my men in shape, there's great hope of bringing them up to his standard." He loped up the steps and enveloped his mother in a bearlike embrace. "How's my gal?"

Clytie was beginning to feel as fragile as the contents of a china closet invaded by a bull when Pete was around, but it would take more than splintering and clinking to repel his onset. He lifted her off her feet and swung her about.

"You surely are *cossetung,* honey pie." Cossetung was his word for kissable, and he sniffed puppylike at her cheek before he set her down.

"What's the news about Georgie?" Jamie asked.

"Georgie?" Pete straightened his tall length, smoothed back his neatly queued fair hair and directed a guffaw at Jamie perched on the newel post. "How come ole Doc Chester wants to know?"

"Just wondered when he was going to get promoted."

Pete and his father both looked startled at the inquiry.

Clytie recalled Adam's outrage that Colonel Washington's rank had been changed to that of captain. . . . Adam, whom Pete would be seeing every day. Her mind went blank. Should she appeal to Pete to make no mention of his visiting cousin?

"By the big bazooks, fellow countrymen—" Jamie grinned at them through his drawn-up knees—"it's like this: Can they get their recruits so long as Georgie stays down on his farm? Nay, brethren. So out they drag him by the hair and restore his rank, and find him a quiet place on Braddock's staff."

There was a moment's silence, then Pete said gruffly, "Pa, what's wrong with your little boy's head?"

"Where'd you hear such a thing, son?" Uncle Peter said soberly.

"Didn't, Pa. All you've got to do is add things up. Like this—" Jamie leaped from the newel post and expounded—"rank restored, will they put George in command of all colonial troops? You know they won't. Why, old Braddock don't trust any colonial, much less Washington. How does he know a wilderness-wise lad like that wouldn't take over his whole outfit—redcoats, puff pants, cocked hats and all—and march 'em up to the forts and *take* the forts without benefit of Braddock? Could do it, you know."

"Ma, your brat's looney," Pete growled.

"All right, sweet brother. But just remember that with George on Braddock's staff everybody's happy but George *and* the colonials."

Pete snorted.

"Could be a way out for them. Could be," his father considered.

Monica sighed and tried to divert the conversation from military matters, but when Pete was around you might as well try to divert the army itself.

"Stopped by to watch the regulars drill this morning, Pa," continued Pete. "Prettiest thing you ever saw the way they——"

"Know about as much of Indian warfare as tomcats know the way of tigers!" Uncle Peter's explosion came so suddenly they all stared.

"Squire!" But Monica's protest was feeble; she looked scared.

"All right, but if Braddock had the brains he ought to have he'd listen to men like Washington who've had experience fighting the redman. Understand he wouldn't even listen to Franklin." He was pacing back and forth.

"You've had experience in such yourself, Pa."

"Wouldn't expect him to listen to me, Pete. But, by Lucifer, somebody ought to make him understand that there's nothing *regular* about Indian fighting, not in this wilderness, and that the French on this continent practice that sort of warfare and nothing else!"

"But—but for taking the forts, Pa?" Pete looked as anxious as his mother.

As Uncle Peter looked down on his sturdy son settled in his chair, the moment's pause seemed to Clytie to be filled with unspoken thoughts.

Then Uncle Peter answered solemnly, "First, he's got to get his army *to* the forts."

When, long afterward, Clytie recalled this scene it seemed imprinted like an intaglio on a deeply submerged part of her mind. She recalled the hard planting of Uncle Peter's feet as he walked back and forth; the rigid lift of Monica's head and shoulders, as if she was listening to some faraway echo; Jamie's solemn eyes and Pete's questioning stare centered on their father's back; while within her own mind sounded the terrifying yells of the Indian boys and Adam's words: "Gives you an idea of what a full-bodied Indian ambush can be like."

"And along a trail hacked through a wilderness that the red savage knows like the back of his hand," Uncle Peter addressed the spaces of the garden without turning around.

"D-dinner's ready. Jamie, go wash your hands." Monica's effort to keep her voice steady was a part of the picture engraved on Clytie's heart and mind.

The next day Pete came home, waving a circular.

"Your friend Ben is getting tough, Pa. Read this. Batch of 'em has been sent to distribute to farmers about the county." Pete gave him the printed slip.

"About the horses and wagons, hey?" Uncle Peter was so excited he handed Clytie the slip and beat at his coat pockets for his spectacles. "Raising 'em, is he? Knew Ben would do what he set out to do."

Pete went in to look for his mother, and Clytie smiled. Dear Uncle Peter! He had forgotten his long anxiety that Mr. Franklin had undertaken to raise horses and wagons where none existed.

"Read it to me, honey, read it." He couldn't find his spectacles.

"He is sure putting the fear of God and the Shawnee into those Lancaster farmers," Pete said, returning. Monica was with him.

"Sit down, sit down," Uncle Peter said.

Clytie skipped the introduction and read aloud: " 'I apprehended that the progress of British soldiers through these counties on such an occasion, especially considering the temper they are in and their resentment against us, would be attended by many and great inconveniences to the inhabitants, and therefore more willingly took the trouble of trying first what might be done by fair and equitable means——' "

"Quiet, will you!" Uncle Peter reproved Pete, who was whispering to his mother.

Clytie read on: " 'You will be paid in the silver and gold of the king's money. The service will be light and easy, for the army will scarcely march over twelve miles a day.' "

"Lily feet," Peter said, snorting. "Washington covered that same route at twenty miles . . . and without a trail."

"And without heavy wagons and baggage train, son. Braddock's line of march may stretch out three or four miles. Read on, Clytie."

"Yes, Uncle Peter." Three or four miles! The black lettering leaped up at her, blurred by her memory of the arrows that had been aimed at her by unseen foes as she galloped across the causeway in Adam's wake. " 'But if you do not this service to your king and country voluntarily, and when such good pay and reasonable terms are offered you, your loyalty will be strongly suspected. The king's business must be done. So many brave troops come so far for your defense must not stand idle through your backwardness. Wagons and horses must be had. Violent measures will probably be used and you will be left to seek recompense where you can find it, and your case be little pitied and regarded.' "

"Rub-a-dub-dub! The commissioner's taking no back talk, what?" Pete interjected.

" 'I am sincerely your friend and well-wisher, B. Franklin,' " finished Clytie.

"That'll fetch 'em!" exulted the squire. "Dunkards, Quakers, or what-not. Ben knows. Printed words look up at a man, make him stop and think. Wants 'em circulated about here, hey?" He turned toward Pete. "Must mean he's finished his job in Penn Colony."

"Reminds me, Ma," Pete said, "that officer you asked me about, Major Mayne, is back."

"Oh, son, why didn't you tell me!" It was a call to arms for Monica; she folded her knitting and got up as though called to duty.

"Didn't know it till he came onto our reservation. . . ."

But Monica had disappeared into the house, and Clytie found herself more than a bit disconcerted by the subtle grin Pete was leveling at her. She tweaked his ear in passing, and followed Monica.

He bawled after her, "If you weren't my cousin, damme if I wouldn't cut all these suitors out, you little witch!"

All these suitors? Now what did he mean by that? There was something cryptic in the grin Pete had given her. Could Adam have spoken to him? No. She dismissed it. Adam was not the kind of man to speak of . . . But she must not count too much on that. The letter; she must write it, now. Yet every time she tried, her hunger for the sight of his dear, slow smile, her ache for the touch of his hand, for the essence of him that she had drained in with his kiss, so blurred the page that coherence eluded her and fear of his pride, resentment, humiliation and anger came to defeat her phrasing of reasons for her actions. But now the matter could not be postponed. Clytie shrugged her shoulders and hurried up the stairs.

"Darling." It was Monica's voice. Clytie turned back. "I have just sent Solomon with a note for Sir Jason to the general's headquarters. Come into my room, dear."

Clytie followed. The supper party was set for Friday. This was Wednesday, and other notes must be dispatched.

"And with the servants all so busy," Monica said, "loading the *Mary Monica,* so much to be done, I shall have to dispatch Phyly with a note to the Carys. Would you like to ride with her, dear, so you can meet Barbara, a girl of most commendable deportment?"

"I'd admire to, Aunt Mony." Was that last remark barbed? Since her escapade with Adam, Clytie knew that to her aunt her own deportment was permanently suspect.

"Now for the other notes." Monica bustled away, toward the library. "Best start at once after dinner, and wear one of your prettiest dresses." Her voice held the force of fatality. . . .

No note for Adam this day.

It had been a lovely ride to the Cary plantation. On the way home Clytie and Phyly walked their horses along the mossy, loamy, trail. The lush country led through farmland that rolled away toward blue hills and indigo distances. The big log plaster-and-plank structure of the Cary house had intrigued Clytie; it slumbered on green turf under great oaks, like a brown mouse of uncertain proportions. Its interior was gracious with the charm of old England. The older Carys had been visiting a sick neighbor, but Barbara—a tall, large-boned, robust girl of more health than beauty—when called from the fields where she had been trying out a new hunter, radiated charm.

When she ordered tea, she confided, "I have so longed to meet you, Mistress DeLancey! But all our horses have been in use to get the planting done before they must be turned over to the general—except Horace, my new hunter—I shall hide him out in the woods. . . . You like the vast forests?" And without waiting for an answer: "They terrify many—my mother when first over from England felt smothered, buried alive by the endless wilderness. Me, I was born in this green ocean and love it! Do you hunt? Oh, you are more beautiful than I have heard! May I call you Clytie?"

"Do, Barbara." Clytie, amused by the rapid chatter of the rosy-cheeked girl, took her tea.

"Oh, you should ride to hounds! Stay until October and we'll give you a wondrous hunt. We are breeding from the Fairfax pack. But, of course, if General Braddock is to take all our horses . . ." She drooped with the thought. "Yet they will be returned by autumn, Pa says. Oh, this wicked war! And Pete Chester home only to be snatched away again. . . ."

Clytie could not remember now all of Barbara's chatter, but the general impression had been of a wholesome girl who had too little companionship and was most eager that Pete should come sparking. Also, she marveled that there was no underlying fear in the girl's heart as to the outcome of the expedition to the forts, or that the country might be threatened with invasion by enemy Indians. All such things, as she knew, sat heavily on Uncle Peter's heart and caused Adam to apply all his vigilance to cementing friendly relations with the neighboring tribes.

"Phyly," Clytie said now, "do you remember the Indian raid on Chestermere, so long ago?" Her thoughts were turning irresistibly to the day in the library at home when her father had first spoken of the menace to this part of the country.

Phyly turned her big solemn eyes on Clytie, and away again, but for a moment she did not answer. She was so picturesque in her well-starched, brown cambric dress, a bandanna splashed with red on her head, sitting her horse so upright—more the indomitable grenadier than ever.

"It was den I lost my little baby, missy, an' my husband, Silas," Phyly said softly.

"Oh, Phyly, I did not know." Jamie had told her so little of the tale; but after all, he had been only a nursing baby.

She heard it all now from Phyly as they continued to walk their horses. When the tale was done she felt closer to Chestermere than ever before, and to Uncle Peter . . . never so valiant as in defense of his home.

Phyly's own part in it was told briefly—how when word came for the slaves to fly to shelter in the big house, she and Silas had been late in hearing the warning, and Silas, with the baby in his arms, had been felled by an arrow. Phyly had grabbed the child and reached the house, but, injured in the fall, it had soon died. A few weeks later Monica's little girl had died. All the cattle had been destroyed, and for some reason they never understood, the milk Uncle Peter had been able to obtain for her had "not set well on her little stomach." But that both her own baby and Miss Mony's were now romping and playing together in heaven was Phyly's firm faith.

A beautiful faith, Clytie thought, and she remembered what her grandfather had told her: "A person's life is but the *scene* of good and evil; his part, or hers, but to find the strength and purpose to meet and overcome adversity." As Phyly, Monica and Uncle Peter had overcome it.

They had quickened their pace and were no more than a mile from the river, which they would cross on one of the squire's flatboats, when they heard raucous shouts ahead of them.

Phyly drew rein.

"Wait, missy. Hit's some o' dem redcoat soldiers, drunk, maybe." The cursing shouts were not pleasant to hear, coming from around a bend in the trail that hid the shouters. "Better wait here till dey be gone. Been actin' mighty nasty, folks say, of late—dem soldiers."

They waited. But when it appeared the roisterers were making no progress along the road, only arousing themselves now and then to shout, Clytie grew impatient.

"It is clear they are not mounted, Phyly. We will simply gallop past them," Clytie said as she started ahead. It was getting late and she did not want Monica to become anxious.

She was galloping fast, Phyly behind her. At the end in the narrow trail the shouts grew louder, and she saw three soldiers blocking the road, hands lifted high. Angry indignation was all Clytie knew as she charged Bob straight at them, her whip ready in her right hand. A grab was made at her horse's bridle amid raucous yells, but she was well past them. Then she slowed down, conscious that Phyly was not behind her. As she wheeled about, the sight that met her eyes was one that blinded her with anger; they had caught Phyly's horse and were dragging her off.

"Ride on! Ride on!" Phyly shouted frantically to her.

Clytie rode, but at a murderous gallop straight at the redcoat farthest from the melee. She rolled him to the ground. She did not care if she had killed him. She wheeled again and brought her leather whip down on the head of the man who had been holding Phyly's frightened horse. He cowered with curses before her, but when he tried to snatch the bridle she made Bob rear. She saw the hoofs descending on the staggering figure. . . . When she wheeled again the man lay inert on his face in the road. Phyly was fighting the man who was dragging her into the bushes; but, unable to reach them, Clytie was forced to give attention to the first man she had downed. Up now, he was maneuvering, with strange oaths, to reach the side of her horse from which her skirts and legs hung down. Somehow she evaded his animal rage, for Bob had sensed the fight, and a blow from his great shoulders whirled the man over like a ninepin. . . .

Breathing hard from rage and fear, she realized that she should scream.

Phyly had been knocked senseless, she feared, so deep among the shrubbery she could see neither her nor the beast that had held her.

Clytie screamed. Never would she have believed she could emit such a piercing sound. There was a chance that someone might hear and . . .

"Ho! Ho, there!" a voice cried.

Was she dreaming that her wild shout for help had been answered? Then she heard the hoofbeats. She screamed again and saw the flash of the redcoat rider rounding the bend.

The rest was blurred: her half-incoherent cries that a soldier was murdering her maid—"There, sir! There!"—the officer's leaping from his horse and plunging into the brush, with a shout of "Stop or I fire!" the echoing of a pistol shot. . . .

And now she was off her own horse, bending over Phyly, saying, "Oh, Phyly, Phyly!"

"I'se a' right, missy, a' right." Phyly opened her eyes, sat up, and rubbed her head where the man had given her a cruel blow. Except for a scratched face and torn clothes she did seem all right, and so brave that when their now coldly efficient rescuer came from the woods, driving before him the soldier who had tried to escape, Phyly helped bind and tie him to a tree.

All Clytie could do was to take account of this angered British officer. He was a slim, bronze-faced man, his brown hair somewhat disarranged from his dash through the woods; in profile he had a thin, prominent, irregular nose, full lips below a not-too-heavy mustache, and a square chin, reminding her of a portrait of some ancient Norman knight.

Now that the culprit was secured to the tree, the officer bent over the two men Bob had felled. In answer to their groans, he threatened, "Don't try to make off, else you'll be stood against a wall and shot. There's been enough felony in the ranks. I give you warning." With the same crisp quality in his voice he turned to Clytie, and said, "Madam, I tend you my deepest regrets that soldiers of the king should . . . should—" His voice trailed away. For the first time he was truly looking at her. Doubtless she had been but a blur as he had plunged to her rescue. Now as he regarded her dangling bonnet, her hair awry, she was foolishly glad that her blue flowered muslin was so becoming. He seemed taken aback "—should so offend," he finished, clicked his heels and bowed. He was flushed in an unexpectedly boyish way.

"Our gratitude is a thousandfold, sir," Clytie managed to say, feeling somewhat flushed herself at recognition of his youth—twenty-five, maybe. "I am Clytie DeLancey, and my uncle and aunt will be——"

"DeLancey?" He grabbed her outstretched hand. "Not . . . surely not Governor James DeLancey's—?" he gasped.

Clytie stared at his insignia of rank: major. *"Major,"* she got out. Then: "Sir Jason Mayne!" She pronounced it with a lift of her voice that was almost a shout of laughter. Such things did not happen, of course. How Jamie would laugh: fair maiden rescued in the nick of time by hero at whose head fate had determined to throw her.

They were laughing together, and he still held her hand.

CHAPTER *Sixteen*

"Jamie, how do you know they are Mr. Franklin's wagons?" His mother was trying to control the excitement he had created when he had returned home from Frederick and said the wagons were on their way.

"Couldn't be anything else, Ma. Old Jim, one of the Calvert slaves, came galloping into town scared to death. Said he'd seen a train of wagons each with a big *haint* sittin' atop it. . . . Hurry, Clytie!"

"May I, Aunt Mony?" Clytie stood halfway down the stairs, as excited as Jamie over riding out to meet the wagons.

"I—I suppose so. But wear your dark cape. The weather looks threatening."

Clytie dashed into her room, tied the dark-blue woolen cape about her neck, put on the bonnet that went with it, and raced down the stairs.

When she reached the barn, where Jamie had the horses saddled, she was glad she had worn it; the sunless day had a chill in it.

Jamie was like a small boy off for a picnic as they galloped along the river trail and made for the northeast highroad, but after they had traveled quite a distance and had met only a farmer's cart, he looked crestfallen. The farmer had neither seen nor heard of a wagon train.

Clytie began to giggle. "Maybe those wagons still exist only in the constellation of Pegasus, Jamie."

"Listen!" Jamie drew rein.

Clytie pushed back her bonnet, heard a distant rumble, and in the next moment they were galloping toward it. When, along the deeply shaded road, they saw the first wagon, she could understand what the Negro meant by "a *haint* sittin' atop it." It appeared to be a white house on wheels.

"Holy Moses!" Jamie yelped. When they were alongside it he called to the driver, "Where'd you get that houseboat?"

The driver grinned and flicked his long whip at the lead horse. "Steady craft she be, mister," answered the driver, "in heavy weather or smooth." His *craft* rumbled on behind the four broad-backed horses.

She and Jamie drew up beside the road to watch, wide-eyed, the other wagons pass by. Their bodies, shaped like boats, sat high over the four great wheels, and were painted blue or red with green or purple trimmings. Towering above the boats were staves rounded at the top to form a sort of Indian house, the whole covered by white canvas. Clytie thought, also, of crustaceous monsters, each carrying his house on his head.

"Seein' ain't believin'," Jamie said, amid his calls to each of the drivers. Before Clytie knew what he was about, he had thrown her the reins of his horse, scrambled up the back of one of the wagons, and disappeared through the rounded hole at the rear of the taut canvas.

One of the drivers winked at her and asked if she'd like a ride.

"If you spread that canvas into wings and take me to the moon," she threw back at him.

And all this magic was Mr. Franklin's!

When the procession of twelve growling, rumbling monsters had passed, Jamie returned and mounted his horse.

"The others were sent to Will's Creek," he said, and informed her that the canvas covers were to keep the supplies for the army dry. "But come on, we've got to see what happens when they show up in Frederick."

They galloped past the procession. When they were well ahead, Clytie demurred. She did not want to go into Frederick; she was fearful of meeting Adam—fearful and yet excited at the thought of one glimpse of him.

"Oh, shucks! That soldier boy's busy at drill. He won't be in Frederick." Jamie's grin was broad. "Don't you trust the DeLancey luck?"

He called it luck that she and Phyly had been rescued from the impertinent soldiers yesterday by Sir Jason. "Tow for sparking," he had said, not knowing the true peril from which she and Phyly had been saved. Rather than alarm Monica they had made up a tale to recount between them, and had advised Sir Jason of it before he left them to dispatch the guard to bring in the culprits. So, all the Chesters knew was that some drunken soldiers had been impertinent, and that Phyly's face had been scratched by the overhanging limb of a tree. Yet Jamie had made it an occasion to declare that Braddock's redcoats had been thieving about the countryside, and that the girls in Frederick who had not been hamstrung by their parents would likely produce a batch of small redcoats to further harry the bailiwick.

Monica had reproved him sternly, yet she had been so delighted over Clytie's encounter with Sir Jason that she had had to force her sternness.

"Got to expect such things around an army camp," Uncle Peter had said philosophically. "Been the same since the world began; will be so till Saint Peter's trumpet blows."

"Holy Hector! Watch!" cried Jamie.

Clytie was watching. It was a drill of some of Braddock's regulars on the field adjoining his encampment. A squad of approximately fifty soldiers was being put through maneuvers, and they responded to the officer's bellows as though they were puppets and he pulled the strings. She and Jamie, riding by the camp on their way into Frederick, had stopped at the irresistible sight. Now the automatons were advancing four abreast, their black boots and buff pants a rhythm of motion. At the officer's shout, they deployed.

"A phalanx, that's what they are forming," Jamie said enthusiastically.

Clytie had heard of a phalanx but had never seen the perfect formation of the packed square. And so expertly was it done that it took her breath away.

"But what's it for, Jamie? Why do they do it?" she asked as the skillful maneuver was repeated again and again. Hadn't Uncle Peter said that was not the sort of warfare to be practiced in the wilderness? But Jamie was too goggle-eyed at the smoothness of the drill to answer.

"Watch now!" he chirruped.

This was musket practice. They moved as one man. Almost quicker than the eye could follow, every soldier rammed the charge, spat a bullet into his musket barrel, and sighted his gun at the target. Clytie gasped as the shots rang out in one volley.

"Glory! Isn't that pretty? Redcoats, I salute you!" Jamie said.

But the big white-covered wagons were heading into camp now, and the drill broke up as soldiers and the townfolk who had streamed out to see the unwonted sight gathered around Mr. Franklin's miracle that would set the army moving.

The streets of Frederick were all but deserted as Clytie and Jamie rode through. They had reached the turn in the road that led toward home when Jamie suddenly remembered.

"Jupiter! Pete! I've got to deliver Ma's message to Pete if I don't want to get waled with a broomstick."

Monica with a broomstick was too much; Clytie gurgled with laughter. "What on earth are you talking about, Jamie?"

"Didn't you know? Ma's short a man for her supper for Sir Jason tomorrow night. Capt'in Johnson's been detailed for some duty for the general, and Pete's got to produce a replacement."

"Where is Pete?" He had not been home for dinner today.

"Colonial barracks, or parade ground."

"All right. You find him." She had come through so far without being forced into a further deception by encountering Adam, and she was taking no more risks. She started off in the direction of home. But Jamie was beside her, gripping Bob's bridle.

"Oh, no, you don't, my pretty!" said Jamie. "What's on your mind? To have Pa take me to the woodshed when he sees you riding home alone? Ma says there'll be no more of that since yesterday."

This was a point Clytie could not argue; she turned Bob about and found herself once more headed toward the gate of the stockade she had passed through such eons ago with Adam—and in as much trepidation now as then, but for a very different reason. She waited while Jamie cantered across the compound to inquire about Pete and cantered back again.

"He's out on the field, this way," he said, and led along a path outside the stockade.

Clytie followed with misgivings. She had put off writing Adam that letter, thinking that perhaps it would be better to wait until he made some further effort to see *Lottie,* and then trust to all that had cemented them to soothe his pride and hurt. Trust to his own heart to divine that nothing had truly changed between them—could ever change. These were all good reasons for not seeing him now, not *now.*

The field where the colonial contingent of Braddock's army engaged in their own tactics in preparation to meet the French and Indians was a wide cleared space of irregular ground. It rose into hillocks, fell away into gullies, and for the most part was strewn with boulders, tree stumps and felled logs. No parade ground, certainly. Clytie drew up behind a fringe of low shrubs. She thought for a moment the field was empty, then she heard a loud bellow: "Ready! Charge!"

It was magic. As though the earth had opened, the field became alive with crouching, racing men, silent phantoms, that, at another bellow, disappeared as quickly as they had sprung up.

"Fire!" Muskets volleyed, toward the far woods, the smoke of their discharge hanging close to the ground, from men behind rocks, stumps, on their bellies behind logs.

There came an instant's silence in which Jamie said, "Reloading, watch!"

Clytie could see movement among the ground-hugging men. Then a figure at the fore of the scattered troopers stood up.

"Keep your head down! Get down, Joe! You too, Mayne." The tall figure stripped to the waist leaped over obstructions and advanced toward a prostrate trooper, on his belly in the dust.

"Adam!" Clytie exclaimed with a gasp. The tall bellower of orders was Adam, and . . .

"Jehoshaphat! It's Sir Jason," Jamie said. "What in all tarnation–?" Adam, after he reached the wallowing soldier, grabbed at his musket, shoved him aside, and lay down in his place; he appeared to be showing him how to reload the musket without showing his head above the rock.

"But Sir Jason? Why?" Clytie was too dazed at what she saw, at the sound of Adam's unholy bellow in her ears, to be coherent.

"Because he's a smart Englishman, I reckon," Jamie said. "Wants to learn *Indian* warfare. You stay here. I see Pete." He headed his horse along the outer fringe of woods toward a bevy of men who were watching the tactics.

But could that half-naked, dusty figure now following Adam's instructions be the immaculate British officer whom she had thought was the picture of an ancient Norman knight but yesterday? Adam had bounded back to his post now, yelling for another advance, and the troopers, appearing the very color of the earth itself, crept forward again, took cover in the gully, and fired from their bellies. Now came the retreat: Adam's orders were for inching backward–crouching, crawling backward to cover. From behind logs, bushes, rocks they fired again at the enemy supposed to be concealed in the woods. They were getting so close to her side of the field that Clytie moved into deeper concealment.

"At ease!" Adam shouted.

Then she heard Jamie's voice: "Hi-yo, Capt'in!" As Jamie came trotting up to Clytie, she saw Adam and Sir Jason laughing together. "Pete says Major Mayne showed up at camp a few days ago and asked to be put through colonial tactics for wilderness fighting. Do you want to stay?"

But Clytie was already leading off in the direction of home. Of all her mixed, bewildering emotions over what she had seen and heard, the strongest was a feeling of insecurity. Adam, Jason and Pete were in conclave. Would the name of Clytie DeLancey be brought into their discourse and Adam be forced to suffer the cruel revelation before she could soften the blow? Did he already know the truth, and was that why he had not sought to see Lottie again?

"Old Pete said he'd fetch a man for Ma's supper party, but that he would not get home until near that time tomorrow himself. There's a big blond rooster who loves the very scent of barracks," Jamie said as they turned from the highroad toward home.

"What is wrong, Sapphira?" The young slave had come into Clytie's bedroom and stood sniffling, rubbing one bare foot against the other.

"Mist'ess say—say take yo' time. All—all de guests ain't come yet." She sniffled again.

Clytie got up from where she had been sitting anxiously waiting for Phyly to take a last second's stitch on her dress. This was because of Monica's criticism. *Yesterday* she had approved every feature of the dress, yet this evening, after Clytie had it on, she had come in to say: "The bustline is too low. Fill it in about an inch, Phyly, with a strip of lace. Otherwise it is lovely." She had hurried from the room.

Phyly was now occupied with her chore in the sewing room. Clytie waited, regretful that she was too late to receive the first guests for the supper party. She pondered the oddness of her aunt's change of mind about the pink dress.

"Mist'ess ain't—ain't herself," Sapphira said in a quavering voice. She had evidently been spoken to harshly. "Hit—hit's sumpin' Mas' Pete done."

Incredible though it seemed, since Pete could do no wrong, Clytie decided that Sapphira was probably right. For Monica had been in a most placid state of mind when he had blustered into the house, singing, an hour ago.

"Mist'ess be mad at the massa, too, 'cause he laugh 'bout sumpin'." Sapphira's big yellow-brown eyes registered her devotion to Clytie—that often took the form of confiding all she knew. She scampered to the door now to admit Phyly with the dress, admitting as well the sounds of arriving guests from below.

"Ought to be all right now, missy," said Phyly, who seemed a little upset herself.

Something must be truly wrong in the household tonight to bring that about. She slipped the dress over Clytie's head and fastened the bodice.

"Oh, Phyly, it's mortal lovely!" cried Clytie.

The skillfully tacked on strip of lace at the bustline had not marred its perfect fit and beauty. Clytie smoothed the overskirt, under which Phyly had affixed whalebones at either hip to make it stand out with graceful fullness. The underskirt was of the same lustrous rosy material, but it was narrow and showed only down the front, from where the overskirt fell back to end in a demitrain. Before the mirror she gave a tweak at each puffed sleeve, which ended in a ruffle of Mecklenburg lace. The same lace made a ruffle about the neck of the bodice, high in the back but with a wide showing of her shoulders in front.

"Phyly, you are an artist," Clytie said. "Nothing just over from London or Paris could be more stylish."

"'Twere you drew the picture and cut the pattern for me, missy." Phyly was taking account of the length of the skirt, and seeing that Clytie's pink satin slippers twinkled properly beneath as she walked about the room to Sapphira's gasps of delight.

After Clytie had brushed her ringlets high on the crown of her head, Phyly secured them there with a ribbon and bow dyed the color of the dress. Then Clytie clasped her grandmother's pearls—those that Colonel Washington had so admired—about her neck. Adam had not seen them, perhaps would never see . . .

"Lawzy! I 'most forgot!" Phyly took a small red rag from her pocket, dipped it in water at the washstand, and came back to Clytie. "Hold still now." She deftly touched the rag to Clytie's lips. "Dere!"

When Clytie turned to the mirror her lips were the color of a deep-pink rose that lighted her whole face; even the pink flush of her cheeks seemed heightened.

"You are magician as well as artist," she told Phyly.

From the smile on Phyly's mahogany face it was not difficult to imagine her in the role of household goddess, or as the priestess of some ancient cult who provided magic and counsel for her votaries.

Yet Clytie went down the stairs slowly, conscious that the time had come when she must choose between the wishes of her beloved father concerning Sir Jason and the deeper yearning of her own heart already committed to Adam—Adam still so cruelly deceived. At the turn in the stairs she felt stabbed by the gay voices from below, but she gripped the railing of the balusters with resolution and followed it downward as though it were a predestined line—the line of her father's wishes. . . .

"Now I know why I came to America," said Sir Jason Mayne as he hurried to the foot of the stairs to greet her.

He was very handsome in his regimentals, and the memory of him on his belly in the dust yesterday broadened her smile. She quipped at him gaily and took his arm, but midway in the hall he stopped to face her with a more serious mien.

"You know, in the charm of this house one feels that new roots from the mother country have stretched out toward a new growth to rival, even excel, the old," he said, with an admiration of her glowing in his eyes.

"Then you grant our soil, sir, the right to nourish as well as direct our growth after its own manner?" She challenged him with laughter, yet with colonial pride.

His brown eyes widened with mirth as he hurdled this issue adroitly. "Let us say that I am concerned with a certain fair blossom, rather than with the rights of the soil that nurtured it. And that I should glory to see that blossom wafted back to old England and there transplanted——"

Clytie's merriment intercepted such ardor. "Has it then become true that *blossoms* are transplantable?"

They were laughing together when they entered the parlor, and she was conscious that the eyes of the gathering were directed toward them. There were only five guests, besides Jason, but Barbara Cary seemed a dozen in herself as she rushed toward Clytie, blotting out the others.

"Clytie, my mother and father did not believe me when I told them that Diana herself had paid me a visit. See for yourself," Barbara demanded of her elders.

The demand was met with compliments and a moment's chatter, then Jason was propelling her toward a tall figure half-concealed by Pete's bulk. The figure stepped forward.

"Greetings, Major Mayne!"

The darkly clad man, an apparition, swam before Clytie's startled eyes as the confident, well-modulated voice re-echoed through caverns of her heart. Pete's "My pretty, pretty little coz" held gay mockery.

Then Jason said, "Mistress DeLancey, may I name for you the man who promises to make of me a wilderness fighter? Appleton——"

"Mistress DeLancey."

Sounds were split into fragments. A *stranger* was bowing correctly before Clytie, pronouncing her name with an emphasis so subtly ironic as to be caught only by her burning ears. His eyes lifted and met her widened ones, but with no flicker of betrayal of having seen her before.

"Your fame has swept the countryside, mistress," Adam Appleton was saying in an easily modulated voice. "May I be permitted to offer my quota of applause?" His smile was as detached as if she were a thoroughbred filly for whose fine points he had an apt eye.

A moment's anger swept her. And for *this,* this moment of her revealed identification to him she had suffered, tortured herself. A sense of humor saved her and, however distorted, enabled her to answer.

"May I be permitted to accept it, Captain," said Clytie, "as from one whose values are reported to be unchallengeable?" She tried to force a smile that would not come. Sir Jason's laughter, Pete's hearty chuckles, and their mingled words that had no meaning were only creating a vacuum about the reality in which she and Adam were held. She felt that their spirits were being rattled about like two dice in a hollow cup.

"If you accept as well, Mistress DeLancey," Adam's metallic voice was stating, "that for *me* henceforth all values are valueless. It is my tribute to your prowess."

The bend of his body in a sardonic salute forced from Clytie the half-muted appeal, "Adam, I . . ." The quick straightening of his shoulders cut her off; her voice rebounded from the ice-carved monolith he had become. She felt Jason touch her arm, heard Barbara's laughter beside them.

Pete reached for Adam as he said, "Come, my lad, your lady waits."

He led Adam toward the fluffy blond girl, Lucinda Dixon. Monica was marshaling her guests toward the dining room.

CHAPTER *Seventeen*

"SIR JASON, you have heard of Preacher Whitefield, I take it, who was sent over from the mother country to convert us *poor* savages?" Squire Chester asked, amid a lull of conversation, as dessert was being served.

Through much of the supper the talk had been of Mr. Franklin's wagons, the miracle he had worked, and of the utility and worth of the wagons. And when someone had asked why they were shaped like boats that sagged in the middle, it had been Adam who explained that it was for the purpose of keeping their cargoes from shifting.

He was seated at the squire's end of the table, between Mistress Cary and the Dixon girl, and diagonally across from Clytie, who but for the two-stemmed silver candlesticks would have felt miserably self-conscious under his eyes. But she was half hidden from him amid the soft glow on silver and the bowl of flowers, which she herself had arranged. When Uncle Peter asked Adam for his opinion of the ability of the wagons to stand the trip to the fort, the authority behind his voice stirred her.

"They are sturdy wagons, sir," he said, while everyone gave attention—even Monica, whose annoyance with Pete, Clytie now fully understood: it was that he should dare intrude this "poor farmer's son" into her carefully chosen gathering. "The strongest and best ever to be built, doubtless," Adam finished.

But Uncle Peter had persisted. "Granted, Captain. But you and Washington have made that trip to Duquesne. Do you think the wagons can stand it?" He looked down the table at Jason. "You see, sir, having supplied these wagons, we would be a sad people to know they had failed your general."

"Then perhaps we had best be content with our prayers that they will serve him," Monica said, attempting to end such conversation.

"Prayers, indeed, mistress," Squire Cary, on her left, said. "If only prayer might remove the savage terrain of the mountains over which those wagons must be hauled." He leaned forward across Miss Dixon. "What's it like, Appleton?" His round ruddy face was solemn.

Monica moved slightly, with a look of distress; her supper party that had started with such gay laughter threatened to become unpredictable. Sir Jason in the moment's silence leaned to observe the discomforted expression in Adam's eyes.

"I have no means of knowing the route to be followed by the woodsmen," Adam said, "whom I understand are now hacking a way across the mountains, sir. But . . ." His look appealed to Uncle Peter.

"Go on, son, tell us what you know."

Adam looked unhappily at those hanging on his words. "We ourselves and our own scouts were unable to find any trail without sheer cliffs, on which no four-footed animal, short of a mountain goat, could descend or climb with safety."

The moment's taut silence was broken by gasps from Mistress Cary and the wide-eyed Dixon girl. Sir Jason's eyes stared into some granite distance. Then Barbara nervously laughed.

"But the brave general is known to be invincible," she said. "He will conquer the mountains of the Alleghenies."

"And his twelve-pounder cannon will conquer the forts," came Pete's cheerful pronouncement.

"Twelve!" "*Twelve*-pounders?" The exclamations came with horrified unbelief from squires Cary and Chester, directed toward Sir Jason, whose expression was as grim as Clytie had seen it when he rescued her from the drunken regulars.

"I myself have but lately learned of the general's decision to engage these guns at the fort," Major Mayne said. "But since he plans to employ a body of sailors from his ships with lief-tackle to hoist them over obstructions, and rafts to float them over the rivers, I think we can say we will find the twelve-pounders effective for reducing the forts."

"What a man, Braddock, hey?" Pete uttered with enthusiasm.

Monica made a quick observation to Sir Jason about the lovely weather they were likely to have for the journey; Barbara Cary interjected a gay reminder that Mr. Franklin would soon return to Frederick; and it was then that Squire Chester, changing from a too-dangerous subject, delivered the question to Sir Jason concerning Preacher Whitefield.

So now they waited, some toying with their unfinished dessert, others eating from the ambrosial dish of brandied fruits, for Sir Jason's reply.

"Whitefield? But yes, yes, that excellent exhorter." He laughed. "Has a way of making you feel, hey, sir, that one foot is already in the fire and the rest of you like to be pitchforked in any minute?"

Everyone laughed.

"That's the man," Squire Chester approved. "And since we've been speaking of Ben Franklin, I thought you might like to hear what happened when the preacher tried to shove Ben into that fire and have him well-roasted. But knowing Ben, you can judge that he's none too shoveable." He chuckled and went on, "Came about like this: Preacher Whitefield was stopping with us for a few days when Ben rode in. It was a fine October day, so I ushered Ben into the parlor where my wife was serving the preacher tea. Travel-worn, but enjoying the hot brew, Ben opined that the air on so fine a day was a benediction from heaven, whereupon the preacher puffed up like a pouter pigeon. Told Ben a benediction from heaven was not so easily arrived at.

" 'And yet,' says Ben, 'the sun shines impartially on all.' And what did Preacher Whitefield have to say to that?" the squire asked his eager listeners. "He told Ben, ' 'Tis no proof, sir, that the sun will shine in the afterworld on *unbelievers*.' Yes, sir, he hurls at Ben '*Damnation* shall be their portion.' "

Everyone gasped. Squire Chester chuckled.

Barbara giggled and exclaimed, "Beloved Mr. Franklin, so deep in sin!"

Laughter was spontaneous until the squire went on, "But did that trouble Ben? No, sir. He opined he'd have another sugar in his tea, since it was so difficult to think of damnation on so fair a day. But the preacher was not done with his baiting. He pointed an agitated finger at Ben and said, 'So what be said of ye be true, sir. Ye be a deist. One had almost said *atheist*.' '*Chalk*,' said Ben, 'one had almost said charcoal.' "

Sir Jason and Squire Cary laughed until they had to use their handkerchiefs, and for a brief moment Clytie caught Adam's eyes laughing into hers. He seemed to catch himself, and turned his amused attentions to the blond girl beside him. But Uncle Peter had not finished.

" 'At the coming of the Lord the unrighteous shall tremble,' said the preacher. And 'twas then that Ben Franklin spoke what my wife and I shall never forget. Might be as well for you young folks to remember such, too." He looked at each of them with solemn eyes. "Mr. Franklin said: 'It would appear more likely, sir, that when on Judgment Day those of different faiths flock together in the hope of seeing all others damned, they will be disappointed, and each obliged to rest content with his *own* salvation.' "

"Magnificent!" said Sir Jason.

"What is a *deist?*" asked Barbara.

"One who believes in God, but not in creeds and dogmas," said Pete. He got up when he saw his mother rising to lead the women away, and pulled out Barbara's chair. Adam was assisting Miss Dixon to arise, and Clytie managed for herself as Sir Jason turned too late from Monica. Glimpsing the worshipful gleam in the blond beauty's eyes, Clytie knew now that she had always mistrusted blondes. She knew as well, as she followed the other women from the room, that she had never before loved Adam so much.

She even felt an unreasonable pride in the defeat he had administered to her. She had imagined his hurt and anger when learning of her identity, but he had forced her to bear the brunt of her own deceptions. It was like having a penance imposed for your sins. Now that she had suffered it, would there not be forgiveness? She gathered the hope tightly to her heart. But as the evening wore on, and Jason monopolized her, and she was forced to engage in meaningless chatter and repartee, hearing at anxious intervals Adam's laughter from the portico, mingled with giggles from Miss Dixon or Barbara's unrestrained merriment, her inner depression grew until she forced herself to such gaiety that she laughed foolishly at everything Jason said.

He told her of a hunt in his native Devonshire, and she cried "Tally-ho!" as Barbara might have done. He told her she reminded him of a Watteau painting, and she giggled that he should think her the shepherdess type.

"Say rather the goddess of love, who sits near the fountain—"

"—with cupids tumbling about her. Poor babies! I'll warrant they'd like to stick out their tongues at your goddess, and tweak her lover's nose." She felt a little like tweaking his.

More like tweaking Adam's, or pounding him with her fists, because he avoided even a moment alone with her and bent over her hand in good night with all the correct formality with which he bade Monica good night. The evening had been a heartbreaking failure; she was weeping when Phyly came into her room to get her out of her beautiful dress.

Mr. Franklin had returned to Chestermere to be received as a conquering hero. It was the same in Frederick. Squire Peter reported: "A body would think it Ben, not the general, who was out to save the colonies." As for the general himself, he had rushed from the house requisitioned as headquarters to clap the postal commissioner on the back. "A Bacchus of heroic size, welcoming one of his favorite but lesser gods," the squire said.

But, for all the acclaim, there were still twenty-five wagons missing from Mr. Franklin's promised quota, and it was here that Jamie took a forceful hand in the matter. He had been away from Chestermere for several nights without anyone knowing what he was up to. Now it came out.

"It's like this, sir," he told Mr. Franklin. "We can get those twenty-five wagons from Frederick County. Up to yesterday I'd been able to locate twenty. Got them all now. Some are up Sugar Loaf Mountain way. We can tackle that first," he went on with assurance as his father and mother gaped and Mr. Franklin smiled broadly. "My friend, Joe Toads, a Lenape Indian, knows the trail, and my pals and I have distributed your circulars up that way, so you'll have to make only two speeches to the farmers. One at Hans Stainbach's place, then we'll circle back to Squire MacLoughlan's farm. Plenty farmers will be there, so you can put the fear of God into 'em—into O'Malley and his rumrunners, too, because——"

"Sotweed and cider!" broke in his father. "Looks like you are taking a heap on yourself, hey?" He stopped at Mr. Franklin's gesture.

"I think your plan excellent, Jamie." Mr. Franklin looked hopeful. "Say on, my boy!"

But Jamie cast a baleful eye on William Franklin, who had ridden in with his father and was now also a guest at Chestermere. It would appear that he had never had Jamie's approval, and Clytie could understand why. "Top-loftical old Hanoverian loyalist," he had told her with a grimace. But as far as she could make out, his opinion of William was not shared by the rest of the Chesters.

William was nearing thirty; he had seen military service, and held his compact figure as rigid as he appeared to hold his mind. Yet his manners were impeccable. The general effect he gave was of a handsome, superior piece of parlor decoration.

It was doubtless because of this aplomb that Jamie now made his point quite clear: William was not to attend them on their journey. "Farmers are shy of strangers," he put it, to which Mr. Franklin agreed with a droll but affectionate smile at his son.

"Then, too," Mr. Franklin said, "William has a bit of clerical work to get cleared up for me. This will give him the chance, meanwhile, to enjoy the charm of Chestermere."

The Chesters and William exchanged satisfied glances, so the plans were settled. "Everything *probatum est,*" Jamie said.

Early the next morning he and Mr. Franklin were off. Monica had had big baskets of food strapped to their pack mule, with blankets and whatnot, and Joe Toads was put in charge.

Clytie had found a chance to speak to the young Indian and ask if on his return he would pick up the doeskin dress she wished to send back to Omeme. She had despaired of having Adam return it. Joe's eyes held startled, though friendly, recognition, but she was glad to remember Jamie's assurance concerning his friend: "Indians don't talk of other people's affairs."

"I will meet you at Gabe MacLoughlan's place," the squire threw after the cavalcade as it moved down the drive. Both Jamie and Mr. Franklin waved back at him; one would have thought them off on a lark, rather than on an enterprise that would set an army moving.

Nothing could have been of more unexpected delight to Clytie than to have Monica's consent, two days later, to ride with Uncle Peter to hear Mr. Franklin speak at the MacLoughlan place. This was after Uncle Peter had volunteered the information that Adam was so busy training troops these days he had not been able to give him a receipt for money left at his office a week or so ago.

Monica had appeared to sound this out; her eyebrows lifted. But Uncle Peter had not noticed.

"Can reckon well enough that Adam won't be at his uncle's place to hear Ben speak," Uncle Peter said. "Lives at camp. I take it the MacLoughlans haven't seen him in a coon's age."

"*Money?*" Monica said; her voice lifted in startled resentment.

They were in the library, and Uncle Peter had resumed his reading of Mr. Franklin's *Pennsylvania Gazette.* He had not been in a very good humor this morning; he had been fuming over those twelve-pounder cannon the general planned to drag over the mountains "like the Alleghenies were a bunch of molehills." And it was not like Monica to question him further at this moment, although Clytie suspected her of still smarting over Adam's success as a dinner guest.

"Why should Adam Appleton give you money?" Monica pursued.

"Hey?" He put down his paper impatiently. "Left it as first payment for the Jersey bull and heifer the *Queen* is bringing over for him."

"Then you must return it to him at once, Squire. It will serve to cancel our obligation to him for bringing Clytie to us in safety."

It was the first time Clytie had ever seen Uncle Peter angry. His sullen eyes followed Monica's movements about the room. "Clytie?" he questioned sharply. Then, perhaps because of Clytie's own frightened look, he began to chuckle as if all had become clear. He winked at her.

"I see what you mean, Mony," he said. "Been figurin' along those lines myself. But it won't be money I'll offer the lad—it will be the jog I give Governor Sharpe for that couple of hundred acres of rich bottom land I have in mind for the lad and which Sharpe promised. Adam's a born planter. Will be a credit to this colony, time all this trouble with the French settles down."

Clytie wanted to hug him.

Then, before Monica could comment, he questioned with a decisive change of subject as he picked up his *Gazette,* "What do you think Braddock calls our colonial troopers? *Bobtails.* Calls 'em bobtails." He growled.

But a few hours later Clytie could have wept for him, he was so upset over a matter that concerned his beloved friend Mr. Franklin.

Just before dinner she came downstairs and found Monica, Uncle Peter and William Franklin in the parlor. She had put on her pink chambray, as Monica suggested, and was carrying her pink bonnet, for she and Uncle Peter were to set out for the MacLoughlans' as soon as dinner was over.

William bobbed up from his chair when she went in; when she was seated he continued with the subject that she could see was distressing Uncle Peter.

"And so you see, Squire Chester," William said, "that I have had enough of seeing my father barter away the savings of a lifetime on this venture." William pounded one of his stout thighs and rubbed a restless hand along it.

"But Braddock gave Ben eight hundred pounds, hey?" Uncle Peter challenged him in a disturbed voice.

"A drop in the bucket, sir." William's smile was unpleasant. "The truth is that my father has taken upon himself full responsibility for the rent and hire of every wagon, horse and driver so far acquired. And which to date pledges him to the extent of almost twenty thousand pounds, for which he has given his bond."

"Heaven help us!" Uncle Peter's voice was hollow with desolation. Monica looked at him anxiously. Then he said with vigor, "Money to cover all that cost has been pledged by the different colonies, all but Penn Colony——"

"None of which is forthcoming, sir," added William. "Hence these *so-patriotic* farmers, knowing my father had money of his own, demanded——"

"The money will be collected and repaid, William," Monica soothed, but the squire rose angrily to his feet.

"Monies appropriated by the colonial assemblies may not be collectible by General Shirley. The brunt is on him as resident head of the king's forces." He emptied his pipe in a receptacle with a forceful gesture, and William looked at him, alarmed and apprehensive.

"General Shirley was to appoint a paymaster, sir," he said.

"But who *is* this paymaster? Does anyone know? And where is Shirley? Anywhere on the high seas from Nova Scotia to Carolina." The squire walked the floor. "Anywhere on land from the coast to the lakes. Meanwhile, Braddock marches, and all Ben Franklin has in the world goes with him. Like him—like Ben Franklin—pledging his all for the colonies, knowing the matter could not wait."

William's mannerliness did not cover his outrage over his father's patriotism and generosity. But it was the anxiety of the squire and Monica's unease that aroused Clytie's rebelliousness; she wanted to cry out against such disloyalty toward Mr. Franklin's judgment. *He* believed in the success of the expedition to the forts; why should anyone else doubt it? The haunted look on Monica's face checked the avowal of her own confidence which Clytie would have made.

They were nearing the MacLoughlan home when Uncle Peter told Clytie not to be disturbed by the rugged aspect of some of the farmers: "Good men, all of them, except the rumrunners—a nefarious set of men engaged in the rottenest trade in the colonies, selling rum to the Indians. Robbing them. Taking their pelf and hides for rum that makes thieves and criminals of them, and that the poor red devils would sell their own hides for." He spoke with deep resentment, but cheered up when he told her of the MacLoughlan family. "There's a girl, Sally, near your own age, I reckon. Meg is a mite younger. Pat is as smart a lad of nine you'd ever meet, and Rhoda, their mother, is a fine woman."

They had reached the high picket fence that enclosed the rugged ground in the midst of which nestled the MacLoughlan log cottage. Clytie was dismounting on the upping block when a boy and a barking dog raced toward the gate.

"Ma! Pa!" he called over his shoulder. "It's Squire Chester!"

From the door of the house a stocky little girl leaped out, her skirts billowing as she ran, crying, " 'Tis Clytie DeLancey come wi' the squire! 'Tis Clytie!"

An older girl, whom Clytie thought must be Sally, followed more demurely with a cherry-faced woman from the house. A tall, spare-framed, eagle-beaked man with smiling eyes came from the garden, and soon the whole welcoming MacLoughlan clan was upon them, with such an uninhibited and voiceful welcome as Clytie had never received before.

"Oh, ye be like a picture in a book!" chirruped Meggie as her mother tried to restrain her.

But Meggie grabbed Clytie's hand and led her up the walk, her blue eyes dancing in her little freckled face. Pat, with his barking dog, skipped beside her.

"Ye rode through the wilderness wi' our cousin Adam," Meggie said to Clytie, "an' wi' a document bearing the king's seal. The bravest o' the brave!"

Clytie choked at this. The countryside had indeed heard of her, so *Pete* was not so guilty as she had thought.

The voices prattled with delight until the craggy man, following them to the door with Uncle Peter, said, "Dinna let my brood raddle ye, ma'am. But wild-wilderness growth they be."

He and Uncle Peter went off toward the barns, and Pat shouted after them, "The farmers be comin' soon, and Mr. Franklin and Jamie!" He followed Clytie into the house.

Rhoda, their broad-bosomed, sweet-faced mother, was quietly making her welcome, but the fair-haired, elder girl admonished her younger sister: "Ye be no' mannerly to call Mistress DeLancey 'Clytie'!"

"Ha' off your bonnet, *Clytie,*" said Meg defiantly.

Clytie, smiling, untied the strings and gave her bonnet to the younger girl.

"Her hair be like gold autumn leaves, Ma," Meg exulted. She popped the bonnet on her own head and ran to preen before a small mirror, which was fastened on the log-and-plaster wall.

"Take it off at once, ye little dunce!" Sally admonished her.

"Now, girls, girls!" said their mother with mild reproof. "Be seated, Mistress DeLancey, an' we'll ha' ye a cup o' tea in no time." She busied herself in front of the big fireplace, where a steaming kettle hung from a crane.

Clytie was enjoying the novelty of her reception and the spontaneity of their delight. But now Pat, planting himself sturdily before her, demanded, "Since ye come through the wilderness so brave, Mistress, can ye wring a chicken's neck, skin a rabbit, or stick a pig and cut him—?"

"Pat!" With a shout, Meg grabbed him and wheeled him around. "Dinna ye say such things!" Clytie's bonnet fell to the floor in the skirmish as Pat headed for the door.

Clytie yielded to laughter, in which their mother joined with shaking head. "Likely 'tis the springtime," she said with droll humor. " 'Twould be as easy to restrain the birds and blossoms. Meg, fetch the honey cakes."

Both the tea and cakes were delicious, and as Clytie enjoyed hers Meg sat at her feet, gulping tea and gazing rapturously at the visitor. Sally sat more demurely in a chair. But from their casual deportment Clytie was certain that among the MacLoughlans there was no thought of her class being superior to theirs. Then why *Adam's* determined attitude? Had his association with the Washingtons taught him ideas of class, while robbing him of his Scotch accent?

Rhoda was inquiring as to how Clytie was enjoying her visit to Maryland, when Pat stuck his head into the doorway to yip, "Squire Abe Wilson be ridin' in wi' two other farmers." Whereupon Meg giggled and Sally blushed.

"Squire Wilson be sparking Sally, but she will no' bundle wi' him," said Meg.

"Mannerless little magpie!" cried the sylphlike, bright-haired Sally as she put down her tea and got up. "Excuse me, Mistress DeLancey." She made a well-poised flight toward a door that appeared to lead into another room.

The cabin had a warmth, orderliness and charm. A big bed was in one corner, a trundle bed beneath. Animal skins hung on the walls, brass and pewter gleamed about the room, and there was a shelf with books; it was a homey room.

Mrs. MacLoughlan tut-tutted at Meg, but Meg said, "She dinna deserve so fine a man—she that will no' bundle wi' him." But she lifted her eyes to Clytie and inquired eagerly, "Ha' ye bundled wi' a suitor that comes asparkin', Clytie?"

Clytie looked at her in bewilderment, and Rhoda reproved, "Nay, Meggie, such 'tis said be no' practiced in New York town."

"What—what is it you bundle?" Clytie asked.

"*Yourself* in bed wi' a suitor on a cold Sabbath evening after supper," Meg delivered.

It came so glibly, Clytie's face grew hot. She could see her mother's icy stare from across miles of ocean that a maid in bed with a man should be openly spoken of. Yet to blot this out came the memory of Adam's arms about her in the Indian hut.

"Ha' ye ne'er bundled?" Meg persisted, to Clytie's confusion.

"But I . . . Yes—no . . . I don't know. . . ."

"It be an honorable custom," Rhoda said, to cover Clytie's bewilderment. "One long practiced by our Scotch and Welsh ancestors. And a goodly one in a new country, so say Mr. Franklin and Preacher Whipple."

"O-oh," breathed Clytie. So that was what she and Adam had done in the forest and in the Indian hut. Then if she should answer Meg's question truly . . .

"In Philadelphia town it be said lassies bundle in their nightgowns, but wi' a knot tied about their feet," said Meg, who could be no more than fourteen, with a giggle.

"Shame to ye, Meggie!" Rhoda reproved. "She be no' old enough to bundle herself, Mistress. Besides, bundling be no' matter of sliding knots—it gi'e place to marriage, the knot that canna slide."

"Marriage?" Clytie's hopes leaped; she had to ask, "If rolled, each in blankets, you sleep near by. Is that—is that to bundle?"

She thought Rhoda smiled, but before she could be answered, Meg leaped to her feet with a shout: "Adam!" She projected herself toward the doorway.

"Body would think Mistress DeLancey be a stranger to ye, Adam," Rhoda said in her soft English-Scotch accent as she poured his tea.

"He didna see her in so beautiful a dress in their ride through the wilderness," defended Meg.

Adam took his tea, but his big hands trembled slightly. This time he had been the one to be startled into speechlessness, Clytie observed, even as her heart drummed that he was here.

"I saw Squire Chester," said Adam, "but he did not tell me . . . No, no—" he resisted their urgings that he sit down—"I learned that the rum-runners would be here, and feared Uncle Gabe might find trouble on his hands, so I rode out . . ."

Meg, who had shoved a chair behind him, pulled at his coat, and he sat, though unwillingly.

Meg giggled, then said, "Ye see, Clytie, he be that stubborn he has to be tricked. And we love him so!" She kissed his cheek.

"But not too stubborn to forgive *your* tricks, Meg," Clytie said quickly. "Harmless tricks, not intended to be hurtful." So much appeal had crept into her voice that Meg looked baffled.

"Intentions can be far outweighed by facts, Mistress DeLancey," Adam said; his eyes were on his teacup as he placed it on the table. "Facts that no man can change, however wishful his thinking." His brief smile at her was bitter. He started to the door, but Meg yanked at him.

"Dinna go. Mr. Franklin ha' no' rid in." She squealed as he tweaked her ear playfully. "We be talking o' bundling," she said, to intrigue him. "Clytie ha' no' heard o' such, but she ha' slept wi' a man bundled in blankets——"

"Meggie!" Rhoda reproved her sharply.

"But if it gi'e place to marriage——" Meg quoted with an impish grin, to be cut off by Adam's harsh laughter.

"Blankets, bundled, *marriage?*" His laughter increased in volume and bitterness. "I fear, my Meg, that Mistress DeLancey's imagination is as lively as that in your book *Gulliver's Travels.*" He strode out the door.

Meg stared after him, open-mouthed. But Clytie was conscious that Rhoda's eyes had shifted understandingly between her and Adam, and when she dropped her head the older woman said gently, "A fresh cup of hot tea, dear?"

CHAPTER Eighteen

THERE were twenty or more farmers gathered on the MacLoughlans' sloping lawn, at the highest point of which Mr. Franklin stood prepared to speak. Another group of six men stood apart, with a sneering, defiant attitude toward the others.

"It be John O'Malley and his gang," whispered Meg. "John be the big one—a wicked, ungodly man."

Clytie had come outside the house with the two girls, but Rhoda was not permitting them to go far from the doorway. The aspect of the man Meg spoke of was indeed frightening; with his unkempt red hair and bushy whiskers, he looked like a carnivore searching for prey.

Yet as Jamie came across the scrubby lawn he hailed the man with a grin: "How, John!" But that was Jamie, Clytie thought tenderly, no one could hate him. He went toward Adam, his father, Mr. Franklin and Mr. MacLoughlan.

"John and his fellows be jail rats brought over from the old country," whispered Meg again. "They be rumsellers."

So these were the ones Adam had feared would make trouble. Clytie was reminded of a letter published in Mr. Franklin's *Gazette* that had made her father laugh heartily. It had been addressed to the proprietaries responsible for bringing such prisoners to the colonies, and in it he had reminded his readers of the hordes of rattlesnakes native to America, with the suggestion that, since these snakes too were felons, they should be transported to the pleasure parks of London in repayment for the jailbirds.

"My fellow patriots," boomed Gabe MacLoughlan's big voice, "ye be welcome here today that our postal commissioner may set forth to ye, strong and true, the need of the king's soldiers for——"

"Soldiers need help, hey?" came O'Malley's hectoring voice. "Fancy beggars, come no' to fight, but to rob."

"Quiet!" yelled a score of farmers. But the O'Malley group shouted in answer: "Liberty we want i' this country! Liberty! Freedom!"

Adam Appleton made a movement toward the noisy group, but

stopped as Mr. Franklin put up his hand; the very dignity and authority behind the gesture overrode the threatened turmoil.

"Liberty and freedom are magnificent words, my friends," he said, then in the subsequent quiet he lowered his voice, "but they are words that can be easily misunderstood, and selfishly and unworthily applied. Liberty and freedom for this vast continent can come only from the way we make use of the freedoms accorded us today."

"Freedom to be robbed, hey?" bellowed one of the O'Malley gang.

"Say rather, freedom to possess. Freedom to hold your possessions. But this you may do only until the French and their savages break through our narrow line of forts." His voice grew in timbre: "The French covet our whole country, and are resolved to possess it. They will work through spies, and with hatchet and torch toward that end. Therefore, the king's soldiers must be equipped with supply wagons so that they may march for defense of our forts, now held by inadequate numbers of brave and loyal men. For it is only by the strength of our forts that the enemy may be held back, an enemy now gathered on our lakes and rivers. And they are prepared to press *down* these rivers, my friends, to butcher and slaughter." His voice rested for a moment, but there was only a restless stirring from the O'Malley group.

"From Erie they will push down the Allegheny and the Ohio. *Down*, my friends. Always they may push downward with the currents, while we may not ascend the rivers *against* the currents. That is why we must look to our forts along these rivers for protection—forts rightly manned to hold this savage enemy in check. The king's soldiers must reach the forts, and we must do our part to get them there." The bleak faces of the farmers reflected the earnestness of his words; the grim O'Malley men remained quiet.

"Don't think, my countrymen," Mr. Franklin continued in a softer tone, "that I do not know what most of you, and your fathers, have endured for the freedoms we cherish. Even as you sat down to your daily meals there was the hovering fear of the arrow and torch of the unseen foe. Each night's sleep bore its dread of slaughter, and the howl of your dogs caused your mother to grab her youngest to her breast, that a baby's brains might not be dashed out by a merciless, savage raider." He paused to resume with hard emphasis: "This must not happen here again. But it is already happening on our northwestern borders. And because of this, because of your children, your homes and the land you love, I am here to ask your support for the expedition of your king's soldiers to defend your forts." His eyes scanned their faces in solemn silence.

The farmers shuffled their feet, pulled at the hats in their hands, lifted their heads and fingered ragged coats; they knew what was expected of them, and a look of difficult sacrifice was in their faces: their fields must go unplowed, their families go hungry.

Then came the raucous voice of John O'Malley: "Our horses and wagons wi' a musket at our heads, that hit?"

"Let 'em try!" bellowed one of his fellows. "No king's troopers gits my horses fer——"

"Rumseller!" bellowed back an angry farmer; his accusation was upheld by other lusty shouts.

And then it happened: The long-smoldering hatred of the honest farmers against John O'Malley and his evildoers broke forth; the solid ranks of the farmers advanced. The culprits cursed, drawing their knives against the unarmed farmers.

Not even Mr. Franklin's exhortations could allay the bedlam of shouts and fights. Cut off from the doorway, Rhoda was huddling the girls close to the house. Clytie tried to smother her cry of Adam's name.

He leaped into the fight and tried to wrest the knife from O'Malley, who struggled and writhed. The farmers disarmed the others of the gang, but the bull-like O'Malley was standing up against Adam's wiry strength, the knife high held as Adam twisted. Clytie saw the knife fall, saw Adam stagger from a blow, leap again, then the two were down, rolling, fighting.

It might have been a minute or a year of terror before she heard laughter from the farmers. There were scorn and derision in their shouts: "Ye heft be rum-soaked, O'Malley!"

Clytie, with Meg behind her, pushed through the crowd and saw Adam standing over the fallen man.

"Git off my place, ye louts," bellowed Gabe MacLoughlan.

The other rumsellers were already heading toward the gate where their horses or mules were hitched, and with muttered threats and curses O'Malley was up and following.

"Came but to make trouble. Had your fill?" the others shouted after him.

Then amid the laughter rose Clytie's shrill cry: "Bob! Bob!" She raced toward the gate. The shouts that came after her were confused; she heard Jamie's outcry, and Adam's "Get off that horse, you thief!" as he sprang past her.

Jamie reached for Bob's bridle at the same moment Adam grabbed at the man in the saddle. She called, "Good Bob! Quiet boy!" In a trice the would-be horse thief was picking himself up from the dust. He reached his mule and rode off down the lane behind his fellows.

Meg and Pat, with excited chatter, had raced through the gate to claim Jamie, and Adam was hitching Bob to the post. Clytie stood alone beside him.

"Oh, thank you, Adam!" she said devoutly as she caressed Bob's neck.

"Would have been a pity to lose so trusted a friend, ma'am." For a brief moment the real Adam smiled at her, but then he caught himself.

His voice chilled her, yet she pleaded, "Oh, please, Adam, nothing has really changed. Does a *name* matter so much to you?" And when he did not speak, but only stared grimly into the distance, she said, "It would be mortal generous of you to forgive and forget everything, and let us start all over again."

"Depends on what you mean by *everything*, Mistress DeLancey." His lips twisted into a hard smile. "All water under the bridge, hey?"

"Oh, no, just another start—a different . . ." She felt so taut, so helpless; the right words would not come. She turned from him, fearful of the tightening in her throat as she remembered all their blessed moments.

"Different!" He seemed to seize the word and twist it into embittered, distorted shapes. "It's not hard to calculate how different matters now stand between us, Mistress DeLancey."

"Not hard for such stubborn *pride* as yours." Clytie wheeled on him, her own pride and anger flaring beyond control at the hard tenor of his voice. "Yet in your heart you know that nothing ever will be different between you and me, nothing but your own false values."

He looked startled, but answered sharply, "My values are my own."

"And 'valueless' I believe I heard you say. Then keep them, Captain Appleton. I have better ones to serve me." Dimly she heard Pat calling Adam, so she turned from his granite eyes. The boy was standing beside them. She hurried through the gate.

She had surrendered to unworthy pride and anger. Her spirit battered in pain against the barriers she had only strengthened between them.

Adam had ridden away with the farmers. Inside the cottage Mr. Franklin sipped his tea, cheered by its warmth and stimulation. After the farmers had left, he had appeared crumpled and weary. They had pledged to him every horse and wagon among them, and yet it appeared the quota promised General Braddock was not filled.

"Mr. Franklin, sir," Jamie began as he put down his tea. Meg and

Pat ceased their whispers to him. "We are to date six wagons and twelve horses short."

Mr. Franklin sighed and eyed Jamie with a wan smile. "So it would appear that you and I must make further pilgrimage, eh?" he said.

"Pardon, sir, but it would profit nothing unless we traveled far east. But this O'Malley and his gang have the horses and——"

"Six good wagons," put in Gabe MacLoughlan. "Yet none but king's soldiers be like to collect 'em, Jamie."

"Just what must not happen, sir. I mean, that's what Mr. Franklin wants to avoid. But for the honor of Frederick County we've got to get those wagons."

"Right, Jamie! Right!" yelped Pat and Meg.

The others in the room looked startled. Mr. Franklin smiled, and Jamie went on: "Point is, there's a way to do it, sir, if you——"

"Wi' your friction machine," said Pat, who could restrain himself no longer. He squared himself boldly in front of Mr. Franklin. "Did ye fetch it to Chestermere? It be said ye brought it." His eyes danced.

"He brought it, Pat," answered Squire Chester, with a wink at the surprised Mr. Franklin.

"Then if it be true that in a thunder gust ye brought down lightning to kill a turkey cock," Pat exulted, "ye can—"

"—kill off the rumsellers," finished Uncle Peter with a loud chuckle. The philosopher-scientist smiled; laughter filled the room, and Clytie joined in, a delighted spectator.

"Now, look, everybody," Jamie said, "this is not as cockhoot as it sounds. It was Pat's idea, and a good one. For with your friction machine, sir, we can put the fear of God into those rumsellers, as not all the king's soldiers could do. First of all, they could not catch them—too many wilderness hiding places." He appealed to Mr. Franklin: "And since you did bring your machine, hoping for a little leisure to experiment before the army moves, why not experiment on the O'Malley gang?"

Pat and Meg made such eager noises that Mr. Franklin said, "Be careful not to ally me with the Almighty, my young friends."

"But if you have shocked groups of men, sir," Jamie went on, "even shocked yourself once into insensibility . . ."

"You would like me to shock O'Malley into *sensibility*, eh?" Mr. Franklin's eyes twinkled, and he permitted Rhoda to refill his cup with steaming tea.

"Right, sir," said Jamie, and his cohorts shook their heads in agreement.

"Ye'll ha' to catch 'em first, Jamie," Gabe MacLoughlan said.

"With *honey!*" exclaimed Abe Wilson.

This came so unexpectedly and with such fervor that Clytie joined in the hearty laughter. Abe's attention had been lingering hungrily on the honey-colored hair of the lovely Sally; the trend of his thoughts was understandable. He was a slender, sweet-faced boy, blushing now to the roots of his blond hair.

"Wi' honey would be a wondrous way to catch John O'Malley," Meg defied them in her sturdy way, her indignation directed at Sally's giggles. "Long ha' he wanted a crock o' Squire Wilson's honey, but no' willing to pay the price."

"Good, sound idea, bee farmer." Squire Chester applauded.

Within another moment the whole company had gone into a huddle over a plot, with Jamie sifting each idea for what it was worth. In brief, it came to this: Abe would collect the gang at his farm on the pretext of presenting to each a pot of honey, to make customers of them. Whereupon, Pete, Adam and some troopers would appear under the guise of collecting victuals for the army. They would relate to the rumsellers the magic of Mr. Franklin's machine, which could knock them all off their feet at the same moment, and so engender bets as to whether or not it could be done.

"They will swallow nothing so quickly as the chance of winning a good bet," Jamie said. "And Adam, Pete and Abe will make bets to goggle their eyes!"

The farmers were to bring their wagons and teams to Chestermere, where the experiment would be made.

"But when they lose, what if they still refuse to give up their wagons and horses?" Jamie anxiously asked Mr. Franklin, but it was his father who answered.

"Have troopers there to drive the wagons straight to Braddock's camp," Squire Chester suggested. "Once there, no law nor curses can pry them loose." He shook with laughter.

Everyone glowed but Pat, who said solemnly to Mr. Franklin, "*Can* ye knock 'em flat, sir?"

Mr. Franklin gave him a wry smile. "I had not thought of employing science to support wagers, Pat. But since these trying moments of our history seem so largely a matter of risk and wager–" he paused to look about at the eager faces–"yes. If to knock a man down, Pat, is to make him stand up for his country, we will attempt to serve this plan you have worked out and thus bestir these men to their duty."

CHAPTER *Nineteen*

THE next day was Sunday. Pete returned exultant from the rendezvous he and Adam and Abe Wilson had had with the O'Malley gang.

"All six of them," he explained, "fell for our bets of land and cattle against Mr. Franklin's being able to bring lightning down from the skies to knock them flat, gay as peckerwoods sharpening their bills."

But that was before Mr. Franklin announced that not he but *Jamie* was to perform the experiment, because his own presence was requested at a conference with governors Sharpe and Dinwiddie at the hour set for the show, late Monday afternoon. Both Pete and his father looked gloomy for a bit over this turn of affairs; it appeared to give the rum-runners a chance to win their bets. Yet as the afternoon wore on, and Mr. Franklin and the delighted Jamie remained closeted in the squire's office, where the friction machine was kept, the atmosphere of Chestermere mysteriously brightened. And when later that evening Clytie saw Pete, Adam and Abe Wilson crossing the garden, heading for the office, she felt a happy anticipation: perhaps when they came to the house she would be given a chance to tell Adam she was sorry she lost her temper at the MacLoughlans'.

For she was sorry and humiliated; it was just not the sensible way to approach Adam's festering pride. Her grandfather had warned her so often that to lose her temper was to lose her every advantage. In her heart she knew she had not been so angry at Adam as at her own inability to say and do the helpful thing.

But neither Adam nor Pete came near the house before they rode back to camp, and the mystery of all that had happened in the office was only deepened by Jamie's abstracted air at breakfast the next morning. At Monica's unease, that things might not go off as planned, Mr. Franklin assured her he had often taught others to use the friction machine and none had proved so apt as Jamie in mastering, not only its mechanics, but the fundamental principles involved as well—insofar as he himself understood the nature of electricity.

"A principle to change all industry, all life," his infatuated pupil said enthusiastically, "and bloodlessly."

But Mr. Franklin cautioned him, saying, "Don't go too fast, my young friend. Such discoveries come slowly, are perfected more slowly still."

Now ten o'clock had come and a gloomy gray sky still hung over the valley, which caused Clytie to doubt Jamie's success with the experiment. Only fair weather could bring the right results with the machine, Mr. Franklin had said, yet Jamie, unmindful, was still locked in the office with it, denying admittance to everyone.

Clytie was depressed, too, because she had just said good-by to Bob. He was to be taken to Braddock's camp, along with Uncle Peter's two wagons and all his horses except old Molly, his riding mare, who was too old. Monica had been annoyed that Clytie should give Bob up, and even Jason had protested on their way back from a ride yesterday afternoon.

"He is a New York horse," Jason had said, "and subject only to your father's jurisdiction."

He understood how much she loved Bob, yet since he was the only contribution she could make toward the success of the expedition that would so soon take Adam away, she would not be diverted from her sacrifice. It had been hard to give him his last lump of sugar this morning; she had not been ashamed of the tears she had shed upon his soft muzzle. He had been a part of her dearest happiness, and it was like surrendering a precious slice of it to see him go. "Carry a brave soldier to victory," she had whispered, yet resentment had mounted that these dear friends of man should be sacrificed to war.

"Do you think it is going to clear, Uncle Peter?" Clytie asked, coming upon him and Monica on the portico.

"Sun'll break through by dinnertime," he told her cheerfully. "You'll see! Five o'clock's the time set for the show, hey?"

Monica said that it was, and hoped that when he rode into town, after waiting for old Molly to be shod, he would make no mention of the experiment to anyone. "Mr. Franklin would not like it to be made into a sensation," she added. There was suspicion in her voice concerning the whole enterprise—mainly, Clytie thought, because Uncle Peter had insisted that the whole MacLoughlan family be invited to supper.

Uncle Peter promised as much, but voiced his own gloomy thoughts at the mention of Mr. Franklin. "A scientist!" he said growlingly. "Maybe if Ben wasn't so good a scientist he'd be a more practical man."

"But you have always said there was no more practical a man," Monica said, amazed.

"Well, I was wrong," he admitted. "What practical man puts himself in a position to be beggared?" He humped lower into his chair. "Came near telling Braddock yesterday when he asked me for a donation of tobacco . . . glad to let him have it. But what I wanted to say was 'Always heard an army travels on its stomach, but my word, sir, your army will be traveling on Ben Franklin's stomach!' . . . Moses!" he bellowed angrily, "they going to take all day to shoe Molly?"

"Ain't no use gittin' yo'se'f into no lather, Colonel," called Moses from where he was clipping a boxwood. "De day be young." Since their Indian-fighting days together, the master had remained 'the colonel' to Moses.

"For all that," said Uncle Peter, turning back to Monica, "what Ben Franklin has done is already having effect on our young folks. Heard Pete and the Johnson boys talking about the dirty practices of the proprietaries, but when talk of payment for the wagons here and all those at Will's Creek came up, one of 'em said, 'Mr. Franklin is *nationly*. Few more such patriots and we'd *be* a nation.'" He chuckled. "Looks like the older lads find as much to argue about as Jamie and his students, times being what they are. But one thing they agree about, that we are lucky to have British laws, institutions and the Magna Charta, instead of the rotten tyranny of the French Bourbons."

Uncle Peter seemed to be relieving his mind by these pronouncements. He got up from his chair, flexed his stout legs, and as he turned toward the steps the boards of the portico groaned. He was not paunchy—just bone, gristle, meat and man. Clytie, seated on the porch rail, smiled at him as he turned back to deliver: "In this skirmish it's a good time for us all to remember that old England, whatever her present faults, has had the grit to hold on to these colonies she planted here for nearly two hundred years, and we owe a heap to her early settlers, who suffered that *we* might be here. We can prove our worthiness by defying French prostitution of all that's decent, in spite of the fool bungling of parliament." He mounted his horse, which Solomon had just brought, and his polemics faded away.

Jamie was going to perform the miracle in the rear garden. "Soft turf," he told Clytie. "Although it would serve those devils right to bust their heads on rocks. Give me a chance to sew 'em up, sew up a couple of cockleburs inside O'Malley's head."

The MacLoughlans had arrived and had been served tea. The tension and excitement mounted concerning the success of the experiment. As the hour drew near they gathered in the garden. Meg and Pat were in a tizzy, and Pat was racing back and forth to report what was happening in the barn.

"Pete, Adam, Abe and hunks o' troopers ha' come," he told them, "so's when the bets are won the troopers can drive the wagons and teams o' the rummers lickerty-split for Braddock's camp." He did a somersault for joy.

But no such confidence seemed to exist among his elders; they sat speechless under the big maple tree near the dining-room door. The O'Malley gang had not arrived, and it could be they had decided against risking their teams. The weather, however, was doing its part; it was still and balmy—hushed and brooding, Clytie told herself, as if nature took a dim view of this new science which was to be exploited.

Her grandfather had had great faith in "the science of tomorrow." One day on the way up to his farm, when her youngest brother, Steven, had complained of the slowness of the wagon, her grandfather had said: "Before the day be done, sonny, ye may travel swiftly over land and sea by the power of *steam.* Steam travel, when science be given a chance." Yet Jamie had no steam, she thought nervously, to aid his experiment; he must draw down lightning from the heavens where there was no lightning.

"They be comin'—be comin'!" Pat shouted as a rumble of wagons was heard on the lane that led from the highroad to the barns. He headed for the compound but turned back quickly when a small squad of soldiers from Pete's company came through the wicker gate.

The squire got up to receive them, and advised that they stand near a stout table which had been placed to hold the apparatus of the friction machine. The slope of the green lawn was terraced into a foot-drop midway between the house and gate, and above this drop the table stood. Another table was placed near by for William Franklin, who came from the house carrying his ledger. He looked discomforted, as though he were aiding and abetting a distasteful crime. But a procession from the direction of the office distracted attention from his martyrdom.

Jamie, Solomon, Moses and Jake were each carrying some piece of equipment, as for a holy oracle. At Jamie's solemn direction these were placed on the table, while he placed there, amid an awed and reverent silence, something covered with a white cloth.

"Keep back everybody," he ordered. Then he directed that the soldiers stand three at either end of the oblong table.

Clytie, ten feet away, gazed at these instruments of magic. There were two large glass jars, coated part way up with tinfoil, into which Jamie was pouring spring water. He stopped when they were two-thirds full. She had often heard of the Leyden Jar, and wondered if these were such. There were a glass tube, and a rod of some kind, and something else under the white cover. The friction machine? She dare not ask. It would be too much like inquiring of a stringy young jinni how he had emerged from one of the vessels. Jamie with his absorbed, impressive manner appeared just that, as if he must be wary of the moment when he would again disappear within. He wore no coat, his waistcoat, stockings and neckerchief were awry, and his red hair, free of its ribbon, hung about his neck—he was the very picture of some ancient necromancer arranging the apparatus of his wizardry. As the raucous laughter of the rumsellers was heard approaching, he whispered something to William at the other table.

Pete, Adam and Abe came through the gate with the six nefarious O'Malley men, jesting in friendly fashion. And the six were of such brawny, wiry strength that Clytie experienced a moment of breathless fear as to the success of the experiment. Monica, who stood near her, registered the same fear. Not only did they fear for the land and cattle Jamie might lose, but they also feared that his failure might discredit Mr. Franklin's reputation as a scientist.

These six gangling giants to be felled simultaneously! That was the bargain. No wonder the giants grinned.

Clytie, her fear acute, sensed that she must have communicated it to Adam, for she caught his brief but somehow reassuring smile as he stationed the men just below Jamie's table.

"Glad to see you, boys!" Squire Chester was welcoming the grinning stalwarts. They were all neatly dressed, and their faces were shaven and their hair smoothed.

Monica, never lacking in hospitality, asked if they would like cake and ale before the experiment, at which each rumseller yanked off his bonnet and stuffed it into his pocket.

"No thankee, lady," O'Malley answered for the group. "Better we git what we come over fer."

"Messers O'Malley, Riker, Dunning, Skinner, Tennent and Waring," pronounced Jamie impressively, meeting in turn the eye of each, "we welcome you in the name of patriotism versus profits." His bow was formal. "This is Mr. William Franklin. He has something to say to you."

William got up from his table, his austere manner evincing the distaste he had for the whole business.

"My father," he said, "wished me to say that in the event Mr. Chester succeeds in felling you, and your wagons and teams become forfeit to General Braddock, you will receive the same wage and hire for your property as that pledged to all other such owners." He reseated himself, amid sibilant whispers among the rumsellers.

"Shut up, you!" O'Malley was threatening one of his fellows when Pete interrupted.

"First of all, O'Malley," Pete said, "we must have it clearly understood just what these wagers are." He took up some papers from William's table.

"Wagered good bottom land, he be," said a surly-voiced cohort, "but *me*—what be I wagered? A sow wi' six shoats." His scorn was directed at Jamie.

"Tut-tut, Mr. Skinner," Jamie reproved. "Such lack of farmer perspicacity all but suggests that farming is not your trade." He grinned at the man, whose mouth fell open. "Why, the swine themselves would decry such lack of appreciation of their biological perogatives." All the farmers were laughing now, at Mr. Skinner's expense, but Jamie reassured the angered one: "Within a year or so those seven shoats I wagered you will total fifty-seven."

Mr. Skinner was appeased, but another demanded, "What be I wagered?" His features had the menace of a hatchet.

"We will get to that, Tom Tennent," Pete said. "First, yours O'Malley. The exact limits of the land Squire Wilson wagers you are here set down. Will you read this and sign?"

O'Malley took the paper given him, scratched his head, but when a cohort tried to help him read it he shoved the fellow away with an angry scowl, stared for an instant into Pete's honest face, stalked impressively to William's table and signed with a flourish. And when the man next to him looked helplessly at his paper, O'Malley gave him a shove.

"Sign," he demanded. "A cross mark will do."

Mr. Riker made his cross mark. With the same authority, O'Malley saw that Mr. Skinner signed for Jamie's sow and shoats, and that Mr. Dunning made a cross mark for Adam's wagered heifer and bull due to arrive on the squire's *Queen*.

All Adam possesses in the world, Clytie thought, while she in her self-righteousness had once doubted his patriotism. She had learned that he did not even possess the horse he rode; it belonged to Colonel Washington. She watched with absorbed tenderness the strength of his bronzed profile, the breadth of his high forehead, and remembered with poignant emotion the soft texture of his hair. Oh, Adam, Adam! Not a gentleman born? Nonsense! He was fine-grained all through. Yet she doubted if he had ever known a day's leisure in all his life. Her heart beat fast for the success of the experiment—for his sake.

"Now then, for you, Tennent, and you, Waring, no wagers have so far been assembled." Pete looked toward his father.

"Make it good, Squire Chester." Tom Tennent leered. "A strong-bodied slave——"

"Silence!" Adam shouted thunderously, and with an authority that cut off the grins of the rumsellers. "Slaves are not for barter."

"Make it a hogshead of tobacco, son," Squire Chester said to Pete.

"N-a-r!" Tennent snarled.

"A barrel of good grape wine——" said the squire.

"Barrel o' good aged brandy did ye say?"

"Blast you! Speak respectfully to your betters," Adam threatened.

"And stop your foolin', Tennent," said John O'Malley. "Ye'll take what ye git! Hear me?"

"Go shed your hide! My wagon an' team be stouter 'n yourn, and——"

"Strike a blow, and all bets are off," Pete shouted as fists were raised. The troopers moved in closer.

"I'll pledge ye two hives of bees, Tom Tennent," Abe Wilson called out, sober-faced.

The tension broke. The rumsellers guffawed. Abe reddened, and Meg moved closer to him, her defiant eyes on those who baited him. The lovely Sally stood aloof, scornful.

"Take him up, Tom," one of his fellows said, laughing. "Ye got enemies, trade 'em the bees."

"Be gone wi' ye wagers!" The angry Tom Tennent started for the gate, but O'Malley grabbed him. "Why you sot-bellied rattler!" roared O'Malley. "The paper states the six o' us must stand together, or——"

"Four gold crowns I pledge you, Tom Tennent." Clytie made her voice loud to top the curses. Silence ensued.

"Taken!" Tom Tennent yelled. He regarded Clytie with porcine eyes, then lunged toward William's table. "Write it down. You heard her, write——"

"No, Clytie! No!" It came simultaneously from Pete and Uncle Peter, and was topped by Jamie's shout: "The bet is made. Let's get on with it, for pity's sake!" He looked anxiously toward the west, where the sun was sinking low; a dark cloud was on the horizon.

Clytie and the leering man signed the paper. She felt relieved that money had been acceptable; she had seen none used since her arrival at Chestermere.

But now the sixth man, for whom no bet had been found, was shouting at his fellows, "You hyeared me! It be nothin' I be askin'. I be *givin'* me wagon an' team to Ben Franklin, ye—ye lousy-livered swine!" He evaded the grabs made at him, and was shoved behind the soldiers' bayonets.

"Hurray for you, Waring!" Pete clapped him on the shoulder.

But he shoved Pete off. He was leaner than the others, and there was about his hickory-dried face a suggestion of decayed nobility.

"I been a skunk," Waring said. "But a body can git his belly too full o' stink. I be done wi' 'em!"

"You'll have to stand with the others for the experiment, Waring," Adam told him.

"Yes—yes, I'll fall wi' 'em. But I'm hanged if I'll stand . . ." He chortled at his fellows' angry faces.

Now that the bets were settled, the rest was up to Jamie.

"You see that these two jars contain but spring water not fully charged," Jamie was explaining.

"Wi' what?" one asked.

"With electricity," answered Jamie.

The men were goggle-eyed. It was clear that a sort of ague was attacking the group. The word meant nothing to them.

"You will not be hurt," Jamie went on. "It is possible you will not even feel the shock as you fall."

"If—*if* we fall." O'Malley's bravado was tremulous.

Jamie arranged the men in a semicircle, O'Malley at one end, Waring at the other.

"Now, each of you," he directed, "place your hand on the head of the man next you." Skinner's hand came down hard on Waring's head, and Jamie warned, "Take care that none presses too hard on the other's head—the result will but bring peril upon yourself. Now!" He stood off to regard the picture. "You must hold that position with each other without moving if our contract is to be fulfilled."

Too much was at stake for the men to disobey. Looks of suspense and fear were mingled on their faces. On those of the spectators, awe was mingled with hope . . . and fear.

"Take this in your hand, Waring. Hold it firmly." Jamie gave him a chain connected to the two jars. "Steady now," Jamie warned, "while I place this rod on O'Malley's head." And when O'Malley's eyes glinted as he looked at the long shiny rod, Jamie said, "I won't hurt you, John. I'll place it gently on your head, so . . ."

The rod touched O'Malley's head.

To Clytie and the astounded onlookers, what happened appeared as one movement: the contact of the rod and the crumpling of the men's bodies to the ground. They did not stagger or go down lengthwise; they folded, doubled up, as if their bodies had become strings. They lay there, huddled, scrambled. The spectators uttered muffled gasps; in the hush that followed the song of a thrush in a treetop seemed loud. Pat's shrill cry was the first outburst.

"D-dead! They be dead!" He cavorted with joy. "Hiyee! Dead an' dinna know it!" He pointed at O'Malley's popped and vacant eyes.

"Gi'e us a penny an' we'll close your eyes, O'Malley." Meg, too, howled at the scrambled men. "The devil's got ye!"

"Ye got wings, Tom Tennent! Git up an' fly to hell-fire!" cried the troopers, who had joined in the raucous outburst of joy. The house servants, who had been peeping through the hedge, approached the fallen ones, wide-eyed. Meanwhile, a shrill blast sounded from Pete's whistle; it was a signal for the troopers at the barn to seize the wagons and start for Braddock's camp. Jamie gave sharp orders to Jake and Solomon, who took the precious apparatus and carried it toward the office.

O'Malley groaned and sat up, wild-eyed. Then the others sat up, groaned, and rubbed their heads.

"That itch ye got is pinfeathers o' patriotism sproutin'," taunted Abe Wilson.

"Ye been twistin' the devil's tail too long, O'Malley. He's hit back," jibed Pat.

O'Malley staggered to his feet. His eyes glared like those of a wounded beast. "Who—who hit me?" he bellowed. "That—that brat o' Satan! Where be he?"

But neither Jamie nor his equipment were in sight. O'Malley came up against the troopers' bayonets.

"Nobody hit ye, ye copperhead," exulted Waring, who had refused to take a bet. "We all got felled, good and honest, like the bargain said, an' ye lost your wagons to the army."

The rumble of wagons being driven out onto the highroad was heard.

"Cheats! Robbers!" The rumsellers were on their feet now, adding their cries to O'Malley's: "Tricked us, by heaven! Tricked . . ."

The rumble of the wagons faded. With bellows and curses, the gang started toward the gate and the barn.

"Git! Git! Git!" shrieked Pat.

Clytie turned about and saw Uncle Peter and Gabe MacLoughlan holding their sides with laughter.

A supper of cold meats, buttered bread, cakes, pies, ale and milk had been served to everyone, in the garden, and their mood had been so gay that Jamie had brought two of the slaves up from the slave quarters with banjo and flute, and Pete and Mrs. MacLoughlan had led the company into a dance. The troopers had done some wonderful jigs, and everyone made merry—everyone but the trooper Pete had dispatched on horseback to follow the rumsellers.

Now the trooper was back, and they all gathered eagerly around to hear his report.

"They didn't know I was following, sir," he said to Pete. "They was runnin' so hard down the highroad, tryin' to catch up with their wagons an' cussin' so loud, they didn't look back. But they ain't got a chance to catch up with them wagons goin' lickety-split."

Waring, who had not followed his erstwhile comrades, and whom the squire had urged to stay to supper, laughed so loudly that everybody joined in. The trooper had followed all the way into Frederick and had watched them go into an alehouse.

"So I says to myself, sir," he went on, "reckon I'd better warn the constable, knowin' with liquor they'd maybe make trouble." So Constable Svarz had been watching and waiting when the gang began to fight among themselves. By that time they were so drunk and noisy that he arrested the lot, and locked them up for the night in jail.

"It may put an end to the dirtiest business in the country," Gabe MacLoughlan said, "selling rum to Indians."

He and the squire went into the house, followed by everyone except Pete, Adam and Clytie, who concerned themselves with seeing that the belated trooper was well fed. A short while later Clytie found herself, by chance, left alone with Adam.

"More lemonade?" she offered. He had been drinking only that, but he shook his head.

"Looks like rain," he said.

The valley was misty in the late-evening twilight, but Moses had hung up some lanterns, which gave an eerie light. When she began to talk about the magic of the experiment, as though no harsh words had ever passed between them, he sat down beside her on the seat that encircled the big elm. His mood was distant and formal, but she was determined not to be dominated by it.

"My grandfather believed in the possibilities of science," she said, chatting with less self-consciousness than she felt. "I wish he could have known our postal commissioner. He would have been so proud that Mr. Franklin has made the service pay. My father says no one else ever has, and become a great scientist as well."

"And a great pamphleteer." Adam seemed to catch her mood. "Poor Richard brings a heap of comfort to a lot of people. But that's not all. He teaches himself French, Italian, German, establishes a great university and a fire department, invents a stove to keep people warm. Holy saints!" He banged his fist on the garden seat. "If only we could learn the secret of his success!"

"He told Jamie that any man could achieve the desire of his heart by study, application and work," Clytie said quickly, stirred by this declaration of Adam's ambition. She then added gaily, "Jamie avows that Mr. Franklin will yet become the midwife of a new nation."

He turned to her, and in his transforming smile she glimpsed his desire again, and her pulse warmed, then chilled. He gained control of himself, and with a jerk of his shoulders turned away.

"Work, huh?" He addressed the deepening twilight. "Man can work his heart out—no answer in that. Takes genius, I reckon, to bring success."

"But, no, all genius is not success, nor is all success genius. At least that's what my grandfather used to say." She wanted so to say the right thing, to bring him out of this mood of depression and feeling of remoteness. "I am not sure what he thought success was. Something in a man's own heart—wisdom, maybe, or knowledge of himself. I only know he did not rate true success as wealth or power or . . . The motto on my grandfather's coat of arms is: 'Set bounds to your desires.' " She looked at him, hoping that she had cheered him, but his profile remained flinty. She suppressed her hurt, sensing quickly that he was tired, worn down. She had never seen the lines in his face so drawn. From his inner conflict, she told herself. She yearned to draw his head into her arms and comfort . . .

"Thanks for reminding me, Mistress DeLancey, that some men *don't* come by a coat of arms." Without turning to her, he clutched the edge of the bench on which they sat.

Clytie held tightly to herself, smarting from his unkind taunt. The tinkle of the harpsichord, mingled with song and laughter, came out to them through the parlor windows, clashing discordantly on the tension between them—the barrier that Adam was walling high.

"Doubtless Mr. Franklin had no coat of arms," she said quietly, "yet it did not interfere with his usefulness." If only she could breach that wall. . . .

" 'Experience keeps a dear school,' " he turned to her and quoted in a caustic voice, " 'but fools will learn in no other.' " He jerked away again, with sharp laughter. " 'Use no hurtful *deceit.*' But perhaps you don't hold with Poor Richard's maxims, Mistress DeLancey?" His smile was twisted and dour.

She met it, wide-eyed, hurt. His spirit must be sick.

"Oh, Adam, please." Her voice wavered with her appeal. "You can't believe that I intended to hurt——"

"*Facts* I believe. And that fools learn only when they can see those facts clearly." His words came quickly, as bullets meant to wound. "Facts that were made into a *game*—oh, a skillful, tricky little game! First in the wilderness, eh? Forcing me to search for a dispatch I was not likely to find. And all to break a man down, break his will power, then, well-broken, toss him into the fire——"

"A-Adam, stop!" Her voice trembled and seemed to stick in her throat.

But without a look at her, he went on, his great hands rubbing together, his eyes glinting in the faint light of the lanterns. "And at the Indian camp you watched him burn. Burns well, the nincompoop does, hey?" He jerked to his feet. "So with the guts torn out of me, and my scalp hung up to dry . . ." Both his body and voice were shaking as he walked away a few steps, then smashed his fist into his palm.

Clytie's breath was cut off by tears and anger; her heart and spirit were bruised by this distortion of the truth, the picture of her wanton guilt with which he tortured his mind. A nightingale sang away in the treetops, taunting their bitterness, and she heard her own voice, as from a distance.

"You are lying, Adam. Not to me, only to *yourself*. For *I* know you don't believe what you say." Her voice was steady, but when she got to her feet her knees trembled, and she dropped onto the seat again.

He swung around to face her. In the light from the windows it was not a face she had seen before—it was twisted into a mask of pain and anguished pride. She expected an outburst and was startled at the complete control of his voice.

"In which case, Mistress *DeLancey,* permit me, at least, to do your grandfather the honor of observing his motto 'Set bounds to your desires.' G-good night."

His voice wavered, but before Clytie was able to make a sound he was hurrying with long strides toward the garden gate. The night swallowed him. Clytie shivered. The tinkle of the harpsichord was mingled with the taunting sweetness of the nightingale.

CHAPTER *Twenty*

"THANK God, they are going to set out at last!" Uncle Peter said with a grim sigh of relief.

Word had just come that General Braddock and his troops, accompanied by the colonial contingent, were to march for the forts within five days. Clytie tried to concentrate on the reason for Uncle Peter's relief as the words "five days" made a threnody in her heart: at the end of five days Adam would be marching away. She had not seen him for almost two weeks, heart-hungry weeks.

"Whole county can breathe easier now," Uncle Peter continued.

She forced her thoughts to follow him: so many refugees from the northwest country had arrived in Frederick with tales of burnings and slaughterings that there was fear the enemy was even now encroaching southeastward. . . .

"Your uncle wants the whole countryside invited to the ball," said Monica; her mind was on that event, set for the night before the army left. "But we will have to draw the line somewhere."

She went toward the library, and Clytie followed. There were notes to be written to the county families.

"All the nice young people, of course," Monica went on, "and the general's subalterns. Sir Jason can notify the staff. . . . Is he coming to supper tonight?"

"N-no, not tonight, Aunt Mony." He had come so many nights, and the days had been filled with such gay events. . . .

"Anything wrong?" Monica turned from her desk in anxiety.

"No, I just wanted a little time to think. He asked me last night to be his wife." The time for confession had come; she could not put it off. But her heart was responding only to "five days." Five, and Adam gone.

"I am so glad, darling!" Monica's eyes shone. "Don't delay your answer too long. Oh, I know it has been a hasty courtship, but such an ardent one. And now with the time so short . . . Oh, how happy you will make your father, darling," she ended persuasively.

Clytie turned away, mute. Since that heartbreaking night when Adam —hurt, believing that she was no more than a Jezebel, a Delilah, out to ensnare and betray him—had flung himself away from her, it had often seemed that obedience to her father's wishes was the only reality, that the Adam she had known was but a figment of her dreams. Yet sometimes she could see the pattern of his self-torture so clearly before her that she felt she must do something, find some way to force her own truth on him. But no way had come. She had found no light to guide her.

"Surely Sir Jason has everything a young girl could desire," said Monica somewhat impatiently. "And such devotion as one rarely sees. There! I'll say no more." She got up from her desk. "If you don't feel like writing the notes——"

"I'll write them, Aunt Mony."

"Thank you, darling." Then she said, in a softer, more persuasive voice, "Happily, I know you to be one who will never discard her beloved father's judgments." She turned back from the door and said, "Don't let me forget that Jamie is to tell each of the young men to assist some young girl to arrive here on the night of the ball, and to tell Pete to have Captain Appleton bring that girl, Peggybelle Brawn, whom he is said to be courting." Monica hurried out.

Courting, Adam, Peggybelle Brawn? Clytie's breath came short, and the three ideas would not connect. Had there been a design in Monica's revelation? She could not tell, the words had so stunned her. Yet why not another girl for Adam? Clytie pulled off her hair ribbon and twisted it about her slender fingers, twisting incongruous thoughts into a pattern. Why not, indeed, when the whole countryside knew that she was being courted by Jason?

During those first days with Jason she had adopted a gay inconsequent manner, pleased with his stimulating companionship, but later she had been forced to employ every wile and art in order to postpone his declaration of love. She might as well have tried to postpone the moonrise. "I love you wholly," he had said last night, "with a love that has had no beginning, that just *is,* has been a part of me, I feel, since I was born."

Often, because of her response to his charm, she had tried to imagine how she would feel with his arms about her; yet she had not been prepared for her complete lack of response, except compassion.

"Don't answer me now, darling," he had urged, fearful of her refusal. "I will wait and pray that you may come to love me."

In the desperate hope of being able to fulfill her father's wishes she had offered him her lips; no magic had stimulated her. Her spirit had cowered. While when *Adam* was near exquisite vibrations had reached into her blood and bones, and ecstasy into her heart. With Jason the moon had but showered them with disdainful light; a night bird's call to its mate had been a discord.

And on Wednesday morning both he and Adam would leave for the forts. Perhaps if she could only see Adam again, she thought desperately, just once again see his transforming smile, he might reveal some light to guide her, some light in this fog and bewilderment.

No light had come for Clytie. It was Saturday morning, and as she and Jamie joggled along in the oxcart toward Frederick a ray of hope sparkled in her heart: she might see Adam today, just might. Last night Mr. Franklin had asked her and Jamie to assist William in assorting some stores for the general's subalterns that had been donated by the Pennsylvania assembly.

"When it was represented to me," Mr. Franklin had told them, "by Colonel Dunbar, who is in charge of the army's supplies, that in this 'dear country' the subalterns could ill-afford to lay in the stores necessary for so long a march through the wilderness, I undertook to make an appeal for such supplies."

Yet his brow had been knit in bewilderment, Clytie recalled, at the amazing items which he read off to them. But there had been no reproach toward William, who had selected the supplies, such supplies as might have been assembled for a tea party. Not even Jamie had quipped at William as they copied Mr. Franklin's list. Their duty now in Frederick was to assort the supplies and pack one of each item in individual sacks for the twenty subalterns.

"Giddap, Mercury!" Jamie urged the slow-plodding bullock.

It was the best travel Chestermere could afford. William, who had passed them a few moments ago, riding his horse, had made no offer of it, to pull the cart. In passing he had called out: "Stores will be in the shed behind the English church." She and Jamie had only smiled, as they usually smiled at the enigma that was William.

Now as their cart with its two big wheels rumbled through the cool green woods, Jamie shifted his somber eyes from the roadway to her face.

"A beauteous maiden driven behind a white bullock to sacrifice," he commented. "Fact is, moppet, I think you fancy yourself in the role of a martyr. Otherwise, you wouldn't act so snuffed out, spirit gone, no sense of humor left."

Clytie did not answer for a moment. It was the first time he had spoken of the truth of her problem, which he sensed. She did not want to discuss it, but she found comfort in his understanding.

"I am snuffed out, raddled, Jamie," she said. "But I would make a poor martyr." She took off her bonnet and smoothed the skirt of her blue cambric dress.

"Every martyr's a poor one except a saint. Huh! Martyrdom appeals to their white-wings-in-glory urge. But don't get the idea you'd get any thing out of it, my pretty, except to be sorry you did not take your own damn time about this marriage business. Giddap, my winged steed!"

The ox ignored such importunity.

"Thank you, Jamie, but I . . . That's just it—I have no courage for making a decision, not *this* decision." Clytie's voice was faint.

"Takes guts, hunc? Like fire it does!" His laughter was bitter. "Takes a soft brain or a heroine in some novel to get the idea *any* decision's going to do her any good with a war like this in the offing."

"Oh, Jamie, don't!" The loud crack of his whip smothered her unhappy cry.

"Unc, hunc, but that's the way it is. Way it's always been—if not war, it's something else from around the corner to knock all your decisions into a cocked hat."

It was the unusual bitterness of his voice that aroused Clytie to an understanding of his own problem, which he was expressing as well as her own, for the war now made an irony of his own decision and dream to become a doctor. If anything happened to Pete, and Jamie inherited the wealth and burden of Chestermere, that dream would be dead.

"But, Jamie, dear——"

"Ha!" he interrupted. "The Greeks had the right idea about decisions: only the gods made 'em, good or bad. All you could do was propitiate the gods and take what they dished out. Hi, Constable! How, gun toter!" He called the last to a stalwart man who turned about on hearing his cry.

They had reached the main street of Frederick, and Clytie was glad to have his mind diverted from unhappy thoughts of Pete. She had noticed often of late that when Pete was home Jamie followed him about like a small boy wistfully worshipful of his hero.

"This big bazook is Joseph Herkimer Svarz." Jamie introduced the constable, who walked along beside their cart and with whose height and over-all durability Clytie was impressed. "He can outrun a deer, outyell a panther, and shoot a hawk in the left eye."

"What trouble's this fellow, who traffics with lightnin', aiming to drag you into, Mistress DeLancey?" the grinning constable asked. But before she could answer, he remarked, "Hear how them rum-selling rattlers signed up with the general to drive their wagons to the forts?"

"Not O'Malley? Skinner? Tennent?" Jamie exclaimed.

"That's it," the constable affirmed. "Can't operate their dirty trade without wagons and teams. You done this county a service, young man."

Jamie was still expressing his delight when they reached the open shed. To their amazement they found William, sleeves rolled up, hard at work, opening the big crates that held the supplies. He had two volunteer helpers; and a big wide trestle table had been set up on which to assort the items to be packed in the twenty sacks.

To facilitate matters, Clytie took a piece of chalk and marked off twenty places. She had started to assort the various parcels when, because of the dust of the dirt floor, she lifted the front of her skirt and pinned it about her waist. She noted the townfolk who had gathered about the shed to witness this odd activity of assorting supplies take smiling note of her lace-ruffled petticoat, but she was too busy to feel immodest.

"No, Jamie, not two Gloucester cheese in that place." She shoved one of the heavy parcels aside. She must bring some order into this. She lifted other articles and explained: "Those are the bohea—put one green and one black tea in each number, Jamie." The supplies that William was unpacking were well marked, but Jamie continued to heave them at random onto the table. She took out her list and read aloud: "One package raisins in each place, six pounds loaf sugar, six pounds plain sugar, ground coffee, six pounds chocolate. . . . Oh, Jamie!" She stopped her assortment of the items and stared at him.

He was heaving the big parcels of hams and dried tongues onto the table with a surliness that astounded her. Sleeves rolled up, unbuttoned waistcoat flapping, hair awry, he appeared ready to pound the whole table of supplies until it collapsed. And she quickly saw why his face was so red with embarrassment and anger: the townfolk were agape at the display of luxury. Doubtless never before in their hard-working lives had they seen such lavish stores. As she turned quickly back to work she found herself in sympathy with Jamie's resentment, remembering, too, the salt pork and corn pone on which Adam and his troopers had fared on their trip through the wilderness.

"Madeira wine, Jamaica rum, ham, cheese, white biscuits, butter." Jamie, reading in a loud voice from a list, stopped to sling a twenty-pound keg of butter onto the table. "It is the *best* butter, folks," he informed the onlookers. "Now then, we have raisins, chocolate . . . Hey, no cookies, William?" William ignored him, but Jamie was not put off. "Now I ask you, my countrymen, should the king's subalterns be forced to march through the wilderness for protection of the king's lands without *cookies?* Where's the justice?"

William had stopped to glare. But an interruption came from a black-coated, fierce-eyed man who advanced, shaking a horny fist. "Devil-begotten rum," he denounced, and looked ready to upset the table himself, but Jamie caught him.

"Now, now! Brother Hawkins," Jamie said soothingly. Then he whispered something in the man's ear. "Yes, sir, that's right. We got orders from high up to take the devil along—may need him. See?"

"An' hit ain't fer our soldiers—hit be fer the king's men, Deacon," a woman in the crowd told him. The deacon, muttering maledictions, disappeared.

"The white vinegar is ready to be assorted, Mistress DeLancey," William said in an unperturbed voice.

Clytie had just turned to take up a parcel when she heard several of the crowd say: "How, Capt'in!" and then the familiar voice: "Yonkee donkee dandy! What goes here?"

Clytie's knees weakened. Her heart hammered.

Adam Appleton, legs wide-spread, arms akimbo, stood regarding the loaded table with amused amazement. The crowd laughed, welcoming him. To Clytie his presence was surely an answer to prayer, and in the moment in which his startled eyes met hers there was so much unguarded delight that her heart wanted to sit down and rest, as at a milestone of life, and make no further journey toward decisions.

"Top o' morning, ma'am!" He doffed his coonskin cap to her.

And as she smiled she wondered if he had worn his buckskins because he had been scouting among the Indians.

"How, old scout!" Jamie welcomed him.

Flushed and hot, Clytie had just bent to lift up a heavy parcel when familiar hands closed over hers—the familiar electric touch, but of short duration. Adam took the parcel from her and placed it on the table. But as she bent again, his head knocked hers, and for a moment their laughter seemed to blot out eons of heartbreak. What he had said scarcely registered, for almost at once she was assaulted from the other side.

"Oh, Mistress DeLancey, let us help!" two young girls implored, their eyes dancing. "I'm Marta Brawn, and she's Sudy Hammond," said the elder, who was about twelve years old, by way of introduction.

"Certainly! Marta, Sudy, fall to!" Jamie commanded.

They fell to, and with a zest that delighted Clytie, who was so tired of lifting parcels that her arms and back ached. . . . But *Brawn,* she thought, hadn't she heard . . . She was soon to be advised, amid the girls' eager activities, that Marta was the young sister of Peggybelle. Adam's Peggybelle?

"Well, well," Adam said with a mock-rustical drawl now to Jamie, "looks like yo' all be providin' handsome fer us po' bobtails."

Sudy and Marta giggled. The spectators sniggered and hung eagerly on Jamie's reply.

"Why you po' benighted bobtail," Jamie answered, "this hyar's fer soldiers that *be* soldiers. An' this hyar butter be to grease the wilderness trail fer the redcoats."

"All the articles are assorted now and on the table," said William sternly. "We can start to fill the individual sacks."

Marta and Sudy pounced on the sacks he held out.

Clytie and the girls were taking turns at holding open a sack while the other two filled it. Adam and Jamie in low-voiced raillery were engaged at the same task on the other side of the table, when all at once their voices became very distinct.

"Sho', rabbit meat be all a bobtail gits," Jamie was saying. "Ain't nobody a rabbit loves more 'n a bobtail."

"Yes, sir, they jes' hops into a bobtail's pocket," Adam agreed, "beggin' to be b'iled fer supper."

The girls grinned, but Clytie could scarcely believe her ears: Adam in this comedy mood! And she had believed that he lacked a sense of humor!

"But one time, when a spry young rabbit done make a mistake, an' he jumps into a redcoat's pocket," Adam went on—he heaved things into the sack that Jamie held, but without interrupting his tale—"an' was that rabbit scared! But by an' by, when he 'lows that free ride was gittin' mighty slow, he up and jumps onto the redcoat's shoulder an' let out a yell. 'Injuns!' he yells. Lawzy, lawzy! Mister Rabbit near died fer shame, 'cause that redcoat run so much faster 'n he could hisself. So wasn't nothin' to do then but tell the redcoat how to skin him and b'il him fer supper."

The girls chirruped with delight. The few spectators left drew nearer. Adam lowered a keg of butter into the sack, while Jamie contributed, "Yes, sir, honest, tender rabbits is like that."

"But they ain't minded to be washed down nobody's gullet wi' Maderia wine." Adam shook his head at the wine jug as he lowered it into the sack and went on. "No, sir. When that rabbit finds out what that redcoat was minded to do, he lit out from there. Hit ain't no luck fer an honest rabbit to git et with wine."

"Couldn't he git et with rum and not feel bad?" Jamie regarded the rum Adam lifted.

"Rum ain't so fancy," Adam said. "Not fer a bobtail. 'Cause a bobtail's got to have a mite o' rum in his pocket to trade in to an Injun fer his scalp. Even a rabbit ain't friendly with a bobtail that's got no scalp."

Clytie gave vent to her pent-up laughter. The two girls squealed with delight. The spectators sniggered. But William straightened up from his work to eye Adam as an offensive interloper. His manner was disdainful.

"All very enlightening, Captain Appleton," he said with smug disapproval. "But we are not here to listen to elegant observations on rabbits."

The silence seemed to sizzle, and the onlookers' mouths hung open. Adam straightened and, with the cool menace in his eyes that Clytie knew so well, he moved toward William in a slow, stalking way.

"Maybe you'd better say those fancy words again, mister," Adam said with an oily softness.

"Adam, please!" Clytie darted around the table and planted herself before him. She felt his gentle effort to push her aside but, defying him, she wheeled on the taut William and said, "Have you forgotten, Captain Franklin—" she used his Pennsylvania militia title—"that in Maryland Colony there is freedom of public assembly *and* freedom of speech?"

William glowered, his face white. But now she whirled on Adam and made her voice loud enough for all the remaining townfolk to hear.

"These supplies for General Braddock's subalterns, at the thoughtful and kind request of Mr. Benjamin Franklin, were donated by the Pennsylvania assembly. And if it may appear to us that the items chosen are those of luxury, it is not our business, it's Captain Franklin's." She pointed to William. "*He* chose them. Let us hope they will afford nourishment for the officers on their long way to the forts."

William looked as if he could brush her into limbo; he turned back to his work. And in the next second, Adam's amused but vibrant smile was on her—it was the smile of the *old* Adam. In the brief moment that their eyes met, he was the Adam of the wildwood, of the Indian camp, of that glad morning when he had ridden home with Lottie, who was in the Indian dress—he was the Adam whose endearments were still buried in the fiber of Clytie DeLancey's heart and flesh. Oh, Adam, Adam! She knew her flushed face cried it and that the air was pulsating with his own awareness of all that had been. Then the grim mask was again clapped on.

"How, Sir Jason!" Jamie's cry blotted out that vital moment. Adam's old defensive armor shrouded him; it seemed to Clytie that she could hear its discordant clang as he hailed Jason, who was coming toward them.

Jason had borrowed a horse for her to ride, then he had called at Chestermere, had had her saddle put on the horse, and had followed her to Frederick.

The twenty sacks were filled, and Sudy and Marta, ecstatic over Clytie's romance with the handsome Sir Jason, had unpinned her skirt from about her waist, had brushed the dust from her shoes, and had given advice as to how much starch powder was needed on her nose. She had felt hot and sticky and tired; but now that she was mounted she knew that a good canter was just what she needed to restore her mental equilibrium. She smiled at Jason, not knowing how soon that prized equilibrium was to be destroyed.

"How!" Pete called to them as they cantered past the greensward, on which numbers of townfolk were assembled. He and Adam were ahorse and chatting with a number of pretty girls.

Clytie could not give attention as to which of the girls was the favored Peggybelle; she was too intent on adjusting to her strange mount.

"How's that Injun war whoop, Major?" Adam called.

And Pete added, "Hear you are a hellcat at it."

She and Jason drew rein as the two riders joined them.

"It wants practice, Captain," Jason said, laughing.

"Hit it like this," said Adam. Then, as with some diabolical intent, he gave a "wa-waa-waahaah!" that curdled her blood.

Pete's voice joined the incredible outburst, then Jason's. Their volleys seemed to split her ears, and in the next confused second, three yelling demons released from the nether regions were galloping away, as if attacking enemy legions.

Clytie, stunned at the suddenness of their action, held in her horse. But the animal's nerves, as were her own, were not adjusted to such bedlam. He reared, caracoled and pulled savagely at the bit. He was pawing the air when a man grabbed his bridle.

"Let him be, sir!" she cried; she kept her seat only by defying gravity. She heard screams, which seemed to well up around her. She released her restraining hold, gave the horse his head, and galloped away in pursuit of the howling savages.

Her mount was well under control when she drew rein along a wooded stretch of road. Her bonnet was dangling and the ribbon was loosened from her hair, but her battle with the horse had released a tautness in her spirit. She patted the neck of her mount and laughed. She should be outraged at the three war-whooping pigwidgeons, especially Adam, but she was not. As she retied her hair ribbon she giggled at the way Jason had met the challenge of the other two and had worsted them; the resonance of his whoop had topped theirs. She jerked up her head to listen as the muffled echoes of their yells came rolling back.

The sound diffused itself in the wooded glade, faded in ghostly cadences, and died away. Clytie sat rigid, her whole being penetrated by some dread foreboding. Never at any moment of her life had she felt so alone. It was as though that dying echo had come back to her through a narrowing corridor of time, cutting her off, closing in on the three Indian fighters, imprisoning them in a bleak eternity of silence.

Warm sunshine filtered through the trees, but an icy wind had attacked her spirit, and the scent of the wildwood became that of the mold of a thousand springtimes—wilderness mold on the hearts of men who had fought and . . .

Clytie aroused herself with a sense of urgency; she had promised Monica never to ride out alone again. It was clear to her now that since the road ahead bent back toward the town, passing one of the blockhouses, the three war whoopers had ridden back, around the loop, expecting to find her where they had left her. She lifted her knee and hung her bonnet beneath it on the horn of her saddle. She had just lifted the reins when she saw a figure emerge from the undergrowth close to her horse's head.

For a terrified second she believed it a hallucination. The brown, half-naked body had the color of the roadway, the immobility of the forest, but his eyes were looking at her. "Half-breed of sorts," Adam had said. It was Wawa, the cruel-faced Wild Goose, who had leered at her that evening in Big Corn's camp. She had neither switch nor crop to force her horse to leap ahead, so she flicked the reins and dug in her heel.

The movements of the Indian were incredibly swift; he caught the horse's bridle, but her own effort to gallop ahead and throw him off caused the animal to rear. In the next second, iron claws had torn her from the saddle. . . . She was standing in the roadway in the illimitable loneliness of the forest, the Indian beside her. The only sound was the clatter of her horse's hoofs as he raced away.

CHAPTER *Twenty-one*

THE Indian was rum-soaked. Nauseated by his savage grip, Clytie had fought to the limit of her strength against being dragged through the underbrush. She still fought at intervals as she was dragged deeper into the forest, but she was unable to break his foul hold on her arm. Her dress had been torn by briers, and the fact that her captor had taken no notice of the telltale bits of it left here and there was evidence that his savage cunning was befogged. At times he staggered, but the fierceness of his grip never relaxed. Each time she screamed he clapped his hand over her mouth; her last cry had been only a throat-rasping croak.

"You will die for this. I know you, Wawa, and you will die," she told him.

He said drunkenly over and over again, "Good squaw. Make good squaw."

He had seen her in the white doeskin dress at the Indian village, and she knew that his savage mind was remembering as well his hatred of Adam. Oh, Adam, Adam! her soul cried.

Now they were nearing the peak of a hill—no more than fifty yards from the highroad, she thought. Though her agonizing fear seemed to have lasted a lifetime, her stumbling journey had lasted less than a quarter of an hour. But where was he taking her? Every step cut off her rescue. Her riderless horse must have reached the blockhouse by now, and . . .

"Wawa—" with every ounce of her strength she jerked him to a stop—"I will give you much money to buy rum, much rum, if you let me go." She had no money with her, but wanted only to detain him.

"Good squaw, good." He yanked her cruelly up the slope.

An icy madness attacked Clytie. She must find some way. Blessed God! Some way to defeat the fiendish lust in his black beady eyes until the sound of the searchers could be heard. She stumbled on. As the ground sloped downward the undergrowth thinned. A sapling stood in their path, and Clytie, with a lunge, wrapped her free arm about it and held tight. He turned back with a fierce guttural sound.

"Wawa, your squaw tired." She forced a smile, and wooed him by saying, "I make good squaw, *good,* yes?" To detain him for a moment, if only for a moment, as her every nerve listened. "But your squaw tired."

She did not know how much he understood, but such a savage look had come into the half-breed's face that her breath came short and she pressed tighter to the tree. Incredibly, his hold on her wrist loosened. Her arm hung aching at her side.

He stood below her on the slope, his glassy animal eyes on her, drooling a guttural sound. With an obvious gesture he grabbed for her neck, one hand on his hunting knife. At one moment as she had fought him he had lifted her from the ground by her hair and made a scalping gesture. Now, fearful to move, she watched his head shift from left to right, his eyes focused on the ground.

"No good place . . . make squaw good," he muttered.

When he lunged toward her and grabbed at her body, Clytie was steadied by her hold on the tree. His animal howl ripped into the forest as he pitched backward, rolling down the slope.

She had landed a hard-heeled kick delivered with every ounce of her strength directly in his groin. From the top of the slope she looked back and saw him, knife in hand, crawling upward.

She ran in leaps and bounds, and the undergrowth tore at her clothes. She was too terrified to scream, but hoped that she might reach the highroad. As she looked back through the branches and saw the fearsome Indian running just behind her, she tripped and fell . . . staggered up as shouts split the air and she heard the pounding of galloping hoofs.

"What happened, Clytie, in God's name?" Pete's arms were around her; she buried her head against him, trying to shut out the appeals all three were making—Jason's tortured voice, and Adam's. Adam had reached her first as she broke through the shrubbery to the road, and because of all she had seen in his eyes, and because of her longing to throw herself into his arms, she had grabbed at Pete and clung to him.

"Clytie, please . . . Why? What?" stammered Pete.

"May—may I sit down?" she said weakly against Pete's questioning.

She felt calmer now, and she felt the terrible need to think before she spoke, before she told them anything. Aunt Mony—she had to think of Aunt Mony and of the dreadful fright this would cause her. Think too of all the still-wilder fears which would be stirred up in Frederick—the fears of such girls as Marta and Sudy—if it be made known that not only advancing enemy Indians were to be feared, but also those in surrounding tribes.

Pete lowered her onto a felled log. She looked up at Jason's tortured face and cut off his anguished words by saying, "It–it was not anybody's fault but mine. I–I got off my horse to–to pick some whortleberries, and–and when he got loose from where I had tethered him, I–I was frightened and tried to find my way. . . ."

"Stop lying like that!" Adam's voice thundered. He had just come out of the undergrowth from which she had emerged.

"Appleton! Good God!" Jason protested.

"You were dragged from your horse by a soldier? By an Indian?" Adam demanded. And when she did not look up he pulled her to her feet with a hard grip on her arms. "Answer me! Who are you protecting? Which way did he go?" At her silence he shook her, shook her hard. "Tell me!"

"Now look here, Appleton——" But Pete restrained Jason with muttered words.

"I–I don't know what you are talking about," Clytie defied Adam. And with fire in her eyes she said, "Let me go!"

"When you tell me the truth." In rage and fear he shook her again. "You struggled with an attacker. Do you think I'm a fool? The evidence is there, in the woods. Tell me!"

"I-I'll tell you nothing, *nothing!*" Her voice had mounted with hysteria; she wanted only to throw her arms around him and cling . . . "I want my horse, want to go home." She wrenched free of his hold and started toward her horse, which they had caught.

"Women! Good God!" Pete swore.

"But darling, please," said Jason as he followed her. "Appleton only wants to know, to follow the trail of the beast, so why not–?"

"Because she is a little fool!" The words burst from Adam. "Ready your gun, Pete." Adam was unstrapping his own gun from his saddle. "It was an Indian who attacked her–I saw his moccasin tracks in the woods. And if she thinks it makes sense these days to defend——"

"Adam Appleton, don't you dare repeat that!" Clytie rushed toward him, her tattered dress trailing, her hair disarranged. "Don't you say that and let it come to Aunt Monica's ears! Don't you dare! Don't you frighten all those girls in Frederick——"

"Ho, ho! So that's it!" Adam whirled on her. "You admit the truth but won't have it known, is that it?" He again started toward her, but she clung to Pete. "Can't you see it, Pete? But then you haven't traveled the wilderness with her as I have." He examined his gun. "You don't know the beatings she can take and not squawk. . . . All right, *Lottie*—" his voice softened—"keep as fool mum as you like. Nobody will hear of this, nobody. Pete, Major, get it? Nobody. But I'll crucify that Indian before I kill him. Take her home, Major. Come on, Pete." He plunged into the woods, Pete after him.

In miraculous answer to her hope, Clytie had been able to reach her room without being seen by anyone. She and Jason had dismounted at the barn and had hurried through the pear orchard. Because it was the midday hour, when the slaves ate and Monica was busy, she had been able to rush up the back stairs unnoticed. Her tattered dress now rolled up and hidden, her body scrubbed from toes to hair, she felt better; even her spirit seemed cleansed of the frightful nightmare.

She was grateful that she had been able to hide the cruel bruise on her arm by wrapping the strings of her retrieved bonnet about it. She must put on her long-sleeved, pink, flowered dimity so that Monica would not notice.

When she came downstairs she found Jason and Uncle Peter conferring on the portico. She drank deeply of the wine and mint Ephraim was serving, while Uncle Peter resumed their conversation.

"So you are going to meet at dinner today, Major," he said, "the greatest Indian scout this side of glory."

It was clear he had Jason's interest, so he elaborated: "Christopher Gist is his name, and he has a body of Iroquois scouts he's trained himself—dependable, loyal. And that's not all the scouts we've got on hand," he emphasized, regardless of the fact that Jason looked vague, not understanding what all this meant. "George Groghan can furnish a hundred Indians. The point I'm getting at, Major, is that your general is going to need these scouts whether he thinks so or not."

"Yes, sir, but——" Jason began uneasily.

"Oh, I know you can't force the general to see it, any more than the rest of us. But there's no harm, hey, in your meeting Gist? Ephraim! More of that punch," shouted the squire.

He was so wound up in his subject now that he was indeed, as someone had suggested, acting as godfather of the expedition. "Ben Franklin's the man to put the truth before the general, remind him of that four miles of men, ammunition and supplies you'll have for the enemy to try to throw into panic by sniping. That's their game—to wear your line down by fear and panic. . . . There's Gist now!" He got up to welcome the rider coming up the driveway.

Jason had followed Uncle Peter's words with profound interest. He whispered to Clytie that he had heard Gist was a friend of Colonel Washington and was the only white man who had swum his horse across the wide Ohio. Clytie had heard as much, but had been inclined to think Chris Gist was legendary. At sight of him she felt thrust into the legend herself. He was not so much a man as a gnome carved out of weathered oak. When she gave him her hand, his sun-dried face wrinkled into hummocks and troughs with a pixie smile.

He had responded to Jason's friendliness, but watching him later, during dinner, Clytie divined in him a craftiness as old and wise as that of some heathen god. This gnome-man had braved the sunset lands beyond the wide Ohio and had come through many perils with Colonel Washington. She recalled, too, Jamie's saying that Adam had learned much of his woodcraft and scouting from Christopher Gist. . . . Adam who, but this morning, she had prayed to see again in the hope that she might resolve her dilemma about Jason, and who now assumed a more anomalous place in her heart than ever. She envisioned his terror at the sight of her riderless horse, recalled his breaking into fierce anger at her effort to lie—a heartbreaking reminder of their days in the wilderness—and his calling her Lottie.

Clytie wanted to sob over that reminder, even though she was at dinner, but Jason's hand covered hers on the table, as if he was sensitive to her thoughts, and she smiled. Jason too had won her heart with his self-reproach for having left her in his mad ride with the war whoopers; her need to comfort him had lifted her out of her hysterical reaction to the danger. She had even been able to jest: "Admit then, sir, that our wilderness has reduced you to the rawest elements." He had answered: "I'll admit to but the most elemental of all—I love you." And he had said *that* when she was torn, tattered, red-faced and tangle-haired. She had believed only Adam could love her amid such ugliness. The morning had indeed brought no answer to her problems.

Monica, who had borrowed Mr. Franklin's horse, had ridden into Frederick with Uncle Peter and Mr. Gist on some mission that concerned the ball on Tuesday night.

"Solomon will set the tea table for you and Jason under the great oak in the rear garden," she had said. "And perhaps Mr. Franklin will join you when he has finished his letters."

And now Clytie and Jason were walking about the front lawn.

"If you could know how long the time has been, my darling, since you asked me to wait," he began.

"Yes, Jason, I know." This was the day she had promised to give him her answer. But she had no answer.

"Clytie, my heart, I know that I can make you happy." He arrested their walk and grasped both her arms tenderly. "I shall hold in my life that thought only."

"But the time has been so short, and I don't know. I don't *know*, Jason," she said desperately, and turned from him. She felt deeply now the tug and appeal of her father's wishes, felt as well Jason's charm, his tenderness. She knew that her mind was attuned to his but that her heart was attuned only to the mysterious harmonies that Adam could draw forth, even in his wrath. "Love, gender," Jamie had said. But if it were these that sparked her love for Adam, did not such binding forces contain a spiritual element as well that augmented, compelled and completed their urgency?

"Yes, my love, the time is indeed short and the waiting, while I am away, will be long."

"Oh, Jason, Jason!" She turned back on hearing the patient sadness in his voice and held out her hands. "Some part of me loves you, dear, some part but not all. Oh, couldn't we be happy while we wait, until I know the truth about myself, find my reality?" she pleaded.

A shadow crossed his face, but he drew her close and kissed her tenderly. "Yes, darling, we *will* be happy while we wait."

They walked on toward the river, and in admiration of the myriad greens that flanked the far shore and climbed to the blue mountains, he said, "What a wondrous life, this life of the wilderness!" And, looking at her with a heartfelt smile, he said, "All life can be wondrous, my dear, so wondrous!"

His words struck familiar, intuitive chords, and she heard a voice that seemed to say: "Never forget that Jason has said, 'Life can be so wondrous.' "

"When are you going home to your father, dear?" he asked anxiously as they walked back across the lawn.

"When Uncle Peter's ship the *Queen* puts in. But why, Jason?" She looked at him, startled. "Now, you are not to worry about this morning."

"Not that alone," he said. "But if, after the departure of the army, enemy Indians should penetrate the native tribes . . . Oh, I don't know, darling, but I feel so troubled about leaving you here. And now that Adam Appleton . . ."

Clytie caught her breath. She tried to smile to hide her trembling. There was nothing she wanted so much as to keep him from knowing of her feeling for Adam—for his own sake, more than for her own. He was so sensitive that to add this knowledge to his uncertainty about her would be cruel in the face of his long trek into danger. But had he already divined, because of this morning . . .

"Appleton too will be leaving with the army," he went on; she began to breathe again. "And I am told that only he is capable of keeping the sharp watch needed on the native tribes."

She could not dispute that, but she tried banter and gay words to relieve his anxiety. By the time they reached the tea table, which was set in the rear garden, she had brought the conversation around to his recollections of a hunting party in his native Devonshire.

As she poured the tea she said, "Tell me of Blount."

"Blount," he echoed. There were happy memories in his eyes as he spoke wistfully of his home. "It is a hoary old Tudor pile, my darling, that stands in a park of ancient oaks, but to me it is the dearest place on earth. And when this campaign is done this gray old warrior of twenty-six hopes to return there for always. . . . Umm! Fresh dairy butter." He nibbled at the buttered bread Solomon had served. "You colonials have everything." But when Solomon had gone, he said, "Shall I tell you the picture I see when my dreams return to Blount? It is *you*, bringing youth and charm to those gracious old halls. It is teatime there—" he looked into the distance—"and on the south terrace, hedged about with blossoming hydrangeas, the scent of myrtle and heliotrope, my wife Clytie awaits me. . . ."

"Jason . . ." She stretched out her hand to him, so moved by compassion that she was insecure as to the truth in her own heart. She so needed such tenderness, devotion, love; she needed not only to give love in anguished uncertainty as she had given it to Adam, but some abiding, sustaining affection. "Jason, I . . ." Her voice faltered with her desire to tell him her deepest feelings about Adam, to throw herself on his wise, tender judgment.

"Waa-waarraawaah!" The Shawnee yell was close to them, and Clytie's nerves cringed. In a daze she saw Jamie, who, after leaping like a young savage, slithered to a stop on the grass beside the tea table. "Ch-charity! Charity, sweet lady!" whined the supplicant, now in cockney. "Ain't had a mite to eat, so blimy——" He grabbed a slice of bread from the table and stuffed it into his mouth.

Jason laughed. But Clytie spoke in a severe voice as she said, "Why didn't you come home for dinner?"

"Why, *why!*" mocked the miscreant. "Mean little word, a pet with women. But don't let her get away with it, sir," he advised. And, at the sight of Solomon, he squealed: "Food! Bring food, King Solomon! Cold ham, chicken, pickles. . . . Hi, Pete! William!" He waved at the two, who were standing in the doorway. "Clytie's gonner give us vittles."

Pete and William came from the house and, knowing what she wanted to hear, Pete leaned over her amid the medley of other voices and whispered, "Traced the red devil to the river, then lost him. Don't worry, sweet! The matter is dropped in the well. Feel all right?" He caressed her arm, and she nodded and smiled as she poured their tea.

Solomon arrived with platters, and the feeding began. All went merrily enough until Jamie waved a drumstick in the air and shouted irrelevantly, "Hurrah for William and Mary, and good Queen Anne!"

"Why not Edward the Third or good Queen Bess, my Wyandot," Jason said, smiling, "since one is as dead as the other?"

"And pity 'tis, 'tis so." Jamie sighed. "But you got to whoop it for some of them, now and then, just to remind yourself that old England once had sovereigns *worthy* to wear a crown. . . . More ham, William?" he chirruped when William looked indignant.

"Look here, what's all this about?" demanded Pete.

"About how God's got to have a little help, sweet buddy, if such quacksalvers as the Hanoverian Georges are to be kept from a throne." The imp grinned.

"God save good King George!" William was up from his chair as if there were pins in it.

Jason hid his smile, and Clytie suppressed her own to say, "Aren't you forgetting that Sir Jason is an officer of the king, my young dissenter?"

"Oh, don't mind me, sir," Jamie appealed. "I'm just one of the younger generation of 'uncivilized colonials,' what? Or *do* you mind, sir?"

"Not at all, Jamie," Jason said in an easy voice. "I could do neither the king nor old England a disservice by hearing the point of view of you younger-generation Americans."

"He's just thinking up some way to start a fight at school," Pete said.

"Or a *revolution,*" Jamie said blandly.

Jason's eyes widened, but William straightened his shoulders and wore such an outraged expression that Clytie said quickly, "What a word, darling, for so lovely an afternoon!"

But William gnawed at the bone. "Whether you like King George or not does not signify, Jamie. His father was rightful heir to the throne."

"So am I, sweetheart, if you go back far enough." Jamie then gave his attention to Jason. "Point is, sir, you in England can afford to laugh at the fact old George can't speak English and that his grandson, who will some day be George the Third, is distinctly a nimcompoop." He hurried on before William could interrupt. "But over here it's different. We need a symbol of royalty that has dignity, and we could do with a little honor if we *must* have royalty. But what have we got? A goggle-eyed mid-European, a whip-cracking, tax-busting, whiffle-whacker, an old fool, who tries to repeal our charters and add taxes every time the court favorite squeals for a new wig, and——"

"You'll squeal for a new head if you don't shut up," Pete threatened.

At the sight of William's purple face, Jamie threw up his hands and said, "All right, sweet children!" He lay back on the grass, from where he addressed the sky. "But, Mister God, you can't say I didn't warn them when the big fight comes."

"W-what big fight?" William pulled at his collar.

Jamie sat up. "Know what the battle cry will be, my children? 'Liberty! Freedom!' " he bellowed. "Liberty for a land that stretches from ocean to ocean."

"Oh, Mr. Franklin, sir!" Clytie stood up when she spied him in the doorway. "Help! We do so need your help."

He came toward them, smiling. Jamie leaped up and placed a chair for him near the tea table; and Clytie called to Jake for another pot of fresh tea.

"You have just spared me, sir, from having to take this young imp of Satan to the woodshed," Pete said.

"Tut-tut! I had not recognized you as such, Jamie." Mr. Franklin met Jamie's impish grin.

"Nor am I, sir," answered Jamie. "I'm a prophet. And I leave it to you if prophecy should be discountenanced."

"By no means." He took the cup of strong tea Clytie served him. She had remembered he liked it well steeped. "Thank you, my dear."

He helped himself to sugar and stirred the tea for a minute thoughtfully. Clytie wondered if he had heard Jamie's talk of revolution.

"I have often suspected that the eyes of youth might divine what others may not see," he said slowly with veiled meaning.

"Truth is, sir, he's been squawking like a jay," Pete said.

The philosopher smiled. "Well, well! I fear we must all squawk a little in our time. It would appear the only means of determining our true note." He sipped his tea, then asked, with a twinkle in his eyes, "Were you squawking, Jamie? Not in prophecy, I hope, which should be solemnized with mystic sound."

"Well, sir, truth is," said Jami
a concourse of atoms—" he indic
is more apt to be heard. Yet with
my epilogue."

"If a good squawk needs an
permitted Clytie to refill his cup

"I will need your permission,
his feet, smoothing his hair and
assent and Jamie added, "If yo
write it. I only mean to uphold
began: "Fellow countrymen an
just government is founded on f
that would assume to be of divin
man's reason. The power of go
in the people, the good of eve
of his rights—liberty, estates
and continued the delive
exercise of their sovereig
they judge to be for t
absolutely but *cond*
feited if the condit
be the true end, t
and dropped on

Jason applau
Jamie."

Jamie gri
moment or
ders a lit
Jamie's
preferre
she ha
vast st
as he
quer

H
he
sti

o

ER

two

the ball, which was to be held
ay at Chestermere. In the long
en removed and the wide floor-
s and slippers might glide easily
Consoles and tables of oak or
Cromwellian chairs, with their
nity, though thrust close to the

uet Jason had taught her
rtsy and came up with
inked knowingly, re-
ad participated long

Mr. Franklin had
g ago. She and
s so little she

ught of him
here would
rowd, the
s widen-

ad told
he no
snare
her

art,
me
er,
h-

ened by Monica's reference to the girl in Frederick whom he was "courting." Monica would not lie, not for a cruel purpose would she lie.

Clytie straightened her shoulders and went out into the bright sunshine of the garden. She was inspecting buds on the rose bushes, hoping to find some blossoms with which to decorate the house for tomorrow evening, when Uncle Peter came through the wicket gate.

"See that moss-rose bush," he said. "Planted by my grandmother. Been trampled down many a time, but there 'tis, healthy and hearty." He spoke of the Scotch brier and tea roses brought from England. "And that cabbage rose, gets cabbager every year. Can't kill it."

"Where did the yellow roses come from, Uncle Peter?" They were showing buds that would be just right for tomorrow, she thought.

"Blessed if I know. Many plants came over with the boxwoods years back. Not those pink climbers, they're native here. Transplanted from the fields." Then he called to Monica, who was standing in the doorway. "Mony, I told the boys to tie up twenty turkeys, 'long with a dozen ducks. You figure that'll be enough, what with the hams and terrapins and the barbecued lamb?" He went toward her and Clytie followed, astounded at such an outlay of food for a party.

"Yes, yes, Squire." Monica sat down in a chair on the brick walk that ran close to the house, shaded from the morning sun. It was evident that something was troubling her. "You want the library left just as it is?" she asked. "For the general's use you said, for conferences?"

"That's right, Mony." Uncle Peter looked a bit guilty.

Monica sighed. "Conference with Mr. Gist, is that it?"

The squire's face set itself in firm lines. "If by tomorrow night he has not consented to talk with Chris Gist about taking Gist and his scouts along, *that's it.*"

"And you don't think it a violation of our hospitality to——" Monica began.

"No, Mony, I don't. There's too much at stake. If he remains stubborn as a mule about the safety of his army, I'll ram Gist down his throat with the terrapin and my best liquor! And Ben will uphold me." He turned and stamped down the walk toward his office.

Monica shook her head slowly. "Still determined to play godfather to the army," she said to Clytie. Then, with a wistful faraway look in her eyes, she said, "God grant they may persuade him to use the scouts! George has written Pete how necessary it will be to have the Indians."

"Won't Colonel Washington be here tomorrow night, Aunt Mony?"

"Yes, I hope so. But if Braddock won't listen to Mr. Franklin, he won't listen to George. Yet, young as he is—" her expression became strangely rapt—"I would more willingly entrust my son on an expedition George headed into the wilderness, than . . ." She blinked as if awakening from a trance. "I'm not talking rationally, my dear."

"I think you are, Aunt Mony. And I believe every mother in Frederick would bear you out." Clytie, too, was giving vent to a long-smoldering resentment which she had caught from so many things said and left unsaid.

"No, no. We must not think that way. Braddock may be stubborn, but he is a great general." She got up. "Don't let me forget to remind Pete of the British flag we must put up over the front entrance. Tomorrow will be time enough to drape the ropes of smilax the slave girls are making about the hall and parlor."

Clytie followed her into the house.

"Is your white dress for the ball finished?" Monica asked.

"A dream dress, Aunt Mony. Will you come up and see it?"

"Not now. But I think your idea of placing a jar of big white magnolia blossoms on the stair landing is excellent. Hadn't you better look at the trees, see if they will afford enough blooms?"

The large magnolia trees stood at the far end of the front lawn where the ground began to slope toward the river. Clytie had been fascinated when the big buds first appeared on the trees, and she still marveled at the waxy white beauty of the large blossoms. Many of them seemed to have lost a petal or two, but, yes, she spotted buds high up that would be just right for tomorrow. Jake and Sapphira could climb the tree and gather them, cutting long stems for the tall crock that would hold them. She was still circling the tree, only vaguely aware that she had heard horses gallop up the driveway, when she heard Pete shouting to someone. Across the grassy lawn she saw a figure emerge from the boxwoods, coming toward her.

Adam! He had sighted her bright-pink dress; her spirit lifted into the breeze as each long swinging stride brought him nearer. She felt like a magnetized needle turning toward its loadstone, and the saying of some ancient came to mind: "If this pole—" she was the pole—"were then turned away a thousand times, a thousand times would it return to its place by the will of God."

"Give you good morning, Mistress DeLancey," her figurative loadstone hailed.

Clytie waved her bonnet. His white shirt was open at the throat, he wore no coat, and his sleeveless jerkin revealed the rolled-up sleeves of his shirt, from which swung his sun-baked arms. His smile swept her up and sounded her out as if she were a bell it pleasured him to ring.

"I have come to offer my apologies—" his face was sober-looking now—"for losing my head the other morning, but I reckon I was just about insane, time we caught your horse and reached you."

"Oh, yes—yes, Adam, I know!"

He was twisting his hat, his eyes grim. "See now why you wouldn't talk, guessing the furor it would have stirred up against the tribes, and——"

"Please, let's not talk about it any more. Let's just forget it, can't we, Adam?" she appealed.

"Not so easy to forget." He looked at her with narrowed eyes. "If we had caught the red devil, or knew what tribe he came from . . . Sickens a man to be going away before he can kill him."

"No, Adam, please—please don't feel that way!"

A moment before, she had had the feeling that she should tell him the Indian was Wild Goose; now, sensing his need for vengeance, she realized that she must dispel it. She could not let him leave for the forts with his heart full of gnawing failure to avenge her.

"Besides, the Indian was drunk," she said. "And I was not truly in danger, only frightened—mostly because my horse had got away, and I felt so lost——"

"Look," he interrupted her, almost savagely; then he eyed her curiously. "What sort of liar or angel of mercy are you?" He threw his hat to the ground. "I can't make it out. I know what you went through. I saw the bruises on your arm. Just don't try to gammon me. It won't go down." He squared himself.

"No, Adam," she said meekly. Her wits had never felt so futile as now, confronted with his strength. But as the flicker of a smile crossed his face she rallied. "But there is one thing you can do for me, now that you are going away—" her voice broke in spite of herself—"you can *forget* it, as I am determined to do." His helpless shrug and gesture encouraged her, and she said, smiling, "Time to sit down?" She flopped onto the ground.

Adam regarded her for a moment. " 'Women!' as Pete would say." He growled it, but lowered himself, in that agile way he had, to sit beside her.

"Now, let's talk about you," she said, "and about—about your going away day after tomorrow." She pulled at the grass, struggling inwardly for a poise that she could never achieve, certainly not at this moment—precious moment with him alone, the first since the heartbreaking evening when he had denounced her as a Jezebel and had recoiled from her—the *last* that she might ever have. It was not likely that on the night of the ball there would be time to talk with him alone.

"Yes. . . . Take it you . . . you'll be gone, hunc, when we get back from the forts?" His voice was strained.

They were two puppets held in restraint by invisible hands. Or were they wearing masks, Clytie wondered, each fearful of being unmasked by the other?

"Maybe. But you," she said, "when you are back you will be married to Miss Brawn, I—I guess." It was out, forced out, and now she shrank from the answer, not daring to look at him.

"Married? Brawn? Me?" Adam threw his head back, and the loud guffaw that followed his words was the sweetest sound Clytie had ever heard. Yet his face, as he looked at her again, was changed with bitterness; some fire might have swept up, consumed him and left him charred. "No, ma'am, I don't plan on anything any more." He snapped a twig into fragments and threw them from him. "Much less marriage. Figure I'm through shootin' at stars, thinkin' I might fry 'em for breakfast." He directed his eyes into the distance.

Clytie sat very still. Her relief concerning Peggybelle Brawn was tempered by her own unhappiness concerning Jason and her father's wishes. Then, too, she had the helpless feeling that Adam by all his fierce resistance to her had reduced to drifting wreckage the bridge that she had so joyously erected to span the distance between them. Any cry to him she might make would only be rebuffed by his pride, his bitterness. Yet never before had she heard him speak with such careless contempt of the future.

"But you—you do expect to become a planter, Adam," she questioned, wide-eyed, yet with a feeling that her words were meaningless, "after you return from the forts?"

"There you go, with those big blue suns for eyes." But his bemused glance at her was brief. "Now what in all tarnation would I be a planter for? No, ma'am." He sat straight and crumpled a magnolia leaf viciously in his hands. "Man's got to have ambition to be a planter——"

"But, Adam," she wailed.

He took no notice. "Figure a man I met up at Will's Creek has an idea suits me. Dani'l Boone's his name. Plans, after we take the forts—if we take 'em—to set out and travel south. Find out what's behind those Carolina hills. Figure I'll go along with him and just keep on going, *going*—" he spoke emphatically—"southwestward."

"Oh . . ." Clytie's throat tightened.

"What's the matter with that?" he said sharply. "Ought to be good enough for a rustic like me."

"S-stop it!" Her outburst was beyond control. "You are just prideful and—and blind, deceiving yourself." She got to her feet and walked away from him, struggling against the things she must not say.

"Not so blind as not to see things straight, *milady*." His voice was sardonic, and the thought behind it, she knew too well, was Jason. He was up now, brushing leaves from his breeches.

"Straight!" she cried in such quick anger she was startled by her own voice. "So straight that—that all I have ever been to you was only a lie from the beginning!"

"Hey, Adam! Adam!" It was Pete calling from the porch, snuffing out her anger and almost reducing her to impotent tears.

Adam answered with a shout. Voiceless and contrite, she fitted her steps to his slow ones across the lawn: this was indeed the end. But his lack of resistance to her flare-up amazed her.

"Well, ma'am, I—I reckon all dreams are lies," he said slowly. Then, in a tighter voice, he said, "But a man's got to face that . . . best way he can." Eyes on the ground, he kicked at some object in his path.

"But—but you can't run away from dreams, Adam." Clytie stopped and faced him, recovered now, her voice pleading. "They will haunt you."

"Yeah," he answered quickly. "I'm prepared for that, Mistress DeLancey." He stressed that name, strongly, meaningfully.

Clytie's own pride rushed up to strengthen her poise. To touch further on their personal feelings was hopeless, but there was one thing she must say in the hope that he might carry with him at least one truth obtained from her.

"Adam, your ability to become a great man is no dream," she said with conviction, "and right here in Maryland. Oh, don't laugh. I know it. I feel it. And so does Uncle Peter. He so hopes to help you, and—and Maryland needs such great men——"

"Great, ma'am, like a sinkhole is great, hey?" he broke in angrily. "Think a man don't know when the ground has sunk under him? But no matter, ha! Well, the war's not over yet." He straightened his shoulders. "No good ditching myself till that's finished. Then keep on moving. . . ."

"Hey, Adam, Colonel Washington's back. Sent a messenger for us." Pete's voice rang like a gong; he was mounted, waving at them from the boxwoods. "Shake a leg, old racoon. How, sweet cuz!"

Adam moved swiftly from her. But at the hedge he turned back, and for a brief second his glistening eyes buoyed her up with a truth she hugged to her heart.

"G-good-by," he stammered; then he disappeared beyond the boxwoods.

Clytie stood voiceless. The quick clatter of his horse's hoofs seemed to bracket her whole life. He was gone. She had let slip through her fingers the chance to tell him her true feelings. "Keep on moving," he had said. Meanwhile, time for her would move on in an eternity of loss. . . . She crossed the lawn again and threw herself down on the crushed grass that his body had touched.

Laughter and chatter streamed in from the portico, rippled through the hallway into Pete's and Monica's rooms in the left wing, where the guests left their coats or bonnets, flowed out again along the receiving line in the parlor, and poured into the colorful pond of gaiety already filling the long room.

"Orphington! Mistress . . . Greetings, Garland, Schmidt!" boomed Uncle Peter, who was echoed by Monica's charming, warm voice, and by the voices of Mr. Franklin, Clytie and William Franklin, on her left.

There was no holding Pete or Jamie in line, and Clytie feared that if she laughed any more at Jamie's activities, the red rose in her hair would topple out. He had constituted himself major-domo, by-passing Ephraim's dignity, and for the first time in her memory his red hair was well secured by a green ribbon, which Phyly guaranteed would stay secure. But it would be well not to count on his green damask coat; it might come off at any minute as he laughed and jested over the manner of each guest's arrival. He reported that mules and bullocks were dragging the carts of the most distinguished guests up the driveway, and that four girls had arrived atop one worn-out old mare.

As for Pete, a magnificent sight in his blue embroidered coat, violet waistcoat and dark-blue velvet breeches, his fair hair shining, he was looking for something *cossetung* before Barbara should arrive and claim all his attentions. He should find it: the girls were lovely in their pretty dresses.

"Mister and Mistress Clayborne and Miss Clayborne, Miss DeLancey," pronounced Mr. Franklin, his eyes merry.

Clytie loved his leaving off the second syllable of "mistress" for the unmarried girl; it was so practical and succinct. She greeted them and they passed on with gay chatter to others, but Mr. Franklin's twinkle remained on her.

"I am favored to have the white dove of peace so near me," he said, his admiring eyes focused on her dress. "Even though she wears two red roses."

She laughed, delighted by his admiration, and touched the red rose she had stuck into the low-cut bosom of her dress. It was a splendid dress, made like the pink one but without trimmings, just the lustrous white fabric. The color of her lips was a part of Phyly's magic.

"The man speaking to your uncle now," William whispered, "is Jeremiah Dixon, one of *the* Dixons."

William had been giving her information all evening about the social status of guests. He was very handsome in his rich maroon-and-gold outfit, which was quite a contrast to his father's simple brown homespun garments that, to Clytie, set the elder man apart from all the other guests, emphasizing the aura of quiet charm, dignity and wisdom that radiated from him. But William's words had drawn her attention to Uncle Peter, not the distinguished man he was greeting. She wanted to laugh at his white well-curled peruke; it was slightly awry. He had submitted to Monica's insistence that he wear it, but had stormed: "I'll have it off before the evening is done."

"Yes, yes, Mistress Dixon," Mr. Franklin was saying, amid the hubbub, "my Debby, like an orderly providence, goes an unchanging way in health and human kindliness."

What a lovely thing to say!

The Dixons asked about her father, and she told them his last letter had come from Albany, "where he will make his headquarters until autumn."

"Colonel Johnson, the Johnsons of Rose Hill. Sons are leaving in the morning for the forts," William informed her.

"You make a man long for his youth, my dear," Colonel Johnson, who had the great beaked nose and bright eyes of a Spanish grandee, was saying. "Memories, memories." He bent over her hand. Dreams were in his eyes.

His daughter was fair and lovely, even if his wife was broad-beamed and had a petulant mouth. Clytie thought the former must be some compensation. "Compensation," the word filtered through her mind as she greeted the Calverts—"Not *the* Calverts," William had said—compensation for the loved and lost. Time, that defeated all reckonings, might it heal all hurts? Had some other girl in a past era of the old house stood here in a white dress, her lips the color of the red rose she wore, awaiting in perturbation the one she had loved and lost? White dove, indeed! She was but a white sepulchre.

Her hand was out, her smile ready, her voice welcoming the inflow of guests, then *he* was standing in the doorway and on his arm leaned a tall, healthy, ruddy-faced girl with gleaming blond hair.

"Welcome, Adam, my boy! Greetings, Mistress Brawn," she heard Mr. Franklin say.

"Yes, Mistress Calvert, I hope to remain at Chestermere for a month or two." Clytie hoped her voice sounded normal; it was pitched a little high, she feared, as Adam reached Mr. Franklin. Two men in dark homespun.

"Mistress DeLancey—" the tall, fair girl by-passed them and eagerly held out her hand—"our household has heard nothing but excited talk of you since my sister Marta helped you with the sacks the other day."

Oh, Adam, did she have to be so lovely! Clytie held the girl's hand and met her generous admiration with friendly words and laughter, but she was thinking in spite of herself of the ideal wife this hardy cabbage rose of a girl would make the *planter* Adam. "Can't kill it, gets cabbager every year," Uncle Peter had said. But smile! Smile! Poise must not desert a DeLancey, not even with Adam bowing over her hand, the warm touch of his lips on it, dividing a formal smile impartially between her and Peggybelle Brawn, his words those of a stranger in casual greeting—he, going *another* way. Scent and sounds of the wildwood, drumming rain, rolling thunder, the dark of night, and she close in his arms—these memories assailed her senses, battling against the laughter and mannerly chatter she was affecting.

"William!" Pete's voice, close beside her, had the sound of a call to arms. He and William made their way hurriedly into the hall as a cavalcade clattered up the driveway.

Whispers of expectancy ran about the room, a girlish giggle trilled out and died in a breathless hush. Like magic a path was cleared from the hallway door to the parlor. A heavy tread on the portico was heard, a fullsome "Aahh!" was heard from the same direction.

"Braddock! Braddock! Huzzah! Braddock, huzzah!" came the concerted cheer in the hallway. It rose to a crescendo. "Long live the king!" The rafters of the old house quaked.

Then sudden silence. A white-uniformed figure, adazzle with medals and decorations, loomed in the parlor doorway—a figure of majesty and might. A juggernaut, ark of the covenant, Clytie thought, drawn up before its votaries. She made obeisance, as did every other woman in the room, to this highest of all representatives of the Crown on colonial shores.

"Obligements to ye, sir and madam, in the name of His Most Gracious Majesty, that ye so honor his servant and my officers," boomed the general to his host and hostess.

His scarlet-coated staff now crowded the hall and doorway. The medley of voices mounted. Mr. Franklin was greeting the general when Clytie caught the widened, sportive eyes of the general on her. At the "aahha!" that rolled in his throat she made a profound curtsy, sensing that he would be pleased. He was, for he laughed.

"We give you gratitude and great welcome, General," she said.

"Blast my eyes! It be the white rose of York, old England's finest!" His stout hand grasped hers, he bent over it, and his mustache tickled like drooping and abortive vines. "Transported to the colonies, hey?"

"No. Indigenous, General."

She was enjoying his astonishment when his staff, crowding behind him, began to chaff their general and edge his magnificence away. Captain Halket, the first to reach her, outboomed the general with his compliments, but was routed by Lieutenant Shirley, who asserted his rights because of her father's friendship with his father, General Shirley. Lieutenant Morris, with whose father she had dined in Philadelphia, edged the others out, as they all, with jests and quips, closed ranks against Sir Jason's efforts to reach her side. When he had defeated them a concerted groan went up in recognition of his priority.

They were shephered to a group of pretty girls by William and Pete, while Jason led Clytie toward the hallway. He was very distinguished, wearing the Order of the Garter decoration and other military honors, and his possessive smile lifted his full generous lips and crinkled the tiny wrinkles about his eyes in a warmly provocative way. He gave her confidence in herself. Clytie recognized it, and clutched his arm for protection against all the dark uncertainties besieging her heart.

"Greetings, Colonel Washington!" Clytie said eagerly.

They had met the dark-velvet-coated figure, the only one of the general's staff who had not fought for a place beside her. He turned, towered over her, grasped her extended hand and smiled in a somber, perplexed way.

"So you don't recognize the muddy-faced, ragged messenger to whom you were so kind?" She gave him her brightest smile.

"Not . . . Mistress DeLancey!" His healthy smile showed an uneven row of teeth—it was a youthful smile. It did not flatter, yet she loved it. He summed her up and accredited her with being a *person,* not merely a pretty young girl. "When I learned you were still here, I anticipated this meeting," he said.

But that his anticipation was so quickly diverted to discussing military matters with Jason did not surprise her; nor that her own attention wandered from their words to a consideration of the power and strength in his rock-ribbed personality.

"Jason," she said, after someone else had claimed the colonel, "George Washington bestirs me to dreams."

"Now look here, my girl," he threatened.

"But a poor frivolous creature like myself wouldn't have a chance. It is just that time and generations get jumbled when he is around."

"Choose partners all!" Pete called.

Her schoolgirl vaporing was interrupted. The harpsichord player struck a loud chord; the fiddlers began to tune up. When Clytie saw that the two MacLoughlan girls, who had arrived late because their mule had balked at a hill, were without partners, she hurried Lieutenant Shirley toward Sally and steered Squire Wilson toward bright-eyed Meg.

The elderly people had ranged themselves against the walls, and under the generalship of Pete, with William and Jamie as top sergeants, the line for the grand march was soon completed. Colonel Washington and Mr. Franklin had disappeared into the garden.

The musicians struck up a gay saraband, and Monica and the general led off, followed by the staff officers and their ladies in a colorful procession—into the parlor by one door, out by the other, circling through the hallway. At a signal from one of the musicians they swung around in a circle, then came another signal and they reversed the movement and swung in the other direction, skipping, and singing the tune.

Somewhere during the swinging Clytie lost Jason, her partner, and when the heeling and toeing began she found herself circling with Adam. It was her first sight of him since his greeting to her on his arrival, and she found herself gloriously dizzy at this unexpected encounter. Each couple was doing a caper on its own, and Adam was leading her into a merry one, their faces flushed, eyes smiling. She followed him easily; he was as light on his feet as when he moved pantherwise in the wildwood, and his swiftly changing movements she met with a challenging delight. He swung her away from him, swung her close.

"A dream dances before it is done," he whispered, then whirled her giddily about, caught her up, lifted her off her feet, and let her slide slowly down his body. She felt like a white satin feather, without substance, whirled on a delicious, warm wind. Their hands overhead, she circled around him, whirled off, was caught close again.

"Hear the cock crow, my heathen goddess," he whispered again. "Time runs out."

She was so close to him now there was no time, there was only this dream fragment in which they were held together, as cavorting couples obscured their pause by jostling, dancing and laughing around them. His breath was on her cheek, and then came the musician's signal.

"*Kaput,*" he said—that old German word—and launched her in the circling line that was re-forming. She headed in one direction, he in another, amid the dancing, laughing crowd.

By the time she reached the hallway, feeling as if she were all feathers and rubble, Monica and the general were diverting the crowd with their own fancy steps.

"Know 'The Dull Sir John' or 'Fain I Would'?" he called to the musicians as he danced. He was having a wonderful time. He capered and clanked, flinging his heavy legs about like a ponderous, restless Satyr, delighted with the applause around him. Monica, in her stately way, encouraged but failed to follow his cavortings.

Clytie paused only long enough in the hallway to see Monica lead the puffing, blowing general into the library for a drink, to the accompaniment of gay laughter, before she dashed up the stairs to repair her hair and steady her heart throbs.

Mr. Christopher Gist arrived during the supper hour in fringed buckskins. When Clytie saw him, she and Sir Jason took him in tow; but when he was introduced to some of the magnificent staff officers, eyebrows were lifted at this wilderness species. The wise old scout stared back with a twinkle in his eyes, as though they were children dressed for a charade.

Most of the young people, carrying plates heaped with food and mugs of ale or punch, had gone into the garden, where gay lanterns were swinging, leaving the dining room to their elders. A small table had been provided for the general, and with his host, Mr. Franklin, colonels Johnson, Cary and Dixon he was enjoying the terrapin, made into a fabulous dish, the smoked guinea fowl, wild turkey and malmsey wine. He regaled his companions, meanwhile, with episodes of his campaigns on the continent of Europe or in Ireland.

Clytie was listening with one ear to Lieutenant Morris and with the other to the general's hearty voice, when Abe Wilson touched her timidly on the arm and said, "Mistress Clytie, J-Jamie wanted me to ask you to—to . . ." He stuttered under the scrutiny of the lieutenant. She took Abe's arm and moved away.

Jamie was in the hallway, surrounded by a group of young colonials who appeared to be eagerly plotting some coup. He seized her eagerly.

"Listen, angel, we want you to get Mr. Franklin away from the general's table," he told her. "*Now,* before the general finishes eating, because . . ." He held up a finger for quiet as the others gathered round.

When their plan was revealed she consented to do her part, but she quaked as she approached Mr. Franklin at the general's table.

"Your pardon, Excellency, gentlemen," she said, then she whispered low to Mr. Franklin.

When he arose, wide-eyed, the general quipped at him, "Lucky fellow!"

She tucked her arm in his and as she led him toward the parlor she said, "You are summoned, sir, by a committee of the Inquisition. Some heresy you've been spreading abroad."

"Had all torture been dispensed by such a Hebe . . ." he began. He was wearing such a bewildered expression as she planted him in the center of the deserted parlor floor that she giggled.

In another second she was forced to flatten herself against the wall to avoid the onrush of boys and girls. They came in a long line, hands clasped, and prancing, skipping, laughing; the snakelike line encircled Mr. Franklin. Jamie counted a note and the song began.

"Poor Richard, Poor Richard, Poor Richard 'tis he!
None greater, none dearer, none wiser there be!
Po-po-po-po-poor Richard!"

They stamped for emphasis, widened the ring about him, closed in with a "Hurrah!" widened again, circling with their song.

"Poor Richard, Poor Richard, hearts ne'er say him nay!
Poor Richard, hurray! Hurray! Hurray!"

The shouting assaulted the walls. Guests crowded the doorways. Poor Richard himself appeared dazed but delighted. Jamie raised a hand for silence; the object of such veneration appeared ready to speak.

"Poor Richard thanks you, my young friends," said Mr. Franklin, "from the bottom of his grateful heart. And being but a gay young lad himself, if sometimes given to philosophical discourse–" he smiled at their eager faces–"he would wish me to say to you on this late May evening, when the springtime of hopes and joys fills your hearts that–" he paused to meet their expectant looks, then said, his eyes twinkling–"the joys of love all joys excel, and lovin's adoin' mighty well."

They gasped, then shouted: "Hurray! Hurray! Poor Richard!" The line broke and they headed for the door, repeating with glee: " 'The joys of love all joys excel, and lovin's doin' mighty well.' Hurray!" They vanished into the garden as their elders claimed Mr. Franklin.

Clytie felt a light touch on her arm, and to her speechless surprise Adam Appleton stood beside her. Without a word he drew her hand through his arm and led her out to the portico. No word was said, none was needed. His firm hand that held her arm in place on his was like a seal set on a compact made before the world began. Yet a voice within her echoed: This is but further torture of parting. Tomorrow he will be gone, leaving me nothing, nothing.

Gay laughter came from the boxwoods edging the driveway. The air was close and sultry. A beetle hurled itself against one of the dim lanterns. The portico was empty; at the shadowed north end he released his hold on her arm and leaned against the railing. His low laughter had a sharpened edge.

" 'The *joys* of love,' " he quoted sarcastically, and hugged his arms. "You believe that?"

"Yes, Adam." Her words came slowly. There was an ache in her throat, her mind was confused, her emotions were in control of all her faculties.

"So with you 'lovin's doin' mighty well,' eh?" It was a bitter reference to Jason's devotion.

"N-no, no." She dared not look up at him, faint before the great truth that touched her every fiber.

"Too bad," his voice rasped. Voices were heard from the doorway, and he turned his face toward the night. "Well, who knows," he went on more evenly. "When this fight's over and I head southwest with Boone, could be–might *just* be–I'd find again my wilderness girl." He banged his hands on the railing. "Might be worth traveling all the way to the other ocean to find Lottie again."

Clytie turned about, placed her hands on the railing, and as for a breath of eternity they stared together into the night her truth welled up and out: "I love you, Adam." She said it firmly, resolutely, softly.

The second's silence was split by a low sound from him. A groan?

Gasp of joy? Disbelief? She was unable to identify anything but the lift of his shoulders, his turning to her, for other sounds followed her words and drove them into the night: raucous laughter—Pete's punch-bowl laughter and Barbara's peals of gaiety crashed at them.

"Hey, Adam! That you, old fox?" called Pete as he lunged toward them. "Bar-ba . . . Barbara here says we can get us some g-greased pigs to ride for the Fairfax hunt." He, accompanied by Barbara's husky laughter, reached them and punched at Adam. "Hi, pretty cuz!" he said as he gathered Clytie into his bearlike arms.

"Clytie, darling, Sir Jason is looking into every corner for you," Barbara contributed.

Dazed, shaken by her recent emotional strain, Clytie had no power to wrest herself from Pete's arms, but stronger arms threw Pete's aside, and as Pete staggered backward Adam put an arm about her and propelled her toward the steps.

"Clytie! Oh, here you are, dear!" Jason, issuing from the bright hallway, stood before them. "Our coffee is in the library . . ."

What happened next was too full of jumbled sounds to reckon with; it was chaos breaking around her: Peggybelle was in the doorway—other guests behind her—saying, "Adam, Mama said we must be home by twelve."

"Are you ill, Clytie?" asked a disembodied voice.

Adam had dropped his hold on her. Jason held her arm. Adam's tall frame streaked to the doorway, vanished into the hall.

CHAPTER *Twenty-four*

"TERRAPIN? Manna, mon! Manna!" boomed the general's voice at the library door.

She and Jason had just come in to drink the coffee she had ordered sent there.

"You are tired, darling," he said, and she tried to smile, hoping the hot drink would restore something of her shattered nerves.

"No, yes. Just battling time, I guess, time," she answered, still confronting the dark cloud that had cut her off from Adam, trying to see through it, to find his true reaction to what she had told him.

Now the general was entering. Clytie put down her coffee cup and got up. This was escape, escape from Jason's tender, half-bewildered scrutiny. He took her arm and they stood aside, awaiting the opportunity to slip out, but others barred their way. Mr. Franklin, colonels Johnson and Dixon were entering, and behind them Colonel Washington and Uncle Peter.

"Ho, ho, my white rose!" the general exclaimed with robust delight. "You, too, Mayne, hey?" He regarded them, twisting his massive mustache, his legs wide-spread.

The others, with grave smiles, scattered themselves about the room as she and Jason edged toward the door.

"No, no! Sit down, sit down, both of ye," boomed the general.

But no, no, she could not. The guests would be leaving, Adam leaving, and . . . She tried to tug away from Jason, only to realize that this was an order from the general—protocol, hospitality—she had no alternative but to submit.

She caught Uncle Peter's sober nod and permitted Jason to lead her to a seat in the embrasure of a window. So this was the conference Uncle Peter had spoken of, in which he intended to ram Mr. Gist down the general's throat. Clytie sat taut, knowing she had no real right to be here.

Colonel Washington, with his darkly brooding face, was drawing his chair into a shadowed part of the room, and she remembered with discomfort a remark she had overheard him make to Mr. Franklin earlier in the evening. She had been here, in the library, filling a glass with old brandy for Mr. Gist, since he did not drink punch, when the two had entered, and before she could make her presence known, Colonel Washington had said: "I find him to be a man incapable of argument without heat or passion, or giving up any point he asserts, however incompatible with reason or common sense." She had known he spoke of the general.

"No better food than in the colonies, hey, Mayne?" The general flexed his great legs and took from Uncle Peter a big snifter glass of brandy.

The atmosphere in the room, the solemn faces of the men, forced a truth upon Clytie: the general was only using her presence and Jason's to divert the conversation from any advice these stolid colonials might offer him.

He whiffed his brandy, drank, smacked his lips and burped just as colonels Johnson and Dixon were being served.

"To our good host," he toasted. "And to our white rose of York!"

Clytie stood up and bobbed, and waited for him to resettle himself in his chair before she sat down.

"Ah, if I were but younger, I'd gi'e ye a race, Jason, my lad. Aye, once I remember . . . No matter, no matter." He drank deeply, swept the other men in the room with a crafty look, and settled his eyes on Mr. Franklin. "Well, Mr. Franklin, well?" But before Mr. Franklin could speak the general said, "Let us hope, Mayne, my boy, that on our march to Fort Duquesne we'll find brandy one-tenth so good, hey? Some little inn, tidy little inn, along the way." He gulped his brandy.

Jason's face reddened.

Then came Mr. Franklin's solemn voice: "No, General, you will find no inn along the wilderness route."

"Hey?" The general jerked upright. "Hear that, Mayne? What a country!" He sighed lustily. "Well, after taking Duquesne, we'll on to Frontenac!" He waved his goblet, chuckled, and because the faces about him remained solemn, he said, "And when 'tis done, good sirs, we will ha' made for ye colonists a good war. Aye, an' a peace o' no mean sort."

"There never was a good war, sir, nor ever a bad peace."

"Hey?" he brayed at Mr. Franklin's quiet words.

The squire refilled the general's glass with brandy.

Meanwhile, Mr. Franklin said firmly, "Considering the narrow line, General, the extremely long and perilous line your troops will be forced to follow through the deeply wooded mountain passes, I believe, sir, you will agree with us that the Indian scouts we are able to furnish you will be a necessary protection."

"Scouts? Indian?" asked the general.

"More than a hundred, sir, to guard your line of march," Mr. Franklin answered.

An explosion seemed to threaten the sultry air. But the general relaxed and gave a belly-deep chuckle. "Ho, ho! Indians, hey? So a tatterdemalion of savages be necessary to protect His Majesty's regulars! Well, well, my friend Franklin, the French may be of peril to ye colonists, but to my own trained troops, nay, mon, nay!" He plumped his glass down on a near-by table, and emphasized his dissent by waving and rubbing his big hands.

But Mr. Franklin gave no ground as he continued: "The peril for your army, sir, stems not from the French troops but from their savages, from ambush."

"Ambush? Baah!"

"Ambush, sir!" Jason was on his feet, his voice firm. "May I recount, General——"

"No!" the general thundered.

"Oh, please! Hear him, Your Excellency." Clytie made her appeal with such swift urgency that she was unconscious of her impertinence until all eyes were turned toward her. Her face grew hot, but she emphasized her plea. "Please!" For a moment General Braddock's look flogged her.

"Humpf!" he grunted. Then he reached for his brandy glass, drank deeply, and looked at Jason. "What may you recount, you—you young hotspur?"

"What I have learned from the scout Gist, sir," Jason answered, "concerning the inferior number of French troops that guard Fort Duquesne. And it is because of this, sir, that they will be forced to employ the murderous tactics of harrowing our line of march, and—"

"Baah!" he snorted.

"—resorting to ambush." Jason rushed ahead. "These Indian scouts know every wooded height, valley and stream between here and the Ohio. They know where the French Indians would be likely to set traps, and if you would but consent to talk with Gist——"

"Talk! Talk!" The general was on his feet, snorting and stamping. "Consult! Consult!" He glared at everyone. "Little I ha' had since landing on the shores but *talk*. Consult! Advise! And nought but meddling advice, except from Franklin, who ha' secured me transportation."

He jangled to the door, swung about, and fixed grim-looking eyes on Jason. "And now ye prattle o' native scouts to help the king's general fight red savages. Ha' I not fought savage Turks and Arabs, hey? Ha' I not fought the bloody French through Holland? And now ye, who ha' followed me right willingly to victory——" He broke off, planted fists on hips, and asked, "Be ye feared then, Major, o' red Indians?"

"Yes, sir." It came so readily from Jason that the general's mouth flew open. "Afraid of their savage cunning, of ambush."

"General, sir." The words came from the shadowed part of the room. Colonel Washington was on his feet, but as the general swung round and fixed him with sword-point eyes, Squire Chester laid a hand on Washington's arm and stepped in front of him.

"As an old Indian fighter, may I be permitted a word, General?" the host appealed.

General Braddock stared, shrugged off his anger, gestured at such intercession, walked to his chair, sat down, and drained his brandy glass. "Say your say, mon. Say your say." A shining boot agitated itself as it swung from his knee.

The squire refilled the general's emptied goblet, and then he spoke quietly: "There lives no man who would question the unexcelled exploits of General Edward Braddock, nor his victories for King and Crown. But in this wilderness are conditions and terrain as have never before been faced by a European contingent of troops, nor has any army in all history gone forth to encounter an enemy more superior in savage cunning."

The general made a baleful sound in his throat, yanked forth a huge kerchief and wiped his mustache. But the old Indian fighter was not deterred, he went on in an earnest voice.

"The French in this primeval world have adapted their warfare to the Indian's stealth and trickery. Civilized methods are not employed—not ever."

During the brief moment that the squire paused to receive the nodded approval of colonels Johnson and Dixon, Clytie noted a flicker in the general's bleared eyes that was akin to stark fear. A lift of his head, a jerk of his shoulders, and it was gone, as though every motivation of his life, every well-fought victory discountenanced that brief disloyalty to his own prowess. But her heart went out to him for the long miles he had come, for the trickery practiced on him by the lords of trade and the court favorites for their own selfish designs. Jamie was right: government was a *moral* force, and when honesty gave way to greed . . .

"It is the invisible attack from the hidden foe that is so deadly, sir," Uncle Peter went on. "And when they have reduced your troops to panic, it is then they swarm over you out of nowhere, a sea of red devils with war screams of hell. It paralyzes the brain, leaves the steadiest hand unsteadied, and, forced to meet it, you survive by the grace of God alone." The general made an impatient movement, but the old Indian fighter's own dread memories aided him in speaking a poignant appeal. "Don't meet it, General. Don't let it come. Protect yourself from it with our Indian scouts. It is civilized man's only hope——"

"Hell's trumpets!" The general leaped to his feet and stamped to the door. But his hand on the knob stayed itself as if beaten down by the gay laughter and voices outside; he swung about. His voice had no kinship with his former bellow when he said, "Now then, gentlemen, that I ha' heard what ye ha' to say, I take it ye didna know the king's general be provided wi' his own scouts, trained, veteran scouts–" he flung his words at them–"scouts who ha' never failed me, never." His suppressed anger emphasized his accent. He looked at Jason. "In my long campaigns ha' ye ever known my scouts to fail me, Major?"

"No, General." Jason stood erect.

The general's hard eyes challenged the others in the room. Outside a fiddle wailed–some phantom in pain, Clytie thought quickly; then she shuddered. Outside Adam awaited. Or would he? Panic seized her.

"Yet I pray you, sir, out of my long loyal service, talk with this scout Gist, and——"

"Oh hear him, sir, for me and for all women who will be waiting, praying——" Clytie pleaded.

"Ho, ho!" The general's shout took Clytie's breath away. The appeal she had added to Jason's was being derided. "So, 'tis the beauteous white rose that ha' bewitched my young major into fear o' redskins." His chortles bombarded her. "In which case all be forgiven, my lad. Out! Out wi' your beauteous lady!" He waved them toward the door, and returned to his brandy glass.

Clytie reached the door, but Jason turned back from it.

"As seal on your magnanimity, sir," he pleaded, "grant me *one* favor."

"Why, ye wily scalawag! Hey?" He sputtered into his brandy.

"Grant the scout immediate audience."

Clytie held her breath. Disgrace, dishonor seemed to leap at Jason from the general's purple face.

"Blast your eyes!" he shouted. "Out ye love-sick hound, and–and fetch this Gist. Fetch him!"

Clytie looked back and saw hope dawn on Mr. Franklin's face and Uncle Peter's.

"Good night. . . . Good night. . . . Good night." Caught amid the stream of departing guests, Clytie forced her smiles and words in spite of the panic in her heart. Adam—where was Adam? Not gone? Oh, no, not gone! "Good night, Sally." Lieutenant Shirley clung to the fair girl's arm; their faces were alight with the joy of each other.

"Good night, Clytie darlin'!" whispered Meg, nosing her face against Clytie's. "He dinna love her—Sally. 'Tis myself Abe loves."

Clytie answered her joy with a hug, escaped the onslaught of other guests, and hurried toward the dining room. He was not there; only members of the general's staff clustered about the punch bowl. Her heart grew hollow. Where, then? Where? She followed the other chattering guests onto the portico. "Good night. . . . Good night," she said mechanically as she searched the shadows. Not there! Amid the gay calls and laughter, she retreated into the shadowed place where they had stood when she made her confession, reason hammering against hope. He had gone—without a word in answer to her love, he had gone. And tomorrow at dawn . . .

She forced her heart to submit to the truth, a truth that loomed, terrifying, possessing all her faculties: Adam Appleton had never truly existed; her love had only created him. She had hung on his pine-tree quality all the strength, daring, loyalty—virtues of her own imagining. Now he had shaken them off. Bent and swayed by gossip and appearances, still hugging tight his stubborn belief in her wanton trickery, he loomed before her mind's eye stripped now even of kindliness. Clytie turned to face the night. A sob welled up, she swallowed it as a voice spoke behind her.

"Darling, you are shivering." Jason wrapped about her a cloak he had found for her and held her close.

He had led her through the now-deserted hallway and out into the lantern-lighted rear garden before she became fully aware of his tender solicitude.

"Oh, Jason, Jason!" she said, submitting to his embrace. He too would be riding away in the morning, and to defend a country not his own. Thunder rumbled among the distant hills; the sultry night cut off her breath and her sobs stuck in her throat, trembled in her body.

"Sh, my darling, everything will come right," his soothing voice comforted. "The general has accepted the scouts through your own intervention. And for me, my heart, it is enough that you permit me to love you." And when some terror in her heart made her, still unable to speak, tighten her hold on him, he said, "I shall never cease to love you—" his voice was trembling—"it is all I can say for remembrance."

"Oh, Jason, you—you are so noble, so true, so dear!"

"Mayne! We are off!" came Captain Halket's booming voice from the doorway; his words were mingled with the distant thunder.

Jason answered in a steady voice.

Clytie shivered, within the circle of his arm, as they moved to the light of the doorway, and in the hallway she answered the love in his eyes with a smile that brightened his own. Some part of her loved him, some part that she could not sort out from the pain and confusion that made her spirit a battleground of conflict.

The Chesters and their overnight guests, the Dixons and the Calverts, along with Mr. Franklin, were gathered on the portico to bid the general and his officers Godspeed. The colorful staff made a brilliant picture as they stood beside their mounts in the lantern light.

"*Au revoir,* my white rose!" said the general as he bent gallantly over Clytie's hand.

"God keep you, my General." Her voice carried a prayer.

Straight, steady, in spite of all his brandy, he moved down the steps.

Clytie's eyes caught now the one dark, solemn note in the gay colorful array: Colonel Washington. When she waved and called his name she was rewarded by a smile.

The general was mounted now—every inch the conquering hero. The men sprang into their saddles, and at the same moment a song poured from the throat of every man—from all but Washington, who sat his horse like a brooding centaur.

"*Marlborough s'en va t'en guerre!*" they sang. "*Miraton, Miraton, Mirataine!*" their lusty voices filling the night in tribute to their general, a Marlborough, none greater. "*Marlborough s'en va t'en guerre!*" They followed him down the driveway.

Jason turned to wave back at Clytie's fluttering kerchief; but the fears in her heart and tears in her eyes blurred his face.

"*Miraton, Miraton, Mirataine!*" Rumbles of thunder mingled with the sound. Darkness cut off the sight of the riders, but suddenly out of the stillness came the ghostly clatter of the cavalcade and the phantom echo of their song: "*Marlborough s'en va t'en guerre!*"

CHAPTER *Twenty-five*

"HIT's goin' to rain, Missy Clytie, ma'am, fo' sho," said Jake.

His voice startled Clytie as she hurried down the garden path. He was taking down the lanterns. As the rear door of the hallway was closed, she had hoped no one could see her. She was certain no one had seen her come down the back stairs.

"Don't say to anyone that I am out, Jake," Clytie commanded. "I am only going to walk about the compound."

She hurried out through the wicket gate. It would appear as madness to Monica, who fortunately was busy with her guests, to know that she was out; but to her it was less fearsome than to stifle and choke in her room.

On an irresistible impulse, after taking off her white satin dress, she had slipped into her dark bombazine and had put on the old clogs she had worn during the wilderness journey. Her desire to escape had been too strong to control—to escape into some void. The darkness of the night as she hurried across the compound seemed less dark than the darkness of her own spirit. The great spreading tulip tree near the compound threw it into deeper shadow, while out in the meadow beyond was the gray luminous light of the moon, which was hidden behind heavy clouds. Her restless movements took her to the meadow gate. She left it ajar as she passed through. Out here in the open spaces she could breathe. None of the slaves would see her; all were locked in the stockade, except the house servants.

A breath of wind stirred as, in the ghostly light, she made out the path, inked amid nebulous field grass and wild flowers, that led to the Cabin of Refuge. When she was halfway across it, the strengthening wind tugged at her skirts and unbound hair. Adam! Adam! Adam! Had she invented, as well, the Adam who had held her so tenderly in his arms in the Indian camp? She knew she had not, and that Adam would ride away at dawn—the Adam whom she had invested with the power to draw from her the deepest, dearest things—and leave her empty.

The force of the wind mounted, groaning in the near-by forest. Frogs croaked in the cattle pond—the croak of life that must move on, croaking, croaking. She had moved so swiftly that the cabin on the knoll loomed up unexpectedly. A dark gray shape amid swaying trees—the cabin Adam had spoken of on the first day of their arrival in words that her mind had resisted as with a premonition of pain.

She swung about to retrace her steps, but a gust of wind struck her with such force she had to brace herself and struggle against it, against a deeper darkness. She was off the path; now there was no path, no lights from the house. A flash of lightning lighted the meadow, then was swept away by a thunderbolt that rocked the earth.

Wind-driven rain struck her like bullets. Jagged lightning teeth across the sky again showed her the way. She tried to run, but the washing, pelting darkness took away her breath. A thunderbolt crashed, splintering into the forest; Clytie ceased her struggles and screamed into the chaos her own frenzied release.

"Roar on! Crash, split, hammer out new worlds, better worlds! Better—"

"Clytie! Clytie!" The eerie call pelted her screams. Was the storm itself answering? "Clytie!" was bellowed on the wind.

"Jamie! Jamie!" she shrieked in answer. Only *he* could be out to find her. But her cry was snatched from her, blown back.

Then, in a flash of lightning, a figure was etched in the meadow, then was blotted out, like an apparition. She screamed his name into the storm: "Adam! Adam! Adam!"

"Stand still! I'll find you!"

Not all the wind's fury could drown his cry. A flash of lightning showed him close by, and she shrieked his name again and again.

In another flash their outstretched arms met, their bodies clung, welded by the storm.

"Should have known I'd come back," said Adam, who was kneeling on the rock hearth, lighting a fire from the tinderbox he had found. "Took time to get the girls home."

A flame shot up and lighted the safe enclosure of the white-washed walls of the Cabin of Refuge—heaven's walls. He had picked her up, as he would a feather, and carried her here.

"Had to stable the oxen and get back to camp for my horse," Adam explained. The dried wood crackled with the leaping flames; Adam stood up and faced her. "Meant to find you, come heaven or hell." With mellow laughter he eyed the puddle her dripping clothes made on the floor. "Little wet rat." He reached out and drew her to the fire. "When I saw Jamie starting out to look for you—! *You,* to run away in the night alone!" He pushed her from him, shook her, and hungrily drew her close again. "You knew I loved you, known it from the first, knew I'd been in hell."

His lips were blotting out all that had been. Clytie struggled to believe that her first entrance into the cabin was not on the wings of a dream.

Bunks were built along one of the walls, and Adam found a blanket there and spread it before the fire for them to sit on. Outside the rain and wind beat down and left them secure in this little oasis of time—left their love secure, wrapping it about them.

When they were settled on the rug, their feet toward the fire, she drew away from his arms.

"You were not in such hell, Captain Appleton, as to make you tell me you loved me in all those wasted days." She pushed him away—pushed the moon from its orbit.

"I loved you too much."

"You are not making sense."

"No sense to it, you know that. *Me*—how can I marry you?"

"But—but you *shall* marry me." She pulled in her legs, and sat quickly on her heels to watch him; he, firm-lipped, was staring at the flames. "You shall, because my father——"

"There you have it! Your father." He heaved himself forward and kicked a log back into the fire. He leaned back.

Clytie relaxed and snuggled again into his arms, that held her hungrily in spite of his words: "It's not real, nothing about it's real. . . . Oh, Clytie!"

When their lips parted, she said contentedly, "You must write to my father, darling. Write him the first moment——"

"And say what, good heavens? Say what?" He put her aside; he groaned, his head was in his hands.

"Say—say the truth."

"All right, the truth." He gave her a brief smile, twisted with despair. "Dear Governor DeLancey," he composed, "I love your daughter, and ask her hand in marriage. What have I to offer her, Your Excellency? The poverty of a soldier-farmer. Not even a roof to shelter her. I can offer your beloved daughter only a life of struggle and hardship."

"No, no, Adam!" She threw herself on him, and he drew her close with a fierce tenderness, muttering into her hair, "Clytie, Clytie, my love could never make up to you for all you'd lose, never."

For a moment she was so lulled with his utterance of her name that she did not move. Except for his call to her in the meadow, he had never used it before, yet the very way he pronounced it made her know it had long been in his heart.

"I can't see beyond this moment, my sweet love, can't see," he murmured. "We've got this little hour, only this is ours."

"No, darling. No, it isn't like that." She straightened up. "Listen to me!" she commanded, but he shook his head despairingly. "There will be plenty of money, all we need. I mean, there are the four thousand crowns a year provided for me by my grandfather. So you see——" She broke off, a little frightened at the strange look in his eyes, the hard set of his mouth, but went on anxiously, "We–we can make a wonderful life, and when you get your land grant——"

"A squaw-man, hunc?" He got quickly to his feet. "So you would have a squaw-man for a husband, living off his wife's tribe."

"It is not like that!" She sprang up to face him. "The money was provided to make me free to marry anyone whom——"

"A man who can't provide for his own wife has got no right to have one." He moved back into the shadows of the room.

The rain beat hard on the roof, the wind moaned among the treetops and blew a gust down the chimney. Clytie stared at the trembling flames and tried to steady her voice as she said, "Is it so noble, then, that my love should be sacrificed to your pride, Adam?" She knew his own struggle and respected it, but was forced to add, "If so, it is a heartless pride, heartless."

For a moment he made no sound. Then, from the shadows he answered, "You don't know what you are saying. You've been bred on gold–it means nothing to you. But God above! Four thousand gold crowns a year!" He strode toward her and squared himself. "How many crowns do you think I can find a year, if I'm lucky? *Ten,* maybe." He swung about, then back again in agitation. "And as for this pride of mine that's so heartless–how much for a man's ignoble pride knocked down on the block, eh? How much for the poor love-sick fool's honor? Four thousand crowns a year. Done. Take him away from the sight of his countrymen. He's sold!"

He turned from her widened eyes, and his boots hit the floor hard as he walked. Clytie stood speechless, battered by his cruel outburst.

"And with a man's self-respect gone, what is he? What has he," he went on, "and what's a *woman* got that ties onto him?"

Clytie had not believed his pride could assert itself so cruelly, and for a moment she struggled against her own pride, then she said quietly, "It is not self-respect that will ever fail you, Adam, it is your love that has failed you, failed to surmount four thousand gold crowns."

"That's not true and you know it."

Clytie took no notice. Her voice sounding hollow in her own ears, she went on, "My grandfather told me once what love was." The thought of him brought a comforting strength to express her hurt. "He said that love was the only truth, but that you had to hold to it and believe in it, against all the things that would try to batter it down. And that if you tried to qualify it and measure it by other things, pretty or ugly, it would go away." She gulped, but set her lips firmly and went on. "He said it could never be limited by birth or position, or by four thousand crowns, or lack of four thousand, because there were so many false things to trap it and leave only the trappings. . . ."

As her voice broke she made a dash for the door. She wanted to get away from her hurt, out into the rain, away from this . . .

"Clytie!" His cry held all the force of the storm. Her hand was grabbed from the door, and she was whirled about into his arms, smothered against him. "You know you lie if you don't believe in my love!" His voice was smothered by sobs, and when she touched his face it was wet.

She had never loved him more, for she knew by his very cry of her name that he had broken so much of his pride it would never trouble them again.

When they were seated again by the fire he said humbly, "I'm ungrateful to God, sweetheart, that's my trouble. Ungrateful that He has made you the very breath of my body, the body of a prideful fool."

"We will never quarrel again, never in all our lives," she promised. Yet her heart repeated "all our lives" with a tremor of pain; the *all* might be packaged in these few moments, the moments that were rushing away. The fire was dying. Time was dying.

He seemed to read the dread in her heart, for he said lightly, "Quarrels may be healthy, madam, and what with such a little bundle of perversities as you to live with, I figure maybe I could use some of that money to buy me a cat-o'-nine-tails. Handy to have about in case a wife acts up."

In a spurt of flame from the dying fire their huddled bodies made a fantastic shadow across the floor and on white-washed walls, like the haunting menace of things to come. Clytie shuddered and tucked her head deeper into his arms, while they talked of many things, disconnectedly, conscious of the closeness that knit them, fiber, bone and spirit.

And now they eyed the red embers, which were making ashes of their little hour. The wash of the rain on the roof had ceased, when a hammering came on the cabin door and Jamie called to them.

"You are all wrong about that, Adam," Jamie contended. "Pa's asleep. And if you start rooting him out to tell him about Clytie and you, you'll get a squawk from Ma, set as she is on this Sir Jason business, and make the rest of Clytie's stay pretty unhappy. Can't send her home, you know, till the *Queen* gets in."

"The *Queen*? No, no, she can't go till I get back." He drew Clytie closer, possessively; determined to tell the squire of their love, he was now heedful of Jamie's argument.

"No, no, I can't leave until he's back from the forts, Jamie." The thought filled Clytie with alarm.

"Leave it at that," Jamie cautioned. "Write Uncle James, get his consent, and you've got clear sailing. But, now let's move, let's get back to the house before Ma takes a notion to look into your room, and finds you gone." He picked up his lantern and walked to the door.

They followed the light of his lantern across the meadow, toward the barn where Adam had left his horse. Adam's arm was about her, but, to Clytie, their footsteps were moving quickly toward a fissure in time into which they would be hurled.

"Jamie," Adam said as he stopped.

Jamie dimmed his lantern and turned back.

"Listen closely, boy." Adam went on in a heavy voice. "The last time I rode out to the Lenape camp I didn't like what I smelled out—the look of things. There's a group of warriors there sweating under Big Corn's friendliness with us long knives—a devil's crew. And should some *accident* happen to the old chief-sachem——"

"Blast!" Jamie exclaimed. "And with you gone, fellow, who's got the guts and sense to watch 'em?"

In the darkness a menace more terrifying than any gone before seemed to hover about them as Clytie recalled the evil faces with poorly concealed sneers that had watched Adam's departure from camp on that sunny morning.

"Svarz will dig up somebody among the home guard." Adam's voice was now heavy with significance. "But the important thing you can do, Jamie, is to keep in touch with Joe Toads. They won't spare him if they make up their minds to rid themselves of the chief. Joe's on the alert, all right, but a good thing to do would be to get him away. Think up a job for him. He could be a great help to you and the squire in case——"

"Yes! I'll pretend we are short of hands, what with Braddock having requisitioned Zeke, Pete's slave."

"That's right. Make your tale stand up so they won't suspect you," Adam cautioned. "You'll have Joe to spy on them–there's no better scout. Don't know that they'd try anything against the settlers, not unless——" He broke off and drew Clytie closer. "Time Braddock puts the fear of God into the tribes to the north, everything will be all right."

Jamie took up his lantern. They walked on. Adam had said that about Braddock for her sake, Clytie knew–knew that neither he, Jamie nor Uncle Peter was confident of anything concerning the army, even though Braddock had grudgingly consented to take Gist and his scouts.

Jamie left them to bring Adam's horse out to the driveway that led from the barn to the highroad.

Then came the blinding moment of parting.

"I am taking you with me every mile of the way," Adam whispered, and smoothed her damp hair back from her forehead. A little sob escaped her, and he comforted her by saying, "No tears from my brave love, my own little wilderness sweetheart." Their lips and bodies clung, then parted.

"I'll be on hand to see you off, come daylight," Jamie said. He hung his lantern on Adam's saddle.

Adam swung up onto his horse.

Time caught up the last sound of his voice on the wind, whirled it into the void. Hoofbeats pounded on Clytie's heart. The dark blur of his figure dissolved with the lantern light, lost in a drumming of sound on the highroad.

CHAPTER *Twenty-six*

THE first time Clytie heard the moaning of the slaves was the night after the troops marched away. She had been awakened by the awesome sound filtering in through her window, like a concerted wail of pain. Had someone died? She had aroused herself and gone to the window; she had heard the cries topped by an angry voice, Amos Hartley's. The sounds had ceased and she had crept back to bed, shivering.

She had said nothing about it; but a few nights later she heard the same eerie cries, so she spoke to Phyly about it when she came in to make her bed.

"Pay no mind to dem ole crones, honey," Phyly said as she jerked off the bed sheets with annoyance. "Sis' Liza and Sapphy be mighty ole. Has dreams maybe 'bout Injuns comin'." A glitter of fear came into her eyes. "But dey got no cause to go scarin' folks."

"But don't they know the tribes about here are friendly, Phyly?" Clytie remembered Adam's warning to Jamie, and said with more brightness than she felt, "Besides, General Braddock's army will tarry at Will's Creek until . . ." She stopped short; there was so little anyone could be certain about.

"Don't take much to scare colored folks 'bout Injuns," Phyly went on. "They's heard how folks in Frederick got their kettles het." She pounded the pillows. "Maybe scares 'em, too, dat Mas' Peter be widenin' cellers fo' stores."

"But—but Aunt Mony said that was but a usual precaution when the county was upset."

"Yessum." Phyly tucked in the sheets, and muttered, "Injuns treat colored folks like hound dogs. But don't you worry yo' pretty head, honey. Ain't nothin' gonner happen here."

Yet Clytie soon found occasion to worry her "pretty head" over Sapphira. Sapphira's duties, which were chiefly to do Clytie's bidding, had been defined by Phyly. And since Monica had taken in a family of refugees to occupy the Cabin of Refuge and had turned over to Clytie the heart-warming duty of looking after them, Sapphira, always eager and worshipful, had been of great help to her. But in the last week she had been fidgety. Every time Clytie had sent her across the meadow to the cabin with something for the McCarthy family, she had run all the way and had returned, panting and shaking.

"What are you afraid of, Sapphira?"

The girl had rolled her eyes and gulped when she answered, "Injuns."

"Nonsense." Clytie let it go at that. But only yesterday, when the girl had come into her room with a pail of water to replenish the pitcher on her washstand and had spilled it all over the floor, Clytie had reproved her severely. Whereupon, Sapphira sat down on the floor and bawled.

"They's comin', missy. Sho comin' to kill we alls." There was stark terror on her face. "Sis' Liza and Sapphy knows, see 'em in dreams, comin'."

Clytie comforted the girl, but lectured, too: "When people are aged, Sapphira, their minds are not always clear. But your master's mind is clear. And until *he* tells you Indians are coming to harm you, you are a very wicked girl to believe it."

Sapphira dried her tears, but muttered, "Injuns sells colored folks to mean, bad mens."

Clytie sent her to the cabin to help Mrs. McCarthy do the children's washing. There were three children under the age of ten. The younger two had died during the long trek from the northwest country. And Mr. McCarthy, lean, gaunt-faced, but valiant, had received an Indian arrow in his leg. How he had ever reached Frederick with the festering wound was a marvel to Jamie, whose professional pride was aroused with the avowed determination to save that leg from amputation; while for Clytie the McCarthy family and their needs had come as a sort of salvation, for by helping them she found surcease for her own pain over Adam's departure.

She was sewing now, in the early twilight, on a dress for the youngest McCarthy, stitching vagrant thoughts into the muslin fabric. With head down, ringlets tumbling about her cheeks, she had no chance to give way to any thought, however rapturous of that last happy hour with Adam. She could not let Monica, who was knitting near by, suspect how every cranny of her heart was filled with her precious love.

"Figure Braddock will keep a line open to Philadelphia, Mony," Uncle Peter came into the library to say. "So any letter we'd have from Pete would be apt to be sent on from there." He settled himself with his pipe beside the east window.

The June breeze that threatened rain stirred the summer curtains. He and Monica were marking time until that letter would come. Clytie's own heart raced ahead, already reading the precious lines Adam would write her.

"Best have your letter for Sir Jason ready, dear," Monica looked up to say, "so that when the postrider comes he can pick it up."

"Yes, Aunt Mony." Clytie bent her flushed face lower to her work. It would be a hard letter to write; but it was cheering to recall Adam's generous attitude toward Jason when they had spoken of him: "Can't ask you to knock a good man down," he had said. "He'll need all the grit he's got for what's ahead of us. Time he's back will be time enough to tell him." She had already written her father, confessing everything. *Give us your blessing, my adored father,* she had ended the letter, *for I feel so deeply that you will not reproach me for following the truth in my own heart.*

"Ben's not got the postriders he had," Uncle Peter said. "War's taken a heap of them. But those he's got are whacking at time. Not so long ago it took three weeks to get a letter from Boston town to Philadelphia. Cut to six days now. Day and night riders. Letter I had from Ben few days ago took little more 'n two days to get here from Philadelphia."

"What did Mr. Franklin say, Pa?" asked Jamie, who had come in. He straddled a chair.

"Said Braddock was still writing about stores." Uncle Peter snorted. "If he'd push on he'd not be using up his stores. Army sitting on its tail at Will's Creek, giving the French time to reinforce Duquesne."

"Didn't I hear you say Mr. Franklin would be coming this way again before long?"

"That's right. Round the first of July he intends for a swing around the mountain gaps—Bedford, Chambersburg, up Cumberland way."

"Why, Pa?"

"Why? Because he's commissioned to see that the forts are strengthened. Reckons he'll be coming this way time that's done."

Unspoken anxiety hovered over the silence. Often now it seemed to Clytie that time stood still while they waited—must go on waiting—until that blessed day should come with word that the magnificent army had met the enemy, whose savages so threatened their homes, and destroyed them.

"Cary, Johnson and I have aroused old Sharpe into loosening up on funds to strengthen our own fort and blockhouses," Uncle Peter mumbled into the eastern breeze as he emptied his pipe.

A deeper silence followed the dread significance of his words. Monica's hands lay idle in her lap, her eyes closed.

"Sure hope old Captain Jackson gets in soon with the *Queen,*" Jamie said brightly. "Need that gum arabic he's bringing me."

"The *Queen's* got to unload staples and such at Baltimore first," his father said. "Could be a *month* before she gets in."

Clytie looked up with such quick delight that she felt guilty, but only Jamie caught the hope in her eyes. He grinned and winked. She did not wish Uncle Peter's ship to encounter difficulties, but any delay in its arrival would help her sorely. Her daily prayer was that she not be sent home until Adam returned.

The busier the days and evenings, as the June days trailed ahead, the shorter the time would be until that hoped-for letter would come.

No more than a week later it came.

She was on the portico when Jamie loped Rozinante up the driveway and dashed up the steps. He held a letter behind his back, shaking it. Clytie pounced on it and concealed it in her pocket.

Then he called, "Letter from Pete, Ma. Letter, Pa. And one for Clytie from Sir Jason." He gave her Jason's letter in the presence of his parents.

Amid the joy over Pete's letter, Clytie was able to escape to her room to read Adam's precious missive. Her heart and eyes drank it in: *Mistris sweet-art O dreams dont ritely kno ef you herd me tel you I luv you maybe dreams cant here so herewith I rite I luv you luv you luv you like that big pole star up yonder be luvin the nite.*

Oh, darling! Darling! Clytie kissed every misspelled word. The funny scrawl was beauteous. The breath of his lips was in the letter; and as she read on his slow smile that so transformed him, and the very feel of his arms, were with her. There was a bit about his impatience to set out from Will's Creek: *The sooner we get goin the sooner we get back so my dream wife and I can start bildin the bes lif ere was bilt.* He had "rit" to her father "sweatin an fumin that it wouldna be rit rite."

Clytie lay back on her bed and laughed happily. Even her father's frown, after he read Adam's spelling, seemed amusing, for he, too, would likely break into laughter and not judge the man by the formation of the words, but by the words themselves. "Maybe dreams can't hear." Oh, that was lovely! And he loved her as the pole star loved the night. She reread every word of the letter, then sat up, startled: she recalled one morning at breakfast when her father had received a letter from Governor Dinwiddie, and the spelling had been so bad that her father had said impatiently, "Ignorant old fool."

Oh dear! But then, her father was a wise man. Besides, he had met Adam and had judged him to be . . . Jason's letter caught her eye, and she opened it with a little pang of guilt. It was so beautifully written, his devotion so tenderly expressed, that tears came to her eyes. She brushed them away when she read that Colonel Washington had persuaded the general to let him take an advance column ahead, and that he, Jason, was to accompany him. Jason wanted to be on the march, needed to be.

She had just started down the stairs to tell Uncle Peter of this part of the letter, when she heard his outraged voice: "Befouling the Indian squaws! An outrage! Not even Gist nor Groghan can keep those Indian scouts if this keeps up. They'll desert."

Clytie sat down on the stairs. Monica was trying to calm him, but he would not be calmed.

"Then what'll he have to defend his line of march, hey?" he went on, pacing the hallway. "His own scouts wouldn't know a red Indian from a mulberry bush. And with mountain ranges, craggy steeps before them . . . What'd Sir Jason say, honey?" He spied Clytie on the stairs.

When she told him Colonel Washington was going forward, he seemed relieved.

"Thank God, they are moving at last!" he said.

This news so pleased him that he called for old Molly to be saddled, and was soon on his way to spread the news in Frederick.

"Chicken in the bread straw do-ce-do!" Jamie sang as he picked out the tune on the harpsichord. "Do-ce-do!" Clytie added her voice to his and they sang loudly every verse they knew, while now and then she took over the harpsichord and Jamie clogged in his comic way.

Even Monica laughed, which crowned their efforts, for it was to relieve the listless mood she had fallen into of late that they often devised any rowdy play they could think of to distract her. It was in early twilights such as this that her depression seemed worse, not wholly because no further word had come from Pete, no word of any kind had come from the army, but because of an indefinable thought that seemed to weigh her down, sap all her vigor, after her days of tireless energy. Some prescience of evil, Clytie felt, was gnawing at her.

Monica looked at them now with a grateful smile, because Uncle

Peter was applauding their antics; and when Clytie began to sing, "Frog went a courtin' and he did ride, ummummm," he added his big bass voice.

> "Frog went acourtin' and he did ride,
> A sword and pistol by his side, ummmumm!
> He rode up to Miss Mouse's door umm-umm . . ."

His humming had a large-bell ring to it, but both Jamie and Clytie knew that his zest was for Monica's benefit. What distressed him most was her insistence on more cellars being dug for storage. She had said tonight at supper: "A cellar for two of the milch cows, I would advise, dear, dug as far away from the barns and outhouses as possible." A far-away look had been in her eyes.

"Er—yes, Mony," he had said, troubled, but without argument, although it was clear he thought she was overrating the danger of an Indian attack.

The big clock in the hallway struck nine. Uncle Peter ended his song, got up and stretched. It was his bedtime.

But to their surprise Monica, as she folded her knitting—she must have made enough socks and mufflers to fill baskets in the last few weeks—said, "The rations were far too short you remember, Peter, dear, after the last Indian raid."

Clytie had never heard her call him Peter before. And after they had said good night he followed Monica from the parlor, his shoulders slumped, his head shaking.

"Ma's seeing things—you'd think she's been hexed," Jamie said as they sat quietly, pretending to read. "See how it is, with all her brooding over Pete and the uncertainties to come. That last Indian attack comes back to haunt her. A cellar for milch cows! That's because little Sister Flora died from lack of milk." He slumped in his chair, brooding. "Queer, the human mind, memories that bob up."

"Not so queer as *prescience* of things to come."

"Now what the old nick do you mean by that?" Jamie's faith in the army had been strengthened from the morning he saw them march away with bagpipes and trumpets playing, banners waving, boots swinging in rhythm. "Course, that's only a part of the army," he had said. "A larger force is at Will's Creek."

Clytie wondered why she was remembering all this as she curled up in her chair; why she connected it with the frown on the face of her grandfather's portrait, with Monica's forebodings. She looked up and laughed at Jamie's scowl.

"Do you suppose, Doctor Chester," she said, "that a psychic sense can be inherited? Or did we DeLanceys spring from some pythoness of old? You know, like a priestess of the temple of Apollo at Delphi?"

"Shades of Charon!" Jamie leaped from his chair. "What's going on around here? You mean, are the DeLanceys nimtopsical, or just plain crazy?" As Clytie giggled he asked, "Are females folks?"

But the long summer twilights remained a problem. No longer did that lovely, mellow evening song sound from the slave quarters; only the thrush and whippoorwill added their sweet notes to the creeping shadows of the June nights. The days were busy enough for everyone; but one evening when the squire was fidgety, and not even Mr. Franklin's *Gazette* could interest him, Jamie dug up an old map of the Monongahela country that Washington and Gist had made a year or so ago, and pegged it to the library wall. His father was delighted, and it made a diverting game for them to follow in fancy the army's advance.

"About here now, Pa." After counting the miles Jamie would stick a pin in the spot, and they would speculate about the terrain. He also found ways to introduce stimulating arguments.

"Reckon we'll ever have peace on this continent?" Jamie launched this question at all of them one evening.

It was raining a slow, dismal rain, and Clytie was thinking of Adam plodding along in it or sleeping on the soggy earth. She thought of times when the rain had sung; the louder it pounded, the sweeter its song because they were together. Peace, that was all she wanted in the world—life and peace in Adam's love. . . .

"Why not, son?" Uncle Peter, interested, stuffed his pipe. "In the course of time our increase of settlers will push the savages westward, I figure."

"And keep on pushing, hey?" Jamie added. "Folks sure have itchy feet when there's hope of grabbing land, peace or not."

"Give a man too much peace and he gets soft, chicken-livered," Uncle Peter pronounced. "The fiber of our settlers has been hardened, hearts made stout, by danger."

"But lordy, Pa, civilization can't go on with a man toting a musket every time he goes to the privy."

"Jamie!" Monica reproved.

"Who says it can?" boomed his father. "What I say is, a man's musket and courage will weed out savagery—got to—with the aid of Christianity, Christian laws upheld by God-fearing men."

"Have we always been Christian with the Indians?" asked Jamie.

"Tried, wanted to be. But a few evil, avaricious men can undo the work of the peace-loving majority. But *this* country," his father emphasized, "is not the only one in history where a new civilization has been introduced. And wherever it happened there's been bloodshed, the old fighting the new. But Christianity will win on this continent, because it is the best civilization man has ever known, when it's kept out of the hands of fanatics." He warmed to his subject. "It teaches a man to make safety for *himself*, to establish freedom under a Christian government that leaves him free to protect himself. Without that sort of government you are apt to end up with a nation of slaves."

"Squire, please, keep your voice down," Monica said.

"Hunc?" He shifted in his chair belligerently. "What's wrong mentioning slaves? Did I invent bringing over Africans as slaves?" He growled and for a moment appeared to turn his thoughts inward.

The discussion had veered so suddenly that Jamie looked helpless; it had got beyond his control. The squire was touchy about his slaves.

"New countries are built up by any means that come to hand," he went on, "but I'll say this—" he aroused himself and looked at Jamie—"no government such as must finally be worked out for this continent can offer anything better than freedom for every man, not peace. Any government that offers that offers a lie. The Greeks and Romans found that out."

"Right, sir." Jamie ran his hands through his hair, and the argument rested.

Jamie and Uncle Peter had advanced the army on the map part way over the Alleghenies. Jamie in his imagination found defiles here and there, while Clytie gave them Jason's description of the defiles of Will's Creek, a valley lying between cliffs nearly a thousand feet high, with bald, white eagles wheeling about the summit of rock towers that were like giant fortifications. Their anxiety so increased about the fate of the wagons and the twelve-pounders that they deserted the map and left the army atop the highest peak. They could not get it down.

So the days crept unnoticed toward July, but they left the Chester household and every household in the countryside taut with expectancy.

Jamie brought back the fears he heard from the huddled groups in Frederick: Had there been sniping along the lines? How many had been killed and wounded along the line of march? As refugees straggled in from the northwest country with grim tales of their neighbors slaughtered, their cabins burned, the vast surrounding wilderness grew more menacing, and no news of the army came as reassurance.

It was on the twenty-seventh of June that news of the army came in a letter to Clytie from *Adam.*

"Adam Appleton? To *you?*" Monica spaced her questions with mounting disapproval.

"Let her read it, Mony. Read it, honey," urged Uncle Peter.

Clytie opened the letter the moment he gave it to her; their need for news of the army must transcend her longing to read the letter in privacy. She held on to all the fortitude she could summon, praying that her emotions might not wholly betray her. *My own dere darling,* she read to herself, then she scanned quickly the following lines of endearment, steadied her voice, and was able to overlook the bad spelling as she read aloud:

" 'We are encamped on a high plateau of the second range of Laurel Hill—" she skipped the endearments—"One of my men is being sent back to Dunbar's supply camp, and if there is any way of getting this letter through he will do it—" she skipped a few lines—"The squire will want to know how things are with us, but with time to write but one letter . . . Tell him that the wood choppers who mapped out this trace ought to be shot. There's no easy way of getting over the Alleghenies, but with Washington last year we did not scale such peaks. Swamps are much the same—same venomous snakes. . . . Not such yelling as the redcoats let out. We overtook the wood choppers a few days back, hacking through a forest of giant hardwoods where day was night. Most of the supply wagons have already been wracked to pieces; down a defile a couple of them tumbled over the horses, carrying all to destruction.' " Clytie caught her breath, and the squire groaned.

"Ben's wagons—wagons he bartered his all for!" he said.

She had been able to make the letter sound coherent in spite of the hasty scrawling and bad spelling, but as she came to the next page the endearments made her blush. Yet she held steady until she came again to firmer ground.

" 'Tell the squire,' " she continued, " 'he was right about those twelve-pounders. Been held up at every river while rafts were made to get them across. The horses are so weakened by the heavy loads that the troopers must help, heaving, staggering, while the general bellows defiance at men, beasts, mountains and God. Playing God himself, looks like he'll get the army across the mountains no matter how little is left of it.' "

Clytie stopped for a second as she became suddenly aware why Adam wanted Uncle Peter to know all of this: It was to warn him to be prepared for anything, with the fate of the army so uncertain.

"No sniping, hey? No sniping?"

Clytie read on: " 'Colonel Washington advised that all the wagons not dashed to pieces be sent back to Dunbar's camp and to go forward with pack horses, but the general would have none of it. The colonel's been mighty sick with the bloody flux–" Monica interjected a little sound of terror–"He is better now. But when he was too sick to be told about it or do anything to prevent it, every last Indian scout pulled out and left us because of the inhuman treatment of their squaws by the redcoats and their officers.' "

"Gone, hey? Gone–Groghan, Gist?"

"That . . . that's all, Uncle Peter." The rest was but of his love. She turned to the next page and saw Pete's writing. "Oh, for you!" she said and gave Monica the page. With their attention thus diverted she was able to escape to her room.

She had reread the whole letter, savoring with released emotions his loving endearments, and as she came to the last lines her excitement grew: *I'm telling my trooper to look up a trapper friend of mine, and see if he wont fetch you this letter so'f he does–name's Tom Sims–you giv im one fer me an maybe the good God will see I get it.*

Oh, yes, darling, yes. She would find Jamie, and he would take it at once into Frederick. Her hungry eyes still on the last loving words of Adam's letter, she sat down and wrote hastily: *My Heart's Beloved, No greater blessing could have come to me, save only sight of your dear face, than your precious letter.*

CHAPTER *Twenty-seven*

To HELP *me through these days—eternity of days—with my heart sounding but one rhythm: you, you, you! Listen to the winds of the wilderness, dear love, and let them tell you . . .*

"Cover that white thing, lad," said Gist.

Adam Appleton, rereading Clytie's letter for nearly the hundredth time, looked up with a grin when he heard Chris Gist's whisper beside him. He would risk an Indian arrow or gunshot any time for the sight of those written words, for the sight of her smile that filled the page, her lips, her eyes, the whole magic sense of her that flowed through him. But he folded the letter and put it in the inside pocket of his frayed, rust-colored homespun coat; Gist, on a scouting expedition, mistrusted the show of anything not the color of leaf mold.

"What'd you smell out?" Adam said.

Gist took a swig of water from his canteen and squatted beside him. Adam's two troopers, Hank and Zeb, whom he had trained in scout duty, moved silently toward them to hear the old scout's report. They had waited in this deep forest of giant poplars, which lifted branches a hundred feet above them, while Gist scouted eastward, alone.

"Scouts, Ottawas, from the fort are moving down eastward of the river," Gist said. "To watch Braddock cross to westward tomorrow morning with the main body of the army, I figure."

"Snipers?" Adam said.

Gist shook his head. "Not enough of 'em."

But in that shake of the old scout's head there was an anxiety that Adam did not underrate.

They sat silent amid the din of crows and swallows in the treetops. It would be foolhardy now to move to their objective north of the clearing, which they could see through the trees to the west, until deep twilight. The sun was already down, but no matter how restive they felt, they must wait. It was that clearing that was giving Colonel Washington so much concern. "Get to north of it," he had said. "And if there is no activity there by nightfall we can get the army across before they can prepare any sizable ambush."

It was the perfect place for an ambush. Adam Appleton leaned back against a tree and considered how his colonel had kept that clearing in mind since last spring when Half King, the friendly Mingo chief, had pointed it out to Washington, Gist and himself from a high lookout along a ridge of the foothills just east of this valley.

So, just after Washington had crossed the Monongahela two days ago to wait for Braddock to come up, Adam had done some scouting on his own and had reported: "It's a clearing nearly two miles long, sir. I'd say the French at some time back cleared it for planting, since the north end lies no more than ten miles from the fort. Good arable land—nothing there now but stubble and bracken."

"How wide? How bordered?" Washington, gaunt-faced, worn from the diabolical sickness, had asked anxiously.

"Half a mile wide for the most part, sir. But just beyond the north bank of the river—" That damned winding river! The whole army would have to cross it again from south to north in the morning—"and the woods where the clearing begins there's a long stretch of it, sir, no more than a couple hundred yards wide."

"The natural route for the army to follow, hey?"

"Leads directly to the fort. Westward there's a gully between the clearing and the thick woods—the dry bed of a brook, sir," Adam had told him. "Eastward the land rises to the foothills, toward that ridge with the lookout."

He had known what his colonel was thinking—what he thought himself: that it would be the first clearing encountered by the army since, oh, away back. Couple that to the fact there had been no sniping, and he pretty well knew what would be waiting him from the woods along this clearing. Washington knew, too, how Gist and Groghan and their Indian scouts could have kept the woods cleared. . . .

"Blast your din!" Gist muttered at the squawking crows.

Adam blessed the old scout, who, because of his friendship with Washington, had stuck by him and had come along with the advance column.

The forest was darkening, not a leaf moved, there were nothing but stinging gnats and mosquitoes. The birds were almost silenced when the shrill call of a whippoorwill sounded to the east. It was answered from beyond the clearing to the west. Gist gave the signal, and they all rolled onto their bellies, dug their moccasined feet into the leaf mold, and lay still.

So enemy scouts were on the watch to westward as well, Adam considered as he lay there tortured by insects, his finger on the trigger of his musket. What tortured him most was his anticipation of the general's attitude toward whatever report he and Gist would bring in concerning enemy preparations for ambuscade. Flushed with triumph from having conquered the mountains, ready to bring his army up in the morning, old God Braddock would not be apt to let anything deter him from pressing on to the fort, no matter how Washington pleaded that these woods first be cleared. No good worrying about that till they made out what was going on north of the clearing.

Adam brought his thoughts back to the miracle of his receiving the letter in his pocket, and the outlook for the army's success in reaching the forts so brightened that he heaped blessings on the stubborn old general's head. True, he had played God, but he had got that army across, very near intact, too! Got a lot of wagons across, even, by Hector, the twelve-pounders! You could not rob a man of that achievement. But of all Edward Braddock's achievements, Adam Appleton rated first the general's putting Clytie's letter into the official pouch received by Washington last evening.

"It would appear that the general has respect for the DeLancey coat of arms on the seal," Washington had said with an approving smile as he gave him the letter.

Adam had gaped, hurried from his colonel's presence, and sat up with nose, lips and eyes buried in the missive until the hour before dawn, when he and Gist and the boys had crossed the river. Maybe he'd had a cat nap or two; he did not remember. . . .

At Gist's low signal he got to his feet. The deep-blue twilight filled the woods, and like a phantom band they moved northward along the east side of the clearing. It was plain that if French Indians were trickling southward toward the river they were doing so along a trail deeper in the woods to eastward. For Gist, Adam and the boys had reached their objective, the woods north of the clearing, before they heard a sound. It was a vague sort of rumbling noise, and Adam resorted to an old Indian trick: he stuck his knife into the ground and put his ear to it. The sound became amplified.

"Gun carriages," he whispered to Gist, dumfounded, "in the rocky gully west of the clearing."

It was a risky business to move farther westward, toward the sound, but the significance of what Adam had heard struck too deeply into their vitals not to be investigated. Gist was not one to take supposition for fact; yet a vague resistance tugged at Adam's mind, and for the first time he questioned the old scout's judgment in advancing. There was but one thing that rumble *could* mean: the French planned a full-scale ambuscade with cannon. And every second lost in getting back to report to Washington . . .

Adam was following Gist when the sound became unmistakable; he touched the elder man's shoulder. They made their way to the outer edge of the woods, and Adam skinned catlike up a tree. From this vantage point he found it difficult to believe what he saw. Under the clear blue-white light of the stars he made out a line of guns, four-pounders, being dragged along the rocky, dry, creek bed, moving southward. And among the swarm of heaving, grunting Indians, he heard the driving notes of a French voice, and he could distinguish the white coats of the French uniforms.

"Twelve cannon, swarms of men," he told Gist when he was again on the ground.

"Ottawas," whispered the old scout. "We've got to travel, lads, and reach the river by moonrise."

To Adam Appleton that next hour's journey was the longest in his life and was weighted with significance. He wanted to leap into the clearing and run the two-mile stretch, but discretion held him. In the open he would be spotted, draw attention to the others, and the army would not be warned, Washington not warned. His heart was beating gonglike with his urgency as they moved like shadows among the trees. The deep woods continuing to their left might be filled with savages, and the breaking of a twig by one of them could result in the destruction of a whole army. When he became conscious that the wind was rising, affording them a cover of rustling sound, he thanked God. Now he was repaid for the long weary hours which he had spent training Hank and Zeb for scouting.

Across the clearing they could see the stretch of woods to the west; they had reached the section where the clearing narrowed. This would be the spot where the cannon would be concealed in the woods, where the line of march of the army would be within gun range. Diagonally across the clearing, brightening now under the light of the rising moon, the wooded stretch just north of the river showed up darkly. But they would make it, thank God! They would reach . . .

Adam stopped, swung about at a faint sound, and saw that Gist too had stopped. Zeb was behind him, not Hank. They leaped as a body into the undergrowth, toward the thrashing sound, the strangling gurgle. Gist's knife came down again and again on the savage atop Hank, and the next moment the old scout shouted as a swarm of slinking forms emerged from nowhere and surrounded them.

"Run! One of you will make it!" cried Gist.

Adam leaped into the open. The life of an army was at stake. The lives of many men depended on his swiftness and stamina.

Adam Appleton glanced quickly behind him as he ran, but he did not see Zeb or Hank, only his three Indian pursuers fanning out to cut him off from reaching the woods along the river. Their crested heads and flying bodies looked like vultures in the blue-white night. Crouching low, he put every ounce of strength into his stride. He cleared a knoll and an arrow whizzed past his ear. Now amid brambles and stumps he forced his muscles to relax. Easy, fast and easy, his brain said. If he stopped to fire his musket the other two would reach him before he could reload, and now he was gaining distance. Indians were fast, but not the fat, pampered kind around a fort.

His breathing came easily, but he was hampered by his musket. Another arrow sang past him, and he stumbled as another struck the pack on his back. He regained his equilibrium, but, making a swift decision, he dropped to his knees behind a tree stump and fired. His nearest pursuer fell, and Adam dropped his gun and raced on; they could not use it against him without powder. He made swifter headway, feeling the pressure now on his lungs. God give him strength to reach the river! His eyes were glued to the ground, uneven ground here; he must make no misstep.

He was in the shadow of the stretch of woods along the river, his lungs in a spasm of pain, when he turned amid the brambles to look back. His two pursuers stood silhouetted against the night in the place where he had dropped his gun. A cold fear attacked him: if they no longer pursued, there was reason for it. That reason was *in* the woods—snipers were there. He headed swiftly westward, just outside the woods; some distance ahead a trail had been cleared yesterday for the army. If he could reach that . . . He had reached it, had seen the glint of the river beyond, when instinct, rather than his aching lungs, stopped him. There was movement in the woods which neither sight nor hearing could divine; sounds jumbled amid the croak of frogs along the river-bank. Yet, reach the river he must.

Along the blazed trail he moved swiftly, cautiously, in the moon shadows. Another twenty yards and he would clear . . . Adam stopped. Blood pounded his brain. Every tree to his right, to his left, moved, and there closed in on him a solid wall of devil-like shapes, crested, naked. The stench of savage bodies seeped into his aching lungs.

For an indeterminate time Adam, Gist, Hank and Zeb had been stumbling through the deep woods, their arms bound tightly, prodded by their Indian captors with kick or knife whenever they lost their balance.

After Adam's escape to the river had been cut off by the squad of Indians, he had been captured. A Frenchman in white uniform and cockade gave the order that the prisoners be taken together to the fort for questioning, which could mean but one thing after the questions and tortures: hanging.

Gist to be captured and hanged, after all his long years of scouting! Adam, his face and clothes torn by the tangled undergrowth, from which he could not defend himself, was trying to understand how they had been trapped. There was only one answer of course: the horde of savages had gained the south woods by a detour along the wooded eastern slope of the foothills, then had closed in to cut them off from the river. But his own fate, that of Gist or the boys, was of minor importance compared with the picture in his mind of Washington's awaiting their return, and with the painful realization that he had failed to report to his colonel the trap set for the army.

"Kaw, kaw!" Adam heard from one of their four captors, and from another, with guttural violence, *"Ugh, ugh!"* He had thought they were Ottawas, but those sounds meant "yes" and "no" in Iroquois, a language of which he had learned much as a lad from an old trapper.

This sort of quarreling had been going on ever since the Indians had been directed by the Frenchman to take the captives to the fort, and by the roundabout way they were traveling, it was clear they were not heading directly for the fort.

The gray light of dawn was now seeping through the forest, and as the traveling became easier Adam gave ear to their fierce grunts to one another. He made out the words *"gaganaesa,"* which meant scalping, and *"pauguk,"* death. And from one, whom he noted was older than the others, he heard repeated often *"ininewug,"* which implied that their captors were to be used as pawns in a game. That these words were

Iroquois confused him; the Iroquois were friends of the English. Then he remembered that tribes near the Great Lakes often mingled with the Ottawas.

They were threading through a small ravine beside a shallow brook, and as the day grew lighter Adam could see the war paint of their captors—white, black and vermilion streaks over their faces and naked bodies. They wore only a breechcloth and knife belt. They carried no muskets like the ones he had encountered with the Frenchman, but their heads, hairless except for the scalp lock, were crested with colorful feathers.

Adam, his mind, body and soul tortured, tried to reason that there must be some wit and cunning which civilized men might employ to free themselves from bondage by these gruesome painted devils; the safety of a whole army was at stake.

"Ugh, ugh!" "Kaw, kaw!" The argument of their captors went on.

The eldest Indian, whose *"ughs"* were the most ferocious, laid hold of Adam, forced him back against a tree, and bound him to it with withes and ligaments taken from the knife belt. The thongs cut into his arms, chest and legs, but he made no sound. Zeb and Hank were bound to near-by trees, and he watched Gist maneuver so that when he was bound they faced each other. Hank cried out from the cruel tightness of the withes, and one of the younger Indians made a scalping gesture and said, *"Gaganaesa."*

"There's a higher price for us delivered alive than for our scalps," Gist said to comfort Hank; he received a knife prick for doing so.

The two heavy-set Indians were squatting on the ground, but the two lean young warriors stood, arms folded, their eyes blazing defiance of their elders. This glen, miles from the fort, appeared to Adam to be a sort of hiding place.

Why were they stopping here? He formed this question with his lips to Gist, then made out Gist's answer: "The price of live prisoners will be higher *after* the ambush."

Scalps then would be too numerous, hey? Adam writhed in his bonds. He recognized his own musket, knapsack and powder horn piled with those of the other men, near the two squatting Indians. The eyes of the young warriors were on them as well.

"Napahwin," muttered the eldest Indian, but the moment he stretched out to sleep, the younger warriors pounced and grabbed at the muskets. The snarls that ensued became a volley of throaty sounds.

"The young warriors want to be off to the ambush to gather scalps."

Gist's words went unnoted by their captors amid a turmoil such as Adam had never seen before among red men.

The younger two were silenced, but their painted bodies trembled like animals held in leash. The sun was rising now, dispelling the fog, and Adam's tension grew as in agony of mind he prayed: Oh, Christ, God, show me a way to prevent the ambush! Show me a way!

Braddock must have come up by now with the main army. Would he listen when Washington warned that there must be an ambush, otherwise his scouts would have returned? Almighty God, delay their crossing the river! Delay them! Delay! His anguish prolonged itself as the sun rose higher; his unconscious writhings had caused the ligaments with which he was bound to cut through his ragged coat and burn into his flesh.

The two Indians stood, macabre sentinels, listening. Then came the roar for which they had listened, crashing like muffled thunder through the ravine.

Adam Appleton's blood rushed to his head in blinding torment, and he heard himself yell, "It's come! There it is! There!"

But his own frantic words were drowned by the fiendish war whoops that knifed his ears. The two young Indians leaped and writhed in the contortions of a dance. Another cannon boomed. To reach this ravine they must have circled back to within half a mile of the river. Now the eldest Indian in authority was topping the sound of the cannon with some sort of oration to the others that quieted their yells.

But Adam's ears were for the cannon, a solid mass of sound, making a single impact on his ears. Then came a quieter interval, and he could distinguish between the roar of the twelve-pounders and the smaller more distant French guns. On the wooded slopes? How many savages? But Braddock had got his big guns in position. A wild hope swept over Adam's despair: God Braddock and his well-trained force could not be overcome by an ambush, Washington could not be trapped. The French were no match for well-trained colonials, veteran regulars, and twelve-pounders blasting at their ambush . . . and his own company, under Ben Johnson, firing from their bellies. "Keep 'em down, Johnson! Keep their heads down!" He was bellowing in a demented way when the frenzied yells and actions of the Indians brought him back to reality. They were gathering fagots and brushwood, piling it up about his feet, Gist's feet and the boys'. Unable to appease their blood lust with scalps, they would torture and maim their captives. Shrill cries of terror came from Zeb and Hank. One of the older Indians was tearing into Adam's pack. He found the tinderbox, a spark flashed from it. A torch was being applied to the brushwood about Gist's feet as an idea leaped into Adam's brain.

"Burn the bloody spy!" he shouted, looking straight at Gist. In Iroquois he said to the Indian who held the flint, "*Muska! Muska!*" The Indian turned to him, and with all the hatred he could force into his voice, Adam cried in Iroquois, "He is no Yengeese. He is one of your own Canada fathers. Burn him! His tongue is as false as the cry of a wild cat. He is a spy for the commandant of your fort. Burn the spy!"

The war yells of the Indians died. There was silence in the ravine except for the intermittent explosions of faraway guns. The savages gathered around Gist to regard him solemnly. Adam thanked God they had understood his Iroquois. The elder savage grunted a question at Gist. It was answered by a long speech in Ottawa, which Adam could not understand. Then, unbelievably, they untied Gist's bonds.

Gist flexed his arms and legs as he said, "I feared you would run away to gather scalps in the battle, my brothers, and rely on me to take our captives to the fort. Had the Yengeese overpowered your commandant's friend, you would have fared badly. And I know you, Dahinda, to be a brave warrior." Gist smiled his admiration.

The old Indian grunted, beat on his chest, and repeated the name he had been called. But how in God's world could Gist have known the name? Adam wondered, amazed at Gist's skillful handling of the matter.

"You, Opeechee," the old scout addressed one of the younger warriors. "Want to go to the ambuscadc to gather Yengeese scalps, hey?"

Opeechee and the other Indian beside him strained like wild beasts at the smell of blood.

"Go, young brothers! Go!" Gist waved them off.

With yells they unsheathed their hunting knives, leaped into the air, and raced away, down the ravine.

Adam called out a curse at Gist. But he was marveling at the disciplined response to authority displayed by these French Indians. The French had a hold on the tribes which the English had never thought it worth their while to effect. Gist conferred with the two savages, delivering a sort of oration, of which Adam caught only a part: "The Great Spirit that made men brothers colored them differently. . . ."

"W-water," came as a hoarse plea from Hank. His head rolled in feverish pain from the cruelly tight thongs and from the biting of insects.

For pity's sake, couldn't Gist find some excuse for cutting them loose from the trees? He was emptying powder from one of the horns into his cap, then he gave it to the second Indian, whom he called Onewa, and told him to fetch water from the brook.

Hank and Zeb drank thirstily.

As the water was put to Adam's lips, Gist cackled and said in Iroquois, "Drink, Yengeese dog! You'll have no throat to drink with when you are gibbeted by the commandant."

The two Indians grunted, and the conference was resumed.

Adam strained to hear, above the maddening chatter of the birds, any further sound of the big guns. None came. Had Braddock won the fight, then, so soon? A faint thudding echo came on the wind. One of the smaller cannon. Not French? It came again and again. Now another unidentifiable sound. Concerted voices? Impossible!

Wracked with anguish, he heard the volleying savage yells, volleying death across earth and sky—the death of those he had failed to save. Failed! Failed Washington, his men. Failed *her*. The letter in his pocket burned into his heart, and his spirit cried out her name, over and over, numbing his pain. He began to indite her a letter: *Heart's dearest* . . . He could go no farther; the drone of Gist's voice forced up his head, and reality bit into his flesh. . . . *Ninth of July, my heart's love . . . ninth of July* . . . He was writing the date in red, red that could not be rubbed out. *And no tomorrow, my love, no tomorrow* . . .

Red . . . Red . . . Adam's head dropped forward, hung limply, inert.

"Sh! Don't make a sound," said Gist, who was bending over Adam.

His first thought was that he was blind. He sat up, rubbed his head, and realized the truth: it was night. He lay under the jutting edge of a small cliff, and the dark forms of Hank, Zeb and Gist stood beside him.

Gist thrust bread and a canteen of water into his hands, and commanded, "Eat, fellow."

Adam ate the hard crust ravenously, and learned from the low voices what had happened. Gist had bided his time, delaying the Indians from setting out to the fort by promises of a rich reward. He had sent one Indian to the brook for water, stabbed the other in the back, and then he shot the first one as he bent over the brook.

Gist had cut the boys and Adam loose. But yes, yes, Adam remembered that. Remembered staggering . . .

"You'd had no sleep for forty-eight hours, lad," Gist told him.

"God help us!" Adam said as he leaped to his feet. How could he have slept without knowing . . . "Let's be off!"

But Gist held him for counsel. Their only safety had been in resting here until darkness. There was no knowing what had happened down there on the clearing, but whatever it was it had been finished before they could have reached it. They must take no chances by traveling due south to the river, but must head east toward the wooded foothills.

"Like hell we will!" Adam swore. "Let's get to the army. If they have suffered casualties, they'll have re-formed by this time, making ready to march on the fort."

"Listen, son." The old scout's voice arrested Adam with its quiet wisdom. "Your tortured young body slept. Mine awakened too often to the sound of victorious war whoops."

"Vic-tor-i—" Adam strangled on the word.

"A man can't know for sure," Gist said, "but it will help nobody, our playing fools."

Adam's arguments were cracked wide. The old scout was right; no use to plunge like fools into danger again. They'd be safe enough in crossing the river from the east. As they shouldered their recovered muskets and headed toward the foothills, safety seemed all at once to Adam an important matter. Their narrow escape had pointed up the advantages of having a whole skin, whole except for bloodied knife-prick wounds and the seared flesh of legs and arms.

The last glow of twilight had disappeared by the time they were midway up the ridge and headed south, feeling their way along what seemed to be a Stygian darkness. Never had a trail seemed longer to Adam Appleton, who was sweating in his anxiety. They should reach the river near where it bent, flowing from east to south again, and once they had reached the camp . . . Oh, God, to reach Washington's tent, to see him, to hear his voice, to know that he lived!

Into Adam's thoughts and the blackness of the hillside shot a great white glare from the west. He sighted Gist and the boys a few feet above him on the ridge. The eerie light that sifted through the wooded slope showed them to be open-mouthed with astonishment.

No more than an eighth of a mile away Adam could see the clearing in the blue-white light. Had the army gone mad?

"Gunpowder sprinkled . . ." he said, watching the light move along the earth, then die down, leaving the hillside darker than before.

Then came Gist's voice: "Adam, the lookout atop the ridge's no more 'n a couple hundred yards ahead, once we reach the top."

Adam turned left, leaping up the hill slope, his brain on fire. No sooner had Gist spoken than he had sighted the promontory with the lookout in the flare of light. Falling, stumbling, climbing boulders, sometimes on hands and knees, he struggled up the grade, sensing that he was climbing toward a hell that could not be reasoned about.

After he had reached the sparsely wooded crest of the ridge and had turned south, lights again sprung up to westward—steady glares filling the horizon. He was running now along the well-worn Indian trail that led to the lookout, and as he swerved to reach the jutting point the boom of a cannon thundered across the ridge. Other sounds pierced its echo.

He was past being able to reason, to think, as he drew up on the flat rock; his brain refused the sight and sound of the devil's caldron spread out over the narrowest section of the clearing.

Bonfires made great yellow holes of light, over which naked horsemen galloped with frenzied shrieks amid drumbeats and the calls of trumpets. Snakelike lines of dancers, serpent-streaked, encircled the fires, leaping contortedly. Wagons and cattle dotted the open space. Bright red-coated objects lay on the ground, multiple dark objects . . .

"Oh help us! Save us!" someone moaned near Adam. Zeb was there.

"Bodies!" Hank cried. "Hundreds scalped! Our men scalped! There on the ground!"

Gist gave a pain-wracked moan.

Adam was not able to speak as he gazed into the nightmare of savage triumph. His glazed eyes took in white objects—French uniforms—that stood out amid the lurid glare of the devil's Sabbath.

The roar of a cannon split the heavens. Another, then another. Braddock's twelve-pounders, dragged over the mountains by the sweat and blood and death of men and beasts, were playthings now for howling fiends.

Adam Appleton turned from the sight and retched, his very guts spilled onto the ground.

They had crossed the Youghioghen at daylight, and now slogged along in the woods, following the eastward trail. Bands of Indians were still following the retreating army, to collect the scalps of any stragglers and to gather up, as well, kegs, bales, food or ammunition, the broken or discarded things of an army in flight. From the trail they heard drunken shrieks and panther cries.

"Picked up a keg of Braddock's ale," Gist said.

It was not easy traveling in the brush; at this pace they would not soon overtake the army. They dared not get too far from the trail that wound about the foothills, or they would run the risk of losing it altogether in the vastness of the woods. Soon, perhaps, the persistent savages, drunk not only with discarded ale and wine, but with triumph, would have done with their pursuit.

During that part of the night in which they had rested, Adam and Gist had made one speculation after another as to the cause of the debacle of the army.

"Couldn't have been more 'n a few hundred ambushers," Gist had said. But there was one thought he had given Adam, concerning their failure to warn Washington, which had drained some of the poisonous despair from his mind: "Listen, my young self-torturer," the old scout had said impatiently. "A man does the best he can. He is no all-seeing god. Nor is young Washington a fool. Our failure to get back to camp was proof enough that the woods were full of snipers."

"Then why? Oh, why?" cried Adam.

"Because Braddock wouldn't listen to him, that's why. Vaunty, after conquering the mountains. And with the fort so near he busted ahead, his troops marching in solid platoons, I'll bet."

The sun was rising now, and as they moved cautiously through the still-darkened woods they sighted the glint of red coats on the trail. It was a band of savages, fantastic scarecrows, wearing the garments stripped from the dead. The coats flapped grotesquely about their naked bodies. Because of the yells they heard far ahead on the trail, Adam, Gist and the boys moved back deeper into the woods.

While crossing a small brook they had stopped to douse their faces in the cool water, when Adam sighted the Indians stalking them. Their four muskets fired at once, and the Indians fled.

They had stopped to reload when a snakelike, painted thing dropped from a tree beside Adam and landed on its feet. Adam dropped his musket and leaped for the upraised knife. He had never felt more strength, augmented by grief and rage, flow into his muscles than as he gripped the savage throat. Never again would death's gurgle sound so sweet.

But now that they had been forced to fire their muskets, their presence in the woods was known; they moved more cautiously still. Many of the savages they had seen had been armed with the guns of their victims, and some of the Indians had long been schooled in the use of firearms by the French.

The attack followed sooner than they expected. Slinking forms were closing in on them from all sides; arrows sang through the woods. With his back to a tree Adam fired, felling one savage, but another came on. Before he could reload, the savage leaped to wrest away his gun. The struggle was brief; with the knife of the Indian's former victim, Adam stabbed, stabbed and stabbed again, stabbing out his vengeance.

The firing had ceased by the time he recovered his musket, and he heard Hank's joyous shout: "That's done fer 'em!"

So they were all right. He was about to call out when he heard a shot sound behind him. An impact hurled him forward, pain ripped into his side. He staggered against a tree, turned, and saw the smoking gun in the arms of the crested savage wearing the shining gold-braided red coat of a British officer. Through a blinding fog he heard the next shot, saw the red coat spin and fall in the darkening woods. Then he heard Gist's voice: "All finished now, boys!"

The hand that Adam fastened on his side was bloodied. The forest reeled. . . . Finished, all finished, my little love. In darkness . . . Adam toppled forward; his face became buried in the damp leaf mold.

CHAPTER *Twenty-eight*

It was on the afternoon of the seventeenth of July that Mr. Franklin returned to Chestermere. The day had been hot and breathless, and the squire sat on the portico in his shirtsleeves, where he could receive full benefit of the slight breeze that had sprung up.

Clytie was sitting on the front steps, fanning herself with a big paper fan, when she saw the way-worn traveler on the tired, dejected-looking horse coming up the driveway. She could scarcely believe her eyes.

"Uncle Peter!" she cried.

"It's Ben! Ben!" he shouted. He heaved himself up; his gloom and inertia were thrown into limbo. "Ben Franklin!"

Clytie dashed toward their welcome visitor with excited greetings; Uncle Peter was not far behind. But, remembering Monica, she rushed into the house again and found her reacting as to a bugle call.

"Tea for Mr. Franklin, Ephraim. Phyly, have a hot bath prepared in his room, and fresh linen and socks in case . . ."

The household awoke to new life. It was the first rift in their all but unbearable anxiety for more than two weeks. And he was bringing news!

By the time they had seated him in the parlor, Uncle Peter had extracted enough to exhilarate him.

"Indian runner into Chambersburg said the army'd made safe crossing of the mountains, hey?" he repeated. "Good! Good! Jamie, open those west windows."

"Reliable, I am inclined to think, Squire." Mr. Franklin's smile was tired, but it brightened as Ephraim brought in tea and Monica poured out a steaming cupful.

Everyone was agog with questions, but held them back as the squire exulted, "Likely crossed the Monongahela by this time, hey? No more 'n fourteen miles from the fort? Once there he'll take it with his superior force." His elation was good to see after his long weeks of anxiety. "Maybe the general was right, hey? He'll sweep on to Niagara."

Jamie tried to put in a question about the possible penetration of enemy Indians behind the line of march, but Monica cut it short. Their guest must have his hot bath and rest before supper. She even had him started up the stairs before he got round to telling them that he had traveled from Hagerstown with Governor Sharpe, who was now inspecting the fort in Frederick.

"Coming out here? Sharpe's coming here for the night, hey?" It was routine that Uncle Peter's friend, the governor, should do so when in the vicinity. But Mr. Franklin's answering smile was to Monica. "It was my impression, Mistress, that you might expect him, with all his staff." He said the last with wry sympathy.

But Monica was not disconcerted. The need to provide for a large company stimulated her generalship and lifted her as well from the gloom of her abstracted thoughts and premonitions. The mechanics of Chestermere's hospitality went into full swing. And her orders were precise.

Clytie rushed to her room to fulfill those given her—which were to put on her prettiest summer dress, and to make ready to entertain the young officers. But her mind and heart were far away: Adam's safely across the mountains! That much was known. And with their superior force they must have taken the fort by this time. Adam led his men over the walls; he will be a hero.

She let her thoughts gallop at will. It was her first urge toward optimistic release for so long that she felt the dark walls crack that had held her spirit prisoner. She was even ready to believe that Adam had received her letter, which Jamie had given to the old trapper. My darling, my darling, with the fort taken, soon you will return. In her released hope for happiness, her need for happiness, she felt a little dizzy. Darling, oh, to be happy, happy with you!

She had sponged herself, had slipped into fresh linen, and was putting on her pink ruffled muslin, her heart leaping forward in time, when a present reality brought her to earth: Mr. McCarthy's soup for supper! Since care of the little family had been entrusted to her the sick man depended on the strong nourishing broth which Phoebe, the cook, made. Clytie herself always took it to the cabin at sundown. The children too would be waiting for her good night, hoping perhaps that she would stop to read them a chapter of *Robinson Crusoe*. She could not neglect the McCarthys.

Dressed, her hair tidy, she raced down the steps and through the garden to the kitchen door. Phoebe had the soup ready and the lid closed on the pail, but to her surprise the chocolate face of jolly, fat Phoebe was streaked with tears.

"But, Phoebe, news of the army is good," Clytie told her.

"Y-yessum, missy." Phoebe wiped her eyes with her apron.

Zeke, Pete's slave and Phoebe's son, had been requisitioned by the army. Clytie had taken the pail and was hurrying toward the meadow before Phoebe's tears fully registered in her conscience. Phoebe would not be crying because a large company was coming to supper, nobody loved company like Phoebe. A hand squeezed at Clytie's heart.

She put down the pail, closed the meadow gate, and leaned against it. Could Phoebe's tears be connected with another fearsome prophecy the slaves had made? She had become so superstitious since their dreadful wails on the night of July 9 that she could no longer force herself to discountenance their behavior. Not since the eerie things that had happened to her on that very day . . .

She tried to break away from her haunting thoughts. She picked up the pail, then set it down again quickly and strained, listening, into the westward breeze, thinking she heard the stroke of a bell.

Oh, no, no! It was but her fancy recalling that dreadful day of July 9, when she had heard the vesper bells from the little church in Frederick.

It had been at just this time in the late afternoon. Although Frederick was far away by the road across the swampy part of Uncle Peter's land, it was not too far away when the wind was coming from the right direction for you to hear faint echoes of the bells. All that day she had gone about her duties with an iron band around her heart, her insides hollow with a nameless fear. Adam's voice, Adam's presence, had been all about her, calling out to her with anguish. In the late afternoon the vesper bells had brought release, like a comforting, peaceful presence, the touch of a loving hand.

Then the wailing of the slaves that night had awakened her from fearsome dreams. The next morning her anguish had only increased, but she had fought it. Oh, dear God! For the sake of the others she had tried so hard to put it aside, but not even her prayers had soothed her.

And now, today, Mr. Franklin had come, and with his news her hopes were restored. Phoebe's tears had no power now; the army would conquer, and Adam . . .

The loud cawk of a raven pierced her thoughts. Its dark wings were spread against the afterglow of the sunset sky—against purple, saffron and rose, and a blue as clear and infinite in depth as the cry of her own heart. Clytie picked up her pail and hurried across the meadow.

A cow mooed, Jamie's dog barked, a thrush called its sweet evening note, and she forced her heart to become calm. Then her name was piped in shrill childish chorus; the McCarthy children were racing toward her, like an elfin brood, out of the painted afterglow.

"We hyeared bells, missy!" cried Jeff, the eldest, who reached her first. "Dingedly queer bells!"

"Yonderly bells," Cynthia raced up to say.

"The vesper bells?" Clytie asked. Then perhaps she had heard . . .

But the children were protesting this. Little Mary, the youngest, slipped a hand into hers.

"Bells like a funeral," Jeff said. "Listen!"

They listened. Then one deep-toned note of a bell moved like a ghost through the valley. Clytie held her breath. Another stroke—a tolling bell—diffused itself under the lurid sky.

"Somebody dead," Jeff whispered.

Terror struck at Clytie's heart: funerals were not held at this time of evening, but bells were tolled on news of disaster. Disaster to . . . Panic seized her. She gave the soup pail to Jeff, cautioned him and the children to hurry to the cabin, then turned and fled toward the house. On her way across the compound she saw two slave girls, who had set their baskets of washing down; their arms were lifted and they were moaning incantations.

Near the garden walk Moses, head bowed, muttered as she passed, "Save him, little Lord Jesus! Save him!"

Save the young master, Pete? Oh, then, they *knew* that the tolling bells meant disaster to the army! In a frenzy she rushed into the hallway to find Uncle Peter, only to come up against Governor Sharpe's military staff and their gay banter.

"But, Mistress DeLancey, if a messenger has arrived in Frederick, he must have followed close on our heels, since we have just come from Hagerstown," said Lieutenant Harwood, who was smiling his deprecation of her anxiety, as the governor had smiled at first.

Uncle Peter had not smiled. He had ordered Solomon to ride into town, but Governor Sharpe had sent two of his aides instead.

"If a messenger has ridden in, bring him here at once," he ordered.

Clytie had been certain that his hand trembled as he took up his liquor glass. He looked tired and worried in some secret way, she thought, but not so old as when he had worn his black garments; he [illegible]pressive in his military regalia, red-coated and with shining [illegible]d orders. He had long been a military man.

[illegible] standing now on the portico with Lieutenant Harwood and [illegible] aides, trying to give attention to their flattery as Ephraim served them punch, but her ears were attuned only for the sound of horses' hoofs.

At long last it came, with a rumble of cart wheels. Constable Svarz drove the cart, and in it was the inert body of a large, heavy man.

Jamie was the first down the steps, and he called back to his father, who had come out onto the portico with the governor, "It's John O'Malley, one of the wagon drivers!"

John O'Malley, leader of the rumrunners, Clytie's mind registered. They were lifting him from the cart, standing him on his feet, supporting him. He was blear-eyed, muttering resistance: "I ain't . . . ain't done nothin'."

"Good old John! Come on, John, you are among friends now," Jamie coaxed. And when John pulled back Jamie said, "Easy, John, you've got a bad wound. I'll take care of you."

His right arm was matted with dried blood, his head, face and clothes covered with dust. A pitiable sight.

"Got me . . . got me wi' a tomahawk," he muttered, more docile now.

"Indians? Where'd they get you, O'Malley?" the squire questioned.

Meanwhile, the governor had been questioning the constable and Mr. Franklin had come out.

When O'Malley looked up and saw them gathered on the portico, he cried out in a suffering whine, "Leggo! Leggo! Ain't done nothin'. Ain't done nothin' but—but a letter."

Jamie and the constable held him now, trying to soothe him, but it was Mr. Franklin's quiet voice and manner that drew out the whimpering words: "Nothin' but a letter in his pockets. Dead . . . dead, he was scalped." O'Malley's head dropped on his chest.

"John, was the man a messenger from the army?" asked Jamie, but he got no answer.

The lusty, powerful O'Malley had fainted. They got him into Jamie's room, undressed him, and put him to bed.

Clytie had fetched bandages and the distilled seaweed Jamie used to dress the fearsome wound in the flesh of his arm. Jake had found a letter in the patient's tattered clothes addressed to Mr. Franklin, and she took it out to him with a message.

"He is regaining consciousness," she reported. "Jamie thinks he has been days without food, and that after he has been fed beef broth and brandy he may be able to talk."

"Deserter, hey? Deserter from the army," Governor Sharpe muttered to the other anxious faces around him.

But everyone was too intent on Mr. Franklin as he opened his letter to respond. Monica sat stiffly, as though in unbearable suspense; and Clytie was shaken with apprehension. Mr. Franklin's solemn face only crystallized her fears.

"From General Braddock," he said in a strange voice. "An order for a thousand pounds he owes me." He gave the letter to Governor Sharpe. Then he said to Uncle Peter, "But no news. It is dated July the eighth."

July the eighth, one day before the unhappy *ninth,* Clytie was thinking. And this was the seventeenth. The old clock in the hallway seemed to be swinging its pendulum toward eternity.

"Where'd O'Malley come from? What'd he say when he rode in?" Governor Sharpe impatiently asked Constable Svarz, who had just come from Jamie's room.

"He was too spent to talk, sir," the constable said. "But when we got him off his near-dead horse, and he kept mutterin' 'Dead, all dead,' somebody started tollin' the bells like—like it be our troopers he be talkin' of." The constable's head went down.

Clytie looked at Monica in wild-eyed fright. But to her astonishment Monica stood up, and, as if to discountenance such rumors, said graciously, "Gentlemen, shall we go in to supper?"

Jamie had stimulated O'Malley with beef broth and brandy. Propped up in bed, he seemed to be rational now, and as the squire summoned them into Jamie's room it was odd to see the eyes of the erstwhile ruthless rumseller linger on Monica with a look of compassion.

"I'm that sorry, ma'am——" O'Malley broke off and sat up with a jerk, seeing Governor Sharpe in the doorway in his general's uniform. He cried out in frenzy, "He's dead! D-dead!" Jamie held him, and on the other side Mr. Franklin soothed him, but he continued to blubber with terrified sobs, "Dead, I tell you! Saw him buried. Washington b-buried him, b-buried . . ." Sweat dripped from his brow.

Jamie and Mr. Franklin forced brandy and hot milk down his throat. Governor Sharpe, his face seemingly aging, reached toward the bedpost for support.

"Buried whom, John?" asked Mr. Franklin quietly.

swallowed, wiped his mouth, and turned to the soothing to a deliverer. "Braddock, sir," he said huskily. "General

Death stole into the room and made itself at home among them. And Clytie heard echoes: *"Marlborough s'en va t'en guerre."* . . . "Good night, white rose." Uncle Peter started to speak, but the governor's rasping voice cut him off.

"The man's mad! Mad! Harwood," he cried, "take a squad, ride to Will's Creek——"

"One moment, Governor."

But Mr. Franklin got no farther. O'Malley shouted defiantly, "Mad, is it? When I seen 'em butchered, slaughtered, wi' my own eyes? 'Twas me that was there, me!" He pounded his chest, strong now in his anger. "I saw 'em go down like flies, them redcoats, ambushed they was. Ambushed wi' cannon, cannon hid in the woods, an' us in a clearin', a clearin'!" His shout filled the room. "Bullets, arrows, cannon, right, left, afore! Down them platoons o' redcoats went, down! An' them left arunnin', runnin' yellin', runnin' away! Runnin'—!" He toppled over, face forward.

The room was stilled, except for the whispers between Mr. Franklin and Jamie as they ministered to the wounded man. Governor Sharpe eased into a chair and slumped forward. The squire's face was stricken. Monica sat unmoving, unseeing, staring at phantoms. Clytie struggled to hold onto her reason—the governor was right: they were heeding the tale of a madman. She wanted to leap toward the insensate heap on the pillows and shake the truth from him, the truth about Adam. Adam! Adam! She gripped hard onto her longing to cry out his name.

A lifetime of movement began—quiet footfalls, Jake bringing in lighted candles, Lieutenant Harwood bringing brandy for the governor, Uncle Peter went out, then came in again, Jake entered with a steaming potion, Phyly was standing behind Monica's chair—a movement that measured their aching uncertainty.

"All right now, John?" asked Mr. Franklin.

The patient had opened his eyes and was watching Mr. Franklin as he stuffed pillows behind him. Jamie held a mug of milk and brandy before him. O'Malley put his mouth to the mug and gulped greedily. Everyone hung on the smack of his lips, as on the hope of divine compassion.

"Could you tell us more of this battle, John?" Mr. Franklin asked gently.

O'Malley stared for a moment, a little wide-eyed, then shook his head. When he spoke, he sounded rational.

"'Twas no battle, sir, 'twas slaughter." He reached for the mug Jamie held, and gulped again. He eyed their anxious faces. "Brave man, the general, mighty brave." He heaved himself higher on his pillows, winced with pain, but went on in a stronger voice. "You ain't seen him gallopin', ridin' through them bullets like he was God. Four horses was shot under him. *Four!* Washington had two shot under him, four bullets through his coat never scratched him. Thing got a man's gall was them runnin' redcoats."

Governor Sharpe made a restraining sound, but O'Malley only shouted louder: "Me? I was there! Shootin' wi' a redcoat's gun after I biffed him down, 'cause I hyeared that officer yellin': 'Don't leave yo' general to be scalped!' Blast it!" O'Malley threw this at all his listeners. "*Our* boys wasn't runnin', no, no sir! They—they was jes' *dyin'*, them not on their bellies." He grabbed at the mug again, gulped, wiped his lips, and eyed Jamie. "Redcoat officers was all right. Firin' cannon 'cause them skunks run away. Two of 'em went down acarryin' off the general. *Our* boys took him up, got him away. Ain't one man-jack redcoat officer left alive——"

"Not *one,* John?" Jamie said quickly.

"Hunc? One, sure, name was Orme. I know 'cause I ketched him a horse. He was wounded."

Clytie's head went down. Jason! Oh, Jason, Jason! her heart moaned. But her spirit rebelled as her memory reminded her: "Life can be so beautiful, my heart, so beautiful."

"Can you tell us more of how the colonials fared, John?" Mr. Franklin's voice sounded hollow. A deadly quiet had fallen over the room as hearts and souls hung on the rambling words of the incoherent tale. O'Malley, sensing fully now his importance, spoke with resentment.

"Tell you how *I* fared, 'cause I ain't got no wagon nor horses no more, and I ain't got no pay——"

"You will be paid, John, every farthing," Mr. Franklin said. "But you were saying about the colonials," he urged the surprised, yet still surly-faced O'Malley.

"Ain't sayin' nothin' I ain't seen wi' my own eyes, 'cause I was with the colonel's forward command, handling pack horses. I didn't see them scouts go out, night before Braddock come up wi' the army, but I know all the troops be mighty worried when they didn't come back. Yes, sir, when they didn't come back we knowed them woods be full o' Injun snipers, knowed the colonel knowed it, like we knowed his scouts been scalped or took to the fort to be hanged. Leastwise, they was dead, an' that's what he tried to tell Braddock, but——"

"What scouts?" The squire's voice had a metallic rasp.

"Gist. He didn't leave us when his Injuns left. So him and that feller Adam Appleton went ascoutin'."

"Steady, honey! Steady . . ." Clytie heard Jamie's voice through a swirling, blinding darkness, felt his arms binding her. Fire was at her lips now, down her throat, she was gulping fire to warm someone else's quivering body.

"Courage, dear—" not Jamie's whisper, another's far away—"courage, DeLancey courage, my little one." "Life but the scene of good and evil." "Yes, Grandfather." Her numbed hands gripped the chair. She sat straight, perceiving—beyond feeling, beyond knowing—a comforter.

"Pete Chester—what of my brother, John?"

Clytie opened her eyes when she heard Jamie's voice and focused them on O'Malley's; she saw him shift his eyes to Monica, then to Uncle Peter. She heard words, but for a moment could force no meaning into them; there was only the void that sounded: Adam, Adam.

"Boys told me it happened when Washington's second horse got shot down," John was saying. "Said Pete Chester leaped up off his belly, like he'd been keepin' his men down—saved more 'n any other company—an' caught a horse. Run wi' him to the colonel, he did. Wouldn't nobody have got out alive but fer the colonel." O'Malley stopped, and Clytie's eyes turned to Uncle Peter's stricken face, to Monica's which were staring into the unknown. "He, Capt'in Chester, never got back to his men, sir, never got back. . . ." O'Malley's voice died away.

There was no sound in the deathly stillness. Mr. Franklin laid a hand on Uncle Peter's shoulder. Monica made no movement; her eyes were lifted. She seemed to be listening to a voice from another world.

CHAPTER
Twenty-nine

NEWS of the defeat of Braddock's army had rolled back to Frederick County in a lethal tide of fear. It numbed the citizens with unbelief, then terror, as the stories grew of the vast savage horde that had engulfed the magnificent army. The townfolk of Frederick had watched the great general, sent from the mother country for their protection, ride forth on that misty morning with only a fraction of his unconquerable troops, and they had marveled: "Banners flying, red-coated ranks stepping out." "Beelzebub! Can they march!" With the skirl of bagpipes, the shrillness of the flutes, the beat of drums echoing from the far hills, they were made more valiant still by the brave colonial troops and the rumble of the homespun thunder of Ben Franklin's white-covered wagons.

How then defeat, except by such a vast sea of savagery, inherent in the northwest country, that it might soon sweep down to destroy them all? Yet no panic reigned in Frederick County. Other generations of settlers had endured, and had found faith and courage to meet savage encroachment; they in their turn prepared to meet it with what means they had.

And with the courage of her ancestors, Clytie DeLancey prepared to meet the challenge of heartbreak dealt out to her. During the first long sleepless night after O'Malley's return, her numbed mind and senses had refuted the truth of his tale, remembering Jamie's description of that unconquerable army: "Siege guns, ammunition, supply trains rolling . . ." They were rolling through her head and calling Adam's capture and death a lie, all lies. At one moment during the tortured hours she had thought of rushing into Mr. Franklin's room, shaking him awake, and demanding to know how he could believe such lies.

Prayer had saved her. There was a point beyond which the human heart could not go in suffering, and when morning came she had found herself on the floor beside her bed, where she had knelt to pray. Endurance came, and with it a diamond-hard calm that lay beneath her conscious mind—a calm that contained hope and faith, faith that Adam had escaped his captors. She could not explain from where it had come; it was just there—a miracle born within herself and that connected with all the other miracles of life: love, birth and deathless spirit. Her hope had a continuity without beginning, without end.

It was given nourishment later that morning by Mr. Franklin. But he spoke first of Jason: "A truer gentleman I have never known, my child. He died a hero's death."

A sob escaped Clytie, unashamed. "To die, to be buried, so far from Blount," she said, "the home he so loved."

But when Mr. Franklin had spoken of Adam, that calm faith and knowing, which she could not explain to herself, obtained. "I dare to believe," he said, "that Gist and Adam, both so wise to savage cunning, may have devised some way to outwit their captors."

His words were a great comfort to her. But there had been little comfort for Mr. Franklin in the words of Governor Sharpe. "You must muster a regiment, Franklin," the governor had said. "No man can enforce enlistments as you. Morris will commission you a colonel, and you must build a line of forts, fortify the old, hey?"

Mr. Franklin was no military man. But the burden of defense was now on the colonists themselves, and by the quiet calm of Mr. Franklin's rejoinder one knew there would be no dissent to any duty he might perform for the colonies. He stood to lose his all through the destruction and loss of the wagons that he had collected with ceaseless toil. The thousand pounds Braddock had sent him the day before his death was but a small fraction of the monies due him, yet his thoughts now were only on further service to his countrymen. And it was clear that his own trials set less heavily on him than his sorrow and sympathy for the Chesters.

He rode away that morning with two of his postriders toward Philadelphia. Governor Sharpe was riding toward Will's Creek in the hope of intercepting Colonel Dunbar and his service of supply force that had remained behind the army. But before he had left he promised Uncle Peter that he would dispatch from Baltimore two hundred trained guards for the fort in Frederick, which was so woefully undermanned.

But now that a week had passed, and other wagon drivers had returned to Frederick to corroborate O'Malley's tale of the army's defeat, the fear grew of roving bands of emboldened enemy Indians now penetrating the country this side of the mountains. Abe Wilson had returned, but he could add little to what O'Malley had told of Adam's fate.

"He and Gist must have been but a few miles from the fort when they were trapped by the whole body of advancing savages," he said.

Yet Clytie's faith and hope were not shaken.

It was from the small number of surviving troopers who made their way back to Frederick that they learned how the colonials, too, had been decimated. Out of three Virginia companies, three hundred men, only about thirty-seven men were left: a monument of dead to Braddock's refusal to listen to Washington: "What? A colonial colonel teach a British general how to fight!" But it was Washington who had covered the retreat of the fleeing regulars.

"And except for the cowardly Dunbar running toward Philadelphia for protection from civilians," Jed Hawkins told the squire, "we could have marched on to the fort and taken it, sir. Washington knew it. Knew it was manned but by a handful. And had he been in command after we'd had time to re-form . . . But he wasn't in command, Dunbar was."

As more and more refugees streamed into Frederick with tales of the butcheries of roving Indian bands, the squire's greatest hope was for the two hundred guardsmen promised by the governor. They would not only greatly strengthen the fort and blockhouses, but would afford greater safety to the whole countryside. His greatest distress was for Monica.

She had withdrawn into a remote world of her own into which no one could follow. She moved silently about her duties, inspired by a greater loyalty to Chestermere, it would appear, than ever before; yet her spirit was in a shadow land. Where she communed with Pete? Clytie thought so. It was in the very sound of her voice when she would comfort Uncle Peter by reading the evening prayers: "In my father's house are many mansions. . . . I go to prepare a place for you. . . ."

Meanwhile, Jamie and Joe Toads had been scouting among the two neighboring Indian tribes. As Adam had predicted, old Big Corn had been murdered by his discontented warriors, who made it appear to the county authorities as a natural death. Joe Toads was now a refugee from their murderous intents, but he had skillfully discovered that Senecas and Susquehannocks had secretly invaded the camp, their purpose to bestir unfriendliness toward the settlers.

And though Clytie knew that Jamie's absences were a source of anxiety to Uncle Peter—Monica was never told of his destinations—she did not realize his true danger until one morning when he returned, and John O'Malley said with profound relief, hearing Jamie's voice, "Thank God, he's back! Thank God!"

The care of the sick man had devolved on her, and she, assisted by Jake and Sapphira, had found much solace for her own sorrow in applying Jamie's remedies and seeing her patient return to health. He was so humble and grateful for all that had been done for him that it was hard to believe that he was the vicious man encountered on the evening of the electrical experiment. It was the army that had changed him, and he had explained it in his own way.

"Friendly they was, them fellers, ma'am," he said, "like they ain't got nothin' against ye." The sharp little blue eyes under his impressive forehead had become calflike as she bent over him to thump his pillows. "An' ye . . . your own self, doin' so kindly by the likes o' me."

His big heavy face, clean-shaven, had lost much of its coarseness, and there was an intelligence in its contour—great nose, firm-set mouth and chin—that argued strength and endurance. Clytie had smiled as she gave him his midmorning soup.

"Trouble with you has been, John O'Malley," she told him, "that when they brought you over here from Newgate prison, you started in to bully and cheat your way in a new world that offered you the oppotunity for a free and honest life. You thought everybody was against you, as they had been in the London slums you told me about. And that was unworthy of a man of your intelligence." His big mouth had dropped open with amazement, but she had gone on, "It should interest you to know that many former prisoners, sent to the colonies, have accepted their chance and have become useful citizens. Some hold high offices—mayors, judges."

His eyes had followed her about the room as if she had pronounced some miraculous cure. It was clear that at the age of thirty-four he was beginning to see the light. This morning she had just finished reading him a chapter of *Gulliver's Travels,* when his thanksgiving over Jamie's safe return sent a little chill down her spine.

Pete's death had brought to Jamie the sort of inward suffering that he never voiced; it was bound up with the relinquishing of his own chosen career. For the sake of his mother and father he spoke as cheerfully of his brother as though he were still away at college, and this was helpful to Uncle Peter for it softened the shock and allowed it to wear away gradually. He came in now, trailed by Joe Toads.

"There's something I want of you, you old sinner," he told O'Malley. "We want a barrel of that rum you've got cached away somewhere. So out with it! Got to have it as a bribe for old Gray Cloud."

"My—my rum, Jamie?" Distress as well as doglike devotion was in his attitude.

"Your rum, John. Where'd you think we'd get any other? By Hector! Looks as if you'll be of use to us after all."

"Sure, Jamie, sure. But don't you go givin' old Gray Cloud rum less 'n you tell him what I tell you to tell him. Rum be bad for bad Injuns."

Clytie and Jamie smiled at the reformed rumseller, but Joe Toads grunted and said, "You die you go hell-fire." Joe was a Christian, and John's past iniquities toward the Indian tribes were unforgiven.

Clytie's anxieties about Jamie were not decreased when she found out why they wanted the rum. Old Gray Cloud's tribe, a few miles from Frederick, was composed of Mingos who had formerly been associated with the Shawnee, and Jamie suspected that two or three of that ever-treacherous tribe might have filtered back, for no good reason, into Gray Cloud's tribe.

"Joe found out that some of those young bucks have been war dancing. Gray Cloud's scared, but he can clear 'em out if he's a mind to."

"Look, Jamie—" O'Malley's eyes took on a dangerous light—"you give that old sleeping rattler a keg of my rum, but you tell him Kokojactonoh will hang his scalp up to dry if he don't hide every drop o' that liquor out for himself. Tell him Kokojactonoh will fill his hide full of poison arrows if he drinks it up under eight moons. See?"

Jamie was impressed. He was also delighted with the way O'Malley's arm was mending. The terrible swelling had gone down, and he was out of bed now most of the day. Mr. McCarthy too would soon be able to throw away the crude crutch Jamie had made for him. Meanwhile, between ministering to her patients, reading to the little McCarthys an hour or so every day, and doing all she could for Monica and Uncle Peter, Clytie found solace for her own sometimes-despairing heart.

It had not been easy to keep the resolute hope about Adam that had forced its way into her consciousness during those first days; there had been times of black doubt and desolation, but she was prayerfully schooling herself to overcome these. Loyalty to Adam and his prowess demanded that she believe—*believe* that he would survive any adversity. Compelled to back this up with a cheerful demeanor, she often noted Jamie watching her as if she were some phenomenon.

"Is it occult or hypnologic?" he said one day when he was in one of his own black moods.

Clytie shook her head. "I don't know, Jamie, I just know that if he were dead, I would know it—my heart would know it." That was all she could say. But she did wonder sometimes what Monica thought about her almost fainting that day when O'Malley had given out the news.

"Didn't register," Jamie had said. "Too intent on Pete."

That was doubtless true, but Clytie had determined to tell Uncle Peter about her and Adam if the time ever came when she could catch him alone and idle from his many duties. He seldom spoke of the savage raids known to be taking place to the northwest, or of the danger threatening their own borders; but his storage cellars were being filled. And, for added worry, his ship the *Queen* was now overdue.

"Can't get you away, honey," he said one afternoon, when she found him resting on the portico. "No way to send you away but by the *Queen,* and she's now nearly a month overdue." He was deeply troubled.

"Darling Uncle Peter, I—I don't want to go away," she said. When the full impact of the thought rushed upon her—of being sent away on the *Queen* before word of Adam should come—she dropped on her knees before him. "Please, oh, please, don't send me away! I can't go, I can't!"

Surprised at her outburst, he smoothed her hair. "God knows we don't want to lose you, honey. What would the place be without you? But our promise to your father—our promise . . ." His voice was unsteady.

She told him then about her and Adam, everything from the beginning, and watched him gladden, knowing that he had suspected as much all along.

"Nothing could have made me happier, nothing . . ." His throat tightened; he put out a hand and stroked her shoulder. "Poor little one, poor child," he murmured.

Clytie took his big hand in hers, stroked it a moment to gain courage, then faced him resolutely. "Adam is not dead," she said evenly. "He will come back. And it is for that I must wait, must wait."

His strange silence soothed her. After his first startled surprise had passed he said, "Stranger things have happened in this wilderness." His eyes looked beyond her. "Yet if it's true, as they say, that he and Gist were so near the fort . . . Savage things are practiced there. For all that, it could be. Hold your faith, honey, hold your faith!"

She felt very close to him; her eyes filled with gratitude. But he was still so adamant about fulfilling his promise to her father that she had not the heart to discourage his hope of doing so and assented cheerfully, "Your *Queen* will come sailing in soon, dear Uncle Peter. On a fair breeze she'll come, all her cargo safe."

But in her heart the arrival of the *Queen* became a menace that she was forced to struggle against as the hot, sultry days dragged wearily into August.

Clytie had had no news of her father for weeks, and when at last a letter came her anxiety concerning him was somewhat appeased. But the letter was not in answer to the one about Adam. It was from Boston. He had not been back to Albany for weeks, and at the time the letter was written he had not learned of the army's defeat.

She sat down at once to try to write him the manner of Jason's death, of which Jed Hawkins had told her, but it was still so poignant a grief that her eyes became misty as she remembered his words: "You see, ma'am—" Jed was a little confused himself, having just learned that she was Lottie, but his report was coherent—"Major Mayne was crossing the clearing with his skirmishers when it opened up—cannonfire right, left, afore, demon yells but no enemy in sight. Nothin' to shoot at but cannon smoke. 'Twas said Major Mayne got his men to firin' from their bellies, till the general come gallopin' by. 'On your feet, cowards!' he yells. 'Cowards! on your feet!'—" Jed had groaned—" 'Twere said the major bellowed to his men louder 'n Braddock: 'Keep down, men!' But he himself obeyed the general an' stood up, to be riddled by cannonfire."

Since that report Clytie had heard as in a nightmare Braddock's voice demanding: "Feared o' red Indians?" and Jason's brave reply: "Yes, sir," on that evening so long ago.

She gnawed her goose-quill pen, but at last the report was set down. She wrote of Uncle Peter's activities in strengthening the fort at Frederick, of the two hundred guardsmen promised by Governor Sharpe, of Monica's bravery in the growing anxiety settling over the countryside. And of the stouthearted refugees, the McCarthys. She finished the letter and sealed it quickly. There was so much she had not dared tell him.

There were the burning and slaughtering by bands of enemy Indians that drew nearer the borders of Frederick County; there was the fact that Amos Hartley and his sons, John O'Malley and Mr. McCarthy took turns now at night, patrolling the pastures and cattle pens; there were tales of marauders pushing down the rivers. "Down, always downward with the currents," Mr. Franklin had said. Of these things her father must not be told.

But Clytie's own distress was about Jamie. Last week he and Joe Toads had taken a keg of O'Malley's rum to Gray Cloud, and had come back cheered by his promise to drive the three troublemaking Shawnee from the tribe. Yesterday they had gone out again and had not come back.

She gave her father's letter to Ephraim, to send to the postrider, took up her bonnet and a copy of *Robinson Crusoe,* and went down to the cabin to read to the little McCarthys.

But her anxiety about Jamie still haunted her when, in the middle of the night, she heard someone walking about the house. Uncle Peter? Was his anxiety keeping him awake? Or was she dreaming? It was not until next morning that she learned how near the menace of the enemy had come to Chestermere.

Depredations and thefts by Indians had been unknown in Frederick County since the two mixed tribes had become friendly to the settlers; but last night, in spite of the watches kept, two shoats and a lamb had been butchered and carried off. Moccasin tracks had been found. And Jamie's beloved dog, Monk, had been killed.

Uncle Peter's face was a thundercloud during that silent breakfast. Their anxiety for Jamie was taut to the breaking point. Then they heard his voice. He came into the dining room full of his good news, kissed his mother, straddled a chair, and flipped his napkin open.

"Keg of rum did the trick, Pa. Old Gray Cloud drove those trouble-makers from his village. Said they were not Shawnee but Delawares. Hey, what's wrong, Pa?"

His father told him of the thefts during the night. "Likely the Delawares Gray Cloud drove out, son."

When he learned of the death of Monk Jamie had slipped away. Clytie watched his cold, speechless rage with a shudder. Jamie, whose life had been dedicated to healing the bodies of men, was now committed to the lust of killing on his own. Vengeance was in his eyes.

CHAPTER *Thirty*

SCOUTS from the fort in Frederick had reported that enemy Indians, penetrating southeast of the mountains, had stirred up bands of Delawares and Susquehannocks and were now raiding as far south as the border between Pennsylvania and Frederick County. Because of this, Squire Chester had arranged to have all his cattle driven to Abe Wilson's farm, which lay three miles south of the river and was considered fairly safe from raiders.

The Monocacy River zigzagged eastward, then west before it again took up its orderly flow southward; because of Chestermere's situation on the river, it would be cut off from help from the fort should immediate help be needed. Across an elbow of the river the distance was not great, but the only travel was by the roadway, a distance of several miles. Chestermere was also the most northernly of the plantations in the vicinity of Frederick and the best stocked with cattle. It was, as well, the best stocked with the commodity most coveted by Indian raiders: slaves. These, bound and shackled, could be transported by rafts to illicit slave dealers and bartered for the guns and ammunition most needed by the raiders for ravishment of the countryside.

The slave quarters were guarded at night, but because of a growing terror among the slaves it had been found necessary to guard them by day as they worked in the tobacco fields. The rich crop could not be neglected.

"Won't be ripening for nearly a month yet," the squire said hopefully—largely to reassure Monica, Clytie thought—"and by that time those militiamen promised by Sharpe should be here. This part of the country will be safe once it's known they are within call."

But Governor Sharpe was still at the forts along the mountain gaps. And it was because Uncle Peter well knew that the militiamen could not be dispatched until the governor returned to Baltimore that he was sending the most fearful-minded of his slaves along with the cattle to

Abe Wilson's farm. This would reduce restlessness among the others.

Clytie was watching this exodus with interest. To cross the river all were being loaded on flatboats: squealing pigs, cattle, Uncle Peter's imported prize sheep, squawking chickens. The general clamor was brought into order effectively by John O'Malley's brisk authority. He had become a tower of strength. His arm was now out of its sling. And although his pride in Uncle Peter's confidence in him sometimes made him swagger, he was never lacking in loyalty.

It was O'Malley who had spoken to Uncle Peter one day of Chris Gist within Clytie's hearing.

"Them Injuns and frogs can't finish off that old codger," he had said with assurance. "He'll outsmart 'em. Take that Appleton fellow, he's no fool neither."

Clytie's heart had hammered with hope, but Uncle Peter had shaken his head sadly. "It's been a long time, John. Even the wounded are back."

It was because neither Uncle Peter nor Jamie could force himself to hope that she never spoke of Adam, locking him tighter within her heart with her faith.

The flatboats had now reached the other side of the river, and listening to the hollow echoes of voices, Clytie was reminded of other hollow echoes she had heard, surely in some other life: the lusty yells of three galloping horsemen that had died out against the far hills. Jason, Pete, Adam. It had been then that she had felt forsaken, left alone in a dread corridor of time.

She turned back toward the garden, reproaching herself that memory had just listed Adam as lost with Jason and Pete, when his living spirit was still in the very air she breathed. After Uncle Peter had said that even the wounded were back, she had wanted to tell him that sometimes when she awakened in the night, after hearing Adam call her name, she was certain that he was wounded—somewhere he lay wounded—but she had not found the courage to speak. Hallucinations, he might think.

Yet her heart knew that Adam's spirit called reassurance to hers. Jamie had spoken one day of the vibrations of earth and air on which waves of sound might travel, and had said that these might account for the mystic knowing of the slaves, their uncanny prophecies. "They are closer to the earth than we are," he had said, "more sensitive to its vibrations." And sometimes she tried to think that such might account for the knowing of her heart, but it did not satisfy. There was some perception below the surface of all objective knowing that linked Adam's existence with her own.

But there was little time for such wandering thoughts these days, for Clytie was able to relieve Monica of many of her arduous duties. She spent long hours at the household ledger. As the days wore on—dry, hot and sultry—and tales of the butcheries and burnings drew nearer the border of Frederick County, it seemed at times as if Chestermere's very heart lay bared for a blow that all its gallantry might not be able to parry.

Clytie would sense it at night in the mournful lowing of the two milch cows that had been robbed of their calves and that were kept at night in the new cellar; or in the bark of a fox that she suspected was no fox; or in the call of a night bird, the notes of which so often went wrong, as Adam had taught her to observe. There was also the eerie feeling that unseen eyes watched her as she crossed the meadow to the McCarthy cabin.

Yet there was always brave cheer among the McCarthys. Mr. McCarthy had been able to throw away his crutch and, gun on shoulder, had taken his place with Hartley and his sons, guarding the slaves as they worked, or keeping one of the night watches. Mrs. McCarthy's pioneer spirit excluded fear; her discipline with her children was exacting.

Clytie heard their laughter one afternoon as she approached the cabin, and she asked Sapphira, who followed with a basket of ripened fruit, "Why can't you be as fearless and happy as they are, Sapphira?"

Sapphira had become a problem. She seemed forever in a state of fear. She forgot what she was told to do. She broke things, and often wailed dolefully. Phyly's discipline had not helped.

"I ain't got no mammy like dey's got," she answered dismally.

That was true, and as Ephraim's granddaughter she had probably received too much coddling around the house. But the more Clytie tried to think of some way to put metal into the girl, the more hopeless it seemed. Fortunately, Mrs. McCarthy did not share Clytie's discouragement, as was soon made evident. They arrived at the cabin at a very auspicious moment.

"I did see an Injun. I did. An' I chased him," Jeff, the eldest child, was insisting, in spite of the birch rod his mother held.

"An' he had a painted face, an' he run," one of the other children upheld.

"Excuse me, missy," Mrs. McCarthy said to Clytie. "But he disobeyed me, goin' into them woods." Then she demanded of Jeff, "Turn round."

Jeff turned and yielded his little behind to the rod, which fell resolutely on bottom and bare legs, but with no wails from him; the wails came from Sapphira.

"Now what in all tarnation!" demanded the dispenser of discipline. "Hush that yellin'!"

Sapphira only wailed more. "He seen an Injun, he seen——"

Mrs. McCarthy grabbed her. The switch was plied on Sapphira's legs and behind. Never had Clytie felt such sympathy for the birch rod.

"Shame on ye! Shame!" Mrs. McCarthy held firmly to her victim. "What good be ye to our mistress, sniveling, wailing? It's them that fear that first gits the hatchet." Sapphira's shrieks diminished. "Where be your guts? Ye got a heart brave as anybody's, an' ye have the wits to use it."

Amazing as it seemed, Sapphira was wholly subdued; no further sound escaped her. Shock of the treatment? Clytie wondered. She was to discover the truth on their way home.

"Is—is I got me a brave heart, missy?" Sapphira appealed.

"Certainly, Sapphira, you have a good heart. And try to remember what Mrs. McCarthy said—those that fear are in the most danger."

Clytie had scarcely expected the treatment to last. But, surprisingly, Sapphira's hands steadied, and Clytie heard her telling Ephraim one day: "I ain't scairt no more, I ain't. I ain't gwine to git scairt. I'se got me a brave heart, an' dem as gits scairt gits hacheted."

The cure proved complete when, a few evenings later, a painted savage face appeared at the library window, and Sapphira did not scream.

It happened on a chilly, rainy day. Monica had had a fire built in the library, and was resting before it, her eyes closed. Clytie was reading by candlelight. A blue twilight filled the windows. Sapphira came in with Monica's knitting bag; Clytie looked up and saw the frozen fear in her eyes. The nose of the savage was flattened against the windowpane. His head was bald except for a scalp lock and feathers; the streaks of blue and vermilion on his face were gruesome.

Clytie's reaction was instinctive; she leaped for the gunrack and her musket which was always loaded. By the time she had reached the portico the savage was bounding toward the wooded riverbank. She did not fire until she had reached the cover of the boxwoods; she was sure she saw him stumble before she dropped low for cover. An arrow whizzed into the boxwoods and stuck there.

To her utter amazement, when she was again in the house, Monica still sat by the fire. Alarmed, Clytie knelt close. Not even to have heard the gunfire! But it was sleep, deep sleep from physical and emotional exhaustion. Yet when later Jamie and Joe Toads found evidence of blood on the ground, and traced the savage to the river, where he had escaped in his canoe, Jamie told Uncle Peter proudly: "She winged him!" Monica overheard, and the tale was out.

"The child must be sent away, somehow," she affirmed with resolution. "Sent to safety—to Baltimore. In a small boat if there is no other way."

Uncle Peter argued there was no safety on the Monocacy. "And if we started her off from the Potomac wharf, what safety for a small sailboat—the only kind we've got—with the season of storms hard upon us? It's a long way to Baltimore."

Monica was appeased only when he promised that at the first warning of enemy Indians crossing the border in numbers, Clytie would be sent to the fort at Frederick.

It was because of this that Uncle Peter and Jamie conspired with Clytie to keep from Monica much that happened in the next few days as Chestermere appeared to be drifting, unalterably, toward a fight for its life. Amos Hartley and Mr. McCarthy routed a small band of Indians one night near the tobacco barns. And one night O'Malley killed one sneaking about the slave quarters.

"A renegade old Big Corn kicked out of his tribe months ago," Clytie heard him tell Uncle Peter. "Joe Toads says he was a bad one. Name was Wawa, Wild Goose."

Clytie clung for a moment to the garden bench on which she was seated; but the only reaction she could find in her heart was: Adam's need for vengeance is now appeased. Yet for a moment she shuddered again at the memory of that hideous, lustful face and the loneliness of the forest that had re-echoed her screams.

On the following day another thing happened to fill her with fear, not of the past, but for her immediate future: the *Queen,* Uncle Peter's ship from London, put into the wharf on the Potomac.

This morning Zeke, Pete's servant, who had been impressed into General Braddock's service, came home.

His return was announced by Phoebe's happy shouts from near the kitchen door: "My baby's come home! Glory to little Lord Jesus! My baby's come home to his mammy!"

Clytie and Uncle Peter followed hard on Jamie's heels toward the scene of reunion.

"Good Zeke! Good old Zeke!" Jamie cried, pounding Phoebe's six-foot *baby* on his dusty back, which was bare except for a ragged shirt.

"How'd you get here, boy?" the squire added to the glad welcome.

"Me, Mas'?" The Negro's own happiness shone through his tears. "I walk some, run a heap, I reckon. Rode some, too."

"Feed him up, Phoebe," the squire said. "Take a wash in the brook, lad. See that he gets fresh clothes, Phyly. Then come in, Zeke, and tell us all about it."

Back in the house Jamie maintained that it was evidence that luck had come to Chestermere. "Leastwise, we've got another one to man a gun."

Zeke, Pete's constant attendant since they were small lads, had been well trained to ride and shoot. When he told his tale to the squire he admitted unabashed that he had stolen a horse and a musket to make his escape from Dunbar's fleeing brigade.

"Me, I ain't gwine to go to no Philadelphy town and git put on no boat for no Lon'on town. So I lay me low, and come dark I fin' me a hoss an' I lit out from dere, I did."

He had overtaken some of the wagon drivers from Pennsylvania, but by the time he reached Hagerstown alone, he had been forced to barter his horse for food. He had come from there on foot, hiding for days, because he had sighted a band of painted Indians and had seen the cabin of a settler in flames. As for Pete's death he knew only what he had heard, since he was far to the rear with Dunbar's detachment.

"I ain't believed what dem runnin' redcoats say," he affirmed. But when the troopers of Pete's own command had come up, he had said, sobbing, "I ain't et me nothin'. I ain't slept."

What he had seen and heard of the infiltration of enemy Indians only confirmed the reports of the Frederick scouts. But he added: "Folks say dem frog Injuns burn *our* Injuns dat won't put on war paint an' butcher our folks."

But Jamie found cheer in the very fact that Zeke had returned.

"What we need now, Pa, is for the *Queen* to put in with those four-pounder guns she carries. With those stationed near the house we could scare off an army of Indians. Nothing scares them like cannonfire."

"They did not scare at Braddock's twelve-pounders, son," said Uncle Peter, who was not cheered.

"That's because they were hidden from the guns and officered by the French. Those headed this way would be Delawares, Susquehannocks or Shawnee–such as they used as spies behind our lines–wouldn't they, Pa?"

"Can't be sure of that, son. An enemy Indian is an enemy Indian, of any breed."

Nor did Uncle Peter look hopeful when Jamie said he and Zeke would go to the Potomac wharf.

"Might sight the *Queen,*" said Jamie, "since this is our lucky day."

Clytie later saw them ride off in the cart, to which Rozinante had been hitched. Uncle Peter himself had gone, or had sent someone, every day to the wharf for a sight of his ship's sails; and on this day the long-awaited vision materialized.

The Chester household was assembled for evening prayers when Jamie returned with the news.

In these dark days it had become the custom for all on the plantation to gather in the rear garden after supper to hear the squire read passages from the Bible. And never had his big voice rolled out with such grim emphasis as on this evening.

" 'I shall give thee the heathen for thine inheritance,' " he read, " 'and the utmost parts of the earth for thy possession. Thou shalt break them with a rod of iron, thou shalt break them in pieces like a potter's wheel.' "

An "Amen!" came from Ephraim, to be repeated in a wave of assent by all present.

The squire turned the leaves of his Bible to read further: " 'They and all that pertain to them shall go down into the pit and the earth close over them.' "

"Praise the Lord! Praise the Lord!" The words ran about the garden in a flood of sound. At the signal all knelt in prayer. John O'Malley, who was not far from Clytie, knelt awkwardly, but when the prayer was finished he sat back on his haunches, rubbed his great hands, and looked up at her, awed, perplexed.

"It–it says that in the Good Book 'bout Injuns, ma'am?" he asked in regard to the passages just read.

"About any transgressors or unbelievers," Clytie answered, a little uncertain of her ground in the face of his awakening spirit.

It was at that moment that Jamie's bellow reached them: "She's in, Pa! The *Queen's* in!"

During the resultant rejoicings Clytie sank limply onto a garden seat, unconscious that O'Malley was beside her until he spoke with deepening awe.

" 'Rod of iron' the Good Book said, meaning the cannon, ma'am?"

Clytie nodded. She could see in his eyes that he had been given proof of the Lord's fulfillment of a promise: cannon to repel the enemy. He moved away to speak of such wonders to the McCarthys, while the promise of the Chesters to her father weighed heavily on Clytie's spirit. The *Queen* had put in, so her immediate departure from Chestermere was assured. She was torn between loyalty to those she loved and loyalty to her own deepest wish. Through her deep perplexity she heard Jamie's exultant recital.

"Pirates and freebooters drove her off course," Jamie was saying, "but Captain Jackson said the *Queen* showed a clean pair of heels, till one enemy craft pursued. . . . He held his fire, and when the pirate was hard upon him he let go. He sunk her. . . ." He followed his father into the house.

Clytie sat alone in the gathering dusk. Jamie's account of the log of the *Queen* reminded her of all that had happened since she too had set forth on a voyage—a wilderness voyage. The log of Clytie DeLancey. She too had encountered a pirate in Aunt Prissy. She had not sunk Aunt Prissy, only the Lord could do that, but she had sunk a lot of freebooter fears that had threatened her spirit. And she had escaped into a world that was her heart's true home, with Adam the core and rhythm and light of it. The wilderness had given him to her and the wilderness had taken him away. A sob started deep down, but she held it firmly while her thoughts leaped to Pearl Street, with her father not there, where she would be cut off from the news that would surely come of Adam's safety. Adam's safety! Safety! The trees rustled it softly overhead. It was to these words she must hold, as to salvation. But to hold them in New York through long dreary months, while here at Chestermere word might come soon, soon! And find her gone.

It seemed to Clytie, in her desolation, that she must find a fortitude beyond courage to face her banishment—a fortitude that could spring only from the inexhaustible hope in the deep well of her spirit.

She got up resolutely and went into the house to face Monica's heartfelt relief that she could now be sent to safety.

CHAPTER *Thirty-one*

THE squire's strategy for defense of his home included only that the house itself and the tobacco sheds be defended. With so few men it would be impossible to defend the ripening tobacco crop, the richest in four years, and the outbuildings. The main house was the most vulnerable to firebrands, the savages' deadliest weapon, since it was surrounded by shrubbery; and the woods to the south, now dry from the September heat, could be fired, even though the burning brands might be kept at a distance from the house by musket fire.

"But if it's slaves they want, Pa," Jamie had said, "what profit to fire the house with the slaves in the cellar beneath? They couldn't barter maimed or roasted slaves."

"Savages don't reason, son, when set on slaughter and destruction, unless led by a Frenchy."

The squire figured too that since the savages would undoubtedly come from upriver in war canoes, they would make no attempt to pass the tobacco barns and the defense Hartley and his sons could put up there, to reach the east garden. Attack, if it came, would come from the west. Therefore, two of the fourpounder cannon from the *Queen* had been set up in the rear garden, their iron noses, hidden by shrubbery, directed toward the west. One was just outside the dining-room door, the other outside Jamie's bedroom door in the south wing.

It had been a long journey up the Monocacy from the wharf with the cannon, sailors and slaves bending to the oars of the flatboats. Meanwhile, a friend of Jamie's had arrived at Chestermere with his wife and five children to plead for shelter; they had been welcomed. He was Mr. Stainbach, to whose home Jamie and Mr. Franklin had ridden in their quest for wagons. The Stainbachs had made their escape from the northernly hills before their home could be attacked.

"Roving bands of painted devils all around," Mr. Stainbach told the squire, "harrowing mostly the Pennsylvania settlements."

He was a mingy little man, long-nosed, bearded, but hard-timbered, and with a family he had cowed into servility. Mrs. Stainbach was timid and self-effacing, and her children sweet and wistful, as Monica and Clytie installed them in two of the east bedrooms on the second floor.

It was late afternoon when Captain Jackson arrived with the cannon, and Clytie learned the full truth of the fate that awaited her: the *Queen* would sail down the river at dawn and make for the bay and Baltimore, where she must wait until Mike and a guard could arrive to take her to New York. There was no safety in sailing for New York with the sea full of enemy vessels. Baltimore! Alone for dreary weeks, with only Sapphira to attend her! But she made no comment.

"Go ahead, fire her, son," Uncle Peter was saying as Clytie came out into the garden. "We've got no powder or shot to waste, but you want to get your hand in."

Captain Jackson, a stalwart, dauntless man, who rolled about in his walk as though imitating a sea gull, and four sailors had been giving Jamie instruction about the cannon. It was a breechloader, and Clytie thought Jamie was listening a bit vaguely to their talk of its recoil, the need to keep powder containers at a distance, and other things. But when the gun was loaded he cried "Ready!" and fired.

The thunder of its voice rolled like Jovian anger over the valley. The old house seemed to shade its windows as if in indignant outrage. The very ground, with its long cultivation, seemed to resent the volleying echoes. The smoke and acrid smell were still filling the garden, choking the honeysuckle vines, when Jamie said just the thing Clytie had prayed he would. He was too rational not to question his own prowess. Jamie's fiber was just not of the stuff of which warriors were made.

"Takes practice, Pa. Steady hands and a cool head," said Jamie as he moved restlessly about the garden, running his hands through his red hair. Neither his head nor his hands were steady or cool in the face of what would be expected of him: to man one cannon in the case of attack, and to instruct one of the other men in handling the other.

"I'm not sure," he said with some violence. "Just not sure. *Might* not be if attack came. And too much depends on it."

"All right, son." His father's voice was calm.

And Clytie could see that Jamie's reaction had proved his father's own theory. Uncle Peter had only given Jamie the chance to make his own decision.

"Now then, Jackson," Uncle Peter said to his skipper, "the question is, can you get the *Queen* to Baltimore short of four men, these fellows here to be left with us as gunners?"

It was a pregnant moment, and a wild hope stirred in Clytie's heart as the skipper flapped his coattails, walked with a roll a few steps away from the squire, then back again.

"Figured you might be needin' two, sir," the captain compromised. But Uncle Peter was in no compromising mood.

"Got to be on the safe side, Jackson." His voice grated like iron. "Four trained gunners is what we need." Then he said thoughtfully, "If the devils get this far down, like as not they'll pass us by to attack Frederick. More to be gained there—butchery, plunder—seeing that Sharpe's militiamen haven't arrived and the fort is undermanned. But if they strike at me, Jackson, I've got to be prepared. Got to be."

It was the forthright way in which the skipper's bright-blue eyes met this ultimatum that gave Clytie hope for delay in the sailing of the *Queen;* they seemed to say that he too must be prepared to protect his vessel. For one day's delay, only a day, she prayed. It might prove the very day in which word of Adam would come. . . .

"Lost two men, as I told you, sir, in that pirate skirmish coming over," the skipper said. "Took a chance on fair weather to get her down here from Baltimore, what with her cargo none too steady, seeing all we unloaded there. But knowing as how you were worried . . . Thing now is that it's gettin' on to equinox weather, and with her cargo in the shape it's in . . ."

"How long to restack her cargo, Jackson?" Uncle Peter shot at him.

To Clytie the question sang with hope.

" 'Bout as long as it would take to fill her up with a goodly portion of that prime tobacco in your sheds, sir."

"Then go to it, Jackson." Uncle Peter did not hesitate. "Every slave I've got will fill the flatboats tomorrow with sotweed. Pack her solid——"

"No, Squire, no!" No one had noted Monica standing in the doorway. "The child—Clytie—there must be no delay."

"Got to be, Mony." Uncle Peter's voice was firm. "Got to keep the gunners, and can't risk sending the *Queen* out short of hands and with unstable cargo. . . . Take no more 'n three days, hey?"

"About that, sir."

Three days! Clytie rushed to her room, fearful that her joy in this reprieve might upset Monica—sorry for Monica, gladder for herself. Anything could happen within three days. She moved about among her packed boxes, conscious of her need to think more of Monica, less of herself, of Monica's peril that had horrified her so long ago in the library at home when her father had first spoken of such a possibility. Yet her own need to share that peril now seemed of paramount importance. She, who was to be Adam's pioneer woman, to be treated as a fragile, sugar-coated creature unable to endure hardship and danger, when what she truly needed was some rush of life, some hard charge on her youth and strength to prove her endurance, something to *dispel* endurance of the inward ache, the endless ache by night and day! She faced that thought with resentment. Had she then but beaten her soul into submission? Was her fear for Adam still alive? No . . . no . . .

She heard Jamie's voice below her window. He had made brave efforts to understand the cannon warfare to which he was so ill-adapted by nature. She felt a rush of tenderness for his youth, for his need to defend this little kingdom of culture, this little foothold on a continent that must endure against all the sinister powers of destruction beyond the wilderness hills. The general's great army had failed to defy such savagery. It had only dashed itself into spindrift against the powerful and tricky current ever present beneath the green wilderness sea.

The three days had almost passed. It was the afternoon of the third day. The *Queen* would sail in the morning at dawn.

"We need that trigger finger of yours to help defend the castle," Jamie said. He had followed her into the library where she was replacing a book, and the gesture seemed so final that her eyes became misty.

"Then why not use Captain Jackson and his crew from the *Queen,*" she voiced unhappily, "instead of sending me away?" It was a question long suppressed, yet futile.

"But, honey, whether she sails or not they've got to guard the ship."

"Jamie!" The call came loudly from O'Malley in the hallway. Jamie hurried out.

When Clytie followed to the rear door of the hallway they were talking in low, excited undertones, and the fierceness in O'Malley's face reminded her of the old unregenerate rumseller. They awaited Uncle Peter, who was coming up the garden walk.

"Likely rain tonight," Uncle Peter said mildly.

"Found it, sir, found it," O'Malley interjected in an ominous voice. "Just 'bout where Joe Toads said 'twould be, couple o' miles upriver."

"Evidence of how *many?*" Uncle Peter's voice was anxious now.

" 'Nough to eat a whole calf. Carcass near the hole in the ground dug to roast it. An' around the hole, signs where they'd slept; like they do, feet close to the warm ashes in the hole."

Clytie slipped behind the honeysuckle vines, her eyes on Uncle Peter's grim face. She knew John O'Malley had been scouting all day, and that Mr. Stainbach, who came up to join them, had been guarding the slaves in the tobacco field.

"Where do you figure they've gone, O'Malley?" Uncle Peter said.

"Ain't gone nowheres, sir. Layin' low they be—"

"If they'd been thereabouts, ye'd not got out alive, man," Mr. Stainbach put in.

But Uncle Peter thought differently. "Wrong, George. They wanted O'Malley to think they'd taken to their canoes, gone upriver."

It was a climax. Clytie sensed it so sharply that it was like reaching a bend in the road and finding not the expected vista, but that she had doubled on her tracks and come back to where she had set out from. She was still at Chestermere, still a part of it, while the hour of crisis approached, a part of it when the gray, murky sky closed in at the sunset hour and Joe Toads came in from his scouting trip to report that the Indians had taken to their canoes, but that they had not gone upriver; he had spotted a dozen or more canoes hidden farther down the river under the overhanging trees.

After that, things moved so quickly toward the gray-blue muggy twilight that not even Monica stopped in her swift round of duties to question Clytie's offers to help.

"Take Sapphira and see that all the wooden shutters upstairs are closed," she said quietly, without any suggestion of panic. "Look out for Mrs. Stainbach and the children."

Never had Clytie moved more gratefully to obey; she was one again with their lives, no longer parceled and tied about with loneliness. She raced up the stairs, Sapphira at her heels.

"Mebbe dey–dey come tonight, missy?" Sapphira's eyes held the plea that her recent courage must bring the reward of her safety.

"Maybe not. Help Mrs. Stainbach close the shutters in her room, and be careful when you lean out the window, Sapphira."

From room to room she went, stretching her long strong arms out the windows, releasing the iron fasteners that held back the stout wooden shutters. After she had bolted them she lowered the upper sash of each window, marveling that the sickle slit in each shutter was so placed that if a man rested the stock of his gun atop the lowered sash, the barrel pointed through the slit, leaving room to sight his target. The bolt that held one of the shutters in the sewing room stuck, and she had to hold on to Sapphira while the girl leaned out and her stronger hands unloosed it.

"Now listen closely, Sapphira," she said, "for I'm very proud to be able to trust you. I want you to take these three pallets on which the McCarthy children have been sleeping—" Monica had requested that they be sent up each night—"into Mrs. Stainbach's room. And when the children come up tell them they are to sleep there tonight. Make a pallet for yourself and stay with them. Once it is done I don't want you to leave that room. Understand?"

Sapphira did. And after Clytie had spoken to the docile but trembling Mrs. Stainbach about the arrangement, she felt comforted. The stouthearted McCarthys would put stamina into the other pallid brood. And when the two younger Hartley children joined them there might be fights, but at least there would not be terror.

Ten children in the house, she considered. A gloomy picture, should attack truly come. And if the horses and wagons had not been given over to the Braddock expedition, they might all have been dispatched to the stockade in Frederick. When she went downstairs all the shutters were closed and the front door barred; the house was so stuffy that she went out into the sultry blue dusk of the garden. Not a leaf moved on bush or tree.

"Yes, got feathers, these red blokes," she heard near Jamie's doorway. "Got to pick 'em afore ye hang 'em up to dry. Good eatin' an' ye git enough to make a mess." Chuckles followed.

Then an answering cockney accent: "Henemy, me oiy! Let 'em git 'er load 'er freebooters, an' these folks be larnin' what 'er henemy be."

Half hidden in the shrubbery amid which one of the cannon stood sat two of the gunners from the *Queen*, munching big chunks of chocolate-covered gingerbread, and into Clytie's mind came: "Feared o' red Indians?" An echo of the general's taunting voice. The gunners grinned broadly when they saw her.

"Good eats," one said. "Could do wi' a mite o' ale."

Clytie hurried to the pantry, drew mugs of ale from the keg, found more of the gingerbread, and took a full tray out and served all four gunners—the second two were dozing beside the dining-room door.

When her tray was empty she saw John O'Malley, Mr. McCarthy and Mr. Stainbach come into the garden from the compound, with muskets on their shoulders, and stand waiting. Then came the far cry of a whippoorwill and Jamie's call to them from near the meadow gate.

"That's Joe! Tell Pa Joe's back!" Jamie cried.

It appeared to be a sort of signal for action, for the men went quickly across the garden to the path that led toward the tobacco barns on the river.

Clytie balanced the wooden tray against the wall of the house near the hall doorway, and let her hand rest with affection against the twelve-inch-thick walls of rosy brick, which were lustrous in the blue dusk. She stood off to regard the whole solid structure of the house, which had a personality of its own, and with its barred windows a valor and endurance. Yet in her imagination she saw firebrands whirling toward its defenseless roof, the blazes gutting . . .

"No more than a mile up the river, Pa," Jamie was saying as he and Joe Toads came through the gate and headed toward the shrubbery in front of the kitchen door. Uncle Peter was there. Now, in a sharp metallic voice he was flinging orders left and right.

Shadowy figures moved quickly or ran. Low staccato voices sounded half audible. Night crept down on twilight with stealthy breath. Laughter cackled from one of the gunners, and Clytie moved toward the shrubbery that blocked off sight of the kitchen door. A low wail sounded along the winding path that led past many of the outhouses toward the slave stockade.

"Hang you, *quiet!*" That was Moses' voice. "Move faster."

A long, dark line of slaves, directed by Moses and Solomon, was moving toward the door of the cellar beneath the kitchen and pantries. Women and children first, the line moved in orderly fashion, the eyes of each slave silvered, agleam with fear. A baby cried and was hushed at a woman's breast. It was a sight to stir compassion.

"Dan!" The squire halted the line at the cellar door, and when a big Negro came from the end of the line, he said, "I want you to see that the women and children reach the far end of the cellar."

"Y-yassar, Mas'," the voice of the field hand quaked. But those who might have induced panic had been sent to Abe Wilson's farm.

Dan was the first one to enter the cellar, and as the others moved down the steps the squire told them, "No outcries from anyone, mind you. Keep quiet. You are in no danger. We mean to defend you."

"Delia, I'll send milk down for the children," said Monica, coming from the kitchen door. "Phoebe, keep the old women quiet."

When the last of the slaves was through the trap door, the squire said, "All right, Ephraim." He and Monica moved away.

They had not noticed Clytie amid the shrubbery, and she watched

Ephraim, his dark eyes luminous with Christian faith, as he clutched his Bible and followed down the cellar steps. She heard then the solemn words that issued from below: " 'Let not your hearts be troubled. Ye believe in God, believe also in me.' "

When Ephraim came out of the cellar all murmurs had died. Moses closed the stout doors, barred them, turned the great key in the lock and took the key into the house. Clytie hurried back to the door of the hallway. The gunners from the *Queen* were still chuckling in good-natured raillery among themselves.

Uncle Peter had called the roll of the house defenders and had named the window or part of the house each was to guard. There were: Stainbach, McCarthy, Jamie, Zeke, Jake, Ephraim, Joe Toads, Mrs. McCarthy, Clytie, Monica and Phyly. With Uncle Peter, they made twelve. Moses, O'Malley, Hartley and his two sons and Mrs. Hartley, and Solomon were guarding the tobacco barns.

They were to take turns at sleeping until those on watch gave the signal. The four gunners were already asleep on the floor of Jamie's room.

Only one candle burned in each room, and Uncle Peter, followed by Jamie and Clytie, was moving through the rooms examining each musket and the supplies of ammunition at each window.

"Could be as the town scouts think, Pa," Jamie said, "that they'll pass us by and head for the town. Ma's got that in her head, too."

Uncle Peter made no reply. "Firelock, Spanish," he said of one of the muskets he was examining. "Most of these others, the same. From my old regiment. Well primed. Where's your musket, Clytie?"

She hurried into Pete's room and took it from the west window that had been assigned to her. Mrs. McCarthy had been assigned to the other; she now lay on Pete's bed asleep. Jamie's room was at the end of the narrow hallway onto which both Monica's and Pete's rooms opened, but it had no west windows, only a west door; the one window was to the east. She could hear the gunners snoring peacefully.

"It is the one Mike bought for me in Philadelphia," she said when she gave her musket to Uncle Peter.

"Very good gun," Jamie said, yawned, and went off to his room to lie down.

Monica too was trying to rest, worn out by the momentum of the day and by her despair that Clytie should have been caught in the gathering danger. It was because of this that, when Uncle Peter had approved the gun and she had replaced it by the window in Pete's room, Clytie came back into the parlor, sat down on the sofa beside him, and slipped her arm through his.

"I feel so proud to be with you here at Chestermere tonight," she said. And when he only stroked her hand and did not speak she said, "Please, believe that my father would not have it otherwise, Uncle Peter."

His shoulders were bent as he shook his head. When he looked up his face was haggard.

"That–that pistol you had, honey, where–where is it?" he asked.

"Here. I brought it down to show you," she said as she took it from atop the harpsichord, where she had placed it.

She had made a bag for it and had attached it to a belt which she could strap around her. She did so now, fastening it about her waist over the dark-blue cambric dress, which she had worn so much it was frayed. But every other dress was packed for her departure.

"See! It's a holster. I can slip the pistol in and out without fumbling," she said, yanking it out and putting it back in a show-off manner.

But he did not smile. She placed the gun in his outstretched hand.

"Dueling pistol, hey? Safety catch."

"I kept it by me on my trip through the wilderness."

When he gave it back to her he was staring grimly into a distance beyond her as he said, "Keep it by you. Keep it by you, child." His voice had hoarsened. "And if the worse comes to the worse, *use it.*" Grimly he emphasized, "*Death* is better than . . ." He choked and put a hand to his throat.

Clytie watched him pull at his collar and unfasten it. For a moment his unfinished words so stunned her that she only gaped. *Use* it? On *herself?* Then in a desperate desire to comfort him, she said softly, "Yes, Uncle Peter, I–I understand." Death better than kidnaping, or worse. Yes, she *did* understand. He could not know how *well* she understood!

One of the candles, made after Mr. Franklin's recipe, shone brightly from the mantelshelf and was reflected in the mirror. She thought of Uncle Peter's long worry over his friend's loss of money advanced for the horses and wagons, his long anxiety over the army, his loss of his beloved son, and, out of the debacle of the army, *this:* facing the loss of his home, all he held dear, and the lives of so many dependent on his own valor. And now her own presence was but an added burden.

The candle on the mantelshelf reminded her, too, of that flickering candle, so long ago, on the mantelshelf before her grandfather's portrait.

His *frown. Then, this was the cause.* This day, this night, the reason for his frown. Her moment alone with Uncle Peter in the quiet house seemed like the end to a long, fateful journey—*Mextaub.* She had heard her grandfather use that word; it meant, "it is written." But *death!* Icy fingers were on her spine; she had never thought of death for herself. Not even when she swam the Elk River, with Adam waiting for her on the other side. *Adam.* She could see again his hand held out to her from the riverbank, hear again his shout: "You'll do it!"

And all at once Adam's hand held out to her became, irrationally, the only real thing in the world; his hand brushed all dangers aside. A confidence and hope came to her that was as unreasoning as it was all-pervading. She sprang to her feet.

"Darling Uncle Peter," she cried, "we'll worst those savages if they come! You'll see!" Smiling, she tugged at him, to pull him from the sofa. "You are going, sir, this minute to get some rest."

When she had tugged him into the hallway she threw her arms about him in a loving good night and headed for the stairs. When she waved to him from the landing his face had brightened.

But inside her room the air was stifling. She put her hand through the sickle slit of one of the windows, but no breeze stirred. No sound came from anywhere in the house; all the ten children must be asleep. She had forgotten to bring up a lighted candle, and so left her door open to the light from the hall candle. She knelt and said her prayers, then lay down on her bed without even removing her shoes, as on the trip through the wilderness. She closed her eyes to hear again the wind stirring the leaves of the forest. . . . Adam lay beside her, his arms about her. Adam, Adam! Over and over, she was calling his name, and on a slanted moonbeam his own voice streaked down, calling, calling her, roaring her name now in a blinding light, a volley of light and sound.

Clytie sprang from her bed, dazed by the thunder from the cannon outside, uncertain whether she were asleep or awake, struggling to grasp the meaning of the red glare that spilled through the slits in the shutters. Awareness came; she raced from her room and down the stairs.

CHAPTER
Thirty-two

WHEN she reached the lower floor of the house her actions became instinctive; she rushed to her musket in Pete's room and leveled it through the glowing sickle of the shutter. But she saw nothing to fire at.

Through a lull in the cannon's roar she heard Uncle Peter's voice outside. Conscious now that her worst fear was for Jamie, she put her musket aside and raced to his open door. It was shadowed from the red glare of the burning cattle barns by the shrubbery.

"Gunners, hold your fire till I give command. Jamie, mind the near trees, the roof." Uncle Peter hurried past her to other parts of the house.

"Jamie, keep down!" Clytie screamed against the gunfire that battered the house as he raced from the cannon at the dining-room door to the one near where she stood. He reached the shadows on all fours.

She heard the thud of an arrow digging into the roof. Coming from where? Shots whizzed overhead. Coming from nowhere, everywhere. She saw no Indians.

"Fire!" In the second's lull the squire's voice sounded from the dining room. The cannon at that end roared, rocking the red glare of the night.

Jamie was crouched with his musket in the shadows; Clytie raced back to her post. Her musket was at the slit opening when the smoke cleared, and against the lurid light of the burning barns she saw a dark object in a tree near the picket fence. She fired. The object dropped to the ground. Flames lighted the compound, orchard and meadow, but nothing moved within the glare.

"Fire!" The cannon at Jamie's door splintered the picket fence. Grotesque figures disentangled themselves and ran amid flying debris. Clytie reloaded with steady hands, amid the cracking of muskets at the other west windows.

Fire, reload, fire, kill, kill! Not Clytie DeLancey, another born to the lust of killing.

"Stainbach got two of 'em at the east window. Aim to surround the house if they can."

Her face sweaty, blear-eyed from the acrid smoke as she aimed at those racing figures, Clytie was astonished at Mrs. McCarthy's calm voice and her actions at the other window. She lifted her musket as Clytie reloaded, sighted and fired like a veteran. When she withdrew it from the slit she spoke.

"Smell a *frog* in this," she said. "If 'twarnt so, grapeshot from them cannon would o' scairt 'em off long ago."

"Hold fire at west windows!" boomed the squire from the hallway. "Zeke, east parlor window! Keep 'em out of those bushes."

"They aim to worm around close to the house and git those gunners. Frog's game," said Mrs. McCarthy coolly.

Clytie wiped her sweating brow. Volleys of firing were sounding from the pantry windows that flanked the cellar doors. She glued her eyes on the compound. At the left, bordering the orchard, things crawled, multiple things.

"Fire low to your left. Fire!" The squire's voice was coming from Jamie's door, but by the time he had repeated his shout at the dining-room door the cannon at Clytie's left had *not fired.*

The one to her right ripped into the red curtain growing brighter and wider now, and when the smoke had cleared, nothing crawled near the orchard. A child screamed upstairs. A curse sounded as a low moaning cadence reached up from the cellar. Crack, ping, crack—the noises came from an east window.

Acrid smoke was choking Clytie when she withdrew her musket from the window, conscious that she had been waiting for the cannon at Jamie's door to fire. It had not done so. Musket shot spattered at the walls of the house and Mrs. McCarthy's gun spat back. But with an instinct of frantic fear, Clytie rushed to Jamie's door.

She crossed a slit of red glare into the shadow of the shrubbery, stumbled, and fell over a prostrate figure.

"Jamie!" Her cry strangled her. She lifted the head of the figure; her hands were bloodied. Not Jamie! "Jamie!" She groped, calling his name. Another figure lay sprawled over the cannon. Not Jamie. "Jamie!"

In a shadow cast by the red glare something moved, thrashed about. Shots whined above her head as she crawled toward it—two figures, rolling, locked together. One was naked except for a breechcloth. Now on top, now beneath Jamie's writhing body. During a lull of firing she heard grunts, heavy breathing. Her whole being taut, she moved as they moved. Pistol cocked, she dare not fire. Now the savage was atop, head lifted, Jamie's arms were limp. As the savage raised his arm her finger steadied on the trigger. Her shot smashed his head.

She was forced to stand up to drag the slimy savage off the body which lay so still. "Jamie, Jamie!" she cried.

She lifted his head; warm blood matted his hair. The firing was too heavy for her to call for help, and on her knees she pulled, dragged, straddled his chest and heaved and pulled. A shot whined by her ear, and she fell atop his body, her strength weakening, rallied and dragged again. When she had reached the brick walk in front of the door, he groaned and tried to sit up. She forced him down.

"Crawl, Jamie! You must crawl," she urged.

He muttered incoherently, but dragged himself forward. In the shadowed doorway she stood up, tugged and dragged until he was inside. How she found the strength to close the door and put the heavy iron bar across it, Clytie never knew—only that firing from the other wing of the house had reached a crescendo.

The climax of the struggle could not be far off. The two cannon were silenced. Two wounded gunners had been brought into the house with two others who were dead. Jamie had recovered enough to give aid to the wounded; he had bound up the cut on his own head. He was badly bruised about his body and still a bit dazed.

Clytie's fear was that he would try to get at one of the cannon and fire it himself.

The house was surrounded now. Hammerings on doors east and north were heard. A musket shot from within the parlor, aimed at a hatcheted window, shattered things with its concussion. Vases fell, glass and china crashed.

"Jamie, the pantry window!" shouted his father. "Hold it till O'Malley comes."

There was no defeat in his voice, but he had been forced to send Joe Toads to the tobacco barns for help. The squire had become a man compounded of iron that had no melting point.

A shot from within the library reverberated with Mr. McCarthy's yell: "Dead devils don't hatchet!"

"Powder gone, they start hatcheting," Mrs. McCarthy said, her eyes at the slit in the shutter. "Used up their ammunition. Guns are play toys to them. Look out for that broken glass, missy."

Clytie's shoes had crunched it. She now noted with a shudder the bullet holes in the wooden shutter that had broken the window glass, just where she would have been standing had she not been outside with Jamie.

"Frog led," Mrs. McCarthy went on, "or they'd fired other outhouses. Figure to git the slaves out alive, butcher us quick, then fire the place before help can come."

"From Frederick?" said Clytie, who was reloading her musket.

"Far way to walk," she said grimly. "Likely heard the cannon at the fort all right, but a heap o' butcherin' can be done afore they can git hyar."

"Look!" Clytie's eyes were at the shutter. "So *many!* Out of range of our fire!"

The meadow beyond the compound, lighted by the still-bright glare from the barns, was swarming with grotesque figures leaping about.

"Won't be long. Readyin' they be to make a howling rush to hatchet windows and doors all at onc't."

And there were so many windows, so many doors. So few to defend them. O'Malley's voice sounding from the hallway cheered them. He had made the dash from the tobacco barns.

"Upstairs, John!" Uncle Peter shouted.

But Joe? Had Joe Toads got back? He had been so valiant, so . . .

"You too, Joe, Jake, the west windows," Uncle Peter added.

Oh, so Joe was safe! Clytie relaxed somewhat, then she heard Uncle Peter's further shouts: "Attention all. Hold your fire until they pass the picket fence. No wild firing, understand? Pick 'em off. Mony, you and Phyly hear me?"

They had been firing from the windows in Monica's room, and her steady voice answered, "Keep Jamie in the house. Don't let him try to get at the cannon."

"Don't leave that pantry window, Jamie," the squire bellowed. "Keep that cellar door covered."

Clytie gave thanks for those words.

Now against the fiery glow, phantomlike upright worms gyrated through the meadow gate. Others leaped the fence into the compound—all racing toward the garden, real now, as real as death—their gruesome howls shaming hyenas. Painted demons out of a painted hell, hatchets aloft, firebrands flaming.

"Giving their death holler," said Mrs. McCarthy grimly.

"Fire!" cried Uncle Peter.

Muskets answered from every window. Clytie saw the figure she had picked off drop in the mignonette bed. His firebrand rolled against him. Others writhed among the rose bushes, in the heliotrope beds. She was reloading with trembling hands when she heard Mrs. McCarthy's chuckle.

"Too hot for the beasties. Not a brand reached the house," Mrs. McCarthy cried.

"Where—where are they?" asked Clytie, her eyes at the shutter again. She could see only felled brown bodies, red-and-white streaked, and smoking torches searing the flower beds.

"Death holler didn't stick," answered Mrs. McCarthy. "Pulled back to try the rush again. Listen!" A French voice from the orchard was shouting angry orders. "Frog led. I told ye! Heaven save . . ."

The cry of a child from abovestairs had turned Mrs. McCarthy's exclamation into a moaning prayer. Wailing mounted from the cellar.

Then came Jamie's frantic voice: "Let me out, Pa! Pity's sake! Jake and I can fire that cannon."

"Do as you are told," the squire thundered. "They are in every bush. Go back to your window."

Seconds became years. Help from Frederick! Oh, if only help from Frederick might come! Mrs. McCarthy had faced death so often before for herself and loved ones that she would never waver; but as Clytie heard that French voice, saw movement in compound and orchard, a stark, numbing fear squeezed at her marrow—the children, oh, God, save the children!

Again those howls mounting to paralyze body and brain. Naked painted bodies racing, leaping, their numbers increasing rather than diminishing. Brands flaming, they reached the shattered picket fence, raced on . . .

"*Fire!*" the squire commanded.

The muskets spoke. Some Indians fell, the yowling mass reeled but came on, burning brands held high. Clytie tried to reload. No miracle could save the house now. . . . But the miracle came.

One of the cannon, long silenced, thundered, roared. A mass of savages went down. Those who were alive leaped and ran, to be brought down by musketfire from the windows above.

"Help from Frederick!" someone yelled.

The cannon near the dining-room door roared again—Jove avenging. A concerted yell of triumph went up from within the house. When the cannon smoke had cleared no living thing moved within the garden.

Then Jamie yelled, "Pa, the woods are on fire south of the barn!"

"Axes, men, get axes!" ordered the squire. "Trees near the house must be felled."

This new menace did not weaken the squire's voice. A savage foe was routed, but to save the house from the dry burning woods another miracle would be required.

The cannon thundered again as though for good measure. Men raced and called in a chaos of sound, doors opened; all were hailing their deliverers.

Unsteadied by the new danger and choked by smoke, Clytie ran to Jamie's door, unbarred it, and stepped into the night to draw breath. A fearsome crackle of flaming woods licked at the sky; something stung her uplifted face, pelted her overheated body.

"Rain! It's raining!" Her hysterical shout was smothered by the sudden downpour. It beat at the dry shrubbery, volleyed onto trees, washed down on her. Glorious wash! "Rain! Oh, blessed God, rain!" she cried gratefully to the deluge.

The fearsome glare was dying from the sky. Under the hammering wash of rain a voice shouted from the dining room, "You saved us, men! Saved us!" Then, blurred by the deluge: "Adam, Adam!"—Jamie's cry.

Clytie staggered, cringed. Not Jamie's voice, but a phantom voice made by the volley of rain. Her mind was unhinged. . . .

"Adam! Adam!" The laughter in the sound mocked her. It had been in such a downpour that they had called to each other in that other life, called as in her dream.

"Clytie! *Clytie!*" A sound that could be no sound. Now a phantom, tall, haggard, emerged from the lighted doorway. "Clytie," he called, limping toward her in the eerie light.

"Adam!" she screamed as she ran.

No phantom arms grabbed her close. Adam's own voice was quieting her sobbing cries.

CHAPTER *Thirty-three*

MORE than a week had passed since Chestermere's night of horror. Clytie sat on the portico, quiet and happy, while Uncle Peter related to Colonel Cary all that had happened to Adam, and how he and the two troopers, Hank and Zeb, had come to their rescue on that dread night.

But she was not truly listening; she had proudly heard him relate it so often before. She had just left Adam; she had been sitting by his bed, as she always did, until his eyes closed for his afternoon nap, which was part of the treatment Jamie prescribed, and his hand relaxed about hers. She had closed the door of Pete's room softly and left him, wondering now how so much happiness could be contained in so short a space as nine days. There had been anxiety, too, because of Adam's depleted condition and the fact that his wound was not truly healed. But now that he was so happy, and getting the right kind of rest and food and Jamie's devoted care, he was mending wondrously.

Then, too, her father's letter, that had come so soon after Adam's magical appearance, had added so much to their joy. She had read it as she sat by Adam's bedside. Yet when she saw the date, written long before he could have known of the army's defeat and from one of General Shirley's vessels heading north from Boston, she had been frightened for her father's own safety. Uncle Peter had decried her fears: "Must have got back to Boston, since the letter was mailed there." That was true, yet the fact had not wholly comforted her.

The letter made her proud as she read it to Adam: " 'I can not know when this letter will reach you, my child, but I must not longer delay answer to your letter which has caused me such disappointment. Yet since I have always trusted your own heart to guide you, it would doubtless be an error of judgment not to do so now. It would appear that life has its own patterns and designs for those we love, and in this case it is but a father's part to smooth and make easy, as best he may, the way ordained . . .' "

Adam's hand had gone out to her, and his eyes had been as misty as hers as they finished that blessed letter together.

"What a man to live up to, darling," he had said. "God grant, I will never disappoint him."

And one of the most wondrous things had happened when she showed Monica the letter, with trembling regret for her long deception; Monica had only looked up and smiled as she said softly, "I am so glad, darling. I have long known of your love for Adam."

"Oh, Aunt Mony!" She had buried her penitent head in Monica's lap. Gentle hands had stroked her shoulders.

"But, child, don't you see that your marriage to Adam will mean that we shall not lose you, that this will be your home and his, we hope, for a long time."

It had been blessed to see Monica's smile, because the letter had come on the day after they had buried their beloved Ephraim—and one of Amos Hartley's sons, killed while defending the tobacco barns, and the two sailor gunners. The two wounded ones had so mended that Captain Jackson had had them transferred to the *Queen,* where he could look after them. The *Queen* was still in her dock, being leisurely loaded with prime tobacco, for now that Governor Sharpe's militiamen had arrived to strengthen the fort, and Uncle Peter had so depleted the savage horde, the county was considered safe.

But the death of their beloved Ephraim had been a great blow to the Chesters. It was after Chestermere had been saved that they had found him near the pantry window which he had helped to defend; his old heart had just stopped beating. "From joy, likely," Jamie had said, "when he heard Adam and the boys manning the cannon in our defense." It had comforted all of them to think that he knew before he died that Chestermere was saved.

The week had been mixed with joys and sorrows for everybody. The slaves too had mourned Ephraim, and Hartley's son, and the two sailors who had so bravely defended them. They had gathered up the mangled bodies of the Indians, and Uncle Peter had permitted them to bury their enemies after their own rites. They had dug a great hole in the far woods, and on the mound that marked the mass grave they had heaped large stones so that savage spirits could not escape to haunt them. Satisfied now that the Indian raiding was finished, they sang again as they brought in from the fields the ripened tobacco, and Clytie and Adam would listen to their songs and the strum of their banjos in the evening twilight.

"The bullet went straight through, grazing the thighbone, but 'twas the loss of blood that scared Gist and the boys," Uncle Peter said.

Clytie's thoughts had wandered from Uncle Peter's account of all that had happened to Adam, but as he spoke of Adam's wound she gave attention. This part of the story always made her quiet and prayerful. Their fabulous escape from the Indian captors had been so magnified, as it was told and retold by the townspeople, that by now they had been aided, not so much by their own cleverness as by werewolves; now not even Uncle Peter could always get it straight.

"And not yet out of enemy country, hey?" Squire Cary asked.

"That's right." Uncle Peter went on with the tale. "But they made a sort of litter to carry Adam on. None of 'em had had any food to speak of for three days, and almost no sleep. But they headed for the foothills and the cabin of a Scotch settler, friend of Gist. Looks like they were mighty kind to the boys, did all they could. But Adam's condition got bad, and Gist wouldn't leave him till it looked like the boy was out of danger. By that time, of course, there weren't even any stragglers from the army from which he could pick up news, but he lit out alone to make his way to his own home the other side of Will's Creek. *Then* what should happen—" Uncle Peter gave this grim emphasis—"but that Gist should find his wife near dead with a sickness."

"She—she died?" asked Squire Cary.

"Might have if he hadn't got there when he did. Gist's clever as all gitout 'bout handling wounds and sickness. But by the time he was able to leave her and get to Will's Creek, he still didn't know that George Washington was alive and Braddock dead. If Adam had known Washington had come through without a scratch it might have helped him to get well sooner than he did. Didn't know it till Gist made his way to George's home, and George sent two horses and a trusted man to bring Adam and the two boys out. Like George Washington, never forgets men that have served him." Uncle Peter stopped, a faraway look of grief in his eyes.

Thinking of Pete, Clytie knew, and she was glad when his visitor said, "But how—how did Appleton and his men happen to get here and reach those cannon, to fire 'em as they did?"

"A miracle, Cary. Reckon you couldn't call it anything else. Looks like Adam was making for Chestermere, determined to get here if he died trying, weak as he was. But by the time they reached the trail that turns off the highroad into my property, it had got so dark that they decided to settle down in the woods for the night. It was when the barns blazed and our cannon roared that they headed toward us—they'd had some pretty close shaves themselves with roving enemy Indians. But to reach the house and lend us aid they had to cross the river and come up to the east of us." Uncle Peter's face beamed as it always did at this point of the tale. "Talk about skill and bravery, Cary, nobody equals our colonials, sir. There are no such soldiers for using their brains on the face of the earth. Why, before they could get to the cannon those boys throttled and stabbed three Indians. And by the grace of God . . ."

Oh, yes, yes, by the grace of God! But Clytie was thinking of what Adam had told her of his haunting desire to reach Chestermere, of how he had pressed on, day after day, on that long journey over the mountains—"Near driving the boys crazy because I wouldn't stop to rest. Something goading me, goading every mile of the way to get here." And she thought of what Hank and Zeb had told her: "Looked like 'twant no use to argue. He'd been in a fever to cross the mountains when he wasn't even able to stand up. And when those horses got there and we picked up another along the way, he kept on ridin' like a madman. We sho' thought he'd plumb lost his senses till we seen that barn burnin'."

And once Adam had said: "I knew I wasn't going to die on the way, knew I was going to see you again before my time came, knew it."

Jamie had told him about her deep faith that he was still alive, and she and Adam had just smiled at each other, knowing so well the truth of the mystic communion in their own hearts.

What was going to happen to them now they did not know, except that these precious days of being together must soon end. Adam had sent Hank and Zeb to Colonel Washington's home for instructions as to what he should do. War against the French and Indians must be waged now by the colonials, and as soon as Hank and Zeb returned Adam might set off—whether he had fully recovered or not—to join his colonel. The thought struck at her heart. No sooner were they able to snatch an hour, a few days, of happiness than separation came to tear at them.

"Clytie!" Jamie was at the door, beckoning.

Neither Uncle Peter nor Squire Cary noticed her as she hurried into the hallway. Jamie's face was solemn.

"Look, honey, you've got a blow to face, but try to take it standing up." He ran his hands through his hair.

"Jamie, what? Adam?" she asked as she started toward Adam's room.

Jamie caught her arm. "No, no, not Adam. Ma's had a letter from Uncle James. It's—it's about your going home. Hang it, honey, I'm sorry. . . . Well, let Ma tell you."

Clytie raced into Monica's room. Home? Oh, not *now!* Not until Adam . . . "What, what is it, Aunt Mony?" She knew her face was white as she stood with her back against the door, eying the letter in Monica's hands.

"He had just heard about the army's disaster when it was written, dear, and–and you must go home, *go at once.*" Her own disappointment was in her face.

"No! Oh, no! Not until Adam must go . . ."

"He is mortally anxious about you, and upset. Your father is just back from Nova Scotia, and he has already started Mike and two militiamen to Baltimore to pick you up. This is Tuesday. The *Queen* can sail with you on Thursday morning." She spoke with such finality that Clytie shuddered. And she added: "We can't fail your father again, darling, not after the unavoidable delay that forced you into such danger and–and such unexcelled bravery." Her voice broke and trembled. "But for you Jamie . . ."

"Don't, Aunt Mony, please! We must all forget." She felt suddenly strengthened before Monica's tear-filled eyes. "I will go," she said resolutely, knowing Monica's true conflict between letting her go and her duty to her father. "I will go." She gave her promise with a breaking heart.

Wednesday afternoon had come, and tomorrow she would be gone. She and Adam sat in the garden, his arms about her, his lips on her hair.

He had sat in the garden a little while every day, and had grown so much stronger the hollowness in his cheeks had gone and his wound was almost healed. Their identity in spirit, mind and heart had become so complete in these blessed days that while the old vibrations of flesh were still binding, a deeper harmony now absorbed them.

"This war may be shorter than we think, sweetheart," he spoke into her hair. "We'll soon drive those rats back across the border."

She felt his body stiffen and tried hard to be a part of the urgency she knew he felt to avenge all that the army had suffered. It had been burned into his spirit by the horrors he had seen and passed through, by Pete's death that he had taken so to heart; and while she would not have him feel otherwise, she could but face their separation with desolation. And now to be cheated of these few days before Hank and Zeb returned with his orders from Colonel Washington!

"If only I might know what you–how soon you must . . ." His close embrace of her waist cut off her tearful words.

"Let's think of that day when I come riding like the wind to New York town to claim you." He buried his lips in her neck; but as she lifted her hand to caress his cheek Uncle Peter's voice sounded from the doorway.

"Way I've been figuring it out is like this, Adam," Uncle Peter began. Adam drew up a chair for him and he went on. "With Shirley again in command of our forces, he'll be able to concentrate what troops we can drum up in the right places. We've got some hardy New Englanders. They say those mountain boys to the west of there are wildcats as fighters. And if they will just *leave* Shirley in command, he'll bring unity to our forces." Adam assented and he hurried on. "Devil is, *will* they leave him alone? Ben Franklin says in his letter, just come, that Penn Colony—Virginia, too—is spitting fire over the inferior officers the Crown has commissioned."

Adam banged his hands on the garden seat. "Washington won't stand for that, sir," he said with all his old vigor. "Nor will the Virginians, not this time. They have seen a Crown officer get a good army slaughtered because he couldn't take the advice of a colonial, and by Hector—!"

"How, folks!" Jamie said, swinging out of the house. "Have you considered that it is now September thirtieth of the new era?" He looked at Adam, who reseated himself and grinned. "It is the year *one B.D.*"

"What's B.D.?" demanded his father.

"Braddock's Defeat. From here on we will know things as *before* and *after*. It was the big bell that rang the knell of the empire of Marlborough and Queen Anne."

"Stuff!" said Uncle Peter.

"All right, my sire. But by the time we have finished off the French and Mr. Franklin's long plea for *union* of the colonies has come about, can't you see it? The British will never be able to hold this continent, for we'll be feeling our oats."

Adam smiled. But when Uncle Peter growled, Jamie said quickly, "Constable Svarz tells me that in Penn Colony they are offering more than twenty-five pounds apiece for Indian scalps." He flopped onto the ground. "Said when he and the militiamen went out to clean up old Big Corn's tribe, he was minded to let Joe Toads take the scalps of those troublesome warriors and collect on 'em."

Adam caressed Clytie's hand and they smiled at the memory of their night among Big Corn's tribe.

"Took 'em prisoners, did he?" Uncle Peter said.

"And set Joe Toads up as head man. Brave lad, Joe." Everyone assented to that. "He's taken that pretty little Omeme as squaw, Clytie."

Before Clytie could say how glad she was, Monica was coming from the house to join them as Uncle Peter said solemnly, "There was a message in Ben Franklin's letter for you, Jamie."

"Me?" Jamie drew up a chair for his mother.

"Said that Penn Medical School would be opened, time you are ready for it."

Jamie gaped. Then he picked up a twig, broke it viciously, and tossed it away. "Me, ready, ha!" he said scornfully.

"Lost your taste for doctoring, hey?" Uncle Peter winked at Clytie and Adam.

But Clytie was as bewildered as Jamie looked. Could this mean that with Pete gone they still were willing that Jamie . . .

"Considering that your father and I are still young, son—our combined ages not yet reaching a hundred—" he saw that there was a smile behind Monica's eyes—"we had thought there might be many useful years in which you might practice your beloved profession."

"Ma, Pa! What is this? You mean that I . . . Holy Jchoshaphat!" He doubled up onto the ground and flung his red hair back, his eyes like blue stars. All his long secret suffering because he thought he would have to give up his beloved profession vanished with his eager question: "I can go? You mean you can manage, Pa?"

"Why not, son? Wouldn't be fair to keep you. Besides, time Adam gets back from this fracas and we have him and Clytie with us . . . No place to learn sotweed planting like Chestermere, Adam," he broke off to say. "Meanwhile, we'll get that land for you Sharpe has promised and a house started."

"Glory hallelujah!" Jamie shouted with fervor.

Adam put an arm about Clytie as he expressed his gratitude to Uncle Peter, and she tried to make her own words sound heartfelt; yet there were so many barriers that she could not see across. All they spoke of was so far in the future. Meanwhile, she must sail on the *Queen* at dawn. And once at home, what? A few happy days with her father, yes. Then her *mother's* return: her outrage, scorn and anger at her father's consent concerning Adam. Her mother's rage might mean anything, even that she herself for her father's sake might have to renounce . . . Oh, why couldn't Monica see it? See that she faced not only the long bitter wait for Adam, but . . .

"Listen!" Jamie sprang up. There was the sound of horses' hoofs on the front driveway. "Visitors." He ran toward the house. Men's voices sounded and he called back with a shout, "Adam, it's Hank and Zeb!"

Adam, taking long strides, followed Jamie so quickly that Uncle Peter said, "You are losing your limp, lad."

"Chestermere's cure, sir," he called back.

"The boys must have food and cider," said Monica as she folded her knitting.

She went toward the house. At the sound of Jamie's lusty "Hurray!" Uncle Peter followed.

Clytie sat alone, her eyes on the afterglow of sunset that was edging southward—her last sunset at Chestermere. In a moment Adam would return, and for the last time they would watch it together. For his sake she must drag herself out of this cruel depression, but he did not know her mother nor what she would have to face. She eyed the picket fence, mended and straight again. Before her father's letter came demanding her return, she had thought her sorrow mended for all time because of Adam's return, but she was now like the seared and burned flower beds—burned by her own fears and forebodings. She heard Jamie's laughter from the house and tried to rally. Good news from Colonel Washington? How could it matter, with the *Queen* sailing in the morning, and separation . . .

"Adam!" she cried; he was coming toward her, a letter in his hand, his face radiant with smiles.

"It would not be fair to her father, nor right," Monica said, her face set in firm lines. "No, no, I haven't the right to make such a decision. You should not expect it of me." She turned from them.

Clytie and Adam looked at each other in abandoned hope, but from behind his mother's back Jamie gestured that all was not over yet.

They were all gathered in Monica's room, and the plea they made was that Clytie and Adam might be permitted to marry so that he could sail with her on the *Queen*. It had all come about because of Colonel Washington's letter. He had told Adam that he was going to Boston to meet General Shirley and wanted Adam to accompany him. He would be going first to New York, and, he had added, if Adam were contemplating a honeymoon, the time to take it would be during their sojourn there.

This stampeding of Monica was the result. Clytie thought for a moment she could not endure the suspense of the silence that followed Monica's words. Uncle Peter broke it.

"All right, Mony." He sighed deeply. "It will have to be as you say, but—" his pause seemed to last an eternity—"looks like they might have a chance of being mighty happy for a couple of months. Let 'em get married tomorrow, sail on the *Queen*, and—and when they get back down here it may take quite a time to muster up troops. But I reckon you know best." He sighed again.

Monica did not turn from the window. "I know only that I have no right to violate my brother's confidence in me in leaving the child in my care. And you are making it very hard for me, very hard indeed." Her voice was a little unsteady.

Clytie's hopes revived, but her heart went out to Monica; she was about to plead that her father had already given his consent when Adam said in mellow-voiced sympathy, "We don't mean it to be, ma'am. But 'twould be great and mortal comfort, when I must ride away toward Canada, to leave her here with *you* at Chestermere." He could have said nothing of greater import.

Monica shook her head but not with decision, *indecision.*

Then Jamie said in his philosophical way, "You know, Ma, as I see it, Uncle James is going to have a mighty hard row to hoe, time he comes up against Aunt Lucy's determination to set aside his promise to Adam and Clytie."

Monica looked at Jamie, startled, came back and reseated herself in her chair. The air vibrated with tension, but Jamie went on.

"Course she'll make a row," he said. "We all know Aunt Lucy. But what I mean is, Uncle James's heart being like it is, and always wanting to live up to his promises, looks like it sure would be helping him out if *you* made the decision yourself so Aunt Lucy could not blame *him."*

Monica stared at him, but she was staring at something beyond him too; his words appeared to have penetrated beneath her conscious mind.

"A lot to what he says, Mony," Uncle Peter agreed. "And seeing how you have always eased things up for James, having troubles enough on his hands as 'tis."

Monica got up from her chair, and in the lift of her shoulders and head a sort of other-worldliness settled on her features. It was something like the look she had had, Clytie thought, during the days just after they knew of Pete's death. She gave each of them a faraway look, a soft look, that lingered longest on Adam, before she left the room.

"Oohooo!" Clytie, so tensed with disappointment, expelled an incoherent breath. Both Adam and Uncle Peter looked hapless, hopeless, but Jamie said, shaking a warning finger, "Sh! She's in Pete's room."

They sat nervously, knowing she would come back, sensing that her decision had something to do with Pete. *Why* they could not know. But since Colonel Washington's letter had come, Clytie's hopes had flown so high that she was ready to believe she could reach Pete himself and cry out for his intervention.

It came. Monica stood in the doorway, several of Pete's richest garments in her arms, her tender smile all for Adam. And Clytie knew instinctively why: Adam had saved Chestermere, so beloved by Pete.

"He would wish you to have them, Adam," she said softly, her hand caressing the garments. "This suit, I think, for your wedding."

Clytie's arms and Adam's went round her at the same time. Adam's eyes were wet.

Phyly patted the folds of the creamy-white wedding dress, Monica's wedding dress, and sat back on her heels. "Turn round, honey," she said.

Clytie turned. The dress fitted her so perfectly there had been little to do to it except lengthen the skirt a mite; she was a little taller than Monica had been at her age. The full wide skirt ended in a little train, and Phyly was just making sure that it touched the floor evenly. It was little more than an *hour* before her wedding. She took a few turns about the room in her white satin slippers and stopped to glow at herself in the mirror.

"Oh, Phyly, Phyly! And but day before yesterday I believed that life must always be cruel to love. I feel so humbled and penitent." She eyed the square-cut low neckline, the sleeves that ended below the elbow with rich lace ruffles, and the perfectly fitting tight bodice, and then gazed into the two widened blue stars reflected back at her. "Does one ever come to understand, Phyly, that the very next day, the next hour, may bring happiness instead of the expected sorrows?"

It was still difficult to take in the wonders wrought by the letter from Colonel Washington. Yet had she not always had the curious feeling that he would be some force in her life, ever since Adam told her the name of his colonel that first moonlight night in the wilderness? And now, because of him, they would retrace their way through that same wilderness.

"We will make camp in the same spot where I first fell in love with *Lottie,* my darling," Adam had said last night. Oh, yes, they would retrace their steps, completing their circle. And wouldn't Mike be surprised when he met them in Baltimore? And when she and Adam stood together before her grandfather's portrait there would be no frown. . . .

"No, ma'am," Phyly said with such emphasis that Clytie was startled; she had all but forgotten the question asked her. "Life ain't tellin' its secrets to nobody." Phyly was busy at the other side of the room. "Body's jes' got to trust life to be good, honey, and not go pullin', hawlin' an' kickin' against it. Life can be a heap better 'n some o' dem tales folks write in books."

"It can, it *can,* Phyly!" She pushed in the stray ringlets confined by the white ribbon about her hair, and starched her nose again. The whole pattern of her life had fallen into beauteous design, without her making—as Jamie so decried—any decisions about it. Not one piece was out of place, not for the present. Yet her heart picked up the sound of the enemy cannon Adam must face—but not for months, not until he had been to Boston and they were back at Chestermere. And she must always keep in mind that life was good and kind. And she must trust it completely, as Phyly said, on this holy day, her wedding day.

"Did anyone ever die of happiness, Phyly?" Clytie whirled about to meet the beauty of the wedding veil of Mechlin lace that Phyly was holding high. She ducked under it.

"Put yo' hand on dat little ruffled part, hold it to yo' forehead," Phyly said.

The long length of creamy lace spread over the dress of Lyons satin and trailed back over the demitrain. Clytie had just glimpsed her own loveliness in the mirror when Monica came in.

"Darling!" Monica stood transfixed at the door. Then, a little sadly, she said, "If only your father could see you now."

Yes, that was the shadow on the wonder of the day, but for Monica's sake Clytie said comfortingly, "He would be so happy for my happiness if he could know." Yet in her heart it did not quite cover the case; she longed for her blessed father's gift of her to Adam at the altar. But there was Uncle Peter. And Jamie had been right: her marriage here was protecting her father from her mother's wrath.

Monica smiled wistfully and lifted the wedding veil back from Clytie's face. "I wore mother's pearls, too, darling," she said, seeing the lustrous string about Clytie's neck, "on that day so long ago." Happy memories came to her eyes. "Give her the little bouquet Adam left, Phyly, and get your own bonnet."

Phyly bustled out, and Sapphira peeked in at the door, so wall-eyed that they both laughed.

"See that you behave yourself at the church, Sapphira," Monica admonished, "and don't sniffle."

"No, mist'ess," Sapphira sniffled—largely because she was no longer going to Baltimore with "lil missy," Clytie suspected.

Phyly brought in the little bouquet of mignonette and white sweet alyssum Adam had left, and Clytie held it lovingly. He had been so handsome in the suits Phyly and her women had fitted to him; but as they traveled through the wilderness from Baltimore to Chester, he had told her, he would be wearing his buckskins. That had delighted her.

"Mony! Clytie!" Uncle Peter was calling from belowstairs.

"Tell him we will be right down, Sapphira. He is as nervous as if it were his own wedding." Monica's larkspur eyes smiled; they gave the only color to her black costume. "I am happy for you, darling, for all of us."

Clytie held back her tears as she kissed her—no tears on her wedding day. At the foot of the stairs Uncle Peter was waiting with wide-eyed approval, but it was Monica he put arms about.

"She's a replica of you, honey," he said, "on that day in Trinity Church when I near fainted at sight of you."

The first rosiness Clytie had seen in Monica's face for long months came to the surface. She tapped his ruddy face with her black fan.

"Stop your palaver or we'll be late at the church," she said.

Adam's horse that Colonel Washington had sent him, and old Molly, had been hitched to the long-unused two-wheeled coach, and Uncle Peter was on the box with Moses as they rumbled toward Frederick through the early-autumn woods. Phyly and Sapphira were just behind them, riding Zeb's horse. Long-armed Zeb still only half believed that Clytie was the same girl who had dragged him wounded from the causeway, to save him from being scalped by the Indians. He and Hank were setting out again tomorrow for Colonel Washington's home with letters from her and Adam. Adam would meet him in New York; and she had written in her father's name inviting him to dinner.

"I will give you the signal, dear, just after the guests have supped and the wedding cake is cut," Monica was saying. Clytie had been trying to give attention to all her reminders, but her thoughts kept skidding backward and forward. "Then you must slip upstairs and change your dress quickly, for the *Queen* must be sure of sailing—" she raised her voice—"Squire, does Captain Jackson want the *Queen* to sail promptly at sunset?"

"That's right, Mony, that's right." He was telling Moses how Adam's horse must be got aboard the *Queen*.

Monica was naming over the few guests she had invited for the hastily prepared wedding supper, but Clytie was thinking only of how the sailing of the *Queen* now made a melody in her heart, whereas once its sailing had stalked her like a cruel fate. Now it was her ship of dreams.

Everything had a dream quality: Monica's voice, Uncle Peter's, her lustrous white dress and veil, the scent of the early-October woods, the swaying of the coach, the thudding of the horses' hoofs. Did every girl on her way to her wedding fear that in another moment she might wake up and all the ecstasy vanish?

But the bells were real. They were entering Frederick and the gay, happy wedding bells were ringing for *her*, for *Adam*. The approach to the little English church was thronged with people, waving, smiling. She smiled and waved back. But behind her happiness she saw again the ragged, mud-stained girl who had first ridden into Frederick, laughed at, derided, saw Adam striking viciously at the redcoat who tried to drag her from her horse.

They drew up at the church. Uncle Peter was handing her down from the carriage to the sound of breathless oh's and ah's. Constable Svarz and John O'Malley were making way for them through the crowd. A little German girl reached out and touched her dress reverently: it was Marta Brawn. Clytie leaned down and kissed her cheek.

"All right, folks, she is not a fairy princess," Uncle Peter, holding her arm, told the crowd. "Just a girl getting married, as you pretty girls will be doing soon, I hope."

Everyone was in the church who could get in, but the aisle was cleared to the altar. Phyly was straightening her skirt, Monica pulling down her veil. She was advancing now, holding tight to Uncle Peter's arm; eyes and faces were swimming before her.

Oh, give me your blessing, my Mother! Every girl should have her mother's blessing; gladness came that she knew she had her father's, and grandfather's. Oh, Grandfather, watch over us! Murmurs, sibilant sounds around her, waves on a sandy shore, spindrift of shining eyes spraying her.

Her excitement had expended itself. This was no dream; Adam awaited her at the altar, the altar of love and life. She was a DeLancey now from the tips of her satin slippers to the glad light in her eyes that met the solemn pride and happiness in his. Nor did he appear to be in a fainting mood as Uncle Peter had been at his own wedding. When he drew her arm through his it was with such a mixture of humility and gentle possessiveness that he conveyed to Clytie that this was the dawn of creation. She was certain that she had just been compounded of one of his ribs. The minister's voice pronounced the solemn words. . . . Jamie was fumbling for the ring, wide-eyed—not lost?—Adam's mother's ring. Adam was slipping it on her finger. She heard his mellow repetition of the vows, then her own voice, never more clear and steady. And now they were kneeling before the altar of forever and forever.

"Good-by! Good-by! We will come back soon," Clytie and Adam called from the stern deck of the *Queen* to those on the Potomac shore: the MacLoughlans, Carys, Johnsons, with Monica and Uncle Peter. Kerchiefs fluttered, voices rippled across the water.

"I'll bring you back all the numbers of the *London Pharmacopoeia* I can find, Jamie," Clytie shouted, trying to make herself heard above

Captain Jackson's bellows at his crew in the rigging, the noise of hoisting the big sails.

Jamie and O'Malley were in the small boat in which they had rowed them out to the vessel.

"Bring me some mercurous chloride!" Jamie's voice came back to her. Both she and Adam waved their promise.

The sails drank up the freshening breeze. With the rasp of halyards and the groan of spars the *Queen* moved slowly down the river. The figures on the shore grew smaller. The breeze tugged at Clytie's bonnet, and she took it off—such a pretty bonnet, to go with her dark-blue flannel cloak.

The cloak billowed, and Adam from behind her confined both her and the cloak within his arms. Rainbow colors of the sunset danced on the foam in their wake. But alone at last with this stalwart packet of dreams that clutched her with such possessiveness, Clytie knew a moment's enraptured shyness. She covered it with chatter.

"Mr. Franklin once told me that life should finish handsomely, like a splendid dramatic piece." She was uncertain from where the thought had come, and was startled as he wheeled her about with a challenge.

"Finished, Mistress Appleton? What is finished, madam?"

"Our beginning, sir. This is the end of our beginning."

Adam's laughter was so robust her shyness slipped away. "So we begin another beginning, that it?" He held her off. "Will this one include use of that cat-o'-nine-tails I promised to keep handy? Remember?"

"Set bounds to your desires, sir. You are in the DeLancey family now."

Answer to that was delayed until his lips were withdrawn from hers. "My desire for you will always be boundless."

He led her to a place sheltered from the wind, and they sat down, his back against the poop-deck cabin, hers against him, savoring their togetherness while the afterglow died from the sky. The forested shores of the river made a dark line against the deepening turquoise of the sky as deep and unplumbable as love. The movement of his cheek against her hair was like an unconscious prayer to the night, and the serenity of his happiness measured her heartbeats. It was this quality, having behind it such authentic strength, purpose, integrity and self-discipline, that had made her love him; his sensitivity to sights and sounds was now enfolding her with him in beauty, in prayerful awareness of their hearts' fulfillment. Yet time, that had for so long been a sword suspended above their heads by a slender thread, pricked at Clytie's rapture, forced a reminder of those days and nights to come when his strength would no longer be beside her.

She stroked the back of his hand and said what she felt she must, though it was irrelevant.

"Mr. Franklin said there never was a good war, nor a bad peace."

"Darling–" he drew her closer–"not tonight, not *war*."

"I was just confused about what he meant. This war to drive the French back is a *good* war, isn't it?"

The stars that had appeared swung about as the ship rounded a bend in the river with a clack of rigging. Adam's arms tightened in the silence. Then he said, "Some wars are good, I reckon, honey. *Defensive* wars. Figure Mr. Franklin was talking about the mad dogs that *make* war. But so long as there *are* mad dogs in the world . . ." He sighed deeply.

"And evil men thirsting for power who would impose their will on others?" she supplied.

"Right, sweetest. Savages of any breed."

"Yet maybe he was thinking far ahead when men will no longer be savage–I mean, civilized enough to settle their differences in . . ."

His laugh was mellow. "Utopia, isn't that what the poet called it? The place of perfection. That's where I am now."

She snuggled closer, but her haunted thoughts lingered on those months to come when the strength of his arms would no longer be about her and she must wait, wait as other women had waited throughout the long eras of time, would go on waiting throughout the generations to come, for war to give back their loved ones. Yet would she have it otherwise than that Adam should be at the head of his company? She knew that she would not, and that she would draw strength for waiting from his strength.

He withdrew his arms from about her, got up, and drew her up into them again. They were voiceless with love and desire when he scooped her from her feet and headed for the companionway and the cozy cabin prepared for them.